I0681821

Caesar's Wife Must Be Above Suspicion

Caesar's Wife Must Be Above Suspicion

Bruce D. MacQueen

RESOURCE *Publications* · Eugene, Oregon

CAESAR'S WIFE MUST BE ABOVE SUSPICION

Copyright © 2021 Bruce D. MacQueen. All rights reserved. Except for brief quotations in critical publications or reviews, no part of this book may be reproduced in any manner without prior written permission from the publisher. Write: Permissions, Wipf and Stock Publishers, 199 W. 8th Ave., Suite 3, Eugene, OR 97401.

Resource Publications
An Imprint of Wipf and Stock Publishers
199 W. 8th Ave., Suite 3
Eugene, OR 97401

www.wipfandstock.com

PAPERBACK ISBN: 978-1-6667-0739-7
HARDCOVER ISBN: 978-1-6667-0740-3
EBOOK ISBN: 978-1-6667-0741-0

09/09/21

Contents

Acknowledgements

I wrote CAESAR'S WIFE *Must be Above Suspicion* to fulfill my father's deathbed request. I know this may well sound hopelessly melodramatic, but it is no less true for all that. The very last time I spoke with him, in September of 1989, when we both knew this would probably be our last conversation, he told me of a secret disappointment that had been troubling him for some time: namely, that I had never used my knowledge of the ancient world and my talents as a writer (which he almost certainly overestimated) to produce a book that would reach a wider public than the small circle of classical scholars who knew my academic work. This was not, I feel sure, a criticism of my choice of a career as a scholar, but just a wish that, at some point, I would put aside some time for a different kind of writing. He died the week after we had this conversation. I didn't make him any promises, as easy as that would have been; he was a quiet man, one who knew instantly the difference between a real promise and pious intentions. But though it has taken me a terribly long time to write a novel, the thought was never far from my mind.

Just a few months after I submitted the manuscript of this book to the publisher, my brother, Jeffrey D. MacQueen, died suddenly. Like our father, he was a quiet man (most of the time), so very much like him in so many ways that it was uncanny at times even to hear him speak. I deeply regret that I never even shared with him the information that I was writing a novel, let alone showed him the manuscript. He was busy, I was busy, who knew that there wouldn't be time? There's a famous line from a Polish poem by Fr. Jan Twardowski (I lived and worked in Poland for 20 years and speak the language passably well) that reads, in my poor translation, "Let's hurry up and love people: they leave so quickly."

The next person to whom I feel very much indebted is Friederich Nietzsche. And yes, I do mean the famous late-19th-century German classics-professor-turned-philosopher. One of his lesser-known works is an unfinished essay, left in his notebooks as a compilation of thoughts and opinions on classical scholarship, entitled *We Philologists.* At one point in his reflections, Nietzsche remarks that the only thing of real interest in history is to consider what *might have happened*, had this-or-that not happened. In some way that I can hardly explain, even to myself, this one sentence gave me the idea that brought into being the book you are about to read. What would have happened if Julius Caesar hadn't actually died on the 15th of March, in the year 44 BCE? I've put the question rhetorically to more than one group of my students, but the only answer I ever ventured myself was along the lines of "Well, he probably would have gone off to Parthia and gotten himself killed, like Crassus." But once Nietzsche challenged me to consider that question seriously, I set out to answer it to my own satisfaction.

Hardly anyone in my family or among my friends has ever been aware that I might harbor any ambition or intention to write a novel. When I first told my wife, Weronika (just say "Veronica," this is Polish spelling), about my last conversation with my father, she insisted that I must write a novel and fulfill my father's dying wish. Ordinary nagging is not her style, but she reminded me of it just often enough, suggested that I think about it just often enough, that when I happened to read that sentence from Nietzsche mentioned above, I was primed and ready. She has been patient with my moods and distraction, supportive of my attempts to carve out large chunks of time from a busy schedule, and ready with good advice when I asked for it—which was never, ever often enough.

No doubt it will occur to me, later, that I have failed to mention by name many people whose contribution to the writing of this novel, though made all unawares, was too significant for me to have passed over it in silence. If you feel yourself to be one of those people, please accept my humblest apologies. I mean no slight. You may take some cold comfort, though, in the fact that hardly anyone but you will actually be reading this page, anyway . . .

A Few Words of Explanation

This is a work of alternate history. An alternate history, by definition, describes events that did not actually occur, but would have occurred, or at least might have occurred, if at some point in the course of history one or two things had turned out differently. Those who have watched, for example, the Amazon Prime television series called *The Man in the High Castle* will have some idea of what this means; for those who haven't, suffice it to say that the writers began with the assumption that Germans developed the atomic bomb before the Americans did during the Second World War, and used it to win the war.

In *Caesar's Wife Must Be Above Suspicion*, the event in question is the assassination of Julius Caesar on the 15th of March (a date called the "Ides of March" in the ancient Roman calendar; see below), in the year we call 44 BCE. I've tried to be generally consistent with the historical record as much as possible for the time up to that fateful day, but from that day forward, it is all the work of my imagination.

Some parts of the narrative jump back in time to provide background. My original intention was to label and format these parts differently, using a different type, so that they would stand apart from the rest of the narrative. But boxes or background shading finally seemed more intrusive and cumbersome than they were worth, so I've replaced all that by heading each chapter with the date and place of the action. If you start a new chapter and feel a little disoriented, check the date under the chapter title.

The story is told from multiple points of view. In order to simplify the narrative, though, I've used a third-person narrative throughout, with subheadings to indicate the characters from whose point of view the various parts of the story are being told.

All the characters named in this novel, except for one, are real persons. Several important parts of the story are told from the point of view of the Roman historian, Sallust, whose historical monographs I've had occasion to teach in Latin many times. The real Sallust, like the character in my novel, was a supporter of Julius Caesar in the Roman Civil War, fought with him, governed the province of Africa Nova for him, but was accused of extortion when he returned to Rome. Even though the case was dropped, Sallust withdrew from public life and took up writing historical essays. In my own scholarly work on Sallust, I've tried to argue that he finally came to see Caesar as a symptom of the political disease that was about to claim the life of the Republic; in this novel, I've shamelessly taken advantage of the privileges of the novelist to advance my thesis through fiction.

My portraits of Caesar and Cicero, two figures of enormous importance to this crucially important moment in Roman history, are based on my own sense of what these two men were really like, and not on the way so many great writers before me have portrayed them, rightly or wrongly. Julius Caesar was a paradoxical man: even-tempered and remarkably patient, but with very occasional flashes of a truly terrifying rage; engaging and likable in private contact, but with a strong sense of himself as being essentially *sui generis*, that is, different in some very significant ways from run-of-the-mill humanity; an Epicurean by intellectual conviction, detached, bemused by the common lot of humanity, and yet a man with a visceral sense of his own destiny and historical importance. As for Cicero: well, hardly any figure of his time has been more mistreated by posterity, especially over the last century or so. Shortly after his death in 43 BCE, much of his private correspondence was published, though we really don't know who did this, or why, or exactly when. The point is: whose reputation, past or present, would survive the publication of the letters they've written over twenty years of an active life in public affairs, including those written to family and closest friends, without the slightest awareness that someday the general public would read them? Cicero was a thoughtful man, which means, among other things, that he was not quick to make facile judgments, not always and immediately sure that he was right, and prepared to change his mind when reflection convinced him that his original opinion was misguided. It's easy, but utterly unfair, to represent him as wavering, inconsistent, even cowardly; on the other hand, the Roman Civil War (like so many calamities of history) was precipitated by two men, Caesar and Cato, who knew exactly what they wanted, and never wavered or blinked in the pursuit of their goals. Cicero deserves a lot more respect than he usually gets.

As the title indicates, however, the key person in this novel is Caesar's wife. Calpurnia was Caesar's third wife. The first was Cornelia, a very well-connected woman who died just as Caesar's political career was beginning (69/68 BCE). A little over a decade earlier, Caesar had been ordered by the victorious dictator Sulla to divorce Cornelia (who was related to Lucius Cornelius Cinna, one of Sulla's greatest enemies), but he had refused to do so, even though it cost him much of his wealth and position, and very nearly his life. Two years after Cornelia's death, Caesar married Pompeia, who was, ironically enough, a granddaughter of Sulla; but when she was implicated in a complicated scandal in the year 62 BCE, Caesar divorced her, despite her protestations of innocence. It was his famous response to her protests, quoted by ancient sources, that provided the title for this novel: "Caesar's wife must be above suspicion." Three years later, then, he married Calpurnia, who was at the time younger than his daughter Julia, his only legitimate child. Little is actually known of Calpurnia, though the story that she had premonitions of Caesar's death (repeated by Shakespeare from ancient sources) has been persistent. To my knowledge, however, no previous author, ancient or modern, has entertained the suspicion this novel tries to arouse. But I won't spoil the story by explaining.

The single invented character in this novel is Skaiva, the Briton (that is, a Celtic inhabitant of what is now Great Britain). His name, as the story develops, comes to be Latinized to Scaeva. He is introduced to the story as the son of a British king (tribal chieftain, really) named Mandubracius, who really existed, and really was an early ally of Caesar during his second invasion of Britain, and really did give hostages to Caesar as security against his future loyalty. The name "Skaiva" is an authentic name actually found among the ancient Britons, but I chose it here mostly because it is so easily Latinized to "Scaeva," which in turn was a real Roman name. This is in fact what "naturalized" Roman citizens would usually do: adopt the first and second names of the person who sponsored them, and then add their own previous name as a third name, Latinized. This was even more convenient for my purposes because one of Caesar's legionary commanders during the Gallic War was in fact a man named Publius Sulpicius Scaeva.

My depiction of ancient British life is as accurate as I could make it, given the little we really know about these people and my own desire not to write a story only experts would understand. If there are any such experts among my readers, I hope they will forgive the occasional lapse. Skaiva/Scaeva serves several purposes in the story (parts of which are told from his point of view), one of which is to exemplify the process by which various peoples of the ancient world found themselves part of the Roman Empire, and flourished there. I don't mean to sugar-coat imperialism, but if we demonize empires, then we fail to understand that the power of an empire seldom if ever depends exclusively on force and terror, or if it does, the empire doesn't usually last very long. The Roman Empire lasted for several centuries, a record not matched by any subsequent empire in Europe. They must have been doing something right.

The conspirators who actually killed Julius Caesar in the Theater of Pompey on the Ides of March, 44 BCE, were led by Brutus and Cassius, rendered immortal (ironically) by Shakespeare; they were joined by a third ringleader, a much less famous man, Decimus Brutus Albinus (whom I refer to here as "Albinus," to avoid confusing him with his more famous cousin). When we give center stage to Brutus and Cassius, we run the risk of transforming this complex conspiracy into a simple act of revenge by disgruntled partisans of the losing side in the Civil War. The point here (and this is most definitely not my invention) is that Albinus was Caesar's man, as were roughly half of the Senators who took part in the assassination. Part of my goal in writing this novel has been to explore that mystery: how did it happen that men who had fought and bled for Caesar joined a plot to kill him, a year after the last battle they fought together, alongside the very men they had fought against?

We actually know precious little about many aspects of daily life in ancient Rome. I've done my best not to clutter up the story with irrelevant displays of erudition, but I've also tried to avoid glaring anachronisms or silly mistakes. A few Latin words are used here without English translation, but their meaning will be explained in the text; in my first drafts, there was a great deal more Latin, but with every successive revision I took out more and more of these terms. In other words: you don't need to be a Latin student to read this book; if a Latin word is used, there will be some explanation of it in the text.

References to time in a novel like this are not easy. The Romans did not have clocks or calendars, as least as we think of them. A decade or so after Caesar's death, a Roman scholar named Varro used ancient archives and the Greek calendar to fix the date of the founding of Rome in the year we call 753 BCE, thus giving the Romans a "Year One" for their calendar.

In practice, however, they almost never counted years this way until centuries later. Instead, they referred to a particular year by naming the two men who served as consuls in that year, whose names were all inscribed on a monument in the Forum. For example: in the year we call 63 BCE, the consuls were Cicero and Antonius Hybrida (the uncle of the famous Mark Antony), so Romans would refer to that year as "the consulship of Cicero and Antonius Hybrida." As a novelist writing in English, I've referred to the years using modern numeration in the headings, but in the text I've avoided this as an obvious anachronism.

The Roman months were originally based on the cycle of the moon (even in English, the words "moon" and "month" are related). The new moon was the first day of the month, called the "Calends," and the full moon was called the "Ides." A third date point, called the "Nones," was placed roughly half-way between them. The Romans did not number the days of the month, but counted backward from the next following date point: since March 15 was the Ides of March, March 14 was "the day before the Ides," March 13 was "three days before the Ides," and so forth. I've tried to avoid making all this too complicated for readers not familiar with this arcane system. The problem, of course, is that 12 lunar months do not make up a solar year, which is longer than 12 x 28. It was, of course, Julius Caesar who solved this problem by adding a few days to each of the lunar months to make up a 365-day year divided into 12 months; I've referred to this historical fact several times in the novel.

As for the time of day: the Romans divided the daylight hours into twelve equal parts, which they called "hours" (Latin *horae*) and the night into four "watches" (*vigiliae*). That means, of course, that an hour in December was much, much shorter than an hour in June. Sundials, on a sunny day, could be used to tell the approximate time of day, and there were water clocks, hourglasses, and candles that could be used to measure duration, but these were imprecise and not easily available. The Romans had no concept of "minutes," let alone "seconds," so again, in the interests of authenticity, I've avoided using either term. I hope my readers can forgive me for the occasionally vague references to time.

1

The Ides of March Have Come

March 15, 44 B.C.E.

Rome, at the Theater of Pompey, in the
Campus Martius (the "Field of Mars")

THE MASTER OF THE known world lay on the floor in a curious state, gazing up at the ceiling, intrigued by the shape of the rafters, part of his mind wondering how they held up the weight of the ceiling.

A moment before (he could remember this clearly), the pain from at least a dozen stab wounds had been excruciating, and the rage that came from being attacked, now, in this place, by men he trusted, men who owed him their lives and fortunes, had burned within him even hotter than the wounds. But now the pain had somehow receded. It was not gone, but it really didn't seem to matter to him anymore. The rage had evaporated with it. He could still hear the voices of men shouting, fighting, but the noise came to him as though from a great distance, or rather, as though all the chaos and confusion was happening in another room and didn't concern him. He wondered if he was dying, and then he thought, with real astonishment, that perhaps he wasn't dying: what if he was already dead? What a fool I've been, he thought, to argue all those years, to anyone who would listen, that death would be the end of all thought and sensation. Because, now, here I am, dead, or so it seems, and yet I can think. I can think, but I can't move, can I? And for that matter, I can't say I really feel anything, any sensation that I can identify. Too bad. I could write a book about what everyone really wants to know, what it's like to die, but now that I know what to write, I can't write it.

This struck him as funny, but he couldn't laugh.

Then, suddenly, his mind turned in a different direction entirely. How did she know what would happen? How much did Calpurnia know? How did she come to know it? Could it really have been a dream? Or did she want him dead? Perhaps she was just using his own stubbornness against him, something that she had certainly done more than once in the 15 years of their marriage. But what did she want from him? What reason would she have for wanting him dead?

As he pondered these questions, with no hint of any answers coming to mind, the candle of his consciousness finally sputtered and flickered out. Gaius Julius Caesar fell into a long and dreamless sleep that had almost everything in common with death—except that, in due time, he would awaken, very much alive.

Calpurnia

Calpurnia waited for her husband's return from the Senate meeting at Pompey's Theater with an outward composure that perfectly masked a raging inner turmoil.

This composure was her trademark. Some would say that she shared this character trait with her husband, but that was only true on the most superficial level. Calpurnia had long ago realized that Caesar's calmness, the enigmatic half-smile that seldom left his face, was the key to his remarkable personal power over others. It was essential that he never seem to anyone to have been taken by surprise, or worse, to have lost control over the situation, to have no idea what was happening or what needed to be done. The persona he had created for himself had served him well, to say the least.

Calpurnia, on the other hand, never felt safe. That was why she had learned, from childhood, not to let anyone, anyone at all, know exactly what she was thinking at any moment. When she was younger, she had supposed that one day she would have someone near to her that she would have no reason to fear, and so she would be able to speak out loud whatever she happened to be thinking and feeling at the moment. But she had long ago given up on this dream, and packed it away with her childhood toys.

The turmoil that she was now experiencing resulted from the plans that she had set in motion, which were about to produce results, one way or another. There had been little enough she could do at the beginning of it all, and now, she had no control at all over what would or would not happen next. But not even her chambermaid could be allowed to see a single flicker of anxiety on her face.

All of their lives were about to be changed dramatically, this much was certain. Caesar was utterly unaware of the inferno that would soon devour him if he did not change course, and of his volition he would never change course. Only a desperate gamble could save him. He had to see with his own eyes that some of the men he trusted did not deserve that trust. He believed implicitly in his ability to control the men around him, especially Brutus and Antony, manipulating their mutual antipathy to his own ends. He would have to learn that he could not ever allow either of them, or anyone of their kind, to get close to him. He would never be able to gain control over Rome, the greatest city in the world, in the same way he could control an army in the field; and he needed to learn this very soon, for his own good and that of the enormous empire he now controlled. The only question was whether or not he would survive the hard lesson that was unfolding, this very moment, in Pompey's Theater.

Antony

Marcus Antonius (whose habit on most days was to sleep into the afternoon, even when he had been sober the night before, which happened from time to time) rose very early in the morning of the Ides of March. He awoke as he usually did on the day of battle, well before dawn, immediately alert, his mind already occupied with the myriad of tasks that would need to be performed if he and his men were to survive till the next day.

But it was not a battle that awaited him this time, at least not in the ordinary sense. He had to try and prevent Gaius Julius Caesar, his commander and friend, and now the undisputed head of state, ruling unchallenged over the largest Empire the world had ever seen, from being killed by a group of conspirators, who were coming armed to a special meeting of the Senate. And he had to stop this crime without any particular cooperation from its intended victim, even though—figure that one out!—he knew about the conspiracy; and so Antony had do everything without letting the conspirators know that he was aware of their intentions until they'd been caught in the act—that is, until they had gone at least far enough in executing their plan to be unable to deny that they had intended to kill Caesar.

And if he should fail to prevent this murder, if Caesar should fall—well, a good general, as the Great Man himself always liked to say, always has a contingency plan. Or better, you have three plans ready and use the one that seems to work out best at the time.

The timing, then, would be more than usually difficult. If the trap were sprung too soon, the conspirators might not be caught with the proof of their murderous intent in their hands, and Caesar would let them off, again. If it were sprung too late, Caesar might be killed.

At which point a voice that seemed to come from the back of his head spoke up. "And would that be so bad, really?" The voice, oddly, was that of Calpurnia. Antony was still not entirely sure what her intentions actually were, but the day had arrived, and he would soon find out whether she meant to encourage him, or to lure him to destruction. He shook his head, as though to clear himself of the whispering in his head, and ran over the plan in his mind. But planning, especially this kind of planning, was not something he did well, and he knew it. He wished he felt more certain that he had thought of everything.

He knew what the assassins' earlier plans had been, and then, too, he had been ready. They had first thought of killing Caesar the previous autumn, as he stood alone on the high platform, conducting elections on the Campus Martius. The whole idea of this platform, the so-called "voting bridge," was to isolate the individual voter so that he could not be intimidated while casting his vote. So there had been some sense in the idea: by law, Caesar would be there alone, unguarded. Antony had not worried about this plan very much when his informer first told him about it: the conspirators had obviously not realized that though Caesar would indeed be unguarded, his would-be assassin would also have to be alone, and Caesar was known for his physical strength and fighting skills. On one occasion Antony had even teased Caesar that he had missed his calling: he would have made a first-rate gladiator. The Great Man seemed amused by the joke, but then, with Caesar you were never quite sure.

The plot became less amusing when several of the conspirators apparently realized there was a problem with the plan and revised it. Decimus Brutus Albinus, who was nearly as adept at single combat as Caesar himself (an inherited trait, some gossips said), suggested that he himself would catch the Dictator unawares and throw him off the platform; other conspirators armed with daggers would be waiting below to kill him. To succeed, however, the conspirators would have to be able to control the crowd of onlookers jostling to see the Great Man, and the impossibility of doing that finally led the conspirators to scrap this plan.

Another idea was to catch Caesar off guard, perhaps on his way to see a comedy at one of the city's several theaters. He was known to enjoy comedies (and to sleep through tragedies, when Calpurnia coerced him into attending one), so the plan called for him to be waylaid along the way to the theater or the way home.

Antony had very much hoped for this plan to be accepted, and had even instructed his informer to push the idea. But just at that moment a deranged man with a dagger, shouting something incoherent about Marius and the Cimbri, made a lunge at Caesar as he passed through one of the city's crowded streets. After that, the Great Man was always attended by guards on such occasions, and the conspirators dropped this idea.

The plan they finally developed was, Antony had to admit, ingenious. Caesar as Dictator was entitled to have members of his praetorian cohort near him at all times in public places; his house, or anyone's house where he happened to be, was always guarded. The one public place where he could not go with his guards, not without an outrageous violation of custom and good manners, was the Senate: in other words, the guards could not follow him into any room where the Senate was in session. Not even Sulla had had the audacity to come armed to a meeting of the Senate, or to bring his personal bodyguards through the door of the Curia. To appear at a meeting of the Senate with a bodyguard would be as much as to say, "I am a tyrant"—every educated man in Rome had read Plato on the subject of tyrants and their bodyguards, and Caesar knew that.

Antony had never quite been able to predict how Caesar would react when a matter of protocol raised the question of his real status in the Republic. At times, he was utterly indifferent to protocol, full of himself and his own importance. He wore the red toga of the Dictator almost every time he left the house, and had his curule chair gilded. Not long ago he had neglected to stand to receive a group of senators when they called on him at home, a breach of decorum that seemed to have shocked many in the Senate more than the crossing of the Rubicon. To be sure, any overt move towards *regnum*, towards kingship, or even the mere suggestion that he might consent to become Rome's first king in five centuries, was always rebuffed, but at the same time, woe betide the man who showed too much disapproval of the idea. Antony was certain that this was all strategy, indeed typical Caesarian strategy: evoke total confusion in the enemy camp with a deluge of completely contradictory information. He had seen Caesar do this before a battle so many times.

What made it all difficult was that Caesar the politician, like Caesar the general, never let even his closest advisors know what his real intentions were until the dice were thrown. Antony himself had even tried, during the Lupercalia in February of that same year, to tie a white linen diadem, the symbol of kingship, around Caesar's head. He had ended up feeling stupid and resentful: just when he thought he had read his commander's mind and knew his innermost thoughts, what he really wanted, he was publicly rebuked like a naughty schoolboy.

It was only a few days later that Caesar was explicitly warned against the Ides of March.

In private conversation, among his own people, Caesar often made fun of popular and traditional religion, and seemed to actually enjoy the irony of his position as the *pontifex maximus*, the chief priest of the state cult, to which he had been elected almost two decades earlier. He was the first in Rome's long history who, like Epicurus, his favorite philosopher, privately held the most skeptical views on the value of religion. But again, like almost all members of his class, Caesar was punctilious and scrupulous in all public observances. At home, dining with friends, lying on his couch and at least playing the role of an Epicurean, he would laugh at the Stoic notion that the cosmos was bound in some sort of celestial harmony to human affairs. As a politician, he had been known to use religious observances, including the college of augurs, in a very clever but utterly cynical way. He was not above mentioning the old story that his clan, the *gens Julia*, was descended from the goddess Venus and her Trojan son, Aeneas; and he had reinforced that claim by founding an impressive temple to "Mother Venus," symbolically located between the Forum and the Suburra, the somewhat down-at-the-heels residential district north of the Forum, where Caesar had grown up and still lived, at least most of the time. All this from a man who loved to quote Lucretius: "Religion has been responsible for so much evil!" Privately, of course.

The ostensible conflict between the affected skepticism of the private Caesar and the public show of piety was in itself nothing remarkable: a pragmatic combination of private skepticism and public piety was obligatory in the social and political class to which both Caesar and Antony belonged by birth. Truth to tell, even Cicero's behavior in this respect was not so very different. There was a deeper dimension, however, of which Antony was slowly becoming aware. Caesar truly believed in his

own exceptionality. This belief was so deep and so sincere that it sometimes freed him from the petty arrogance to which lesser men were often
given when they felt challenged in their power and status, and produced
the democratic gestures that made him the darling of Rome's nameless
masses. At other times, though, the conviction that he had been singled
out for greatness from birth caused him to accept as natural certain hon-
ors and privileges that should have made him blush.

But there was no time left to think about all this. Antony rose,
dressed, and set out to Caesar's house, ready to escort him to the meeting
of the Senate, which was to take place in perhaps the most ironic setting
imaginable: Pompey's Theater.

Pompey's Theater was actually a large complex in the Campus Martius, the ancient "Field of Mars" once used to marshal the army, which
was located just outside the ancient walls of the city. The theater building
itself stood at one end of the complex. The high rear wall of the stage
formed the backdrop for the plays presented there, but it also served as
the front wall of a large portico, with a colonnade on both sides. At the
opposite end of the portico was a meeting house, generally known as
Pompey's Curia, with an imposing staircase and a temple-like façade;
this, of course, is where the Senate would convene.

What Antony did was to put together a unit of 20 veteran legionaries from Caesar's favorite Tenth Legion, led by one of his most trusted
centurions. The men were instructed to arrive at the theater in civilian
dress, one or two at a time, armed with the standard short sword, which,
however, was to be carried concealed. They would first loiter about the
portico, which would be filled with people who wanted to see Caesar, or
even speak to him, before he entered the Senate. Then, one by one, they
would make their way to an empty storage room just off the portico, near
the entrance to the large room where the Senate would meet. Antony
would walk behind Caesar, keeping him in view but remaining close
enough to the room where his soldiers were waiting that they could respond instantly to his command. When he saw that the conspirators were
about to make their move, he would call them, and they would move to
defend their commander, as they had done in Gaul so many times before,
when a ferocious Gallic charge had brought wild-eyed barbarians a little
too close for comfort.

"Your first and most important order," Antony instructed them, "is
to save Caesar's life: when I give the signal, form a perimeter around him
and let no one approach. We've been informed that the assassins will have

hired some gladiators for protection, but they, of course, will not be al-lowed to enter the Curia, just as you won't, until it becomes necessary. Use as much force as is necessary, keep an eye out for those gladiators, kill them if they try to interfere, but if possible leave Albinus, Brutus, and Cassius alive. Albinus you all know. If you don't know Brutus or Cassius by sight, when I arrive at the Senate meeting with Caesar, I'll be talking mostly to them. I want them arrested and alive. It's no fun to kill a corpse, no sport in it, and I plan on having some fun this time." This last was said with that impish grin he always used when he said something especially bloodthirsty.

After they had gone over the plan and there were no more questions, Antony met them one day on the grounds of Pompey's Theater, so that they could see the area and familiarize themselves with the layout. It was generally a busy place, so there could be no actual practice. That would draw attention, and if word got to the conspirators, the consequences would be serious indeed. Everyone seemed confident that they knew what they had to do. But every soldier knows that nothing in a battle ever goes quite the way it was planned, no matter which gods you prayed to.

So by the time he had dressed and left his house on the morning of the Ides of March, Antony was nervous and keyed up, more irritable even than on those mornings when he rose with a bad hangover. Several of the household slaves were much the worse for wear by the time Antony was dressed in his consular toga (with a dagger concealed in the small of his back, held in place by a linen bandage wrapped around his stomach) and ready to leave the house.

One of his greatest worries, though, was not a matter of tactics. An essential part of the plan involved Calpurnia, and he was not sure, at all, whether or not she would play her role as they had agreed.

He calmed himself, though, by thinking that the day could end in one of two ways: either he would be the hero who saved Caesar, or he would be Caesar's successor. Neither of those was a bad ending; the only real question was, which was better? As he left his bedroom, he found that he didn't yet know the answer. Well, it was a tactical decision, and when the time came he would decide.

When he walked into the atrium of his house, he found Brutus and Albinus waiting for him, as arranged. The three of them, with a few other senators, would go together to Caesar's house and escort him to the Sen-ate meeting at Pompey's theater, as tradition and good manners required. It amused Antony to think that he knew what these men were planning and why they had agreed to serve as Caesar's escort, but they had no idea what was in his mind.

At Caesar's house, though, a disagreeable surprise awaited them. Caesar was dressed only in a tunic, no toga in sight, red or otherwise, and worse, no sign of any plans to leave the house. When Antony entered first, alone, into the private chambers, Caesar did not even wait for him to speak.

"You needn't look so shocked, Antony. I'm not going."

"May I ask why not? You set this date yourself."

"Caesar does not explain himself."

This shift to the third person in talking about himself never failed to annoy Antony, especially when addressed to him. As usual, he showed his annoyance by elaborately playing along.

"Maybe Caesar doesn't, but how am I going to explain him to the Senate? Doesn't Caesar imagine that the Senate will want some kind of an explanation? Shall I tell them that Caesar is indisposed?"

Every time he spoke the name, he put just a little too much emphasis on it. It usually worked, and it did this time, though it was hard to say exactly why. The corner of Caesar's lip turned up in a slight smile.

"OK, it's not me, it's Calpurnia. She's been worried ever since that street-corner conjurer warned me to 'Beware the Ides of March'"—Caesar's talent for mimicry was extraordinary, it might have been Spurinna speaking—"and last night she woke up at least three times that I know of. This morning she tells me she's had horrible dreams, blood on the moon and so on. You know I don't give a rat's ass for all that stuff, but she's really upset. I had to promise not to go to the Senate just to get a moment's peace from her shrieking and crying and tearing her hair."

All the time, Antony's mind was racing. On the one hand, he knew what Caesar didn't know, or at least wanted to pretend he didn't know: there would indeed be an attempt to kill him. Calpurnia's nightmares were oddly well timed, but he knew why. He would have time later to think what, if anything, to do about her apparent betrayal. So if he tried to encourage Caesar to go to the Senate today, knowing what he knew, was he not cooperating with the conspirators? But if he joined with Calpurnia (whom he now wanted to throttle) in allowing Caesar to stay home, his plans would go for naught. More importantly, perhaps, the conspirators would have to make a new plan, and perhaps this time it would be a better plan, harder to penetrate. This needed to happen now. To put it off would be to tempt fate. Antony was hardly a religious man, but Fortuna was a goddess he did not care to cross.

"So, then, I'll just step out into the atrium and tell my distinguished colleagues that Caesar can't come because his wife won't let him."

This annoyed Caesar, who showed his annoyance, as usual, by keeping his trademark half-smile on his face, while his eyes grew very cold.

"I'm sure, consul, you have far more important things to do than engage in a pointless conversation with so negligible a personage as I, so please, don't let me hold you back. As for me, I've said I'm not going to the Senate today, but, well, of course, if some higher authority says I must, I will surely comply. As soon as I kiss the signet ring of this higher authority. If a Roman consul tells me that I must go, well then, who am I to argue?"

Antony was not a shy man, nor a fearful one, nor even a particularly prudent one. But he knew when it was time to back away from Caesar. This elaborate politeness and the vacant half-smile boded no good for anyone.

It was at this point that Albinus appeared from behind him, quite unexpected. There had been a time, not so long ago, when Decimus Brutus Albinus was at least as much a *familiaris* in Caesar's house as Antony was now, but it had been some time since he had enjoyed that freedom, and his appearance now was something of an imposition. Caesar eyebrows went up and he cocked his head, looking rather like a lion bemused by the impudence of a fox who has stolen a bit of his meat. But the moment of danger suddenly passed, and the vacant smile broadened into a much friendlier one.

"Welcome to my house, Albinus. It's been far too long since we've seen you."

Antony could only shake his head. He would never learn to anticipate Caesar's reactions, except that the Great Man would almost never do the obvious thing. This was not a weakness in the man; rather, it was part of his magic. Keeping the people around him off balance more or less all the time was an old habit with him, and it had served him well.

Albinus sized up the situation in a glance and made his move. "Please excuse me, Caesar, for this intrusion. We were all growing more and more concerned at the delay, fearing that perhaps you were ill, and now I see that our fears were after all justified." He paused and lowered his voice, glanced at Antony and then spoke to Caesar in a more familiar tone. "Has it . . . has it happened again?"

It was always risky to allude in any way to Caesar's occasional attacks of what the Greek doctors called *epilepsia*. A more prudent man than Albinus would probably not have taken the risk. But Albinus was a soldier and an inveterate gambler, and he knew perfectly what the stakes were, and who he was playing with. The shot struck exactly where he wanted it to, and achieved exactly the effect he had intended.

"No," said Caesar, rising abruptly. "I was just getting dressed. Please go and tell my distinguished colleagues, who have done me the honor of attending me this morning, that I shall join them shortly." He clapped his hands to summon his servants and turned his back on Antony and Albinus, giving them to understand that their further presence in his room was unnecessary and might soon be annoying. Neither man missed the message. As the servants hurried in, Albinus and Antony walked out.

Both men had reason to be very satisfied with the outcome, but neither of them, for obvious reasons, could let the other know that. The friendship that had once existed between them, in the camps of Gaul and Greece, had been eroded since Pharsalus. One of them was still close to Caesar, and to power, and the other was not. Both of them felt the awkwardness, but neither quite knew how to break the silence.

"I hope," Albinus finally said, not looking at Antony, "that you've been well. One hears of you on every street corner, but we haven't seen much of you. The Great Man's been keeping you busy, I suppose, getting ready for the Parthians."

Antony was taken somewhat aback by Albinus's use, in Caesar's house, of the nickname for Caesar that his officers had used, behind the general's back but not without his knowledge, in Gaul. Of course, the nickname had become common knowledge in Rome, that in itself was not the problem. But knowing what he knew of Albinus's plans for the day, the reference to Caesar as the "Great Man" brought up memories, the more unwelcome for being warm and pleasant memories of good-humored banter in the officers' tent.

Antony felt the urge to hug his old friend, and at the same time, with equal strength, he wanted to pull his dagger from under his tunic and plunge it into his belly. He covered his emotions with a coughing fit, and then, when he had used the time to master his face and his voice, he turned to Albinus and said with a coarse soldier's laugh, "You couldn't be more right. Wiping out my own tracks with my ass."

By that time, they had rejoined the delegation waiting in the forecourt, and Antony was saved the effort of continuing the conversation.

The waiting senators had been talking to each other in small groups, but all faces turned towards Antony and Albinus as they approached.

"Caesar was briefly indisposed, but he will be with us shortly, and we can proceed," Antony announced. The relief on their faces was so obvious that, in other circumstances, it might have been laughable.

They stood in awkward silence, again, waiting for Caesar to appear. No one showed any inclination to speak. The waiting seemed interminable, but that, again, was one of Caesar's mannerisms: he could never endure to wait for anyone, but he thoroughly enjoyed making others wait for him. He would delay his appearance for as long as he could before people would begin to lose patience and decide not to wait any longer, and then he would appear. And just as he had calculated, his perfectly timed entrance would cause a stir, as everyone turned to see and a murmur ran through the crowd: "It's Caesar! He's here!" As many times as Antony had observed such scenes, he never ceased to wonder exactly how it was done. It would be a useful trick to master someday, but he had never had the knack of it. He would walk into a crowded room, and no one would notice except the people nearest him, or worse, people would turn and look, and then turn back to resume their conversations. How did Caesar do it, orchestrate his arrival in such a way that the moment he came into view, he was the complete and unchallenged center of attention?

On this occasion, the silent tension in the room made the customary effect of Caesar's entrance all the more palpable. The senators murmured their greetings, and as Caesar moved towards the door, his lictors took up their traditional place in front of him, his retainers and aides formed a bubble around him, and the senators fell into place behind him: the higher the rank, the nearer the head of the procession. They were Romans, after all, and senators. They needed no instructions on protocol: every one of them knew immediately, instinctively, where his place in line was, and no marshal could have made the parade more orderly.

And it was a parade, as it always was whenever Caesar left his house. Antony often wondered about the crowd of men, and some women as well, who always seemed to be standing around on the street outside Caesar's house in the Suburra, ready to start shouting and jumping up and down as soon as he came into sight, calling to their hero: "Caesar! Caesar!" Had they nothing else to do? How did they live? What did they eat, where did they sleep? There were, by all accounts (though who could possibly count them?) nearly a thousand thousands of souls in this city, of whom the merest fraction actually had work to do here. How did it happen that these people, whose lives were essentially as hopeless as those of slaves—or even worse, for a good slave was an asset in his master's house and could count on being looked after, up to a point—anyway, why did they idolize this man so much? Caesar was, a patrician, by all the gods of Hades, the scion of an ancient house that claimed to be descended from the goddess Venus herself, a man who, though his life had been far from an easy one, had not the slightest idea what it was like to be poor and downtrodden.

His house in the Suburra, where they all stood just now, was itself a symbol of the paradox. As Pontifex Maximus, Caesar had the right to live in the Regia, the official residence of the chief priest, in the center of the Forum, but he seldom made use of the old palace and preferred to live in the Suburra, where he had grown up, surrounded by tenement buildings, taverns, and brothels. Some said he had purchased this house himself shortly after Sulla's death, when he was still a penniless aristocrat from a down-on-its-luck old family, who had barely survived the dictator's proscriptions. Others said his mother had bought it when he was a boy, because she did not want her son to be spoiled by the luxury and security of the wealthier districts of the city. The truth, however (and Antony was one of the few who knew all this), was that the house stood on property that had belonged to the Caesars from time immemorial, and the Suburra had grown up around it, engulfing the property without actually encroaching on it.

One night in Gaul, during the siege of Alesia, which now seemed so long ago, Caesar himself had explained to his officers, with an ironic smile on his lips, how ancient prophecies held that the family would never die out, so long as the familial rites were celebrated in this spot. This was, once again, the kind of thing that Caesar liked to make fun of when he was drinking with his friends—but which he would still observe scrupulously, winking all the time if anyone seemed to notice.

It suited him, then, for people to think that he preferred to live with the people, but deep down he was as patrician as it was possible to be, and this piece of land was his in a way that no commoner could ever own even the grave he was buried in.

Antony shook his head. None of it made any sense. But, he reminded himself, this was not a good time to get lost in thought. There would be plenty of time for that later, after a few cups of good Falernian wine, when a man felt like asking philosophical questions that could never be answered. Right now he needed to stay focused.

It turned out to be rather later than expected, then, when the most important man in Rome, Julius Caesar, now consul for the fifth time, recently appointed Perpetual Dictator by the Roman Senate he had cowed into obedience, left his home to make his way to the Senate, which was about to convene its last meeting before his planned departure to the East, to Parthia.

The procession moved as it normally did, from the base of the Viminal Hill down to the Forum. The lictors knew the way from Caesar's house in the Suburra to Pompeii's Theater, in the Field of Mars, where the Senate was waiting to be convened that day, and so they didn't wait to be told where to turn the corners. Their route took them close to the ancient Forum, but when they reached the corner of the Basilica Aemilia, instead of turning left to go around the Basilica and enter the Forum, they angled off to the right, through a tangle of shops and stalls, into the new Julian Forum, designed by its namesake, Julius Caesar himself.

As soon as he entered his Forum, Caesar began looking around for someone, and Antony knew at once who he was looking for: Spurinna, the old charlatan who had made such a show of telling Caesar, some two months earlier, in this same, very public place, to "beware the Ides of March." And it came as a surprise to no one, now, that Spurinna was right there, on his favorite corner, waiting for Caesar to pass. The gods, he would surely say, rolling his eyes up for dramatic effect and trilling his r's three times longer than normal, had told him that Caesar was coming, and here he was. Caesar stopped when he saw him, and called to him from a distance, before this show could even begin:

"Well, old fellow, the Ides of March have come, haven't they? And here I still am!"

"Yes, Caesar," Spurinna answered, unfazed, "but they're not over yet."

Such audacity from a person of no real consequence provoked a moment's rather shocked silence, until Caesar broke it with a laugh of sincere appreciation. "Well played, old man, well played!" And he was still laughing as he walked out of the Julian Forum, the lictors scrambling to reform in front of him.

Antony was not laughing. He was sweating, heavily. His plans for trapping the conspirators in the very act of drawing their weapons against the Great Man had still seemed flawless last night, but now, in the light of day, he knew the moment of truth was approaching fast. His customary cockiness was gone. And he was unnerved, more than a little, by the strange aptness of Spurinna's reply. By all the gods, when all this was over, one way or another, there would not be a rathole in this city where Spurinna could hide, until Antony found out what the old man knew, and how he knew it.

The procession took its way through the Porta Flaminia and into the Field of Mars, towards Pompey's Theater, passing on their left a large space that Caesar had ordered to be cleared to make way for the construction of a new theater. He never stated publicly, nor did he need to state, that his aim was to build a structure that would supersede Pompey's Theater—which, of course, featured a bust of its founder, Caesar's defeated enemy, in a place of honor. Characteristically, Caesar had refused to order this sculpture removed after he returned from beating Pompey at Pharsalus, and seeing his head in a basket in Alexandria. More: he had actually ordered the bust to be replaced when the caretakers, in an excess of prudence, had removed it.

The truth was complicated. Caesar had gasped and wept at the sight of Pompey's severed head, when the pathetic adolescent Pharaoh, Ptolemy XIII, had presented it to him, as though it were the finest of gifts. And the tears were real. The two men, Pompey and Caesar, had a history together, and much of it, to be truthful, was the kind of history that made men brothers, not enemies. Pompey had been happily married to Caesar's only daughter, Julia, and it would be hard to say which of these two powerful men had been more devastated when she died in childbirth, while her father was still fighting in Gaul, five years before the Civil War began. In other circumstances, grief might have brought Pompey and Caesar closer. But private feelings are a dangerous luxury for public men.

Antony shook his head, again, as though to clear it of memories. It was time to focus on the moment. The procession was entering Pompey's Portico, where most of the senators were waiting for them, standing and talking in small groups in the labyrinthine gardens. As soon as the lictors entered the archway that led into the portico, these conversations all ceased immediately, and everyone began pushing to the front, eager to catch the Dictator's eye for a moment, or better yet, to exchange a word with him. Antony knew well that for at least half an hour, Caesar would mingle with this crowd, receiving and dismissing petitions, smiling and waving at some, nodding to others, ignoring the rest. A routine day with the Senate. Antony always found all this meeting and greeting a complete waste of time, but Caesar, of course, loved it. "Most of the Senate's real business," he would patiently explain to Antony time after time, "is actually done just before we go in, take our official seats, go through all the protocol, and start the round of endless speeches. Or again, just as we leave." Antony couldn't agree more that the formal Senate meetings were nearly unbearable, but he still could not see the use for all this chit-chat beforehand, either.

And this day, of all days, he was in no mood for chit-chat.

What he meant to do was to break off from the crowd as soon as possible and check on his men, who should be waiting, armed and ready, well hidden in that storage room. Just as he started that way, however, he was stopped by Trebonius—whose assigned task, he knew well, was to keep Antony as far from Caesar as possible. Instinctively, he slipped his hand under his toga, checking to make sure his own dagger was ready to hand. Seeing a flicker of alarm on Trebonius's broad face, he made the gesture into a scratch and smiled.

"It's only mid-March, but it's already too hot in these damn things, isn't it?"

Trebonius laughed in response. "I don't remember feeling much cooler in armor, Antony, unless it was winter in Gaul. But that was a long time ago, and I'm happy to say I've nearly forgotten what that was like, really. Don't tell me you miss the freezing rain, or the snow up to your testicles, because I sure don't. Still, those were the days, weren't they, doing a man's work? We saved Caesar's ass that day in Alesia, you and I, and now here we are, kissing that same hairy ass."

Any other day, Antony thought to himself, I'd love to stand here and talk old soldier with you while the politicians do whatever it is that politicians do, but it's not any other day and I need you out of my way. What he said, however, was naturally just the opposite. While trying to squeeze his way around Trebonius—no easy task on this narrow pathway between hedges in the ornamental garden, especially given Trebonius' considerable bulk—he answered in kind.

"The snow didn't have to be that high to reach my testicles, Trebonius," he answered, "but I'll admit I didn't like dragging them in the cold."

He didn't follow Trebonius's lead to talk about Alesia, about the day when the two of them had led a wild cavalry charge against the rear of the Gallic relief army, disorganizing their attack and giving Caesar time to regroup and counterattack. Just at this moment, it was not a memory he wanted to deal with.

Trebonius moved slightly, apparently innocently shifting his body as he laughed at the crude joke, but actually quite intentionally blocking a little more of the path.

Antony tried to squeeze past him. "Sorry, old friend, there's someone over there I've got to talk to."

Trebonius's friendly smile wavered. "Yeah, well, actually, I've got something I need to talk to you about, and it's real, real urgent." Antony felt a trace of threat in his voice, and stepped back, unsure if he was going to need to defend himself or not. For a moment, the two men eyed each other, no longer smiling.

It was just at this moment that a general movement began towards the doorway to the Curia, the spacious meeting hall that faced the Theater across the Portico. Evidently Caesar had decided that the time had come to start the meeting, rather sooner than Antony had supposed.

Antony looked again at Trebonius, deciding just how much time to give him. A movement caught the corner of his eye, and when he looked around, he realized that about ten men in togas were not moving with the others, but were instead moving straight towards Antony and Trebonius, from different places around the portico. As the senators filed into the Curia, these ten men were converging on them, and removing their togas. From their musculature and movement, Antony quickly realized that they were not senators—they were, instead, almost certainly, the gladiators Spurinna had warned him about, borrowed from the gladiatorial school by the conspirators to protect them from Antony (or anyone else who might try to defend Caesar from their attack). But he had expected the gladiators to surround the door to the Curia, not to stand between him and his men. This was a precaution that his sources hadn't warned him the conspirators would take.

His eyes flicked back to Trebonius—who was now standing in a fighter's posture, his back to the Curia entrance, with a dagger in his hand. The game was on. Of course, Trebonius himself was not the main problem any longer: Antony could take him in a moment. But although he was a born fighter, though he knew he was personally, physically, as dangerous as any man in Rome when the fighting actually began, Antony was under no illusions that he could actually handle ten gladiators. One or two of them might go down; if he had had a sword instead of a dagger, three or four, but eventually they would bring him down. He had been in tight spots before, in the heat of battle, but he had never been alone with eleven armed enemies, and this time, he realized, he was about to die.

Or not.

With the instincts of a fighter, Antony knew that he had about five heartbeats to put down Trebonius and make a break for the door where his men were waiting to be called. He did not even take the time to draw his own dagger, which is what Trebonius was waiting for. Instead, he made a quick lunge and thrust with his empty hand, sidestepped the defensive counter-thrust, and with the speed of a cobra struck the side of Trebonius's head with his own forehead. Trebonius went down hard. Antony dodged the falling body, cleared the two intervening hedges in two long jumps (gymnastic training came in handy at the oddest times), and sprinted towards the door.

The speed and unexpected direction of his attack on Trebonius left most of the advancing gladiators isolated and useless, but Antony still found himself facing three of them, who had managed to position themselves to the left of the doorway of the Curia, where—though presumably they didn't know this—they were blocking Antony's access to his men. Fortunately for Antony, they seemed to be assuming that his goal would be to reach Caesar, which meant that they knew nothing of the mortal threat that lay behind the nondescript doorway just to the left of the ceremonial entrance. The narrow pathway from which they were advancing kept them from being able to surround Antony, and in fact he quickly realized that he would be fighting with one of them at a time.

This was Marcus Antonius at his best, in the kind of situation he understood, a tactical situation that called on his experience and his instincts. He had watched gladiators fight, and even considered himself something of an expert on them. He understood, then, that gladiators were practiced fighters and killers, but they were seldom trained soldiers. They had to attack and kill in order to survive, like soldiers, but above all they were expected to put on a good show: if the kill was too quick, the audience was disappointed, and their boos and catcalls could be as deadly for a gladiator as an opponent's sword. So Antony knew how to deal with them.

The first man went down with his belly slashed open before he really knew that the fight was on in earnest. Antony had flipped the dagger into his left hand while feinting for the throat with his now empty right hand, and then slashed down and to the right with the dagger. Since childhood he had made a point of learning to do everything with either hand, not favoring the right or the left, and now this discipline paid off.

The next gladiator, however, was already making his attack before Antony had fully recovered from slicing open his first opponent, and the only way to parry the blow was to take a sharp cut to his forearm. He pushed against the blade, though, rather than giving in to the blow as his attacker expected, pushed the attacking arm higher despite the searing pain this cost him, and again used his left hand to attack. A quick thrust into the unprotected abdomen and the man crumpled to the ground.

A glance at the door to the Curia told Antony that time was short indeed. Senators were rushing out the door, shouting. The attack on Caesar had surely begun.

Fortunately, Antony's third opponent was not prepared to die for his cause. Whatever they had paid him or his masters, it was apparently not enough. The man started to back away, and at the first corner in the labyrinth of pathways, he turned and ran.

Antony sprinted towards the door of the storage room, but when he got there, he paused and looked around. No one was watching him: all eyes were on the door to the Curia.

He threw open the storeroom door, but before he could give the order to attack, he slumped to the floor. The legionaries waiting inside, swords in hand, came piling out the door, ready for action, but when they saw that Antony was bleeding, they clustered around him, some creating a defensive circle around him, others bending over to help.

He counted to ten, slowly and silently, before he opened his eyes. That should be enough. He waved away the men standing over him and shouted, "Go! Inside! Now!" They charged, and were already inside before Antony, weakened by blood loss, reached the door. He could hear the sounds of fighting inside, and at least one death scream.

He tried to hide his smile, but it didn't matter: no one was looking. Antony was pleased with himself. He had learned Caesar's lessons: he had gone into battle with three plans, with the choice between them depending on what happened, but all three plans ended the same way: he was going to win. He went inside to take charge.

2

The Trial Begins

Late June, 44 B.C.E, three months after the
attempted assassination of Julius Caesar

Praeneste, Italy (modern Palestrina, south of Rome)

Gaius Sallustius Crispus awoke suddenly that morning, rather too
early, well before dawn, with an anxious feeling in his stomach that would
not let him go back to sleep, try though he might. Perhaps his restlessness
had stemmed from his dreams, but these were already gone, dispelled,
forgotten, leaving only this vague, gray discomfort. This was happening
to him more and more often, as he grew older, and he dreaded it. Today
it was particularly bad, this feeling that somehow everything in his life
had gone terribly wrong, would soon grow much worse, and there was
nothing whatsoever he could do about it. He knew it would pass, as it
always did, when daylight came, but this awareness did little to soothe
the crawling feeling in his belly in the pre-dawn darkness of his bedroom.

It was not exactly fear. Sallust wondered what to call it, properly.
Not fear. Fear has a very definite object, a point of focus, it is—how to
say it?—transitive, yes, one is afraid *of something*. When it's fear that
wakes you up before dawn, you know exactly what it's about. He had
awoken early the morning before battle on many occasions, when his
first conscious, coherent thought was, "Will I survive this day?" Surely
every soldier knows that feeling. You know you should try to get a good
night's sleep, then of all times, because a hard day's work lies ahead, and
fatigue can get you killed. Your energy flags, your attention slips, and in a

moment you're dead. But who can sleep if you think the day that's about to dawn might be your last?

This particular morning it was not fear, not exactly. The Greeks surely have a name for it, he thought, they have names for everything. *Taraxia,* I suppose, disquiet of the soul. Would it be *anxietas* in Latin? Probably, except that I just now made up the word. But that's me, as usual, fussing with words in my head instead of actually dealing with the problem. It's the feeling down in your belly that you can't save yourself from the mess you've made. It doesn't matter what you call it.

He could feel Terentia's warm body next to him, and as he lay there, listening to her even breathing, he momentarily considered drowning his anxiety in a stronger passion. But she disliked being awakened early, even for—well, again, a Greek phrase, *ta erotika,* the things of Eros. No Latin name for it, really, but hardly surprising; our fathers did it, of course, but they never talked about it. Talking about it meant you either use barnyard Latin or you switch to Greek.

Anyway, it would be a shame and a waste to awaken her for a momentary pleasure that in all likelihood would end badly anyway. When they had first married, the very fact that he, a confidante of Caesar himself, was sleeping with Cicero's ex-wife had excited both of them, though surely for different reasons. But that had been two years ago now. Yes, she still excited him, but he was no longer in his thirties himself, and she was eight years older, erotically skilled beyond anything he could have imagined, but even so—well, there you have it. They had married each other with the same idea in mind, really, to tweak Cicero's oversized nose, though not a word had ever passed between them on this subject. And that sort of thinking might fire a night or two of passion, but was it enough to keep a marriage alive?

And so he lay there, trying not to awaken her by moving too much, or worse, getting out of bed before dawn, which would mean that she would lift her head and begin asking the same questions, over and over. It would end, as it always did, when he snapped at her, and she snapped back, and then silence in the house for a few hours, until he came to her, contrite, and she would forgive him. There were times this game was worth playing, especially when it ended back in the bedroom. But not today.

He had already decided, finally, definitively, not to go to Rome to watch the trial of the first five conspirators against Caesar. His decision had been announced to his family and household, as well as to his neighbors and friends. Nearly everyone else he knew, except for the very young, the very old, and the very sick, was going to the city to see the trial, a show more exciting than a hundred gladiators. The town of Praeneste would be as empty for the next few days as at any time since the fighting in Italy ended, some four years ago. But Sallust would not go.

There was a day, he thought, staring at the ceiling of his bedroom in the predawn grayness, when nothing could have kept me from the Forum on a day like this. There was a day when I spoke from the Rostra to thousands of citizens, and they applauded me. There was a day when I imagined myself returning to Rome from my province in Africa to be greeted as a hero, perhaps even a triumph. There was a day when I really believed that the grand and noble things the politicians said in the Senate actually meant something.

Now, he was ashamed of his naiveté every time he thought of it.

It really mattered little, either to Sallust the man, or to Sallust the amateur historian, or to the Empire, or to the whole world, really, who won or lost this trial. It had come down to this—that five representatives of the cream of Roman nobility (who were really overgrown children squabbling over their marbles) were on trial for trying to kill the Dictator (who underneath his fascinating exterior was simply one of them, the one who had gathered the most marbles), and a guilty verdict meant death by public strangulation. This very fact was enough for anyone of any intelligence and learning to realize that the Republic was finished.

Tradition demanded that the *judices* for this trial, that is, the jurors who would decide if the defendants were guilty or innocent, should be selected by lot. In fact, the pool of men deemed eligible by the *praetor urbanus* to sit on the jury for treason cases had somehow been reduced to 51, which was exactly the number needed to fill a jury. The odd number insured that there could not be a tie; a simple majority was enough to convict the defendant, though in practice the margins of conviction or acquittal were seldom very close.

Ironically, the trial that was about to open would be conducted according to Caesar's own rules—among which had been his edict that the panel of jurors for a major criminal trial could not be challenged by the defendant or his advocate. Previously, the prosecutors had been allowed to challenge up to five jurors, likewise the defense, but this system had been so thoroughly abused that no one, Populist or Conservative, was really opposed to Caesar's reforms.

The *nominis delatio*, the indictment, had also been quite the farce, from all reports. (Sallust had loudly professed complete indifference to the news from Rome, but in fact he hadn't missed a word from what his neighbors were telling each other.) There had been a very long list of ambitious men clambering for the task of prosecutor, so the law required that the jury vote to select the one who would actually pursue the case. The jurors were instructed to consider two questions: first, by whom does the person harmed, if still living, wish to be represented? and second, whom does the defendant most fear in the role of prosecutor?

In this case, the first criterion had settled the matter, and the second was immaterial. Antony had let it be known that Caesar wished the case to be prosecuted by Quintus Pedius, and that was that.

It was an odd choice. Sallust knew Pedius, in fact rather well, and to tell the truth he thought highly of him, personally. Pedius was no fool, but it would be hard to argue that he was truly equal to the task, especially since he had made what reputation he had as a soldier, not an advocate. Why had Caesar chosen him above all the others? But who could say, really, if Caesar had chosen him at all? No one had seen the Great Man, apart from his family, the doctors, and Antony, since the Ides of March, and there were even whispers that in reality he had died of his wounds, and the conversations with Antony were all faked.

There would be nothing to see at this trial but further proof of how low the Republic had actually fallen. That is what Sallust was saying to anyone who would listen. Some even nodded as though they understood and agreed. But without the slightest doubt they, too, were already started on the two-day journey to Rome, or would soon start. Sallust thought for a moment of the road, the sedan chair swaying as his excellent Numidian bearers carried him down the mountain and up the valley to meet the Via Appia, even more thronged than usual. He reminded himself how much he hated traveling. And deep inside, he almost believed it.

"Of course you will go."

Terentia's voice startled him. He was so sure that she was still asleep. What had long since ceased to startle him quite so much was this ability she had, to know what he was thinking before he spoke. After these two years of marriage, almost, he was still not sure whether he loved or hated this way she had of breaking into his train of thought, as though he had been speaking aloud.

"I will not!" he snapped back.

"If I were inclined to gamble, like my poor sister, I'd wager my fortune against yours that by noon the day after tomorrow you'll be standing in the Forum with all the rest. And by the way, do take little Publius with you, please."

"Whatever for?" Sallust was thoroughly annoyed that Terentia clearly meant to win the main argument by diverting to a side topic. (Do all women do this? he wondered.) "He's just a boy, it's a long journey and there's nothing there to interest him."

"Oh please! Twelve is quite old enough to appreciate history. Besides, he's your son, not mine, he hates me with his whole soul because I'm not his Mommy, and if you leave him here, I'll tell you what will happen. He'll sulk in his room for the entire time, speaking to no one except to scream at the slaves, and on those rare occasions when he allows me to see him, he'll look daggers at me. By the time you return one of the two of us will be either gone from the house or dead."

After another twenty minutes of pointless quarreling (they both knew how it would end), Sallust acknowledged defeat, and called his manservant, who was then ordered to prepare the sedan chair and the necessary supplies for a 10-day journey: allowing six days for the trial in Rome, which was surely more than enough, two days to get there, two days to get back. Runners would have to be sent to friends who lived along the way—he still had a few, after all, in Tusculum, in Gabii—to arrange for lodgings for himself and Publius. Once in the city, of course, he would stay in his own town home, the house he and Publius had lived in, back in the days when he still thought he could make something of himself in the capital city of the world, and still thought he could make a life of sorts with Publius's mother, a woman whose name he had sworn to all the gods never to speak again.

They left well before noon, intending to make Tusculum by nightfall.

Later that day, as he was jostled along in his sedan chair, with the curtains drawn to keep out the dust and noise of the oldest and most famous road in the Roman Empire, Sallust tried to compose his thoughts. Ten years ago, when he had still been a committed Populist, he would have made a point of staying at roadside taverns on such a journey, rather than imposing on his wealthy friends, the way Cicero, Cato, and all those Optimates, the Conservatives he used to loathe with such intensity, liked to do. He was not the same man now. And yes, Terentia had brought a lot of money to the marriage, but Sallust had been a wealthy man before that. And no, he hadn't stolen it from Numidia—surely anyone who knew how things were done in Rome would understand that. The extortion charges brought against him two years earlier, after his return from his province in Africa, were only intended to harass Caesar, brought by men who wanted to test the Dictator's power without confronting him directly. But there no longer seemed much point in denying oneself the comforts of hospitality among old friends, merely to make a political statement he had long since ceased to believe in. Besides, he was too old to go and piss in public latrines, elbow-to-elbow with the-dear-gods-only-know-who. And there was young Publius to think of, he was at the age where old pederasts might . . . well, never mind that. No roadside inns for them.

Which explains why Sallust and his son Publius, properly bathed and dressed after two long, dusty days on the road, would be standing in the Forum, waiting for the spectacle to begin.

Two days later

Rome, the Forum

The trial of the five conspirators began as scheduled, of course, five days before the Kalends of Quinctilis, in the fifth consulship of C. Julius Caesar and the first of M. Antonius, with P. Cornelius Dolabella now in office as suffect consul, replacing Caesar, whose wounds had required him to retire temporarily from public life.

The day had been sunny and warm since early morning, just enough wind to freshen the city's stale air, at least a little. In a month or so it would be far too hot during the day to transact any business, but in those days the heat in Rome was still bearable well into July, even for men in togas. Thunderstorms were not uncommon in June. But even if the day had been rainy and blustery, it would have made little difference to the crowds who were now thronging the Forum to watch the trial. If it had been winter, most would have stood up to their knees in snow for hours, just to get a glimpse of the principal actors in this, perhaps the greatest drama of these times—times that had seen plenty of drama already.

By the time the trial was set to begin, precisely at noon, a rat would have been hard put to find a foothold of free space in the Forum. The senior members of the Senate and their families occupied places of honor in front of the new Senate House, the one that Caesar had ordered built on the old Assembly Ground, to replace the ancient Curia (an angry mob had burned it down almost ten years before, enraged by the murder of their hero, Clodius, an uncomfortable precedent for the situation at hand). The younger senators sat directly in front of the tribunal, filling

most of the open central area between the tribunal and the Cloaca Maxima, the ancient storm sewer that drained the Forum (the lesser the senator's pedigree, the nearer he sat to the Great Sewer, which of course stank
with great dignity). Among them could be seen Gauls, in their outlandish
trousers and peculiar facial hair. Their presence in the Senate at Caesar's
command still offended the sensibilities of many aristocrats (and not a
few of Rome's less privileged), but here they were.

Several ranks of battle-ready legionaries stood along the west bank
of the Cloaca Maxima. The soldiers faced out into the open space that
stretched from there to the Regia, the official residence where Caesar occasionally held court as *pontifex maximus*, chief priest of the public cult.
Not so very long ago, the presence of armed men within the *pomerium*,
the religious boundary that marked the sacred heart of the City, would
have been unthinkable. But so many unthinkable things had happened
in the last five years or so that no one paid any particular attention to
this one.

A group of wealthy *equites* ("businessmen who are wealthy enough
to be important but don't come from a senatorial family and have no
political ambitions," Sallust explained to Publius), men who had enough
influence or knew whose palm to grease for their privileges, sat in the
chairs that had been placed in the portico of the two basilicas (the Aemil-
ian and the Julian, the latter still not quite finished). Their comfort, and
their view, were protected by burly slaves and clients. It was here, then,
that Sallust, who no longer wished to be seen among the senators, found
a place for himself and his son. He had no friends among these men,
mostly admirers of Cicero, but neither had he any particular enemies.

"Why aren't you sitting with the senators?" Publius asked. "You
were a tribune, then praetor, and then the governor of a province, *pro
praetore*." Publius tended to take himself very seriously, and never missed
an opportunity to display his command of public affairs at a level much
higher than what anyone would expect from a Roman boy his age.

"I don't care to be associated with those people," Sallust replied.
"This will be fine. The thin double stripe on my toga suits me far better."

The matter was more complicated than that, but Sallust wasn't inclined to explain it all to his son, just here and just now. Someday, surely,
there would be a better time for that conversation. He had indeed once
worn the broad maroon stripe of a senator, and Publius, for all his young
years, knew that. It pained Sallust now to think of the pride he had felt
then, after his tribunate. But first the censors, too busy purging the Senate

of Caesar's men to think of the responsibility of their ancient and honorable office, had expelled him. Then, after Sallust had been named praetor by Caesar before the African campaign, and then served as a provincial governor of praetorian rank, he had returned to Rome from his province, not in triumph, but to face an unjust impeachment. Even though the case had never gone to trial and he was theoretically innocent, Sallust was too proud to wear the senatorial stripe again, and face the possibility of public humiliation, if anyone were to challenge his right to wear it.

Behind the cordon formed by the public buildings and the lines of soldiers was the *corona,* as Cicero liked to call it: the "crown" of spectators, jostling and pushing to get closer or higher, so they could see and hear what was going on. Some of them were perched in the most unlikely places. The steps of the tiny old round Temple of Vesta were filled with people, even on the side turned away from the tribunal; those who stood there were happy to hear even if they could not see.

Behind and beyond them were even greater masses, stretching off to the south and west, a sea of restless humanity, most of whom would not actually be able to see or hear much of anything. But they would always be able to say, to the end of their lives, that they had been there that day. Some of those who could hear and see something from the *corona* kept up a running commentary for the benefit of family and friends behind them, and their reports were passed back with surprising speed, so that even those who stood too far from the center of action to actually hear anything could still keep up with what was going on.

"It's no longer a common practice to have a trial outdoors, in the very center of the Forum," Sallust explained to his son. "Some people thought that this trial should be held in the Basilica Julia, over there. Other people favored one or another of the old temples that surround the Forum. It would have been more in line with recent practice to hold the trial on the steps of the Temple of Castor and Pollux, at the other end of the Forum. That would also have limited the number of spectators to the membership of the Senate, and probably not even all of them—which, I suppose, is why they didn't do it there."

Publius yawned. Sallust realized with some chagrin that he had been lecturing to his son, not talking with him. No doubt the boy was bored, despite his precociousness.

He also realized, with even more chagrin, that his whole pose of indifference about this whole event was probably hypocritical. He had just given his son a rather detailed account of a rather obscure legal dispute regarding the proper place to hold the trial. And to himself, at least, he needed to admit that he had followed every scrap of news about these things—all the while telling anyone who listened that he meant to stay in Praeneste and skip the whole sordid show.

To his surprise, though, Publius stifled his yawn and asked a question. "So why all this argument over where to have the trial?"

"For some people," Sallust answered, pleased that his son had actually heard his lecture, "never mind all their Populist rhetoric about 'the People,' the actual presence of the urban plebs would be about the last thing they would want at such a politically sensitive moment. But it was Caesar himself, or so I heard, who insisted that the trial must be seen and heard by as many people as possible."

"I thought he was too weak to talk. That's what everyone is saying. They're also saying that . . .". But Sallust didn't let his son finish.

"He talks to Antony, when the doctor lets him. But whether Caesar actually says the things that Antony comes out and tells everyone, well . . ."

A red-faced, corpulent man, who had been standing behind them for some time now, snorted at this last remark, which made Sallust realize that he was really being very indiscreet. He felt a flutter of fear: no doubt the Forum was full of agents today, for one side or the other, just waiting for the opportunity to start a fight. The whole political life of Rome had degenerated in the last twenty years or so into gang fights in the streets, involving gangs that were used by Populists and Conservatives alike to settle problems the Senate was increasingly unable to even address, let alone solve. Sallust had no desire to see a brawl break out right here, with his young son very much in harm's way. He was relieved when the man showed no further interest in what he had said, but merely turned, craning his fat red neck to get a better view of the scene where the great drama was about to be played out.

The praetor's chair had been set up on a dais that now stood directly in front of the Temple of Concord. This was the spot to which Caesar had moved the Rostra, since his re-positioning of the Senate House had essentially eliminated the old Assembly Ground as a public space. The jurors would be seated on the dais, to the praetor's right, while the prosecutor and the defender would speak from the Rostra, as would the witnesses. Again, even the physical arrangements were those of a theatrical spectacle, Sallust thought, and not a respectable trial.

By this time, all the jurors were in place, waiting for the defendants, the prosecutor, and the praetor himself, who would signal the opening of proceedings by assuming his place in the curule chair. The defendants, due to their high rank, would be escorted to their place, not by armed guards, but by senators selected by the praetor for that role.

It had once been the particular duty of the praetors to hear all trials in Rome, from treason and murder to the theft of a chicken or a dispute between farmers over a fence, right here in the Forum, with the bustle of daily business going on around them all the time. But those simple times were long gone, and most cases were now handled by legal experts appointed by the praetor to make rulings, which he would then ratify. This was a special case, however, and so the *praetor urbanus* himself, the most important of the six praetors elected each year, would be presiding.

There was no small irony in all this. Until the Ides of March, the urban praetor had been none other than Marcus Junius Brutus, personally nominated to that post by Caesar (as were all the public magistrates these days: the Populist champion had abolished elections). And it was this same Brutus, with four of his fellow assassins, who was now on trial on a capital charge of treason before the same court over which he himself used to preside.

And there was an even greater irony: the new urban praetor selected to replace Brutus after his arrest was none other than Lucius Antonius, younger brother of Antony, Caesar's co-consul, personal confidante, and currently the only man other than his doctor allowed to see the wounded Dictator.

To be sure, just a month before the Ides of March, Caesar had unexpectedly named Aemilius Lepidus, a thoroughly unremarkable man, as his Master of the Horse (a strange old title for the Dictator's second in command; no one could explain it, but no one wanted to change it), even though this post had previously been occupied very comfortably by Antony. But no one believed for a moment that Lepidus had really replaced Antony as Caesar's alter ego. This was always Caesar's way: he hated to be predictable, and he didn't like his subordinates to feel too comfortable in their positions. Sallust knew that all too well.

With such a judge presiding, and a carefully chosen panel of jurors, the outcome of the trial seemed certain to everyone, regardless of their political sympathies. After all, no one on either side really questioned the basic facts. There had been a conspiracy to assassinate Caesar, the attempt had been made in front of many witnesses, the Dictator had been gravely wounded and nearly died. No one supposed for a moment that the accused, or at least the two primary figures—M. Junius Brutus and

C. Cassius Longinus—would even try to deny that they had conspired to assassinate the Dictator. The third chief conspirator, Decimus Brutus Albinus, was no longer among the living.

Perhaps some of the younger senators involved in the plot would try to weasel out, Sallust thought, deny that they were present at meetings, or claim that they never realized the attempt would actually be made, and never actually intended to take part, or intended all along to betray the conspirators to the authorities. Most of those trials would follow this one, and public interest would not be so intense as now.

In the end, before Caesar had been rescued by Antony's men, seven men had struck blows with the daggers concealed in their document boxes. The rest (17 more senators had finally been charged with conspiracy) could claim that they had only been bystanders. But two of those seven would-be assassins were already dead, killed by Antony's legionaries on the Ides of March, and for the other five there was surely no escape.

"If everyone knows they did it, then why have a trial at all?"

It almost seemed as though Publius, too, had Terentia's odd gift of reading Sallust's thoughts. But that's absurd, she's not even his mother, just his step-mother, who loathes him almost as much as he loathes her. Sallust wondered if he should answer the question, anyway, since it would be hard to answer it honestly without getting into a quarrel. But the red-faced man who had apparently been eavesdropping before was now deep in conversation with the man next to him—about chariot races, of all things. So Sallust lowered his voice and tried to explain.

"Roman citizens can't be put to death without a trial. It's the law. Even though these men broke the law, they are still under its protection. If we break the law to punish criminals, we are no better than criminals ourselves."

"Didn't Sulla do that, have his enemies killed without any trials or anything? I've heard you talking about those . . . What do you call them? Prescriptions?"

"Proscriptions," Sallust corrected. "Yes, Publius, after Sulla won the battle at the Caudine Gate, not far from where we're standing right now, he published lists of people he wanted dead, which we call 'proscriptions.' So if you wanted, you could kill a person who was proscribed, whose name was on that list, and then take his property as your own. A lot of people who sit in the Senate today—or their fathers rather, that was almost forty years ago—they have blood on their hands. But that's just what

Caesar never wanted to do, to cut the throats of his enemies like a pirate. He hated Sulla."

"Why?"

"Well, it's a little complicated. Caesar's first wife was named Cornelia; she was the daughter of Cornelius Cinna, who was an ally and friend of Gaius Marius."

"That was Sulla's enemy, right? Marius?"

"That's right. Marius was a very . . . well, unusual person, the only person in our history to be consul seven times, and the only person I know of who rose all the way from being a foot soldier in the legions to the highest office in the Republic. Sulla was a radical Conservative and hated everything Marius stood for. So finally a civil war broke out, and when Sulla won, thanks to the veteran legions he brought back with him from Asia, he decided to wipe out the whole Populist party. By that time, Marius was already dead, but there was still his colleague, Cinna. Anyway, Caesar was a young man at the time, just married to Cinna's daughter, and Sulla ordered him to divorce her. Caesar refused."

"Wasn't he afraid that Sulla would have him killed?"

Sallust looked around guardedly and lowered his voice even more. "There are lots of stories about why Sulla didn't put Caesar on the proscription list, and quite honestly I don't know the truth. I'm not sure Caesar himself really knows, or anyone else who's still alive. One possibly important fact is that Caesar's mother and aunt were actually close relatives of Sulla. But you know how I hate gossip. Anyway, shortly after all this, Sulla suddenly decided that he'd done his job and wanted to quit, so he just announced in the Senate that he was leaving public life."

"You hate Sulla, too, don't you, Father? Did he kill someone you loved?"

"No, son, nothing like that. What he did was to take a lot of land from my father, your grandfather, and many, many good, loyal Italians like him, and parcel it out to his soldiers when the fighting was over. They were the scum of the earth, those veterans of his, and Amiternum, where I was born and raised, was never the same after that. My father was still a wealthy man, but it broke his spirit. So yes, I hate Sulla's memory, and I'm not the only person in this city who does."

Publius thought this over for a moment, but he didn't reply. Instead, he asked another question.

"These men on trial, are they going to be crucified when this is over? That's what everyone is saying."

"Well, to begin with, son, Roman citizens can't be crucified, that's a penalty reserved for pirates and renegade slaves and scum like that. Anyway, you can never be completely sure how a trial will go. There have been so many surprises over the years."

In fact, Sallust thought, there was only one possible reason for doubting the outcome of this trial: the person of the advocate who would be representing the defendants. This was a man, after all, who had lost very few cases in his long career, and won many that no one would have thought winnable. After nearly 10 years of absence from the law courts, Marcus Tullius Cicero was returning to take on the most important case of his career—and it was one that could not be won. The speeches would be memorable, no doubt. Truth be told, it was curiosity as to what Cicero would say in this impossible situation that had brought fully half of all these people to the Forum today. And that included people on both sides of the lines of troops who kept "the many" at a safe distance from "the few."

The main prosecutor, Pedius, would doubtless be the first to confess that he was no match for Cicero, certainly not in terms of eloquence, or experience in the courts, or legal knowledge. Pedius was an intelligent and painfully honest man, very loyal to Caesar personally, but not skilled at the maneuvering and infighting that was a trademark of the Great Man's intimates. He had served Caesar well, but he had never appeared in such an important case. His military record, on the other hand, was nothing to be ashamed of: it was he, for example, who had so quickly put down the rebellion raised by two of Cicero's proteges, Caelius Rufus and Annius Milo, just before the climactic battle at Pharsalus, when no one believed that Caesar would return alive from Greece. Not everyone thought that Pedius had really deserved the triumph that Caesar later organized for him, but the soldiers who had served under him would never let a bad word be spoken about Pedius in their presence, and that surely meant something.

Publius again interrupted his father's thoughts with a question. "Are they being tried for murder, then? How can they? They didn't actually kill anyone, did they?"

"It's not that simple, son." Sallust sighed: he was embarrassed to hear himself repeating that phrase, over and over. "I'll explain it to you later, it's complicated."

Soon after the attack on Caesar, there had been talk of an extraordinary trial by the Popular Assembly, an ancient procedure that Caesar himself had long ago revived from centuries of disuse, when he was praetor almost twenty years before. But Antony had gone in to see the ailing Dictator for one of those brief "conversations," and had emerged with the decision that an ordinary praetorian trial in the Treason Court would be the most suitable procedure. To be sure, the Treason Court did not have nearly as much tradition as the other standing courts, such as the Violent Crimes Court or the Provincial Extortion Court. But it seemed appropriate to make use, for this purpose, of a law that Caesar himself had proposed and carried three years earlier, which stated that "those who lay violent hands on Roman magistrates are to be tried in the same penal category as traitors and spies who betray the Roman people to its enemies." The only conceivable penalty in such a case was death. The other two courts did not have the legal power to sentence a Roman citizen to death.

This was all laced with a certain irony. Whenever he spoke of his reasons for crossing the Rubicon and precipitating a civil war, Caesar always mentioned two primary reasons for taking arms against the Senate: first, the personal affront he had received when the Senate repealed the laws that had previously enabled him to stand for the consulship *in absentia*, that is, without disbanding his army; and secondly, the outrageous way in which two of "his" tribunes (including both Antony and Sallust) had been manhandled by the Senate. The new Treason Act had been presented and justified as an attempt to prevent anything like the forcible expulsion of a tribune from ever happening again. It was also an attempt to repair an aspect of the criminal law that had previously been based on archaic, unclear, sometimes contradictory, and frequently *ex tempore* laws, including a draconian law passed by none other than Sulla, and then revoked, along with most of Sulla's legislation, when the retired Dictator's body was scarcely cold in its grave.

And this wasn't the end of the ironies, Sallust thought. Caesar defends the traditional rights and privileges of the tribunes by taking arms against the Senate and the consuls. He then passes a law that, had it been in force when he crossed the Rubicon, would have made traitors of Caesar himself and all his soldiers, subject to public execution (which indeed would have happened to them if the other side had won). Caesar began his political career by defying Sulla, refusing to divorce his wife, Cornelia, the daughter of Sulla's arch-enemy, Cornelius Cinna. And now Caesar bears the same title as Sulla, Dictator, theoretically an emergency, ad hoc office, which Sulla had manifestly abused, but which he had never tried to prolong in the way Caesar had done. Down in Hades, Sulla was surely laughing out loud at the formula "Perpetual Dictator," which Caesar had graciously allowed the Senate to confer on him just a month before the Ides of March.

And there was more. As praetor-elect in Cicero's consulship, almost twenty years earlier, Caesar had made a considerable impression during the Senate's debate over the fate of Catiline's five co-conspirators, arrested before they could leave the city to join their leader. When the eloquence of several influential senators made summary execution seem inevitable, Caesar had risen to argue that the majesty of Roman law could not be thus violated, even in such an extreme situation. The conspirators could be suitably punished, he argued, by confiscation and imprisonment for life (a novel idea in itself) in city jails scattered around Italy. His calm reasonableness in an atmosphere of near hysteria made an impression on everyone present, even though the Senate was ultimately persuaded by Cato, who spoke next, arguing very vehemently that such treason could only be suitably punished by death. This was neither the first nor the last occasion when Caesar lost the day, and yet somehow emerged, not diminished, but enhanced by his defeat.

So now, Caesar's own law, calling for those who conspired to murder magistrates to be put to death as traitors against the *majestas*, the majesty of the Roman people, was going to be used against these five senators, who faced almost certain execution. Some thought the five defendants would probably share the fate of the five Catilinarians, for whose summary execution Cato had successfully argued. Though never tried, they had all been garroted in the cellar of the Tullianum Prison by the public executioner, at the order of the consul, with the formal consent of the Senate. And this was surely the fate that awaited Brutus, Cassius, and the others. No end to the irony in that.

And all of this would be done in the name of, and perhaps at the behest of, the man who had argued against Cato, the same man who had so conspicuously avoided using his complete victory in the recent civil war to take revenge on his enemies. The mercy shown by Caesar to the men he defeated in battle, his famous *clementia*, had already become proverbial. There were to be no proscriptions, no lists of "public enemies," whose property was forfeit to any citizen who did his civic duty by killing them. Under Sulla, legalized political murder and robbery had been the beginning or the salvation of more than one fortune in Rome. It had also left a permanent stain on Sulla's name, even for those who had been on the same side, and even though Sulla had not been the first to use this repugnant tool to "clean house" in the Republic: the inventors of proscription were none other than Marius and Cinna.

Caesar in his youth had seen the gutters of the Forum running with blood, not entirely metaphorically, and had no desire to see that happen again. He needed live friends more than dead enemies, whose friends and family would be a likely source of ill will for many years to come—unless they were all proscribed, too.

So it was as much the result of a carefully considered policy, as it was of Caesar's personality, that Caesar had chosen *clementia* over proscription. And that was perhaps the main question at the back of almost everyone's mind just now, a question discussed on every street corner, in the worst taverns and the finest aristocratic salons, in this whole great city: would the attempted assassination, conducted by men who had either fought for Caesar in the civil war or been magnanimously pardoned by him for fighting against him, be taken by the Dictator as proof that the policy of showing leniency to defeated enemies had been a mistake?

No one really doubted that if Caesar were to decide, finally, to reverse his policy of *clementia* and purge the Republic, the bloodbath would be on a scale that would make Sulla's proscriptions seem like a comedy. Even fighting on Caesar's side from the beginning would not guarantee anyone's safety in such a proscription, when half of the would-be assassins were Caesar's own veterans. Few of his generals had done more for Caesar during the war than Decimus Brutus Albinus, but his was the blow that had nearly proved fatal. Albinus, if he hadn't been killed himself that day, would be sitting here now, next to Brutus, Cassius, and the others.

The Forum, which was more than usually noisy with conversations about these and many other topics, grew suddenly much quieter when one of the lesser officials, a lictor, came out to perform his task. Observed by all, he walked out to a spot in front of the Rostra, turned slightly to his left, shaded his eyes, and then walked back inside the Temple of Concord.

"What was that all about?" asked Publius.

"Well, son, there's a story behind this ritual, as usual. Before the Great Sundial was put up in the Forum, there was really no way to say exactly what time it is. That's very inconvenient if you're going to have a trial, because you need to tell everyone involved to be in a certain place at a certain time. So our ancestors, when the Forum was built, determined that the hour when the sun stands directly between the Rostra over there and that odd-looking old altar there, the Graecostasis, is the seventh hour, the exact middle of the day. So now the lictor has come out, determined that the sun is in that place, and the trial can now begin."

"Why don't they just look at the sundial?" Publius asked.

"The sundial has stood in the Forum for over a hundred years," Sallust patiently replied, "and for most Romans, yes, most of the time, this is the ordinary way to measure the passing of the twelve hours between sunrise and sunset. But we Romans love tradition. And very important trials are usually held when the lictor certifies the seventh hour, precisely because there can be no confusion about the time. Otherwise"—but he didn't manage to finish the lecture, somewhat to Publius's relief.

An expectant hush fell over the enormous crowd. The defendants would now be escorted to their places; then the praetor would make his entrance and take his seat, and the trial would begin.

Cicero

The arrival of Cicero, the sole advocate for all five defendants, was intentionally ceremonious. He and his entourage of clients and slaves made their way through the crowds standing around the eastern end of the Forum. This showmanship resulted from strategic thinking and careful planning, and not, as some malicious observers supposed, from Cicero's vanity. It was essential for Cicero to make much of his own status as a *consularis*, an ex-consul, and yet it was equally essential, if not more so, not to affront the populace or appear with too much "senatorial" pomp and arrogance. So Cicero began to work the crowd, something he had not done since the last time he stood for public office, almost exactly twenty years ago; he looked around him as he walked slowly but steadily ahead, pretending to catch sight of familiar faces among them, nodding and smiling to everyone and no one, occasionally raising his hand in such an indeterminate way that hundreds of people could feel that they had been publicly greeted by him. At the same time, his entourage used their shoulders to create and maintain a safe buffer around him, and to enable him to continue moving forward without actually coming into physical contact with anyone. Those who tried to impede this movement or penetrate the cordon to get closer to this famous man were not brutalized, to be sure, but were efficiently removed to a place where they could do no damage.

The effect, then, was exactly what Cicero had planned, and his smile was increasingly genuine. He felt the flush of public attention, something he had not really felt for some time now, and the fact that the number of people who seemed to adore him was almost matched by the number of people who just as obviously hated him—even this did not faze him at all. Without turning his head, he spoke *sotto voce* to his brother, who was walking alongside him.

"Quintus, you know all those things I've been saying and writing for the last ten years or so about the delights of a philosophical life, detached from the great affairs of state and the noise of the Forum? *Ataraxia* and all that?"

"Right. All that philosophy crap." The familiar sarcasm in his voice made it unnecessary for Cicero to turn and look, in order to see the crooked half-smile and squint that Quintus had used since their boyhood to bring his high-flying brother back down to earth.

"I'm afraid so. There's nothing like this, is there? After all these years and after all the disappointments and worse, I still love it."

The entourage entered the Forum from the east, passing between the Regia and the Basilica Aemilia. Many of the wealthy equites sitting there rose to their feet as Cicero approached, and now the ex-consul's smiles and waves were specific and personal. He knew these people, had always championed their causes and defended their interests, and they owed him as much as he owed them. He was, to tell the truth, one of them, as some in the Senate had never really let him forget.

When his eyes fell on Sallust, he showed no sign of dislike, but merely smiled and nodded, giving no outward sign of his momentary confusion at seeing a senator (well, nominally, anyway) sitting among the equestrians.

"You know, Marcus," said Quintus, without ceasing to smile and wave, "I really think the next time these people turn out to see you, all dressed in their finest with all their families, clients, and slaves around them, they'll be coming to see you strangled."

"It's so comforting to know that I can always count on my dear brother's moral support."

"I'm here, aren't it? I'm putting my own head in the same rope, though I wish some god would tell me why, because I can't understand it."

"I've been in worse situations and won, Quintus. You know that, you've been there, too."

"When were you in a worse situation? I can't think of anything worse. You're going to defend someone who makes no secret of being guilty, who's enormously proud of being guilty, and you're going to do it by suggesting that the Great Man, who can kill us with a well-timed frown, is a goddamned tyrant who deserved to be assassinated. Brilliant. You'll go down in history."

"We've been over all this, brother dear, and frankly I'm tired of going around and around with you over it. What would you have me do, right now, this minute, turn around and go home? As your Great Man famously said, 'The die is cast.' I've got to see this through, so please don't distract me right now. I need to be focused."

When they reached the area where the defendants would sit, Cicero's entourage (including his brother) fell back, while the advocate himself took his seat. He sat in his characteristic posture before an important speech, his chin in his hands and his elbows on his knees, his senatorial toga wrapped around him, lost in thought as he mentally ran through his speech one more time.

He glanced to his left. Almost unnoticed by anyone, the prosecutor Pedius had arrived, with no attendants except for a Greek slave who was constantly whispering in his ear. A rhetorical coach, no doubt. Cicero let himself feel sorry for his rival, for a moment: Pedius was about to be humiliated, even if he won, which of course he almost certainly would. Why, out of all those who must have stepped forward eagerly to have the honor of prosecuting Caesar's would-be assassins, had this inconsiderable man been chosen? There was really no consensus about that, in spite of all the talk, other than a general feeling that no one was really eager to be Cicero's opponent in such an important case. There was a long list of senators, living and dead, whose sole claim to fame was that they had been pilloried by Cicero in an important trial. No one wanted to be the last name on that list.

Of course, there were compensations, Cicero thought. Pedius is going to win, and I'm going to lose, as surely as the sun will set today in the west. He could admit this to himself, now, in his private thoughts, and he'd done the same in a letter he'd written the day before to his best friend, Atticus. But to no one else would he admit that his case was lost before it ever began, not even to Quintus, certainly not to his young wife of two years, Publilia, whom he had already decided to divorce. Tiro, his freedman secretary, already knew it, but that was Tiro: he knew things without having to be told.

Cicero would have told his daughter Tullia, of course, if she were still alive. His son, no, there was not much warmth between them: his mother, Terentia, had spoiled young Marcus beyond recovery. But his daughter had been the joy of his life. The year that had passed since her death, one month after she gave birth to his grandson, had not eased the pain.

He shook his head, as though to rid it of these thoughts, and put his mind back to the task at hand. He would speak second, probably not today, perhaps not even tomorrow, depending on how many witnesses the prosecutor called and how long-winded he was in developing and driving home his case. By law and custom the prosecutor always put his case first, presented his arguments and his evidence, including witnesses; then the defense.

Ever since his own successful prosecution of the odious Verres, thirty years ago, Cicero had made it a point never again to be the prosecutor. As he'd explained it to Atticus, "If you successfully prosecute someone, you've made at least one lifelong enemy, and it's not certain if you'll have made any friends. If you successfully defend someone, you've made at least one lifelong friend, and it's not certain if you'll have made any enemies. I need friends, I don't need enemies." It wasn't the kind of thing you'd say publicly, or write in a philosophical treatise, but the logic was impeccable. The only problem with this policy was that he had just taken on a defense that would certainly make him some enemies, and the friends he would make weren't going to live long enough even to say, "Thank you."

It was too soon, though, to worry about the outcome. If he were honest with himself (and for all his faults, he was always ruthlessly honest with himself) the only thing he could do now was to reach the minds and hearts of as many of those present as he could. The point was not to rescue his clients from the painful and ignominious death that surely awaited them, but to plant some seeds that would sprout someday, perhaps not too far off in the future, in a rebirth of *libertas*. That much was within his grasp, if he spoke well; and it was this realization that caused him to reject the unanimous advice of all his *familiares*, his family and close friends, and accept the defense of Brutus and the others.

In fact, on that memorable March afternoon, when one of his clients, the annoying but useful busybody Vedius, had come rushing in, too breathless to waste time with the usual amenities and greet his patron formally, to tell him in a torrent of words that a group of senators had just tried to kill the Dictator, but failed, and were under arrest—at that instant he felt two things with equal intensity: first, a premonition bordering on certainty that he would be asked to defend the conspirators, whoever they were (and he scarcely needed to be told their names), and second, the feeling of having once again been slapped in the face by the Optimates, who needed him and used him but had too little respect for him to include him in their plans.

The latter of these two feelings was of course nothing new. He had realized about ten years ago, finally, that all his efforts to win the approval of the senatorial aristocracy—to which, as a senior ex-consul, he nominally belonged—would never get him beyond a certain point. And without their trust and confidence and acceptance that he was a man of *dignitas* and *auctoritas*, despite his Italian middle-class background, there was no point in trying to convince them of the merits of his ideas. In order to preserve the Republic and the values they had inherited from their ancestors, they were going to have to rise above the narrow interests of their class. But after Pompey and Crassus went to Lucca and patched things up with Caesar, more than ten years ago now, and all the nobles had lined up eagerly to take their turns kissing the three most important asses in the world, Cicero had realized that all his understanding and all his eloquence were only fooling him into thinking that something could actually be changed. It had been the beginning of his most creative period, and he had felt very sure that the philosophical works he had written in his retirement were of far greater value than anything he could have done if he had remained in politics.

Until the Ides of March.

The night after his long talk with Brutus, a few days after the Ides of March, he had begun writing a letter to Atticus. It was his way of talking to himself, of forcing his thoughts into coherent sentences and paragraphs, as much or more for his own benefit as that of Atticus—who always listened patiently to Cicero's thoughts on topics that surely didn't interest him in the slightest. Now, as he felt the sweat trickling down his back, under the toga, he remembered clearly what he'd written to Atticus.

"I've written so much about *libertas* and *humanitas* and all these other *-tas* words," he had written, "and now I must decide if they are just words, the pieces in a board game played by philosophers, or if they actually mean something in the real world. For the last ten years I've kept on saying that I wanted nothing more than *otium*, an honorable leisure. I thought I'd come to understand the hollowness of the fame and glory that a statesman can win, that I'd grown out of the need to be applauded by people who would applaud just as hard if they were watching me being killed by a gladiator. I had finally realized, or so I thought, that the Optimates would never really accept me, and more, I didn't really want to become one of them. I'm a smarter and better man than any of them, and in a rational universe they would be standing at my door every morning, hoping that I would nod and smile at them when I step outside.

"I had the villa in Tusculum, where I could see the city without having to hear it or smell it, so what more could I want? It has been, as you know perhaps better than anyone, a most productive period. If I died tomorrow, I'd be happy to leave behind me as my sole monument the essays I wrote after I stopped going to the Senate. The year I spent as governor of Cilicia did nothing to change my attitude, and in fact, just as you told me it would, it all just strengthened me in my conviction that *humanitas* is far better served by thinkers and writers than by warriors and politicians. The string of disasters that began at Pharsalus, in Greece, and ended at Munda, in Spain, made it abundantly clear to me that neither I nor anyone else could possibly do anything to prevent the collapse of the Republic.

"I don't need to tell you, of all people, that my lack of enthusiasm for Pompey and his cause was not the result of cowardice on my part, though I know there are many who think so and say so, more or less openly. Caelius Rufus was right: it made little difference which of these two dictators actually won, either way the Republic was already dead, long before Caesar crossed the Rubicon. So I made my peace with Caesar, again, and threw myself into my writing.

"But the moment that old fool Vedius came rushing in to tell me that the Great Man had been gravely wounded by a group of senators, all these convictions about philosophy being a higher calling than politics burst like a bubble. It doesn't matter to me that I was not there and knew nothing about it. Well, yes, I see your eyebrows lifting, even though you're not here. It does matter to me. But that's not what's most important here. In my writings I've made it clear enough that I consider the Great Man to be a *tyrannos*, an illegitimate monarch, and that tyrannicide is the only form of personal killing outside of war, self-defense or state-mandated execution that can be morally excused, and in many cases is morally necessary. You know all this, and you can take it all with the necessary distance and humor: the more serious I become, the more you remind me how silly I sound. And of course all you Epicureans avoid any kind of political entanglements and spend all your time in the garden reading poetry with friends—well, except for the Epicurean who is now Perpetual Dictator.

"Sorry, that was a cheap shot.

"But anyway, Brutus is an impressionable man who takes ideas seriously. What was he doing there with a dagger in his hand? With all due modesty, the answer is: he'd been reading Cicero, listening to Cicero carry on about saving the Republic before it's too late. He'd read too many of my polished sentences, making him out to be the 'last Roman' of the old, virtuous type. So it's truly my fault that it came to this. I invited these men to a symposium and poured the wine; so what difference does it really make that they started drinking without me?

"I know what your advice would be, and it would be good advice. I've never come out well when I've ignored it. But I've put myself in a position from which I can't extricate myself without either ending my life or making what remains of it utterly false and worthless.

"Forgive me for quoting myself, dear Atticus, but here is what I wrote in my *Republic*:

'For it is not enough to possess virtue as though it were just another art, unless you put it to some use. The arts, even if you do not use them, can be maintained by knowledge alone, but virtue consists entirely in being put to use. And the greatest use to which it can be put is the governance of a nation, the realization of the ideas that philosophers sit and talk about, and not some sort of logical perfection.'

"Now either I am an utter hypocrite, or the time has come for me to put on the toga once again. If I held back after Caesar crossed the Rubicon, that, as we both agree, was not cowardice, but only bending to the inevitable. If I hold back now, I am exactly the coward and vacillator that some people consider me to be.

"I know you will wince at this. Nothing of your Epicurean calmness of spirit in this decision of mine. But I also know that you'll support me, as you always have."

Remembering all this now, in the very heart of the Forum, Cicero sighed. It had not taken a month before Atticus arrived in Rome, having left his beloved Athens on a moment's notice. He had been there since, passing through the homes of the rich and powerful in the whole city, moving quietly and discretely in that inimitable way of his, trying to limit the damage. Atticus had the most remarkable ability to maintain friendships with people who were at each other's throats most of the time, without actually being false to anyone. He could go to dinner with Antony himself and listen to him just as sympathetically as he listened to Cicero, and never say a word that would actually commit him to being on one side or the other. He was, in this respect, the consummate Epicurean, and Cicero liked and admired him for his consistency in this, even though as a philosopher he disagreed with Epicurus on almost every significant point.

This line of thought was interrupted by a crescendo of noise from the crowds. Cicero did not really need to turn around and look to realize that the defendants had arrived in the Forum.

There were five of them: in addition to Brutus and Cassius, three other would-be tyrant-killers of senatorial rank had also survived the events of the Ides of March, and were now on trial: Quintus Ligarius, Gaius Trebonius, and Gaius Servilius Casca. The last two, like the late Albinus, had been Caesar's men all through the war, but Ligarius, like Brutus and Cassius, had fought for Pompey and then been pardoned by Caesar, thanks in large part to an impassioned defense speech by Cicero himself. There had been others, that was certain; at one point, just before the guards intervened, it had appeared that a group of 20–30 men were gathered around the Dictator, daggers drawn. Some of them had later protested, however, that they had drawn their daggers to defend the Father of his Country, and when asked why, in violation of very old and very sacred laws, they had brought weapons to a meeting of the Senate, they had replied by talking about the rumors that were circulating in the whole city, and the famous prediction of the degenerate soothsayer Spurinna, who had cried out to Caesar some weeks earlier, "Beware the Ides of March!"

What they said was at least halfway plausible, so allowances were made, prosecutions were stopped, at least in the case of those who were known to have fought for Caesar. They were, at any rate, men of little account, the followers who are always on the fringes of great events without ever really taking part in them, one-eighth participant and seven-eighths observer, informer, hanger-on. If Caesar had gone down that day as planned, they would surely have stuck their daggers in him and swaggered about later with bloodstained togas. When things suddenly went very wrong very fast, in the blink of an eye they had switched sides.

The guards' attack, though delayed almost too long, had been fast and deadly. Just as not all of the men who had come to kill Caesar that day were identified as assassins and arrested, so not all of the senators who fell before the guards' flashing swords had actually been conspirators.

Antony himself had called their deaths "regrettable," and they (unlike the dead conspirators) had been given senatorial funerals.

So these five had been taken with weapon in hand, along with seventeen smaller fry, ex-Pompeians, who would be tried in due course. Antony had ordered them to be escorted to their homes under guard and held there, with 10 legionaries forming a perimeter around each house. In the Senate, Antony had explained that these measures were necessary to protect the accused from the fury of the people, who loved Caesar and naturally hated those who would have deprived them of their greatest champion. Several of the lesser defendants had already chosen suicide, and undoubtedly several more would do the same, after this trial was over and their own was about to begin.

Cicero had to admit that there was more than a little truth in what Antony professed to fear. He could see it now, in the rather ominous quiet that fell over the crowd when the five men, led by Brutus and the senators who were escorting him to his trial, as custom demanded, entered the Forum and made their way to the seats in front of the praetorian tribunal.

Oh, well, thought Cicero, at least they're not screaming for their heads.

Brutus was, of course, the key. He was a mass of contradictions: the favorite of Pompey, but clearly fascinated and even dominated by Caesar personally; a would-be philosopher who liked to be regarded as the leading spokesman for the Stoics, even though he was utterly unable to construct or even follow a complex philosophical argument; a man widely respected for his morals, even among the common people, but one who had amassed a fortune making high-interest loans to provincial cities to pay their tax levies, and then using his friends' legions to collect the debts.

Cicero was reminded more than once, looking at Brutus, of the "spirited hounds" that Socrates used as a metaphor to begin building his ideal state in Plato's *Republic*. That was exactly how he looked now, led by the arm which he pretended not to notice, his nostrils flaring with excitement despite his obvious efforts to keep a Stoic's calm detachment on his face. He still understood nothing. In his imagination, he was a Liberator, a tyrannicide, and the people would surely be strewing his path with roses now if they were not so afraid of Caesar's (mostly Gallic) legionaries all around them. He would have been utterly baffled if he could have read the minds of some of those who now stared at him with expressionless faces.

Life was simple for Brutus, as it had been simple for his martyred father-in-law, Caesar's last really dangerous opponent after Pompey was defeated, M. Porcius Cato, already called "Cato of Utica." In the dream world Brutus inhabited, a good man simply knew the right thing to do in every situation and did it, whatever the cost, without vacillating. Brutus was far more respectful of Cicero's learning than the doctrinaire Cato had ever been, to be sure, but he had never really grasped the principled pragmatism and skepticism of Cicero's thought. Brutus' passion and integrity made him, at times, a good orator, but he lacked one quality that would have made him great: he could never see the other side.

They had quarreled once, vigorously, over Cato. It wasn't until the Ides of March that Cicero had realized what the argument was really all about.

3

The Conspiracy

Autumn, 45 B.C.E., about half a year before the Ides of March

Tusculum and Rome

THE PLOT TO KILL Caesar had really begun, oddly enough, with a chance remark, the previous autumn, in the midst of another discussion that had been going on for two days already at Cicero's Tusculan villa, just south of the city, beautifully situated on a rise that gave a spectacular view of Rome. There had been several such meetings: small groups of carefully selected guests with philosophical interests, all staying for five days, or even longer, in the comfortable guest rooms Cicero provided in the villa, and enjoying the fresh air, the graceful colonnades, the ornamental gardens, the simple but exquisitely prepared food, followed by just enough wine to loosen the tongue, but not enough to addle the brain. By explicit agreement, all topics of possible philosophical interest could be raised, with the exception of politics; by implicit agreement, whatever the ostensible topic, the real topic was never anything but politics.

The discussion had come around to the topic of death, which in turn brought up the question of suicide.

"Both Plato and Aristotle," Cicero remarked, "as a general rule condemned suicide as a kind of abandonment by the soul of the body to which God, for his own reasons, has assigned it. We are to stay the course until God sees fit to release us; the decision is not ours to make. You Stoics, on the other hand," he continued, turning with a friendly smile to Brutus, "usually say that there exist circumstances in which life is not worth living, and in such a case suicide, if it is physically possible, is not only morally permissible, but the best choice. I've always felt, in fact, that this is one of the main reasons why Stoicism appeals to Romans: we have a certain tradition in this respect. The conquered general is expected to fall on his sword rather than suffer capture, or even the disgrace and humiliation of returning home without a victory."

Brutus stirred uneasily, smarting at the indirect but possibly unintentional allusion to Brutus's decision to surrender to Caesar after Pharsalus, rather than fall on his sword. But Cicero went on without a pause.

"Now, why do you think that is? Is it primarily a question of shame, the whole public disgrace that would occur if a Roman general should be made a captive by a foreign enemy? Or is it more practical? A general in enemy hands would have to be ransomed, which could cost a great deal, or he could be used by the enemy in some way to bargain, or forced under torture to give the enemy information about our plans. So our forefathers, practical men that they were, inculcated in their sons this idea, that the final duty of a defeated general was to take his own life.

"Now I don't know of any other circumstances in which a good Roman should feel impelled, or even allowed, to commit suicide. Your Stoic friends, Brutus, would tell us that a man who has lost all hope of being able to live a free and noble life, even for purely material reasons, would have the right and perhaps even the duty to kill himself. But I just said that, didn't I? Well, anyway, what about this feeling of shame? Plato makes an odd argument in the *Laws*, you know, that a man who feels his own moral character is hopelessly corrupt would be justified in committing suicide, though I have always wondered why a person who is indeed hopelessly corrupt would feel enough shame to end his life that way.

"But that's not my real point here. Was it Cato's Stoicism, or his Roman-ness, his devotion to the *mos maiorum*, the Way of the Elders, that led him to commit suicide at Utica? Or was it simply shame, that he had finally been defeated by the very enemy he had spent most of his life and career trying to destroy, ever since the two of them crossed swords in the Senate in the debate over the execution of Catiline's men?

"Why didn't Pompey commit suicide after Pharsalus, or Ahenobarbus, or any other of the generals who were with Cato at Thapsus and shared his defeat? Well, except for Metellus Scipio, but one always finds it hard to remember him. Was Cato's predicament somehow different from theirs? Or I should say, from ours? Or was it a case of Cato's shame being more than he could endure, having to face the man who had destroyed everything he believed in?"

"My uncle," said Brutus, whose face had grown redder all the time that Cicero had been talking about Cato, "was above all else a man of principle. He chose to die by his own hand rather than become another trophy in Caesar's collection. He could not have done otherwise, and it is unbecoming of you, Cicero, as a man who so admired Cato, to question the wisdom or even the moral justification of his act."

"But if he chose the right way, dear Brutus, then why did we not all fall on our swords? Why were all of us content to go on living if our country is ruled by a tyrant? Was it only Cato who had the guts to do the right thing, and the rest of us were just too weak?"

"He was a better man than any of us." Brutus's tight lips betrayed his efforts to control his rising anger.

"I'm sure he was. But he had no feel for reality, Brutus. He talked as though he were living in Plato's ideal city, not here in the dungheap of Romulus."

There was polite laughter at this. Cicero had once pungently characterized Rome this way in a letter to Atticus; since then, as he often did when he was pleased with his own invention, he repeated the phrase very often, in private conversation if not in his public speeches. The expression "dungheap of Romulus" was now frequently used by some of the city's wits to parody Cicero's style of political commentary. In one of the public bathhouses near the Circus Maximus, someone had written "Dungheap of Romulus" on the wall with an arrow pointing to the nearby latrine. Cicero himself had laughed: contrary to what many people said of him, he had a lively sense of humor.

"At any event," Cicero resumed, "Cato ended up doing more harm than good precisely for that reason. He was incapable of the smallest compromise, unwilling or unable to consider the practical consequences of his ideas, whether or not they were sound. He might as well have pushed Caesar across the Rubicon with his own hands, pointlessly provoking him in every possible way, when it really was possible, in my opinion, to mollify the Great Man with a few symbolic gestures and at least put off the outbreak of civil war until Pompey was ready. It could all have ended very differently. I thought then, and among ourselves, here, in this room, I still think, that Cato was a little mad, at least whenever Caesar's name was mentioned."

"Well, yes, I have to agree," Brutus replied reluctantly. This was an opportunity to defuse the situation before Cicero's middle-class tactlessness caused more offense than he could endure. "Cato misjudged that particular moment. He had a much higher opinion of Pompey than I did, and he may have been reckless when Caesar brought part of his army so close to the border of his province. He never supposed that the great Pompey would just show his heels and run to Brundisium. Cato wanted to provoke Caesar to bring armed troops across the border of his province, to shut up all those who kept insisting that Caesar would not let his wounded vanity be the cause of a civil war."

As Brutus knew, this argument had been Cicero's own, at the time. The man had never stopped insisting that civil war could have been averted, even though many people felt that he'd been proven wrong by the events that followed. In this, Brutus secretly thought he was more right than his uncle Cato had been. It couldn't be denied. There was something about Caesar that made you fear him, even hate him, when he was absent, but in his actual presence Brutus always felt that this was an eminently reasonable man, someone he wanted to like in spite of everything. Cato was perhaps the only man he knew who had actually hated Caesar, personally, viscerally.

"And remember," Brutus continued, his voice rising as he spoke. "Caesar only had one legion with him at Ravenna. Appeasing Caesar at that point would only have given him more time to bring up more troops and whip up the urban mob to support his demands. It's easy to second-guess Cato now, Cicero, when he's dead and can't present any arguments in his favor. But I wouldn't expect a man from Arpinum, like you, to understand Cato's mind, how could you?"

There was an awkward silence. Everyone had instantly grasped the meaning of "a man from Arpinum, like you," and all eyes had gone to their host, to see how he would react. The atmosphere of fraternal equality among philosophers, without social distinctions, which Cicero had worked so hard to create at all these Tusculan meetings, was shattered.

This time Cicero could not stifle his irritation at being reminded of his humble origins. He jumped up from his couch and thrust out his famous forefinger at Brutus, using the full power of his voice: "You pimple-faced aristocratic twit! You and all your pampered friends with your pedigrees and fish ponds! Why aren't you all ashamed to show your faces? It wasn't just your illustrious names that you inherited from your ancestors; you also inherited responsibility for governing the greatest Republic the world has ever seen. And in one generation you've lost what it took four hundred years to build! Out of stupidity, and greed, and exactly this arrogant conviction of yours that no matter what you do, you are entitled to universal respect! Whatever made me think that you were worth saving?"

The quarrel had been ostensibly patched up after dinner that same evening; both men had apologized, and they had embraced. At the time, Cicero probably believed that the embrace had signaled a genuine reconciliation. But Brutus knew better. There are lines in any rational society that can't be crossed.

The conspiracy to kill Caesar was set in motion just two days after Brutus returned home from Tusculum, when he received a late-night visit from his cousin, Decimus Brutus Albinus, who was also his childhood friend and distant kinsman, and Gaius Cassius Longinus, an acquaintance whose adherence to Epicurus gave him few topics in common with Brutus. It was a surprise to see Albinus and Cassius together, since Albinus had been among the victors at Pharsalus, while Cassius, like Brutus himself, had been among the vanquished. All three men were actually cousins, but they had never been close. The *clementia* of the Dictator had forced Albinus and Cassius to endure each other's company, but under the circumstances who could imagine them as friends?

He was even more surprised, initially, at the almost comical attempts they had made to disguise their identities and the nature of their visit: they had come late at night, unattended by any servants or clients, and wearing heavy soldier's cloaks, rather heavier than necessary for an autumn night in central Italy, a little chilly but hardly cold. But they had not spoken long before he grasped the reason for their anxiety and all their precautions.

Brutus had long felt that this day would come, that he would have to make this decision, but he had not expected it just yet. And he was not a man who thought quickly on his feet. He was much like Cato in the strength of his resolution, but lacked his uncle's immediate, automatic perception of the right course, no matter how complex the situation. He needed time to make up his mind.

Albinus made no effort to hide his impatience. Albinus was a soldier: when he was given an order, he obeyed it instantly, and when he gave an order, he expected the same. Soldiers stand up or they stand down, none of this pondering and reflecting. A man who takes time to decide in battle will not survive long enough to reach any conclusions.

Along with the *cognomen*, however, the Brutuses had one more thing in common: both of their mothers had been Caesar's lovers, years before, and both had heard gossip that Caesar was actually their father.

The suggestion was rather ludicrous, since both Brutuses were only about 15 years younger than Caesar: the Great Man, though his erotic prowess was legendary, was not really that precocious. The rumor was remarkably persistent, however, especially because Caesar's affair with Servilia, Brutus's mother, had been long and passionate, while the affair with Sempronia, Albinus's mother, though equally passionate, had not lasted half a year. But then there was the physical resemblance between Albinus and Caesar, which was indeed striking. On one occasion, indeed, in Gaul, while drinking with his officers, Caesar had put his arm around Albinus's shoulder and said, "I love this man like my own son," and then had made a broad wink to the rest of the company, eliciting a roar of laughter.

It was not easy for these two men to cooperate, then, for any number of reasons. Still, Brutus listened carefully as his two late-night guests laid out their reasons for making plans to kill Caesar. Cassius had emphasized the loss of liberty, arguing that even by sparing their lives he had implicitly laid a claim to them: what was his to give was also his to take. Brutus had then turned to Albinus, more than a little puzzled.

"Cassius and I, we're in much the same position: we fought for Pompey, we accepted Caesar's pardon, and now we both feel humiliated by the example of Cato. But I don't understand why you're here, Albinus. You were at Caesar's side through the wars in Gaul, you were there when he crossed the Rubicon, you were there at Pharsalus, at Thapsus, at Munda. He's been more than generous to you, and until now, as far as I know, you've been completely loyal to him. You have everything to gain from the continuation of the dictatorship, and much to lose from his death. So again: I don't understand."

"I didn't fight to make Caesar king." Albinus paused, perhaps because it seemed to him that what he had said was perfectly adequate and self-explanatory. After a moment's silence, though, he finally seemed to realize that more explanation was necessary.

"Yes, I was there at Ravenna when Caesar informed the 13th Legion that he was going to march on the City. We all cheered him on. We'd been fighting under this man's command for almost 10 years, and now he was telling us that Rome was in the hands of a dictator named Pompey. Two tribunes had been forcibly expelled from the city and their vetos ignored. So no, in spite of what you people think, we didn't want a civil war just to have an excuse to kill, rape, and plunder. In our minds, following Caesar to Rome, we were going there to save the Republic, not destroy it.

Nothing happened to make any of us change our minds about that until the war was over.

"Let me tell you something. I've been in more battles than I can count, and before every one of them I was ready to shit myself. But the worst of them all was Pharsalus, looking at those Roman eagles on the other side, wondering how it would feel to charge against them. And then after the battle—almost every bloody corpse I turned over with my foot was someone I knew, or thought I knew.

"But even then I never questioned that we'd done the right thing, the honorable thing, the only thing we really could have done.

"And then the war was over, and what?

"Back in Gaul, and even later, Caesar had this ability, I don't know what to call it, somehow he made you think that he was looking right at you, all the time. It was amazing, how he knew so many of the men by name, not just the officers. He would walk through the camp, stop at every tent to slap someone on the back, tell a dirty joke or two. And all this from a man whose family claims to be descended from a goddess! He was able to come across like another Marius, a simple soldier among soldiers, but there was always that difference.

"He says he loves the Republic and wants to save it, and I used to believe him. I did. That's why I fought for him. Then he starts making a public spectacle of himself with that whore queen from Egypt, he lets her make a Pharaoh out of him and humiliates his Roman wife. And the Senate, trying every day to figure out how to get their noses even further up his ass, and he's just taking it all in. We expected him to use his authority to clean the trash out of the Senate and the Forum, and then put things back the way they were supposed to be. Instead of that, he behaved exactly the way his worst enemies always said he would. He wants to be King of the Romans, anyone can see that now. And that can NOT be allowed to happen. A lot of things needed to be changed, but that's not one of them.

"I don't like the idea of killing Caesar. *Dius fidius*, I still love the man! Sometimes I think, let's just go to Parthia and fight in the desert, never mind all the other bullshit. But if he's allowed to go on this way, Caesar will destroy everything we and our fathers and our grandfathers' grandfathers fought for. I thought it was my duty as a soldier and a Roman to cross the Rubicon with Caesar, now I think it's my duty to kill him."

He paused, amazed at the length of his own speech, and finally decided that he had nothing more to say.

"How many of Caesar's men do you think feel the way you do?" Brutus asked.

"Some. Not all, by any means, some of them think 'his shit don't stink' and that will never change, especially in the ranks. But among the officers and ex-officers, the ones who are senators, I know I'm not the only one who thinks something has to be done. I think I can bring in 15–20 good men."

"And none of them will betray us?" This was Cassius speaking. "None of them will change their minds when the time comes to strike? None of them will be planted by Caesar or Antony or Lepidus or whomever, so we can all be strangled or crucified in one lot?"

Albinus looked at him for a long moment, then replied with an obvious effort to keep his voice calm. "These are my brothers-in-arms. I've been to hell and back with them, I know them better than I know the brothers my mother bore. The ones I choose to tell will be the right ones. If someone betrays us, it won't be one of them." He paused for a moment, as though trying to decide whether or not to say what was on his mind. He plunged ahead.

"But you may be mistaken about Antony. To tell you the truth, I've considered asking him to join us."

Both Brutus and Cassius stared at him, and Albinus laughed.

"I knew you wouldn't like the idea. But listen, he has a string of grievances, and he's about the only one of Caesar's *familiares* who'll tell him right out, to his face, that he's full of shit. After Pharsalus, he said he wouldn't go with Caesar to Africa or Spain, and more than once when he was drunk he told everyone who would listen that Caesar's gone out of his mind and has forgotten completely what this thing of ours was all about, or who helped him get where he is. And he hates the Egyptian bitch Cleopatra almost as much as he hates Dolabella."

"I don't trust him," said Cassius, "I've never trusted him and I won't try to trust him, sorry. Yes, I've heard him, drunk, reciting all the wrongs he's suffered at Caesar's hands, but the next day he's right back to being Master of the Horse, ready to crucify anyone who looks at Caesar the wrong way. No, if he's in, I'm out."

Brutus nodded. Cassius was right, and Albinus—his idea would ruin the whole point of tyrannicide.

"The man has no principles," he explained. "Even if he did decide to kill Caesar, he'd do it himself in a drunken rage. He wouldn't be doing it to save the Republic, but just to get revenge for his own blasted hopes.

Worse, he might do it so he could take Caesar's place. It would be murder, just murder, if he's involved."

"Then perhaps," said Cassius, "it would be prudent to remove him, too."

"No!" said Brutus and Albinus, together. They looked at each other for a moment, each surprised to be on the same side as the other. There was another moment of awkward silence, then Brutus began to explain his side.

"What you've proposed to me, as I understand it, is an act of tyrannicide. This isn't something to be taken lightly, it requires care and deliberation, one must be certain that the ruler is indeed a tyrant and that the only way to save the city is to remove him, physically. In the war between the Marians and Sulla, when our fathers were our age, both sides claimed moral justification for all the killing, but in the end both sides simply set out to murder their enemies. That can never be allowed to happen again. One man is the tyrant, one man must fall, that is enough. Anything more is political murder."

Cassius waved a hand as though dismissing the matter. "I've always admired your feel for the high moral ground. As you know well, though, cousin, I don't share your Stoic philosophy. But then, neither of us are really being true to our philosophical principles, are we? Stoics like you and Epicureans like me agree on very little, but we agree that the goal of a philosophical life is to gain calmness of soul, freedom from anxiety, which can hardly be accomplished if one is engaged in active political life. Plato was right: to say that a philosopher can be a statesman or a statesman can be a philosopher is to utter a great paradox."

Brutus started to reply, but Albinus broke in. "I for one don't have the time or the patience for all this philosophical bla-bla-bla. We've got a decision to make, and I think, Cassius, you're outnumbered on this one. I'll drop the idea of bringing Antony into our project, for now, but I hope you'll drop the idea of killing him, Cassius, and now let's get on with it."

Albinus and Cassius began to discuss other senators they thought might be approached, but Brutus was distracted and didn't seem to be listening to them. Then he spoke, breaking into their conversation.

"I wonder if we should include Cicero."

Albinus snorted his scorn, but Cassius replied in a more conciliatory tone. "Do you really think, Brutus, that he would be of any use to us? Somehow I can't see him with a dagger in his hand."

"No one could have imagined him in command of troops," Brutus replied, "but in Cilicia he took several mountain fortresses after hard sieges and won several battles, and his troops saluted him 'Imperator.' As a soldier, Albinus, you know as well as I that such a salute can never be forced and is never taken lightly by the troops. Anyway, my point is, he is the senior *consularis* in the Senate, and his presence in our midst would be the guarantee that what we're about to do is not a murder, but an act of tyrannicide."

"With all due respect, Brutus," replied Cassius, "he may be an estimable man in many ways, and I know you enjoy his company and even his hospitality. But really, think about it. No matter how many books he writes, no matter how many offices he holds or how many speeches he makes in the Senate—well, he's still a merchant's son from Arpinum. Caesar is one of us, one of the *boni*, patrician still for all his Populist rhetoric, and it is up to us to deal with him. Otherwise they will all say that Cicero once again saved the Republic."

The sarcasm with which he said these last five words, raising his voice in a comic imitation of Cicero's rolling tones, brought a snort of laughter from Albinus. Brutus was slower to react, but after a moment he, too, smiled. The point had been made and taken. Cicero would not be recruited to join a company to which he simply did not belong.

Antony

A month later

Rome

Marcus Antonius had wondered more than once if Caesar really believed, at some level of his psyche, that he was descended from a goddess. And one of the times he had entertained this suspicion very seriously was the day he had learned what Brutus, Cassius, and Albinus were talking about so long into the night.

When old Spurinna (a priest with a reputation for uncanny predictions of the future and a list of sexual perversions that would make a satyr blush) had told Caesar to look out for himself until the Ides of March, lest (presumably) something evil befall him, the Great Man had laughed and made a joke of it: "Let the Ides of March look out for themselves, or I shall write them out of the calendar!" Everyone in earshot had laughed, and not only because it was always a prudent thing to laugh at the jokes of the great and powerful. It was vintage Caesar: at once vaunting his power, reminding everyone of his reform of the calendar, and yet poking fun at himself and inviting others to join him. Whenever a new young officer had joined Caesar's staff in Gaul, part of the initiation process was learning to laugh at the Great Man's jokes—not only when to laugh, but how to laugh.

So on this occasion Caesar had enjoyed the laughter for a moment and moved on, still smiling. Antony, on the other hand, had realized something of great importance. In fact, he knew very well who this Spurinna was and how he worked: the man had amassed a fortune by making a reputation for accurate predictions. Now to a man of Antony's pragmatic turn of mind, there could only be two possible reasons for this success: either the man was incredibly lucky, or he had incredibly good information. The latter seemed much more likely, since any third possibility, that the gods actually spoke to him, was not even worth considering.

The truth was that Spurinna, like the ancient Greek oracle at Delphi, had a very good network of spies, gathering the information that enabled him to know what he would then pretend to learn by divination. When a distraught young officer just home from the wars came to him to find out if his wife had been faithful to him while he was on campaign, Spurinna did not really have to read the entrails of sacrificial animals to know the answer. His prodigious memory was a storehouse of gossip, mostly obtained from the most despised and at once the most reliable source of information: slaves. The trick was to put off the client a day or two until the "auspices were right," so he could consult his files and his sources to find the answer.

It was sometimes a little more difficult if the client were a young woman who wanted to know if Marcus really loved her, but even this information could often be had. Only rarely did Spurinna have to resort to the old dodge: "The signs are unclear, the omens are mixed."

Slaves were the key. They were ubiquitous in the households, not only of the rich, but even in the homes of people who possessed only three bare rooms in a rickety tenement building in the Suburra. As soon as a man made some money, no matter how he got it, he would buy his wife a slave. A man whose wife had to do all the housework herself, without a slave to help her, was a failure, and his mother-in-law would miss no occasion to remind him of it. The servile population of Rome had grown as the Empire had expanded, making slaves relatively plentiful and relatively cheap for a citizen of the capital city. No one knew, or wanted to know, how many slaves there actually were in Rome, but the city was getting close to having a million inhabitants, and it was possible that half of them were slaves.

Now a slave by definition is property in the physical form of a human being. Life in a household with slaves is possible only when the slaves are somehow present and not present at the same time, much like a dog or a cat. Slave owners must always believe that their slaves see but do not observe, know but do not understand, and above all have no reason or desire to share what they know or what they have seen with others. Most of the adulterous wives who were Spurinna's main prey went to great lengths to get their lovers into and out of their bedrooms unobserved by friends and family, but then proceeded to carry on their erotic acrobatics in the actual presence of a slave attendant, who was somehow (from the owner's perspective) there and not there at the same time.

This was made possible by consistently maintaining, among the slaveowners themselves, the convenient fiction that slaves were liars who could never be believed. What Spurinna knew, and used, was the fact that slaves saw and heard nearly everything that went on in the house, and very often felt no compunction whatsoever about sharing what they knew. Far from being inherent liars, they had nothing to gain by lying, no reason not to tell anyone who asked whatever they knew—provided they were sure it would not cost them a beating. So yes, there was an enormous risk involved in talking: a slave caught out in the process of sharing sensitive information outside of the house would be lucky if he escaped with only a severe beating. It was even legally permissible to kill a slave who betrayed a family secret. But there were forms of gratification for a slave that were sufficient to justify the risk. Sometimes it was spite. More often, it was money: there was hardly a slave who did not accumulate petty cash, *peculium*, with the ultimate aim of buying his own freedom. The law even recognized the slave's right to have a *peculium*, within bounds, and to use it in this way.

Several of Spurinna's sources were now freedmen, *liberti*, thanks at least in part to him. Many continued to supply him with information, sometimes obtained by them in the same way, from slaves left behind in the household of the erstwhile master. Tradition and the law demanded from the freedman a polite subservience towards the former master, which the prudent *libertus* strictly observed, but genuine good will was something else.

As his reputation and his fortune had grown, Spurinna had expanded his network and increased his information potential. He still made most of his money from the marital hopes and fears of the city's middle class, but increasingly he was able to find his way to information of greater consequence. He came to know which senator's wives were sleeping with their husbands' friends or clients, and this was a lucrative, though dangerous game. He told himself that he was not a blackmailer, which in a strict sense was probably true: he never asked the errant wife to pay for his silence, but rather gave the cuckolded senator a message, in the form of a riddle that was not too hard to figure out. Or he gave no message at all, earning the undying gratitude of the sinner whose sin was not revealed.

Gradually, through his spreading web of connections, Spurinna gained access to information of a commercial nature, which again he managed to sell in the guise of oracle-like pronouncements. If the son of a certain wealthy merchant had run up debts that would soon bankrupt his father, Spurinna would tell his money-lender client that "the auspices were not good for entering into a financial transaction with this gentleman." Some of his clients knew perfectly well what Spurinna was doing and how he was doing it; others at least pretended to believe that there was something supernatural in all this. It was in the interests of all concerned, however, that the fiction be maintained: Spurinna was a medium, through whom the gods deigned to reveal the truth to mortals. It would be a dangerous thing if Spurinna came to be perceived too widely, overtly, as a purveyor of sensitive information.

As consul, to whom in practice the city prefect and all his lesser officers reported, Antony had no difficulty finding where Spurinna lived and "inviting" him for a private conversation. He had begun by discarding all pretense of piety.

"Very well, Spurinna, I know the gods are very mysterious and all that crap, now, tell me and tell me quickly: what do you know about the Ides of March and why did you say that to Caesar?"

The man's reluctance to talk was obvious, but his fear of the consul's wrath was equally obvious. Antony's temper was legendary.

"I'm not a politician, consul, your honor, Dominus, the gods do not usually speak to me very clearly about matters of state—"

"And that's exactly the bullshit I don't want to hear right now. I think you have information, in fact I'm sure of it, and so I want to know, now, what information you have and where you got it. And if you don't start talking sense very soon, I will find a way to get some sense out of you, and then believe me, all the gods on Olympus or wherever will not do one damned thing to save your sorry ass."

By this time Antony had pushed his face close enough to his sweating victim that it was possible to smell the wine on the consul's breath. This did nothing to relieve Spurinna's anxiety, which was quickly maturing into panic. He began to talk.

The source, of course, was a slave in Marcus Brutus's household, a young Thracian girl named Kallirhoe, who had been genuinely devoted to Claudia, Brutus's first wife. But Brutus had divorced Claudia without even pretending that he had any reason to do so other than his lust for his cousin Porcia, the daughter of Cato, his idolized uncle. There had been some scandal about this divorce: even in the senatorial aristocracy, famous for "serial monogamy," good taste required that some reason be given for a divorce, other than a desire to change partners. But amidst the drama of the civil war no one had much time or interest for yet another marital problem in the aristocracy.

Brutus had clearly transferred some part of his reverence for his uncle to his new wife. This was not shared by Kallirhoe, especially after Brutus had not allowed Claudia to take Kallirhoe with her. To make matters worse, Porcia was a dutiful daughter and did her best to exemplify her father's ideals in all things—which included *severitas*, especially towards slaves. She was never viciously brutal, to be sure, but punishments, including very physical ones, were handed out for minor, even imagined offenses. Kallirhoe performed her duties for her new mistress, of course, with eyes properly lowered, without comment or complaint; but if Porcia had known what Kallirhoe was thinking, the whip would have been too mild a punishment.

The slave with hard feelings for his master has by design no recourse short of the truly desperate. Or so it seemed to the masters, who never seemed to grasp the basic fact that had made Spurinna a rich man: no one can keep a secret from his own slaves. So Albinus and Cassius Longinus had barely left Brutus's house the night of their first meeting before all the slaves in the household knew that the three men were plotting to kill Caesar no later than mid-March, before the Dictator's planned departure for Parthia, far to the east.

And well before noon the next day, Kallirhoe sold this choice piece of information to a freedman formerly of her household, who was a client of Spurinna. The information was of such spectacular importance that

Spurinna himself came to talk to the girl the next time she asked her contact to meet her. The meeting spot was near a shop in the Suburra, where Kallirhoe often came to buy cosmetics for Porcia.

The agreement was easily made: in exchange for the princely sum of one denarius, Kallirhoe would inform Spurinna after every meeting, and as far as possible find out what was discussed and decided.

Spurinna was excited, but nervous as well. For all his dabbling in the secrets of the high and mighty, he had never come into possession of information this important, or sensitive. He knew, though, that if he used it wisely, he could expand his range of contacts to the very pinnacle of Roman society. It was a chance not to be missed.

This is what had brought him to the portico of the Basilica Aemilia on the Forum, where he had called out to Caesar in his best oracular voice, "Beware the Ides of March!" The precision of the date was a guess, of course, but it was an educated guess that turned out, in the event, to be very exact indeed.

When Antony had elicited all this information from Spurinna, he could not conceal his glee.

He had never agreed with Caesar's famous *clementia*; like many of his comrades, he had never understood why they had first faced death many times over on the battlefields of the Civil War to bring down Pompey and the whole senatorial crowd, and then had to watch as these same men were pardoned and put right back in their privileged places. Here, now, was proof that these self-righteous patrician prigs were just as treacherous as Antony had always known they would be.

Worse, however, was the undeniable fact that fully half these would-be assassins, like Albinus, were brothers in arms, men who had fought and bled for Caesar. When Labienus, perhaps Caesar's best and most trusted staff officer in Gaul, left Caesar's camp to join Pompey, before the Rubicon, Antony had felt a mixture of sorrow and anger, but at least you had to respect the man for his integrity. This was something else. It had really hurt to see some of the names on Spurinna's list.

The first task, of course, was to get his own source of information from inside. This, fortunately, proved to be relatively easy. Among the men who appeared sporadically at the various meetings—by design, the conspirators never met all together, but in rotating groups of three to five at a time—was Lucius Minucius Basilus, a member of Caesar's staff in Gaul and later a veteran of Pharsalus and Thapsus. He was an odious little man, always elaborately obsequious to Caesar in person but complaining bitterly behind his back about nearly everything. He had been one of the sixteen praetors the previous year, but Caesar had not seen fit to assign him a province to govern after his praetorship, a slight that Basilus apparently did not mean to forgive.

What Antony knew, from direct personal experience with the man on the battlefield, was that underneath his bantam-cock pugnaciousness, which Caesar apparently appreciated, Basilus was a coward. He was always spoiling for a fight—until swords were actually drawn, and the shields of the first rank began to ring with the blows of enemy weapons. Then Basilus was nowhere to be seen, and never reappeared until the battle was nearly over, when the enemy had broken and was running, at which time Basilus was again close to the front, screaming out his lust for battle. Antony was amazed that Caesar, who seemed to know what every one of his officers was doing at every minute throughout a battle, did not seem to notice Basilus's disappearing act.

Knowing what he knew, Antony had no real trouble turning Basilus. The man was initially outraged at being brought to Antony's house under guard and questioned like a common thief, but he folded very quickly when Antony showed him the extent of his information about the plot. Basilus of course insisted that he had intended to inform Antony and the Dictator in person about the plot, but had wanted first to get more information. His performance was not convincing, but Antony made the tactical decision to pretend to believe him. So Basilus was given the chance to absolve himself from the charge of treachery and rank ingratitude by diligently gathering inside information about the plot to kill Caesar and transmitting everything he found out to Antony.

As soon as he had gathered all the information Basilus could provide, and a date for the attack had apparently been set (the Ides of March after all!), Antony asked Caesar for a private conference (taking pains to have the slaves dismissed, too) and put the matter to him, clearly and succinctly as Caesar liked it.

As accustomed as he was to Caesar's legendary unpredictability, the reaction to his report was not at all what Antony had expected. Caesar looked at the list of conspirators Antony handed him, grimaced, and gave it back. Antony waited a moment for him to react, but he did not.

"So," Antony finally said to break the silence, "what do we do now? Or rather when and how, I suppose the 'what' is pretty obvious, isn't it?"

"No, Antony, my old friend, who has apparently learned nothing from watching me at such close quarters for so long. It's not obvious at all. This information is worse than useless. It seems to be forcing us to take action in a situation where no action at all is necessary or desirable."

"What do you mean, no action? We just let them go ahead and plot your murder?"

"Yes, I think that's just what we'll do."

"Are you out of your mind?! What, are you having another . . ." Antony stopped in mid-sentence, with a great effort, but even so, it was too late. The conversation was effectively over, ending as it always did, abruptly, whenever someone had the lack of good taste or good sense to allude, however indirectly, to the Dictator's occasional episodes of erratic behavior, which on several occasions had ended in a horrifying fit of the "sacred illness," when he would fall on the ground, thrashing and foaming at the mouth,

It took a week before Antony felt secure enough and Caesar seemed to be in a receptive mood, so that the subject of the conspiracy could safely be raised again. To Antony's relief, however, it was Caesar who raised the subject one day, with no warning at all.

"Have you had any fresh information about Cassius and his friends?"

Antony noted with some trepidation that Caesar had referred to the conspiracy without using the names of either Brutus or Albinus.

"Yes, I know who, what, when, and how. The whys we can sort out later. They've made and discarded other plans, what they want to do now is to surround you in the Senate sometime before you leave for Parthia, pretending to have some business to take up with you, but their document boxes will have daggers in them instead of papers."

"Good. Now what I want is for you to tell me nothing more about it. We never had this or any other conversation on this topic. Do what you think is required, but please, don't ruin everything we've been trying to do over the last five years by making me into a petty tyrant. I am dismissing my bodyguard as of today. Don't bother protesting, Antony, my mind is made up. And I'm not suicidal.

"You've neglected your education, Antony, and sometimes it shows, painfully. So be a good boy now, stop squirming and grimacing, and listen carefully.

"The Greeks will tell you what a tyrant looks like. He begins by offering to save the city in a moment when it is both surrounded and penetrated by enemies. He then cleanses the city of rebels, brigands, rabble rousers, and criminal gangs, and all decent men applaud. But then he begins to show his true colors: he brands his personal enemies as enemies of the city and puts them to death. He enjoys killing more and more, and requires less and less of a pretext to do it. And to make it easier for him to kill, he makes a show of the dangers to which he is subjected, and demands that the city give him a bodyguard. Once he has armed men around him at all times to enforce his will, no one can stop him."

Antony was not a well-read man, but he was not a buffoon, and he knew better than to show his impatience with the lecture.

"So now you see," Caesar continued, "why *clementia* was essential, and why I must disband my guards now, exactly now. And why I cannot be the one to raise the alarm that someone wants to kill me.

"The truth is, at any moment a man can step out of the crowd as I'm on my way to the Senate and kill me. Someone tried to do exactly that a few days ago, and if his luck or his timing had been a little better, I'd be in Hades now and you'd be in charge up here. There's nothing you or I can really do to stop that from happening someday, unless I never leave my house at all. And how can I govern a city if I'm a prisoner in my own house? It won't work."

"Why do you care so much if someone were to say or think that you're a *tyrannos*?" asked Antony. "It's just a word, and a Greek word at that, a Greek idea that means very little or even nothing in our Roman reality. You know, I speak just enough Greek to take care of business in a Corinthian brothel, and that's all I need to know. You've read all these philosophers, and all you have to show for it are these weird scruples that prevent you from using your common sense. We fought a war to take power, we won it, we have the power, and we know what we want to do with it. What's the whole point in pretending that this isn't true, when the whole world can see it is true, so we look like liars or idiots?"

"Antony, Antony, what am I going to do with you? You're a good solder, loyal, tough, battle smart. I never want to go into a battle without you, or worse, go up against you. But you really have no political judgment at all, none. A government can be created by force, we've done that, true, but it can only be maintained by force and fear for a time. In the long run, most people have to believe that they are better off being governed by us than they were when someone else was governing them.

"Alexander conquered half the world, but he died young, and as soon as he was dead the whole thing fell apart. He was a great general, but as a politician he failed, because everything depended on him. I can't do that. I can't make that same mistake. I want to leave behind me something that will last, and that will not happen if it all depends on me clinging to my own life."

Antony realized at once the significance of "leaving something behind me," but he was not really as simple-minded and tactless as everyone thought he was. He did not press the point, though the problem of whether being Caesar's right hand would translate into actually succeeding him was keeping him awake nights, and had been for a long time. Instead, he steered the conversation back to the immediate problem.

"So I can take all necessary measures to protect you, provided that no one sees it or knows about it."

This was said with considerable irony, which Caesar pretended not to notice.

"Yes, that's about right. I want no bodyguards, and I want no senators arrested unless you can arrange to catch them with their daggers drawn and no more than a forearm's length from my throat."

Ten days later, Caesar formally announced that the Senate would indeed meet on the Ides of March, so that pressing matters of state could be resolved and decisions made before he left for Parthia. Since his own cautious estimate was that the campaign would last at least two years, it seemed prudent to name the consuls, praetors, and even quaestors for the next three years. This was completely without precedent, of course, but by this time everyone had gotten used to the idea that the ancient citizen assemblies responsible for electing the magistrates of the Republic were suspended, and all the important offices were filled by the Dictator. The fact that he went through the motions of asking the Senate to consider his appointments and approve them made the whole process slightly more respectable. But only slightly.

And there was another matter, though Caesar said not a word that might indicate he was aware of it. Word was flying through the city just now that the college of priests, the ones responsible for reading and interpreting the prophecies found in the enigmatic Sybilline books, had found an obscure passage which they interpreted to mean that the Parthians "could only be conquered by a king."

When Antony saw Caesar the next morning, he could hardly restrain his amusement. "You old cynic, you! Now the Senate will have to make you king before you leave for Parthia. How did you do it? Did you have to buy all 15 of those priests? Or was one enough?"

"Why, Antony," Caesar replied with a half-smile playing at the corners of his mouth. "I haven't the slightest idea what you're talking about.

There won't be time at the Senate meeting for such nonsense, we have to appoint the magistrates, and that will take all day."

This way of choosing magistrates had begun five years earlier, after Caesar had marched into Rome, as a temporary expedient, since it was obvious that when all the magistrates and most of the Senate had left the city to follow Pompey, someone had to run the government. From time to time Caesar reassured the Senate that someday he would restore the citizens' assemblies to their traditional role, but he was never specific as to when this would happen. No one really believed that it would ever happen, though it seemed impolitic to say this out loud.

Antony rolled his eyes to heaven when Caesar told him that he had chosen this particular date for the Senate to meet. It was a typical Caesarian gesture, pretending not even to remember that Spurinna had warned him to beware that very day.

Brutus

A few days later

Rome

For the conspirators, on the other hand, Caesar's announcement of the date of the last meeting of the Senate before his imminent departure for Parthia meant that they would have to act now. Caesar himself would be out of reach, perhaps already wearing the royal maroon, and, as Albinus put it, "If we try to solve the problem by just killing Antony or whoever he leaves to govern while he's off chasing the Parthians around the desert, he'll just come back with his legions and crucify us all."

"If he comes back from Parthia at all," added Cassius, "which I truly doubt. I was there with Crassus, don't forget. It was all I could do to save myself and a few hundred men. It's not Gaul, not a bunch of barbarians. The Parthians are disciplined soldiers, like us, as smart as they are proud, and if you ask me the next meeting of the Triumvirate will be taking place a year from now in Hades."

"Perhaps we are being rash," said Brutus reflectively, "in even trying to kill Caesar now. Won't the Parthians do the job for us? When the news comes that he and his legions are dead, it will take no great effort to remove Antony and the rest, and put things back to right."

"That's not wise," answered Cassius, "for at least two reasons. First of all, I may be wrong, and Caesar will come back with Crassus's eagles and a thousand Parthian captives to march in his next triumph."

"No one expected us back alive from Gaul," added Albinus.

"That's right. And the second reason is that if Caesar does get himself killed by the Parthians, the plebs will insist on his being avenged, and the whole thing starts again. Nothing will actually have changed. Caesar's death has to be a tyrannicide, as Brutus keeps saying, or else it's just a murder that doesn't change a damned thing. The message has to be very clear: Rome will never have a king. Somebody will take Caesar's place, of course, as the darling of the fish market, but whoever he is, he'll know that Caesar's road to kingship is a short road to death."

There was silence as the eight men present in Cassius's house that night mulled over what their host had said. It was Basilus who broke the silence. He had maneuvered himself into the ideal situation: he had been chosen as the conspirator responsible for keeping everyone informed, so he had a compelling reason to be present at every meeting. Then he would spend the next day going to the houses of those who had not been present, informing them what had happened and arranging the next meeting, with a different group of conspirators. The three instigators of the plot, Brutus, Cassius, and Albinus, took part in every meeting, and the final decision, by general consensus, belonged to them. The small group meetings were never held twice in the same house.

"So then," Brutus summed up, "it's agreed. We strike the Dictator at this meeting on the Ides of March. What exactly is the plan?"

"The most important thing," answered Cassius, "is that we all be present. And it would be best if we didn't arrive together or even stand together before the meeting is called to order. Where is it to take place, by the way? I've forgotten."

Brutus answered with a slight smile. "Pompey's Theater." Albinus grimaced.

For eight years now, the Senate had been meeting in various public buildings around the city. An angry mob had used the occasion of Clodius Pulcher's funeral, in the third consulship of Pompey, to burn down the Curia Hostilia, the Senate's traditional meeting house, an event which had prompted the frightened Senate to name Pompey "consul without colleague" for the rest of that year. In the confusion of that year and the gathering storm of civil war, which broke out in full fury three years later, no one had had the time, the money, or the energy to rebuild the Curia.

Now Caesar was rebuilding it, but in a different place, facing out into the Forum rather than commanding the Comitium, as before, where elections were held. The message was pretty obvious: there were to be no more elections.

"Good," said Albinus, passing over the obvious irony of the place where Caesar would fall. "Caesar will pass through the portico that runs from the theater building to the meeting hall at the other end of the complex, where the Senate will convene. We can strike there."

"No, no, no," said Cassius, impatiently. "In the portico, anyone can be present, including lictors or even bodyguards. If we wait until he enters the room where the Senate will be waiting for him, he will have to be alone. We need to gather around him in such a way as to cut him off from everyone else."

"Yes," said Brutus. "It's a good plan. I appreciate the symbolic nature of the setting, too. If we kill Caesar in the presence of the entire Senate, we will be tyrannicides. Otherwise, we are nothing but cutthroats."

He had meant to add, "And Pompey will enjoy seeing his enemy finally brought to justice." But this, he knew, would not sit well with Albinus and his formerly Caesarian friends, and they made up half of the conspirators, so he gave Cassius a glance but said no more.

The time had come to work out the details. Trebonius, who had shared a tent with Antony in the Gallic campaigns, was assigned to intercept Antony in the portico, to prevent him from interfering. Once the Dictator arrived in the meeting room, Tillius Cimber would present a petition to Caesar, while the rest of the conspirators would form a ring around him, elbowing others aside as though they had their own business to bring up with Caesar. Cimber, when he saw that there was no one close to the Dictator who might be inclined to protect him, would give the signal for the attack by pulling Caesar's toga off his shoulder, a gesture which would also make it easier to strike a fatal blow.

Albinus made certain they all understood. "I've seen the man fight, close up. Don't let his taste for elegant clothes mislead you: he's a natural fighter. He's got a grip as strong as a blacksmith."

"How will we bring weapons to the Senate, anyway?" asked Galba. "You can't just put a dagger in your belt under the toga, it's too obvious."

"The whole idea of the toga," said Brutus, apparently oblivious to the effect of his pedantry, "is to prevent men from arming themselves when deliberating matters of state, by wrapping the right arm in cloth."

Albinus could scarcely conceal his annoyance. "As senators we have the right to bring document boxes into the meeting, and no one is allowed to examine them. Put a dagger in your document box. The point is to kill him quickly."

"I can't agree," said Brutus gravely. Cassius winced: Brutus was in one of his contrary moods, when he seemed to be emulating his father-in-law. "We must each strike one blow. This cannot be the act of just one man, perhaps assisted by 'accomplices.' Let each man strike once and then make room for another."

Albinus looked as though he meant to protest, but in the end he just shook his head and said nothing more.

All of this was faithfully reported to Antony by Basilus that same night; the matter seemed urgent enough to wake him from a sound sleep.

The next morning, Antony went to visit Calpurnia. It was time to enlist her help.

4

How Skaiva Became Scaeva

Winter, 54 B.C.E.

Britain

WHEN JULIUS CAESAR INVADED Britain the second time, a decade before the Ides of March and just a year after his first attempt to conquer this remote island, his announced purpose was to mediate in a long-standing dispute between two Celtic kings: Cassivelaunus, king of the Cassi, and Mandubracius, king of the Trinovantes. The latter had accepted Roman friendship, so it was only natural that it was Cassivelaunus who took the lead in offering resistance to the Romans, until Caesar defeated him in a typically swift and successful campaign. The settlement that followed made Mandubracius a "friend of the Roman people" and King of Britain, and the defeated Cassivelaunus was made to swear, if not allegiance, at least non-aggression.

It was a good solution, used in the past by generations of Roman consuls and proconsuls after winning a war: don't annex new territory if it will be hard to govern, just make sure the place is ruled by people who can be controlled, politely called "friends of the Roman people," but more prosaically, "client kings."

Caesar was perfectly aware, of course, that Mandubracius, for all his protestations of loyalty, could not be fully and unconditionally trusted to govern Britain in a way consistent with Roman interests, and so, in keeping with the harshly logical custom of the times, he politely asked for hostages to guarantee the king's fidelity. There was no graceful exit for Mandubracius.

According to custom, then, in good form, the 30 hostages, taken from the children of the leading families of the Trinovantes, were led by the king's oldest son, Skaiva, a young man of 25 years, proud but not arrogant, strong-willed but not hot-tempered, the apple of his father's eye and the delight of his old age. His "uncle" Segovax (actually the son of a distant cousin of Mandubracius' father, Imanuentius) was a Druid, and the king's closest advisor—if one can properly call "advisor" a man who spoke to the king with such authority that his "advice" was usually simply ratified. This was not a personal matter: so delicately balanced were the relations between the Druids and the warrior caste to which the king belonged that neither side was anxious to claim primacy.

Segovax had taken a great liking to his nephew Skaiva, and had taken charge of what the Britons would have called his "education," had they possessed such a concept or been in need of a word for it. For almost as long as he could remember, Skaiva had spent most of his days following Segovax around and listening to him talk, as he patiently explained how things worked, from the minutiae of personal relations and the behavior of animals to the meaning of the cosmos. And on one memorable occasion, he had been taken to the great circle of stones, less than a day's walk from the village, to watch the sun rise on the summer solstice, affirming that the cycle of things was still in order.

He learned, too, the secrets of illness and health, the herbs that healed and those that killed, and how often the medicine and the poison were the same, in different doses or given in different ways. He learned how the vital force is gathered in the head, gazing out at the world through the eyes, protected by the thickest of human bones, the skull. He watched as some men died of the wounds they suffered in great numbers during the nearly constant feuds, skirmishes, and petty wars that kept life in Britain from being insufferably dull, while others did not die, and some even seemed none the worse for a sharp blow to the head.

He often wished he could become a Druid himself, and not a king, a wish he of course kept to himself. It would have been impolitic for him to let his father know what he really thought, watching the way Mandubracius and Segovax danced around each other. He knew that he would become king one day, like it or not. He would rule men, not heal them. This realization gave him no pleasure, but Segovax had taught him, above all, that the verdicts of the cosmos may be inexplicable to our human minds, but they are inerrant and just.

None of what he had learned from Segovax, however, or would have learned if he had been allowed to complete his education as a Druid, came from books. The Britons were literate only in a very basic sense, and did not find the medium of writing suitable for the recording and transmission of truly important information. The only proper repository for divine wisdom, in their view, was human memory. In every larger village, as in a family, there were certain people, men and women alike, whose task it was to remember all the stories that should not be forgotten, including those they had learned from their own parents, and the stories played out under their own eyes.

When he came into his majority at the age of 15, and his uncle Segovax had been dead for a year, Skaiva crossed the Channel, with his father's blessing, and traveled through Gaul, even into the Roman province of Gallia Narbonensis and beyond, all the way into the northern part of the Italian peninsula, which the Romans now called "Gallia Cisalpina," which is to say, "Gaul on this side of the Alps." Though he did not go as far as Rome itself, he lingered for three years in Roman territory, claiming the hospitality of various Gallic families to whom he was at least distantly related, for half a year at a time. And as he lived in their homes, so much more spacious and comfortable than his own, he gradually overcame his initial distaste for the Romanization of his hosts, which at first had appalled his patriotic instincts. Some of these Gauls had even gained Roman citizenship, carried Latinized names, wore the toga on public occasions; they were prosperous merchants, traders, and especially landowners, men who managed somehow to be proud of their Gallic blood and proud of their Roman citizenship, at the same time. Though at first he had regaled them every evening with stories of the feuds and intrigues that kept the British tribes in a more or less perpetual state of semi-warfare with one another, he realized after a time that these men had little patience or understanding for all the squabbling. In time, what had once seemed so important to him, the see-sawing fortunes of the Trinovantes and the Cassi, began to look like nothing more than the petty quarrels of overgrown children. In his own mind, Britain subsided in stature, from the center of the cosmos to a small island on the outer fringes of civilization.

More to the point, for his own future, Skaiva learned to speak Latin, and even a little Greek. He spoke with Greek physicians, and found their methods interesting, though so different from the teaching of Segovax.

So when his father informed him, five years after he returned home to Britain from his travels in Gaul and Italy, that he had been chosen to be a hostage, to live with the Romans for at least the next five years, as agreed between Mandubracius and Caesar, Skaiva's feelings were mixed. Unlike all the other hostages, he was not going to a completely unknown world. Unlike them, he was not leaving behind a world to which he felt he must return, or die.

There was a girl in the village, to be sure, Aia, whose red hair, twinkling blue eyes, and sharp wit had won her a place in his heart. But she was not of the right caste for the son of a king, and so, even if he had been able to stay, he would have had to save goodbye to Aia anyway, and marry someone his father chose. To be honest, it was already much past the right time for a man his age, who would be king someday, to have a wife and breed his own successor. But Mandubracius was not a diligent father. The families with whom he might have wanted to cultivate dynastic ties happened not to have marriageable daughters anyway, and Skaiva was not inclined to press the issue. He went willingly as head hostage.

So the day came that he was presented to Caesar, a man whose name prompted much fear among the people of Britain, even among those like his father, who had chosen to align his own fortunes with those of the Romans. Skaiva could not have known that day, of course, how deeply his own life was to be intertwined with Caesar's, but he did know, somehow, that his destiny would lead him inexorably to Rome. And he felt rather sure that he would never come home to Britain again.

The time would come, long before the five years were up, that he would be free to leave. But he would not go home, because he had read the signs, and they all told him that his place, at least for now, was in Rome, the city of his people's enemy, whom he had come to respect, whose place in the order of things he had finally understood. He was not, could never be, would never want to be, one of them, but he no longer wished, as he had once wished, to see them exterminated. For all the injustice the Celts in Gaul and Britain had suffered at Caesar's hands, they had also seen many fine things, not least of which was an understanding of justice that, in Skaiva's opinion, was much superior to Celtic justice.

Something of cosmic importance was about to happen in the great and terrible city that had given birth to Caesar. The Druid learning he had absorbed from old Segovax told him that there were such moments, when the fate of the world might rest on what a single human being, at one very particular moment, might do or fail to do. He wanted to be there; or rather, he felt certain that he must be there, even though, as yet, he had no idea of the time, the place, the situation.

He recalled in particular a lovely summer day, as he and his uncle had walked together among the sacred oaks, a grove that lay about a stone's throw outside the palisade surrounding the village. Segovax suddenly bent over and picked up an acorn from the forest floor, which was littered with them.

"Surely someone has told you, Skaiva, that whatever is foreordained, must come to pass, yes?"

"Of course, uncle, everyone knows that."

"Nothing is actually foreordained," Segovax had answered, with a sharpness that startled Skaiva. Segovax's face softened slightly. "Look carefully at this acorn. I could crush it between my finger and my thumb, if I had a mind to. We walk here and we step on them, smashing them into the ground, and don't give them a second thought. But this acorn holds within itself all that is needed to make an oak, the sturdiest of trees—though if you did crush it, you wouldn't find a baby oak inside it, would you?"

Skaiva laughed. "Of course not."

Segovax continued. "That is because what the acorn contains is not the tree, but only the beginning of its becoming. Once the acorn has sprouted there are so many things that determine how tall and wide the tree will be, how many branches and how many leaves on each branch, things that the acorn knows nothing about. The whole role of the acorn is to die, to release the life that lies within it, which will then take its course. Do you know why I am telling you this?"

"No, uncle, but it's very interesting, really."

"It's not just interesting, not for a young man who will be king one day. You see, the greatest thing that a man can know is when to become an acorn, fall into the ground and give life, by dying at the right moment and in the right way."

That had been a hard lesson to grasp: Skaiva remembered it, from time to time he would call it to mind and ponder it, but it would be many years before he understood it.

The same was true for another walk-and-talk lesson he received from Segovax, the following spring, when the rains had swollen the brooks and streams into torrents of rushing brown water. Earlier that day, a little girl from the village, not ten years old, had gone out to pick berries and had been swept away by the flood; her broken body was found downstream, caught by a log. Skaiva was sure he would never forget the emptiness of the dead girl's eyes, or the pain in her mother's eyes, wide open as she shrieked, soundlessly, her mouth open but no sound coming out. And he was right: he did not forget, even when he had looked into so many more blank, unseeing eyes, and seen so much more grief.

Segovax stopped at a place where the normally placid brook could be crossed by a wooden bridge. The bridge was gone, only one post remaining to show that it had once been here. The brook was clear out of its banks, making channels among the trees that usually stood on dry land. The two of them stood for a moment, looking, until Segovax spoke.

"Skaiva, tell me, when the flood recedes, in a day or two, will the brook simply return to its banks?"

"I suppose so, uncle, but who can be sure?" Skaiva had learned, by this time, that whenever Segovax asked a question that seemed simple, the obvious answer was probably wrong. So he knew, now, how to hedge his bets.

"It may, but again, it may not. You see where the water has washed out so much soil from underneath the poplar that was growing on the bank, and it has fallen over, across the stream? Now, there is so much water, it flows right over the tree, but when the water recedes, if the poplar is still there, the stream may take another course. Or, it may split. You know, about a day's journey from here, this stream does split into two, and the one creek becomes two, going off in two different directions. That may have been caused by a tree, or a boulder, or maybe, who knows, by something much smaller than that.

"Big things can have very small causes. A pebble can make a boulder fall, which can change the course of a stream like this, and that can change the course of a river."

"So we should all be careful not to move any pebbles," Skaiva concluded, proud of his wisdom.

Segovax laughed. "No one can be sure when the smallest thing we do can change the course of a river. That is out of our hands, it is not for us to know, to control. The point is, the river never stops flowing, but we know where it goes."

"To the sea."

"Yes, all the water flows into the sea. But is that the end?"

"Well, Uncle, I suppose it must be. Where would the water go from the sea? Is there something beyond the sea, where the water all goes?"

"If that were so, Skaiva, eventually the land would all be dry, because the water would all have flowed out, and the sea would be full. But neither of these things happens. Do you know why?"

"Well, the rain comes from clouds, that come from the sea, so the water goes to the sea and goes up into a cloud, then it falls as rain. Am I right?"

Segovax was pleased. "Yes, quite right, absolutely. The rain falls, the water comes together as streams and rivers, and flows into the sea, where the clouds pick it up and bring it back again.

"But notice that the river remains here, in this place, all the while. Or at least it does until some tree or boulder, or the finger of God, puts it somewhere else. The water never lingers, it moves on, but the river stays. Now, if we throw a stick into this stream, where will it go?"

"Where the river goes," Skaiva answered, with just the slightest trace of impatience. "Down to the sea."

"Yes, but when it comes to a place where the river divides and becomes two rivers, which way will it go?"

"I don't know." Skaiva dropped his head, ashamed of his ignorance.

"But you see, no one knows. There is a moment, when the stick arrives at the fork in the stream, and it will go left or right. And its journey will be entirely different, depending on which way it is sent. But the stick knows nothing of this."

"Why are sticks in the river so important, uncle? We've been talking about them for a long time, and it's all very interesting, but . . ."

Segovax sighed, then smiled. "Because I am about to teach you perhaps the most important lesson of all. You see, we are all sticks in the river, and the river is time. It flows different ways, but always down to the sea, which is death. And the water of time rises up from the sea and returns, to fall as rain and begin its journey again, but the sticks do not. And the forks in the river are the moments in time when we must go left or right, and that will make all the difference, though we have no idea of what lies downstream either way—except that it will end in the great sea of death."

Skaiva frowned and shook his head. "I don't understand. It makes sense to say that time flows like a river, that's not hard, but what about the forks, going left or right?"

"The river of time also has forks, though every stream leads finally to the same sea. There are moments when time will take us left or right, but the fact that we go left does not mean that the right fork ceases to exist, because it was not chosen for us. It was chosen for someone else. Someone else is now living the life that we would have lived, had the river taken us down the right fork. We were sent on the left, and this is the life that was waiting for us there. But the river will fork again, maybe soon, maybe late, we can't know. Perhaps we are sticks which think, foolishly, that we can choose which fork we take. But we have nothing to say about that."

This was another, even harder lesson, and Skaiva would never be sure he really understood it. His travels to Italy, which came a few years later, certainly broadened his horizons, but brought him no closer to understanding what Segovax had thought it so important for him to understand.

And then, one day in early winter, when the trees were bare and the air was chilly, but no snow had yet fallen, the Romans arrived in his village. And they changed the course of his life completely. Before he had time to prepare himself, to say his goodbyes, to put things in order for his return, he was taken away, as a hostage, his life and freedom now entirely dependent on whether or not his father kept his word. At least he understood this much from Segovax's difficult lesson: the river had forked, and he was being taken in a direction that had been chosen for him. What he might have chosen, if he could, was beside the point. As they led him away, he caught a glimpse of Aia's pale blue eyes, looking at him. The river forked, there was no going back.

The Roman soldiers who took him away were firm, but not particularly mean. He had learned more than enough Latin to understand what they were saying to each other, but thought it best to pretend ignorance: perhaps, thinking it safe to speak freely in his presence, they would say things that would prove useful. He was, he decided, a small stick that had been thrown into a very large river, but he meant to be a man, and swim, rather than a stick that just floats along.

They arrived at the sea that evening, and then went on board a ship the next day. The crossing was uneventful: the Roman galley handled the choppy water much better than the boat on which he had crossed over to Gaul, some ten years earlier. Skaiva stepped off the ship and into a world that was not actually new to him, but had changed a great deal in his absence.

Northern Gaul

He was assigned, as it turned out, to the custody of one of Caesar's senior officers, Servius Sulpicius Rufus, the general in command of the Seventh Legion, then wintering in northern Gaul. Sulpicius was suitably intrigued to have in his camp the son of a king, even a barbarian king whose palace was nothing more than a hut. So he ordered the other hostages to be quartered appropriately, scattered among the tents of the legionaries, but he had Skaiva brought to his quarters, the Praetorium, for a private interview, with a Gallic interpreter.

"Skaiva, son of Mandubracius, king of the Trinovantes," he began, formally but without deference. "I am pleased to welcome you to my quarters, and hope your Royal Highness"—he permitted the corner of his mouth to flicker at this—"will not find the conditions too primitive. Translate this, please," he concluded, turning to the interpreter.

"This man's services will not be required, *legatus*," said Skaiva in nearly impeccable Latin, using the exactly correct term for the commander of a legion, "and allow me to thank you for showing me such courtesy, which I shall strive to deserve. You may be assured that I am no slave to luxury. I have been trained to sleep on the ground as readily as in a bed, and my father's house, though he is indeed a king, is nothing like the palace of Nicomedes, which Caesar himself, I believe, visited more than once."

Sulpicius was left speechless at this delicately phrased but very clear allusion to Roman gossip about an incident in Caesar's past that no one ever dared mention in the Great Man's presence. For a moment he seemed to deliberate, but in the end a smile first stole over his face, and then he broke out in a laugh.

"Perhaps this is going to be far more interesting than I would have thought. Come, I've ordered a special tent to be set up for you, next to my quarters, and I hope you won't mind sharing my table from time to time." Seeing Skaiva's puzzlement, he went on to explain. "By the laws of war, as I'm sure you know, a hostage is essentially a prisoner of war, and can be treated as such, but Caesar has other ideas, and in this I completely concur with him. You shall be my guest, and I hope that you will feel more a guest here than a prisoner. I'm sure you'd much rather be somewhere else right now, but neither you nor I can change that any time soon, so let's make the best of it, shall we?"

Sulpicius had good reason to attribute the policy of leniency towards "valuable" hostages to Caesar, who in fact always treated the hostages in his own custody with varying degrees of courtesy, depending on his judgment of the hostage's potential later on: if he was someone who could be won over, and would then would go back to his tribe and be a man of influence there, it made sense to send him back as a friend, impressed with the power of Rome and entranced by the allures of its civilization. So Sulpicius, in showing hospitality and even kindness to this intriguing young barbarian, was indeed following his commander's policy, and in fact his explicit orders.

But *humanitas* as a matter of policy was one thing, friendship, *amicitia*, was quite another. Sulpicius could have not have had the slightest idea, just now, that he, a Roman Senator and the commander of Caesar's oldest and finest legion, the Seventh, would come to count Skaiva among his closest friends. He would have scoffed at the very idea.

But it happened, all the same.

It began with the habit of taking a late supper with his guest/captive, which gradually led to increasingly more interesting conversations. Sulpicius was a scholar at heart, now a soldier on Caesar's staff only out of a strong sense of personal obligation to Caesar, who had been an invaluable ally to his father. Sulpicius himself had been praetor, and meant to be consul, so time in the field with a consular army was politically essential. He had never been an ardent Populist, to be sure, but on the other hand, he had little liking or respect for the Conservative senators who hated and feared Caesar with such irrational passion. And no less a figure than Cicero himself had advised him to take a post with Caesar to advance his standing with the electorate, as Cicero's own brother, Quintus, was also doing.

"What Caesar is doing in Gaul right now," Cicero told Sulpicius over an elegant but not extravagant dinner at his Tusculan estate, "is changing the whole face of our Empire. You should be there, you should be part of it. I can't say I fully approve of everything Caesar's done over the last few years, in fact I've been appalled more than once, but there is something about the man that fascinates me, and I keep wondering what could be done if we could win him over to our way of thinking. He's more intelligent than Catiline was, and every bit as ambitious, but he's not half as crazy, and that makes him less dangerous. That is, unless and until his ambition overpowers his intellect, and then may the gods help us all."

So Sulpicius accepted Caesar's flattering invitation to command the famous Seventh, and he had indeed learned a great deal. But he was still an intellectual at heart, and while he turned out to be rather good at soldiering, at commanding troops, he was already weary of the bustle and banter of life in an army camp, the weeks and months of boredom interrupted only by the chaos of battle. What he missed from civilian life was not really the creature comforts of a comfortable home in the city, but intelligent conversation, which required leisure and like-minded companions, both of which were in short supply in an army at war.

The Seventh Legion, which Sulpicius commanded as Caesar's *legatus*, was in winter camp, and the Gallic nights were long, as wet and dreary as the Italian winter, but somewhat longer and noticeably colder. The evening conversations with Skaiva, then, were initially nothing more than an amusing pastime. The man was a barbarian clear through, from his enormous mustache to the trousers he insisted on wearing, instead of the linen or woolen tunic most Romanized Gauls liked to wear. But he was clearly a very clever and capable barbarian, who was never insolent, knew how to listen carefully, when to concede a point, and when to drive his point home. Increasingly, Sulpicius found himself feeling a certain discomfort, and a disquiet that was not simply the Socratic diffidence of a learned man trained in the subtleties of philosophical discourse. It was not long before the two men were conversing as equals.

When Sulpicius caught a fever, late in the winter, in what the Romans called the "febrile month," he fell dangerously ill. It was Skaiva, then, who knew which herbs to brew into a tea that broke the fever and put Sulpicius back onto his feet in a very short time. But this display of medical knowledge was only the beginning of a process that took Skaiva from Sulpicius's hostage to his trusted friend.

Skaiva had been trained rigorously, beginning in early childhood, to watch, to listen, and to remember what he had seen and heard. This particular talent of his proved itself useful within a few weeks after Sulpicius's illness. One night in early March, Sulpicius had invited Skaiva to join him and most of his officers in an evening of drinking the surprisingly good local wine and playing dice. The next morning, well past dawn, Acilius Glabrio, the tribune in command of the first cohort of the Seventh, came to the Praetorium, and respectfully but firmly asked his hung-over commander to pay a gambling debt from the night before.

"You owe me ten thousand sesterces," he proclaimed, rather more belligerently than was perhaps appropriate for a tribune addressing the commander of his legion.

"I'm afraid," said Sulpicius ruefully, rubbing his temples, "that I don't exactly recall, but if you say so . . ." And he went back inside to get the money from the small pouch under his bed, where he kept his spending money.

Skaiva, who had slept on a mat on the floor, cleared his throat, an annoying sound that he was in the habit of making when he wanted to get attention before he began to speak. "Ahem . . ."

"Yes, Skaiva, what is it? My head is pounding and I'm really in no mood . . ."

"I do beg your pardon," said Skaiva, lowering his voice so as not to be heard from outside, "but the truth of the matter is, you owe this man nothing. Indeed, he bet you everything he had on the last roll, then lost. The money he seeks from you is money you won from him."

Sulpicius was still confused. "Then why is he here demanding money?"

"Doubtless he thinks, Senator, that you were too drunk to remember exactly what happened. You are, I am sorry to say, inclined to such lapses when you have . . ." Skaiva completed the sentence with an expressive pantomime that needed no translation. "I overheard this officer telling his friends, when they were commiserating his loss, that you would never remember what happened. Clearly he has decided to turn the situation to his profit and recover the substantial sum he lost. I know little of your Roman customs, sir, but in my village such an act might even be the cause of a death feud."

"We are a civilized people, Skaiva, such things do not happen among us. But to lie to a fellow officer in the matter of a gambling debt—this is a serious matter, if it is true. Are you sure?"

Skaiva then proceeded to recite the last ten rolls of the game: who rolled what number and how much had been bet, by whom.

"And finally, after you accepted his bet of 10,000 sesterces, which was all the money he had won through the night, he called six and rolled a seven, so you won."

"I believe you," said Sulpicius, genuinely impressed, "though I can't for the life of me imagine how you can remember all this. But how can it be proved? If I go outside now and challenge him, I must have proof that he actually lost the last roll. Otherwise I will have defamed an officer, which is at least as serious a matter as cheating."

"Simply remind him that when he was shaking the dice for the last roll, you challenged him to use your dice instead of his own. You must have suspected, sir, that his dice were loaded, and that was why he had won so much money to that point from you and your other fellow officers. And you were quite right."

"Loaded dice?!" Sulpicius roared, then immediately stilled his voice in response to Skaiva's cautionary gesture. "Loaded dice? A Roman officer, an aristocrat, a man whose father has been a consul—loaded dice? I can't believe it!"

"They can be checked, Senator, it is not that difficult to detect, in daylight, though at night, by candlelight, it is very hard. We Celts are at least as fond of dice as you Romans are, and we have ways of cheating that, so far as I can see, you have never thought of. Not that this is anything to be especially proud of." But the slight smile on his lips belied the half-apology.

Sulpicius went back out to where Acilius Glabrio was waiting for him, and asked him to step inside.

"Glabrio, I wish to speak with you in private, because what I have to say is very unpleasant. And in view of your own status and the honor of your father, I would rather settle this matter in private, as two gentlemen. To begin with, I do not owe you any money, since it was you, not I, who bet everything on the last roll and lost. And more seriously, I have reason to believe that you were cheating. Since I can't honestly complain of the way you perform your duties, I am prepared to overlook this, but there must be no repetition. We will say no more of it."

Glabrio's face had been growing redder and redder. "This is an outrage!" he finally exploded. "I won't have it! My family is of consular rank, and who are you to make such an accusation?"

"You were cheating, Glabrio, for all that, and all the money you lost to me is money that you took dishonestly from your fellow officers. I'm amazed, in fact, that you have the nerve to feign outrage."

"It's a damned lie!" shouted Glabrio, "and you can't prove it. Especially," he sneered, "when the whole camp knows how weak your head is after three cups of wine."

"This young man here," replied Sulpicius, pointing to Skaiva, who was standing off at some distance, "drank nothing, of course, and remembers everything. He's the one who realized that you'd been cheating."

"That British hostage?! That mustachioed, trousered barbarian catamite who sneaks around the Praetorium at all hours of the day and night, and as far as anyone knows spends more time in your quarters than he should, is to be believed over me, a Roman officer and the son of a consul? Dear gods!"

Now it was Sulpicius's turn to be outraged: Glabrio had just implied that his friendship with Skaiva was—well, not purely intellectual. Such things happened in a camp, of course, when there was no fighting to do and little decent female companionship available. The Greek vice was no stranger to Roman aristocrats, anyway, though it was not something one talked about openly.

He held his tongue, and for a moment thought how he should respond.

Skaiva, for his part, kept his face and manner completely impassive. He had never expected Sulpicius to mention his own role, and was not pleased. This could end in several ways, none of which were particularly pleasant to think about. But he reminded himself of what he had learned from Segovax: "You cannot change the lot that has befallen you by thinking well or ill of it. Change your mind instead. Only your mind and your heart are your own: all else is something to be given or taken."

By this time the shouting had brought a crowd, and Glabrio realized that there were people outside. He wasted no time in making his case to the crowd.

"He has made a disgraceful accusation with no evidence at all except the word of his prisoner, that British catamite of his, and I demand satisfaction!"

Sulpicius turned to Skaiva. "Skaiva, I will ask you now to explain to these men what you explained to me."

Skaiva replied, "If I could see this man's dice, I can prove that he was cheating."

Glabrio smiled. "Of course, I will present them. But if they are examined and found to be honest, this hostage will be transferred to my custody, and that will be only the beginning of the satisfaction I shall demand." He turned and snapped an order to the slave who had accompanied him to the Praetorium; the man bowed his head once, turned, and ran down the row of tents where the legionaries were quartered until he disappeared into one of them. In a moment he returned, holding the dice in his hand.

"Well then, barbarian," said Glabrio, "show us how smart you are. How did I cheat with these dice?"

"You did not," replied Skaiva, glancing at the dice. Glabrio shouted in triumph, but then Skaiva spoke again. "You did not cheat with these dice, sir, because you did not play with them, at least not when you were cheating. These dice are made of ivory. You played with other dice, made of bone polished to look nearly the same, which you had concealed on your person. After the first three rounds had been played, while the others were drinking, you replaced these ivory dice, which are perfectly honest, with the bone ones. I believe the bone dice are loaded, and I also believe that you still have them concealed on your person."

Now every eye was on Acilius Glabrio.

"Under the law," said Sulpicius finally, "you have the right to deny this, and to refuse to be searched. In that case, however, I have the right to maintain my position and refuse any satisfaction you have demanded."

"Very well," said Glabrio, sensing the mood of the crowd. "You may search me, but I repeat again, as the gods are my witnesses, when I am proven right, I will have this barbarian flayed."

Sulpicius ordered the centurion who was standing guard before the Praetorium to conduct the search, with all respect for the dignity of an officer and a member of a consular family. The search, however, though seemingly thorough, produced no result, and the crowd was beginning to murmur ominously, until Skaiva spoke again.

"Ahem," he said, "Centurion, I believe you will find two dice in a small pocket sewn in the hem of his tunic, just above his right knee."

The centurion felt the hem of the garment and gave a grunt of surprise when his fingers encountered the small, hard squares. He folded the hem of the tunic outward, and the two dice fell into his hand.

"This means nothing!" Glabrio protested. "I had forgotten that I had these. Nothing is wrong with them."

"If you will throw them five times," said Skaiva calmly, looking Glabrio straight in the eye, "you will find that a six will come up at least twice."

Sulpicius himself took the dice from the centurion and threw them five times. The first, fourth, and fifth rolls came up six, both times a double three.

"If you were to keep rolling, sir," said Skaiva, "you would get the same result, and you might also notice that even when the double three does not come up, one of the two dice will almost always be a three."

This was done, and the result was much as Skaiva had predicted it. Sulpicius then examined the dice carefully, and discovered that in both of them, the dots on the "four" side were different.

"I believe you will find," said Skaiva, "that those dots are made of lead."

Sulpicius pried at them with the point of a stylus, and small bits of lead popped out.

The murmuring took on an ugly tone.

"Publius Acilius Glabrio," said Sulpicius, "you have broken no law and no charges can be brought against you. Unless, of course, I were to charge you with defamation for what you have implied about myself and my guest, Skaiva—who, I might add, is indeed unashamed of his Gallic birth, not least because he, in contrast to you, son of a consul, has done nothing to bring shame to his father, a king and friend of the Roman people. If I were you, however, I think I would apply to Caesar for permission to return home now, before the next campaign season begins, because I really don't believe you will find that you are among friends any longer, or will have anything to do in this army. In my legion, Acilius Glabrio, you may count yourself lucky if I allow you to guard the kitchen."

He turned and went back into the Praetorium, Skaiva following. There was a long moment of silence before Sulpicius spoke.

"Skaiva, perhaps you would be so kind as to enlighten me on a few points. How did you know all this, that the dice were loaded, that the first dice he had brought were not the ones he had used to win all that money, and where he had concealed them? Please explain."

"I was once the student of a very wise Druid, Senator, and the gods open many secrets to such men. The oak and the mistletoe—"

"Bullshit!" Sulpicius interrupted, suddenly and uncharacteristically angry. "I won't be put off that way. Tell your simple friends from the village that the gods have spoken to you, but please, tell me the truth."

"You do not believe in the gods," replied Skaiva. It was a statement, not a question.

"I do," Sulpicius answered, "but I don't believe that the divine world, whatever it is and wherever it is, is going to be very interested in where Glabrio keeps his loaded dice, or that the gods are going to be whispering in the ear of one Skaiva to clear up this whole mess. The gods have other things to do."

"Perhaps you are right," said Skaiva. "That the dice were loaded was obvious to anyone who looked at the numbers Glabrio was throwing. He waited, of course, to introduce them into play until the game was well underway, as was the drinking. When it seemed to him that enough wine had been consumed, he slipped his hand under the hem of his tunic and took out the new dice, putting the previous ones in their place. I was watching the game and I saw the movement of his hands, which aroused my suspicion. Then I looked at the dice themselves and saw that, although very similar to those he had been using, they were not in fact the same. There could be only one reason to do this in such a stealthy way; if he had just wanted to use different dice, just to change his luck, as many do, why hide this from his fellow players? Clearly he did not want anyone to realize that he had changed them out.

"Then I noticed that, although he had lost more than he had won to this point, after he made the substitution, he began winning, and won very consistently, always calling six and usually getting it. When I paid attention to the numbers that were coming up on his dice, I realized that threes were occurring far more often than they should. If the rest of you had been fully sober and paying attention, you would have noticed, but there were five of you playing, so his turn did not come around often enough for you to notice that he was always calling the same number and almost always winning. But, Senator, as I said, you must have suspected something despite the wine fog in your head, since on that last roll you challenged him to use your dice instead of his own. He could not have refused without arousing suspicion, but I could see the signs of both anger and fear on his face.

"But Skaiva, however did you notice the difference? I could not. Bone and ivory—they look so similar, and you never had them in your hand."

"I have been trained to look and to remember what I have seen, to see the smallest signs by which nature reveals the truth. Anyone trained as I have been trained can see the difference between bone and tooth.

"As for his concealing the loaded dice on his person: this, too, required no prophecy. One does not keep loaded dice in one's personal belongings, especially in an army camp, where there are many reasons why someone might go looking through one's things. The whole substitution trick requires him to have the dice concealed where no one will notice them, and he can reach them without making large, obvious movements. Hence the hem of the tunic. A lucky guess, that, but not unfounded. And the lead in the fours—you found that yourself. I knew it would be there, but I said nothing."

"You led me to the point," said Sulpicius after a moment's thought, "when even my hung-over head could draw the conclusion, that if it's three that keeps on coming up, four is obviously too heavy. I deserve little credit for that. You have displayed truly remarkable powers, though

I hope you will excuse me if I attribute these to the quality of your mind, and not to any supernatural beings."

"I have done nothing beyond the ordinary."

"I beg to differ," Sulpicius replied. "You've done a fine day's work already, and the day has hardly begun. I shall have my cook prepare something special for our supper tonight. It's the least I can do."

He started for the door of the Praetorium, then stopped. "Skaiva, you are my prisoner, a hostage, not of your own free will, but by compulsion, and you have no reason, or at least not yet, to love Romans in general or this one Roman in particular. You could have kept quiet, let Glabrio swindle me for 10,000 sesterces, and no one would be the wiser. Yet you spoke up to defend me from my own weakness. And you went on to get me out of a very ticklish situation. I'm not at all sure I know why."

"To begin with," said Skaiva, "this 'ticklish situation' you speak of was more than just ticklish for you. Glabrio would cheerfully have crucified me."

"Yes, all right," Sulpicius said impatiently, "your display of logic was necessary in order to save your own skin. But that still doesn't explain why you said 'ahem' the first time, does it?"

Skaiva considered this for a long moment before replying. "The truth is powerful in and of itself, but it does not become truth until one person speaks it. An unspoken truth is a lost chance to heal the wounds in nature made by errors and lies."

"You're quoting again, aren't you? From this teacher of yours."

Skaiva smiled slightly. "How could you tell?"

"When you quote," Sulpicius replied, "you shift your eyes to an invisible point above you and just to the right of center, and seem to be looking at something that isn't there."

"Sir, you give me too much credit, and yourself far too little."

Sulpicius merely smiled in response. Little more was said between them about the dice incident, but the nature of their relationship had undergone a transformation, which was soon to become even more more apparent.

The winter camp had ended badly. Acilius Glabrio, ostracized by his fellow officers, finally did as Sulpicius had suggested, and petitioned Caesar for leave to go home "to attend to urgent family business." But Caesar, inexplicably, had been slow to reply.

Then one chilly morning, late in March, the camp had been attacked just at dawn by a strong force of Gauls, in what would prove to be the beginning of Vercingetorix's last desperate campaign to drive the Romans out of Gaul. Elsewhere, in coordinated attacks occurring at the same time, 15 cohorts were destroyed at Atuatuca, and the Eighth Legion, under the command of Quintus Cicero, was surrounded and would certainly have suffered the same fate at the hands of the Nervi, had not Caesar himself arrived to lift the siege.

The attack on the Seventh Legion, whose *legatus* was Sulpicius, had been well planned, well timed, and well executed. The camp had been built according to regulation, a *castra stativa* for winter quarters, everything done as it should be to prevent a surprise attack from penetrating the defenses. That, in fact, is exactly what Skaiva had seen during his first weeks in Sulpicius's camp: Roman legionaries and gangs of Gallic prisoners digging defensive ditches around the perimeter and building walls, gates, and towers just behind the *fossa*, the moat. All winter long the sentries had been keeping watch on the woods, which had been cut back to leave an open space in front of the camp walls. But months had gone by with absolutely nothing to relieve the boredom, and besides, the feeling was strong among both the officers and the men that the wars in Gaul were already over. Proud of what they had done, they were sure that the spring would see most of them sent home, except for those who might choose to stay in this newly-created Roman province and try their luck as colonists.

It was late March, in the consulship of Domitius Calvinus and Valerius Messalla, and although back home in Italy the spring was well underway, here in central Gaul there were still patches of snow standing in places where the sun could not quite reach. During the night, the day's feeble warmth dissipated quickly, and a powder of snow had even fallen the night before.

At dawn, after spending several hours staring into the snowy darkness at woods where nothing had ever happened and nothing was likely to happen, many of the sentries, if not actually asleep, were at best lost in thought. At least this can be inferred, as none of them survived to stand before their officers to explain why the alarm had been sounded too late, when a considerable part of the Gallic attackers had already penetrated the gates or swarmed over the walls.

Dozens, if not hundreds of legionaries died in their tents without ever fully awakening or having any idea what was happening.

The spearhead of the attack had been aimed directly at the north gate, where the woods came closest to the camp perimeter. A group of 50 carefully chosen warriors had one aim: to break into the camp and make straight for the Praetorium, in the center, to kill the legion's commander. After all the years of war, the Gauls had learned some painful military lessons. Man for man, they were a match for the legionaries, and more, since they were physically larger and raised in a warrior culture, unafraid of death and intoxicated by battle. But the Romans defeated them over and over, due in large part, as the brighter among them came to realize, to the discipline of the legions. The traditional Gallic warrior simply ran straight at his enemy, bloodlust in his heart, and gave no thought to following any orders after "Charge!" The Romans held their ranks, maneuvered groups of men as a single body, moved forward and backward, rotated men to the front ranks to replace exhausted fighters with fresh men every quarter hour or so. And all of this was possible because the Roman soldier always looked for his officers and waited for their orders. In order to win a battle, then, the Gauls had to eliminate the officers, cutting off the head, so to speak, so that the body could no longer act as a body.

So it was Sulpicius, as commander of the Seventh Legion, who was the primary target of the first group of Gauls to get inside the camp's defenses. Ultimately, the perimeter attack failed, as the centurions and tribunes scrambled to get the legionaries into ranks and began to push the enemy out of the camp. At one point, however, the fighting had broken down into a melee right in front of the Praetorium, and Sulpicius found himself fighting alongside no more than six or seven legionaries, surrounded by at least twice as many Gauls.

It was just at this moment that Skaiva entered the battle, swinging a table leg like a club. In the blink of an eye, he had brained two Gauls who had moved around to attack Sulpicius from behind. All the time, he was chanting something in an abnormally loud voice, and it seemed to be this chanting that momentarily distracted the Gallic warriors from their attack. They looked at Skaiva, who was still chanting and swinging his club, and the sight of someone who was clearly one of their own defending the Roman commander, and standing over the bodies of two of their comrades he had clubbed, seemed to be impossible for them to understand.

While they paused for a moment to stare, there came from behind the Gauls the shouts and noise of an *acies*, a Roman battle line, moving to the attack. The legion had recovered from the surprise attack, formed its ranks and driven the attackers from the camp. Only then did one of the centurions look back and notice that their commander was surrounded.

One cohort had reformed, facing back to the Praetorium, and rushed to the attack.

The Gallic attack squad, though now vastly outnumbered, fought furiously, and it took some time to overcome them, one by one. No quarter was asked, or given.

Sulpicius, exhausted by the desperate fighting, stumbled backwards, keeping his guard forward. The three survivors of the men who had been fighting alongside him moved forward as their Gallic opponents turned to meet the Roman battle line behind them, leaving Sulpicius behind. Skaiva, however, was nowhere to be seen.

Sulpicius was fully engrossed in the action taking place in front of him, and failed to notice that someone was making his way towards him from behind, around the side of the Praetorium. The man approached stealthily, dagger in hand, and as soon as he was close enough, he raised his arm to strike.

But the blow was parried—or rather, the would-be assassin's arm was caught in a vise-like grip from which he was completely unable to free himself. For a moment he struggled, but the arm that held him could not be budged, and he felt himself slowly and inexorably forced to his knees, and then to the ground. As the joint in his arm gave way, he screamed in pain.

Sulpicius turned to see Skaiva standing over a man whose arm he held twisted behind him. For a moment Sulpicius and Skaiva looked at each other, then both looked down at the would-be assassin: Acilius Glabrio, who had taken a Gallic cloak from a dead Gaul and thrown it over his Roman tunic, just in case someone were to see him attacking his own commander. It was painfully obvious what the plan had been, and Glabrio had at least enough sense of honor not to deny it. He fixed his gaze on the distant trees and said nothing, not answering or even acknowledging the questions Sulpicius tried to ask.

The battle had effectively ended, but there was much still to be done. Sulpicius did not even have the time to thank Skaiva for saving his life, twice. His legion had been badly mauled, but it was intact, and the attackers had paid heavily for their momentary advantage. There were messages to be sent to Caesar, cohorts to be reorganized. Several of the barracks buildings had been torched by the Gauls, and there were fires to be put out and new quarters to be organized.

And, of course, something had to be done about Glabrio. A soldier of lower rank, caught red-handed in an attempt to assassinate his commander, would have been summarily executed in front of the entire legion, but Acilius Glabrio was, as he never ceased to remind his commander and his fellow tribunes, the son of a prominent Senator who had been consul, and he was a man who could expect to fill his father's shoes someday. Or rather, could have expected. After what had happened, even if he escaped prosecution for a capital crime, his career was finished. His political position in Rome might have survived the cheating scandal, if properly handled, but the attempted murder of a *legatus* during a battle—this was unforgivable. Sulpicius ordered Glabrio sent to Caesar with a letter detailing what had happened; he spared him the indignity of chains, but assigned him a guard of two *contubernia*, 16 men under the command of a centurion.

It was well into the night, then, before Sulpicius was able to return to the Praetorium. He found Skaiva there, sitting on the floor next to the bed, naked to the waist, eyes closed.

Sulpicius was too bone weary and too distraught to be tactful. "Are you perhaps praying for forgiveness for having killed two of your own people to save a miserable Roman life?"

Skaiva opened his eyes. "I was praying, yes, but not for forgiveness. My destiny made me your prisoner and your guest, and as such my duty is clear, and takes precedence over all other loyalties."

"Of course," replied Sulpicius, but his puzzled expression belied his words.

"As for those two," continued Skaiva, "it would be pointless to grieve for them. They were warriors, they fought well, they are already reborn."

Sulpicius contemplated the strangeness of all this for a long moment, before he spoke again.

"You saved my life twice today, once from your own people, once from one of mine. I'm grateful, of course, but I'm also puzzled. Any man would come to the aid of a friend. A soldier would come to the aid of his commander, because that is his duty, and he could expect punishment if he let his commander die, and reward if he saves his life. I have known slaves, too, ready to die for their masters, but these are people born to slavery. You are the son of a king, a hostage for only a short time, you were taken from your home and sent here to guarantee your father's observance of his treaty obligations, and now you find yourselves among people who are in the process of subjugating the whole race of men you belong to. What possible motive did you have for saving my life, when you could have sat on your hands and watched another Roman oppressor go down? If these Gauls had won today, and they nearly did—well, I just heard that a very similar attack was made not far from here, at the same time, and the Roman garrison there was wiped out. You would have been a free man, you could have returned home. In your place I think I might have behaved very differently. Can you explain this to me?"

Skaiva replied calmly, without shifting his gaze to Sulpicius. "I have already explained it. It is a simple matter. I would not be your hostage if the gods did not desire it, so they did desire it. They placed me in a position to save your life, which I could not have done if I had not been your guest. So all of this happened so that I could be here, and if I had not done what the gods clearly intended me to do . . .".

He paused, hunting for the words, and now he looked at Sulpicius. "I know little of your life, Senator, but it was not your destiny to die here today. It is the task of a Druid, even a young one such as myself, destined never to be fully trained, to be just where he needs to be at the moment when his presence or absence means everything."

"I'm not a religious man," replied Sulpicius. "I'd like to understand what you're saying, but I don't. What I do know is that you're an extraordinary man, and you shouldn't be a prisoner. I've decided to ask Caesar to release you from your obligations as a hostage, and I will perform the ceremony of emancipation tomorrow, before witnesses, as the law requires. I would prefer that you stay here until then, but as soon as we have all said everything that must be said, you are a free man, and like any free man you may go where you please. You have earned the right to go home."

Sulpicius was not quite prepared for the reaction he received—or rather, the lack of any reaction. Skaiva slowly bowed his head, once, then turned his eyes away again, resumed his previous posture, and as far as Sulpicius could tell, returned to his prayers. He paused for a moment to see if Skaiva would say anything.

When nothing was said for several long moments, Sulpicius began to feel a certain awkwardness. He had come to this room, the commander's bedroom in the Praetorium, to get some rest. But he had just freed Skaiva, effectively if not yet legally, and now he realized that he didn't really know what to do next. The awkwardness was annoying.

Just when Sulpicius's annoyance was about to get the better of him, Skaiva stood, still not speaking, and took up a position behind Sulpicius, where his valet would have been standing (if he had not disappeared during the battle just now, seen by no one), to help him with his armor. In other circumstances, perhaps, Sulpicius would have wanted to talk about all this, but for now, he was exhausted and childishly grateful to his erst-while prisoner for tacitly agreeing to perform the dead slave's duties. In a few moments, Sulpicius was out of his armor, into a clean tunic, and lying on his bed, with Skaiva lying on a mat before the door. All seemed both very right and very wrong, which, Sulpicius thought just before his exhausted brain shut down, was a clear indication that after this day nothing would ever be as it was.

The next morning he awoke refreshed, and was quite content, though no longer really surprised, to find Skaiva ready to serve breakfast, taking the place of the slave whose disappearance was only explained later that day, when his body was discovered hidden in a bush behind the Praetorium, his throat slit ear to ear. There was no need to wonder who had done this thing, but whatever could be done with Glabrio had already been done, and there was nothing to be gained by investigating the death of a slave, even a trusted and valuable one.

After he had eaten, as Skaiva was leaving to get his own breakfast from the kitchen, Sulpicius stopped him.

"We will perform the emancipation in the presence of my officers, today at midday. Nothing is expected of you except your presence. It will not take long. Will you be leaving at once?"

"Am I expected to leave? Is it required?"

"Well, no," replied Sulpicius, "no, of course not, you can stay as long as you like. I don't consider my debt of gratitude to you fully paid when I have set you free. You will no longer be my prisoner, but you will still be my guest, if you wish."

"I would prefer to stay. But I would prefer to stay, not as I have been, as your guest, but as a soldier, under your command."

Sulpicius could hardly have been more astonished. "Skaiva, I've given you your freedom, why in the name of all the gods, yours or mine, would you choose to remain here, among your enemies? Aren't you a man of standing among your own people, someday to be their king? I've seen how they treat you: even those men who were attacking me seemed to know that you were someone they should respect."

"I am only a learner, the deeper mysteries of the Druid teaching I had not yet learned before my teacher died, and as you know I am not destined to learn them all, ever. But I have learned enough to know that I am here for a reason, and I feel that yesterday's events, important as they were, were not the sole reason for my being placed among you. There is something I have still to do."

"What?"

"I do not yet know. When the time comes, I shall know. For now, if the gods want me here, then I must do my best to stay here. If that means I am to wear Roman armor and even pour your wine, if you command it, that is what I will do. Whether serving or being served, none of this makes me less a man. Following my own will, turning my back on the portion the gods have given me—this is dishonor, disgrace, the death of the spirit even though the body lives on. If, as you say, I am to be a free man and free to choose, this is what I choose."

In the end, Sulpicius freed Skaiva that day, at noon, as he had promised, and then immediately ordered him to be enrolled in the Seventh Legion with the rank of "supernumerary centurion," an unusual procedure, to be sure, but within the prerogatives of a legion commander. As a "supernumerary," Skaiva was not in command of a maniple, like an ordinary centurion, but was assigned to the commander's staff as an officer—outranked, to be sure, by the tribunes and legates, mostly sons of senators or wealthy equestrians. Still, this rank made Skaiva an officer. In this way he remained close to Sulpicius, but no longer in the position of either guest or prisoner.

Summer and autumn, 54 BCE

Alesia, Gaul

Through the arduous campaign that had begun with the surprise attack in the spring and was to end with the siege of Alesia in the autumn, Skaiva served ably and well, and became indispensable to Sulpicius as his advisor. Time and again he proved his value, by his remarkable ability to anticipate what people would do, to somehow hear the important things they were not saying, to see the motives they tried so hard to conceal. He also knew what the Gauls were likely to do, and what they were unlikely to do, though here there was a line that Sulpicius found himself reluctant to cross. He avoided putting Skaiva in situations where his words or his actions would lead directly to the death of Gauls, though at times these scruples seemed rather pointless. Skaiva was indeed an officer in the Roman army, and so it could hardly be denied that he was aiding the enemy of his people. Was he not a traitor? That would have been an explanation, of course, but Sulpicius could not really see Skaiva as a renegade or a mercenary. If the situation had been reversed, if Sulpicius had become a captive in a Gallic village, he would not have acted the same. But somehow that did not seem to mean very much. Skaiva was following a code of conduct that Sulpicius could barely comprehend, that he would once have termed barbaric, but he seemed to be following it very scrupulously.

Interestingly enough, in the course of their many conversations, Sulpicius had realized that there was a logic to it, this Druid "philosophy," which, like any logical system, assumed a set of axioms and then provided rules of inference and argumentation that allowed one to draw conclusions applicable to particular situations. The Druid axioms were different from those Sulpicius had learned, but then again, weren't the axioms of a Roman senator different from those of, say, Aristotle? And once you accepted them, or granted them even provisionally, the process by which Skaiva drew his conclusions was strictly logical, while the coherence between those conclusions and his behavior was nothing less than extraordinary.

What Sulpicius did not know, and would doubtless have been amused to discover, was that Skaiva thought of him in very nearly the same terms. Though he had fully accepted his god-ordained destiny of being under this Roman's personal control, he had never expected that he would come to respect his host/jailer, and even to like him, as a man, as a friend. Sulpicius was a firm commander, as he had been a master, a man used to having his commands obeyed immediately; as a Roman aristocrat, he had been giving orders to slaves since childhood, and although he was not fond of the lash, he was not one to tolerate disobedience or insolence. His slaves feared his anger, but they were also aware that his anger was seldom unmotivated, and he was not, as so many other masters were, capricious or gratuitously violent. Skaiva soon saw that Sulpicius the commander was much the same: stern, strict, allowing no undue liberties, commanding respect, but fair-minded, as quick to reward outstanding performance as he was to punish the lazy and the cowardly.

And yet, despite his firmness, Sulpicius was a man who could still learn something, able at times to step outside of his certitudes and look at things as they really are, and not to see them only as he had been taught to see them.

Nearly every evening during that bloody summer and autumn, the two men sat in the tent they shared when the army was on the move, and talked, often very late into the night. During the day and in public, the relations between them were strictly correct, as legion commander to staff centurion, but when the flap of the tent closed at night, the atmosphere changed, subtly, but noticeably. Sulpicius was increasingly curious about the culture from which Skaiva had been forcibly removed: the Britons were Gauls, of course, but the farthest removed from the influence of Roman civilization. They were Gauls in the purest form, a claim which Skaiva never missed an opportunity to assert, and Sulpicius, who respected them as worthy, dangerous enemies, wanted to know more.

Skaiva was more than willing to instruct his commander. The Gauls of Britain, his own ancestors (and on one occasion he recited the whole list of unpronounceable names, proving that he was related to both Druids and warriors), had built great stone circles to worship the gods and measure the movements of the heavenly bodies, though some said that the stones had been there long before the Druids had come to Britain, that the gods had sat upon them when the world was new, dividing the world into five zones, each the sphere of a different god. Others said the stones were brought to that place from far away to the west, by an ancient race of giants, who drew their strength from them, until a Druid cast a spell on them that reversed their magic. In this way, then, the rule of the giants in Britain had come to an end.

"These are tales for children," said Sulpicius, "and you can't expect me to believe that you take them seriously."

"And your city was founded by orphaned twins suckled by a she-wolf."

"Point well taken," Sulpicius conceded with a laugh. "In our legends, and the Greek tales we heard from our slaves as children, many things happen that a grown man of reasonable intelligence can hardly listen to without a smile, and there are creatures that can only be seen in dreams, or after a great deal too much wine. But there is often a kernel of truth underneath, as Euhemerus taught, an event or a person of some importance, whose dimensions have been exaggerated and rendered fantastical by generations of storytellers. Things that are difficult to explain can be explained away by resorting to the supernatural, and then one is no longer troubled by them."

"What I know," said Skaiva after a long pause, "is that the world makes sense, all of it, but our minds are too weak, too distracted by thousands of things clambering for our attention, for us to see the purpose and the sense in things as the gods see them, whole, all at once. But we can learn to see, to hear, what is available to our senses, and what we see and hear then points clearly to that which we can neither see nor hear. The Druids tell the people that the oak and the mistletoe speak to them, but this is really a—what is that Greek word you used yesterday?—a *symbolon*, a token, a sign of something far larger. It is the whole world that speaks to us, each of us, Druid or not, every moment, if we only knew how to listen, how to read."

"At times, you know, Skaiva, you sound very much like a Stoic. The cosmos as an organism, nature as a sign of what the gods see, past, present and future all at once."

"Oh yes, that would fit among the precepts I have learned from my Druid teacher, very well."

"I'm not a Stoic, of course," Sulpicius hastened to add. "I know several, starting with that self-righteous ass, Cato, and his faithful puppy, Brutus, not to mention any number of lesser lights. I've been at several of Cicero's philosophical soirees, and heard the Stoics, the Epicureans, the Academics, and what-have-you, all going at it, around in circles for hours and hours. They're all a bit mad, you know, caught up in their own thoughts and unable to see the world and people as they are. I come home every time with a capital headache. Not from the wine, mind you, though I see you smiling. Anyway, I promised myself never to go again. But I have to admit that sitting up nights getting drunk with my officers and talking about slave girls, who's sticking what into whom, or what, also leaves me with a headache, and none the wiser for it, either. I think that's why I like talking to you, Skaiva. You're a very intelligent man, but you live in the real world and you're not using your wits the way these philosophers do, like schoolboys competing to see who can run the fastest, even when there's nothing to catch, or hit the hardest, even when there's nothing to fight about, or who can piss the farthest, which is about as pointless as it can be. An idea has to be about something, doesn't it? Not just about other ideas. Or else it's just a schoolboys' game, it's over as soon as somebody wins and no one else has a move."

"You would have made a fine Druid," said Skaiva, "if you had been born a Celt."

Sulpicius looked at him for a moment, wondering if he was being ironic. "A few months ago I would have taken that as a joke, or an insult, or both," he finally replied. "But a lot has happened since then. So, thank you."

It was only about ten days after this conversation that the last desperate battle was fought at Alesia. Caesar's had ordered his men to build two sets of fortifications: one set facing in, keeping the inhabitants of the besieged city penned in, and one set facing out, keeping the relieving army of Gauls at bay. This finally forced Vercingetorix and his Gauls to put everything on one last throw of the dice. They threw—and lost.

Sulpicius and Skaiva again fought shoulder to shoulder (in such a situation there could be no niceties about Skaiva's possibly divided loyalties), and each saved the other so many times in the course of the day that it would be pointless to count the parries and counterblows. When the fighting was ended, the two men sat on the ground together, too exhausted physically and mentally to move, or speak, for quite some time.

"You killed many of your own people today," said Sulpicius. "Again."

"And for the same reason. That is what soldiers do, they fight and kill. Perhaps for themselves, to kill and not to be killed, but often, maybe very often, for each other."

He paused to catch his breath again, then spoke.

"If you were fighting for Rome today, Sulpicius, why did you trouble to save me, and that not once, but many times? My life is far less valuable to Rome than yours is, surely."

"I'm too tired to argue with you, Skaiva. That wound on your arm is deep and needs attention, let's go."

Slowly they stood, helping each other up, and walked slowly and painfully out towards the woods from which, earlier that day, tens of thousands of Gauls had erupted, screaming like the demons of Hecate.

In the heat of battle, as every soldier knows, wounds that are not lethal seem to be nothing but scratches, and deeds of heroism are done that no sane man would choose to do. At the beginning, just before the lines close, there is a horrible fear, which some, to be sure, manage to convert into a screaming rage, but underneath the show of aggression the guts are twisting all the same. Sometimes there is a moment of waiting, when the eyes turn to some object nearby, unconnected to wars and armies, or up to the sky, or distant mountains, or a bird sitting on a branch and singing, and the sweetness of the life that one is about to leave is unbearable. But when the enemy is at hand, when the first blow is parried, there is a certain moment when one of two things must happen: either the joy of battle fills the heart, or fear takes over completely, the legs of their own accord turn and run. Then, as the Greeks would say, the demigod Pan takes over the soul, and there is only running.

When the battle is over, and we've won, there's one final burst of joy, of celebration, exultation. No name for this feeling exists adequate to express its power. The mouth opens and the lungs push the spirit out in an inarticulate roar. There is nothing to match the feeling of having looked death in the eye and lived to see him blink first, of having killed, and not been killed. At this point it matters to no one what the battle meant, what the war was about, what the consequences might be of having won this day, or might have been, had we lost.

And then it's time to pay the bill, and there's a sizable debt to be paid. Every ounce of energy the organism could generate has been consumed, and the deficit is enormous. The spirit lags, the limbs grow inexpressibly heavy, the slightest exertion is impossible. All the wounds that seemed so trivial begin to hurt, all at once, as the mental walls that had kept the pain at bay suddenly collapse. It is no uncommon thing for a soldier who has been grievously wounded to live right until this moment, thinking that he has survived unhurt, only to drop dead, pale as a ghost, a few moments after the last enemy has left the field. The death rattle not infrequently comes as an ironic punctuation to the victory roar.

That is why no general, no matter how wise or clever, can move an army that has just fought a battle, at least not for a day or so.

Sulpicius and Skaiva, without speaking to each other in more than grunts, first washed the blood, sweat and dirt off themselves with several buckets of cold water from the nearby stream. They could now approach with impunity, since the Gallic relief army, what was left of it, had drawn off. The "besieged besiegers" now had only one set of walls to defend. Then they tore strips off their uniform tunics (which were ruined anyway, unfit to wear again and quite beyond repair) to bandage the deeper wounds, of which each man had several. Neither man was still bleeding enough to cause alarm, and they turned back towards the camp, towards their tent.

Both of them had seen battlefields before. The dead, Gauls and Romans, lay sprawled everywhere, like so many sacks of grain strewn from an overturned wagon, and the flies were so numerous already that their buzzing could be heard over all other sounds. The smell was indescribable, and would get much worse. Some of the seriously wounded were still moving, some calling for help, others crawling towards the water from which Sulpicius and Skaiva had just come. Cavalrymen with lances rode slowly among them; when a grievously wounded Gaul was encountered, they struck, without malice or joy, but as one who performs a somewhat distasteful but very routine task. Groups of slaves were moving about, also, finding the Roman wounded who needed help. Others were already beginning to gather the dead for burial. The Roman dead were lain together, in neat rows, officers separate from legionaries; the Gauls were piled where they would soon be cremated.

Sulpicius saw the tears in Skaiva's eyes as he watched all this, but there was no strength left in him to discuss it. All he could do was to slap his comrade on the back. Skaiva simply nodded, compressed his lips together tightly, and kept walking.

The tumult of feelings that were running through his exhausted body was inexpressible.

Every soldier in every professional army knows that the right training, the right weapons, and the right officers can make the difference between life and death in a battle. But they also know that no matter how conclusive our victory, some of us are going to die anyway, and death on a battlefield can find you at any moment. The language changes, the metaphors change, but the underlying thought is as old as warfare itself: if your number's up, it's up.

Caesar's number, for example, was never up. He wore that bright red cape and rode out into plain view of the enemy in the thick of battle, with projectiles flying and angry men with swords all around him, and seemed hardly to notice that death was at hand, that men were dying all around him, that thousands of men were looking at him and wishing him dead, longing for the glory and the prizes that would be theirs if they could just reach this man. His presence on the battlefield, in the melee, a commander who seemed quite beyond the reach of sudden death, had more than once turned the tide of a hard-fought battle. He seemed to spread the cloak of immortality over all his men, so that they found the strength for one more surge, withheld one more desperate enemy charge, performed deeds of valor they didn't even know they were capable of, and sometimes, afterwards, didn't even remember performing.

Sulpicius had now survived yet another battle, wounded, yes, but not too seriously. Still he could not shake the feeling that had awakened him that morning before dawn, the feeling that he would not see another dawn. Apparently the feeling had been a delusion, because here he was, the battle was over and he was alive.

"I am—" he started to say to Skaiva. But he did not finish the sentence.

The blow came from a stone, flung down from a siege tower. During the battle, a group of young Gallic warriors had made a desperate attempt to seize the tower, from which Roman archers had been raining down death on some of Vercingetorix's best men. The attack had almost succeeded, but in the end all the Gauls in the tower had been cut down.

One young Gaul, though, left for dead, had awakened from a stupor, and pulled himself into a position where he could see out from an archer's firing post. A moment's glance was enough to tell him that the battle was over, and had been lost. Vercingetorix, to whom he had pledged his life, was almost certainly either dead or in chains, or worse, was running away. There was only one way to emerge from this with honor intact: to strike one last blow, and die.

Though he had lost a great deal of blood, the resolve to die with honor gave him the strength to lift the stone that the archer had been using for a footrest. He chose his target, a Roman officer walking below him, and flung the stone, then fell back, having used the last of his strength. In a few short moments, his prayer was answered, when a squad of Roman soldiers ran up the stairs, swords drawn, and dispatched him.

On the ground below, Sulpicius lay unconscious. He had been struck on the very crown of his head. Skaiva quickly saw that the surface wound, though it bled profusely, was superficial. His helmet had not protected his head, for the simple reason that Sulpicius, sure that the danger was over, had removed it. The skull seemed intact. Most people, Skaiva knew, assumed that a skull fracture was a terrible thing, but the Druids knew (and so did the great Greek physician, Hippocrates) that worse things can happen inside a man's head when the skull does not break. Then the force of the blow goes right into the brain, instead of being dispersed to shatter the bone.

By this time a crowd of legionaries had gathered, some of whom were from the Seventh. "Is he dead?" one of them asked.

"No," said Skaiva, "at least not yet. Help me get him to his tent."

It was not only Skaiva's nominal rank that earned him obedience. The men from the Seventh had seen what he could do as a doctor; his skills had saved many a wounded legionary, including two of the men who were now standing around Sulpicius.

"Can you save him?" someone asked.

"I don't know," replied Skaiva, "but I can do nothing for him here."

Four of the men picked Sulpicius up, following Skaiva's directions, and carried him to his tent, feet first, while Skaiva walked behind, cradling his friend and commander's head. When they arrived, the soldiers put Sulpicius on his cot and then left, taking up guard around the tent automatically, without waiting for orders.

Skaiva set to work. The bleeding from the head wound needed to be stopped. This was not a major problem, since there were herbs in his medicine chest that would serve to staunch deeper wounds than this. But Skaiva knew well that the gash was, if not the least of Sulpicius's problems, certainly not the worst. From time to time he gently lifted his friend's eyelids and looked carefully back and forth to see if the pupils of both eyes were the same size.

Evening was approaching when, finally, Sulpicius stirred, sighed, opened his eyes, and groaned.

"Thirsty," he said, or meant to say, though the word that came out of his mouth sounded more like "Furry." Skaiva picked up a goblet with boiled water, and said in a calm clear voice, "I am going to give you some water now, but you must look at me first." He knew that many a well-meaning attendant had unintentionally killed a patient by giving him water when he was not conscious enough to swallow it properly.

It was a long moment before Sulpicius turned his eyes to Skaiva and seemed to actually see him. Skaiva then gave him a sip of the water, and when this had gone down without incident, another.

The water seemed to revive Sulpicius somewhat. He meant to ask, "What happened? Where am I?" But all that actually came out of his mouth was "Wha'? Wha'? Wha'?" Agitated by the apparent refusal of his mouth to articulate the words he wanted to say, he tried to sit up. Skaiva gently but firmly restrained him and spoke. It really wasn't all that hard to imagine the question his patient had been trying to ask.

"You were struck on the head by a stone, thrown at us by a Gallic warrior who somehow got himself up on a watch tower, looking for a Roman to kill. He chose you, but you were not meant to die today, and here you are, alive, in your tent, with a very bad headache."

Sulpicius relaxed, lay back, nodded, and closed his eyes. This time, however, Skaiva was not going to allow him to sleep again, at least not yet.

"Do you know who I am?"

Sulpicius did not immediately reply, but finally he opened his eyes and nodded.

"Say my name, please."

"Ska, Ska, Skai, Skaive, Skaiva." When it finally came out, he gave a crooked half smile. "You sumby."

"What?"

"You sum fa by, sun uffa"—some effort to articulate—"son..of..a.. bitch."

Skaiva laughed, somewhat relieved. Sulpicius was having some trouble getting his words out, but he seemed to know what he wanted to say. It was a good sign.

It was still necessary to keep Sulpicius awake for a while. Some men after a blow to the head were perfectly lucid, seemed fine, dropped into a sleep—and never awoke.

Finally, about the end of the second watch, Skaiva felt such exhaustion that he caught himself dreaming while still awake. He decided that the risk would have to be taken, and let Sulpicius drift off to sleep.

It was midday the following day before Skaiva awoke. He immediately stood up from the pallet on the ground next to Sulpicius's cot, and checked to see if his commander was still alive. He was, sleeping heavily, but breathing, it seemed, normally. It was late afternoon before his eyes opened.

"Dear gods!" Sulpicius said, "how my head hurts! How drunk was I? I don't even remember drinking." When Skaiva heard him speaking normally, a rare broad smile spread across his face.

"I'll give you something for that head." He reached into his medicine chest and removed a vial with a white powder in it. "This is ground willow bark, it should help, but you will need to eat something with it or your stomach might bleed."

"Actually I'm starving."

Skaiva had some porridge ready for this moment, and offered it. Sulpicius, who was usually rather fussy about his food and had no use for legionary porridge, took it this time without complaint and ate it. He used the spoon normally, as Skaiva was careful to observe.

The night's rest and the hearty breakfast seemed to have made a considerable difference, along with the willow bark. Sulpicius and Skaiva dressed, in companionable silence, and went outside just in time to hear the trumpets calling an assembly of officers at Caesar's tent.

The entire army was already moving towards the place where Caesar's tent had stood throughout the siege, just opposite the gates of Alesia. The siege machinery, which had maintained a slow but relatively constant shower of stones and projectiles against the Gallic fortifications for over a month, was now still. On the other side of the ditch that lay in front of the inward-facing wall the Romans had built to encircle Alesia, there was a fairly broad, empty plain, littered now with many dead, not all of them soldiers.

Several weeks before, as the food stocks began to run out, Vercingetorix had ordered all the women and children to leave the city, certain that Caesar—already known for his *clementia*, a quality the Gauls did not really understand and mistook for weakness of will—would open the siege works to let them through, giving the Gauls a chance to throw all their forces out in a surprise assault and break through the Roman fortifications. Caesar had refused to allow the women and children to approach, sensing a trap, while Vercingetorix had refused to let them back inside Alesia, where food was already in very short supply. Both armies had watched, horrified at the other's barbarity, as all these non-combatants began to starve to death; and now, whatever pitiful remains the birds, the dogs, and the rats had not already consumed provided a suitable background for the unspeakable scene created by the uncollected bodies of yesterday's casualties, many lying in heaps in the ditch or just under the walls.

When Sulpicius arrived at Caesar's tent, accompanied by Skaiva in a clean staff centurion's uniform, he found the Great Man seated formally in a curule chair in front of his tent, dressed in his best armor, with his trademark red cloak wrapped around him. There really was little need to explain, and the explanation that finally came was laconic (Sulpicius had noticed several times before that Caesar resorted to a very lapidary way of speaking exactly when he was sure he had won).

"Word has been sent from the town, under flag of truce, that Vercingetorix will soon emerge, alone, to surrender. We will draw up a guard of honor to receive him as befits a defeated, but valorous enemy who has earned our respect. Afterwards, I shall address the troops."

Throughout the memorable scene that followed, Sulpicius caught himself mostly looking at Skaiva, trying to read his thoughts from his impassive face. It proved impossible.

There was a silence in the ranks that grew almost oppressive. Vercingetorix, decked out in his finest, slowly rode his trademark white stallion down the road, lined with Roman troops in parade dress, at attention, to the Praetorium. Caesar received him sitting in a curule chair that had been improvised for the occasion, as befitted a proconsul receiving the submission of a defeated rebel king. But at the last moment, when Vercingetorix had pulled on his horse reins and dismounted just before the Pedestal, Caesar stood. He stepped forward and received the proffered sword, standing face to face with the most fearsome enemy he had ever encountered. This was a general receiving the surrender of another general, honorably defeated in battle, and not a Roman governor taking a rebel into custody.

For a moment, in fact, from the expression on Caesar's face, Sulpicius thought he actually meant to embrace Vercingetorix. But the moment passed. Vercingetorix knelt in the dust, then prostrated himself. Caesar looked down at him, then turned away, gesturing to his personal guards, who came forward with the chains they had prepared for this occasion, bound up their captive, and took him away. There were no jeers or taunts from the ranks of the legionaries.

That night, the silence that had prevailed between Sulpicius and Skaiva since the battle was finally broken.

"I can only imagine," said Sulpicius, "how you must have felt, watching Vercingetorix surrender. You wear our uniform now, but I have never had any illusions about it: you surely don't feel yourself more Roman than Gaul, nor do I think you have any reason to feel that way. I never stop wondering about it, no matter how often you've tried to explain it."

"What I can hardly imagine," replied Skaiva, "is what Vercingetorix must have felt. It was the end of everything. Gaul will not rise again."

"I have to admit I hope you're right. But it costs you something to say that, doesn't it? Can't you imagine another day, another leader, another rebellion?"

"No," Skaiva replied. "For us it is over, finally. We Celts are gamblers, you know, and Vercingetorix staked everything on one throw of the dice. Everything. He knew what he was doing, concentrating not only all the armies of the Gauls, but all the power and prestige, in a way that Gaul had never seen before. What would have happened if he had won, I cannot say, but Gaul would have been very different, one way or another. The Celtic way of life would have had to change."

"How so?"

"Our culture is built around the king, the head of his tribe, and the warriors who follow him. There is no higher authority than the king except the gods, and the king answers to no man—though the Druids, who speak the language of the gods, can call him to task. There could never be a King of the Gauls, because that would mean that each king of each tribe would have had to acknowledge the authority of a higher king, and then he would lose all authority over his own people. As for the warriors, they fight if and when their king tells them to fight, against the enemy he points out as his own enemy."

"You've explained this to me before. It's a disgrace to survive a battle in which your king has fallen."

"Yes, that's right. A warrior who returns to his village alive after his king has been killed in battle has no standing, he is no longer a warrior, but the lowest of peasants. People will turn away from him, refuse to speak to him, even his own family, which he has disgraced."

"With us, you know," said Sulpicius, "it's rather the opposite. It's the general who loses his army in battle that's disgraced; he's expected to fall on his own sword."

"I've heard that, though at first I couldn't understand it at all. It seemed to me all backwards, perverse even. But then I realized that a Roman general is not a king at all. In Britain, everyone simply assumed that Caesar was King of the Romans, though I've been in Italy and I know that there's no such person."

"Nor will there ever be. Not in my lifetime, at least."

"You're probably right, I couldn't say. But for us, a tribe without a king would be like a family without a father. It happens, but it's not good for anyone."

Sulpicius nodded. "So what happens if the king loses the battle, but doesn't die on the field? Is he disgraced, does he lose his crown?"

"No, if he retreats or is simply beaten, then he returns home, and his warriors with him, and then he decides what to do next. But as I said before, we Gauls are gamblers, and we have a gambler's approach to winning and losing. When you've staked it all and lost, you lost, that's all, you walk away. That's why our wars usually have only one battle: you win or you lose, and that's it."

"All right, I get the idea. But the situation with Vercingetorix was different. He not only lost, he surrendered himself and became a prisoner. So what do his warriors do now? Do they surrender, too?"

"I honestly don't know," Skaiva replied. "That's what is so hard for me to grasp, this surrender and what it means. But following your king to a valorous death in battle is one thing, following him into slavery is something else. I can't see it, if I were in that position myself. The king isn't dead, but he's not king anymore, so no one will know what to do. Some may choose to go on fighting the Romans, but most, I think, will read this as I have: everything on one roll of the dice, which came up snake-eyes. It's over. I don't think there will be any more serious fighting in Gaul. The Haedui were right all along: the Romans are going to win anyway, so better to be on their side and get a better deal. Cynical and ignoble, perhaps, but what happened to Vercingetorix has proven them right."

"But haven't you done the same thing yourself, Skaiva? Made your own peace with the Romans? Was that a 'cynical and ignoble' thing for you to do?"

Skaiva stood and walked to the door of the tent, looking out into the night. "There are mornings when I wake up, and the first thought that comes to my mind is that I'm a traitor, a disgrace to my father and my people. But they see you Romans as utterly alien beings, not completely human, monsters to be hated and feared, and fought at all costs. Can you imagine how a legion lined up for battle looks to a Celt? Just a wall of shields, all exactly alike, helmets and uniforms that make all the legionaries look exactly like one another, and hundreds of men moving as one.

"And here is this Caesar at its head, a man who always manages to be where we do not expect him, when we do not expect him, and never loses a battle, even when he is outnumbered three to one. Or if he seems to lose, as at Gergovia, he is back again, twice as strong, and somehow even when he loses, he wins. And through it all he smiles a little, like this"—and here Skaiva did a very passable imitation of Caesar's trademark half-smile, which so seldom left his face—"like a horse merchant who has just cheated you exactly at the moment you thought you were cheating him. He is a force of nature, to be cursed at but never overcome. So it's not hard to understand the fear, is it?"

"No, I suppose not. I wouldn't care to face Caesar across a battlefield, either."

"So as I see it, the only thing we Celts could possibly accomplish by resisting you Romans, even if we could succeed, would be to isolate ourselves completely. And that really means, leave ourselves open to be overwhelmed by the Germans, sooner or later. And given the choice, I'd rather be a subject of your Empire than a slave of some stinking German. It's not a pleasant choice, but there it is. The Haedui have seen this all along, or at least their leaders have, until the hotheads gave in to Vercingetorix's eloquence. It's easy to see why some call the Haeduan leaders traitors and cowards, lickspittles of the worst kind, but the hotheads have never been inside the Empire, as I have. On the other side of the Alps, I met Gauls who were Roman citizens, spoke Latin, wore the toga. And their fathers had been born in villages much like my own, and wore trousers like mine. I was young and proud, and at first I despised them.

But then my eyes were opened, and I saw that there are two compelling reasons not to resist Romanization, but embrace it."

"And what are those reasons?"

"First, because resistance is futile. My father is a king, and the whole army he and all his friends and kinsmen could assemble would not outnumber a single Roman legion. And how many legions are there? How many more could be raised if they were needed? Our pride and our quarrelsomeness—how petty it all seems, when you look at it from the perspective of your Empire. My father is so proud of himself because he did a deal with Caesar himself and saw the back of him, but he has no idea how insignificant all of Britain is to a man like Caesar. And Caesar is not even a king, even his power and strength are only a fraction of those of the whole Roman people.

"And second, because Romanization, for many ordinary people, makes life better, not worse. What difference does it make to them to say, 'I am a free born Gaul,' if what that means is perpetual war between one king and another, with the Germans lurking in the forests, hunger every winter because the king is too busy fighting for his honor to take care of petty things like food. My father doesn't understand this. He thinks of his kingship as being the leader of a wolf pack, fighting his way to the top and then fighting off the younger wolves who want to do the same to him, when the truth is very different: that he is a shepherd and the people are his sheep. If he fails to find pastures, if he lets the wolf among the flock, his sheep will die, and who needs the shepherd then?"

He fell silent, and Sulpicius did not feel that he needed to reply, or could have replied if he had needed to. But he lay awake for some hours that night, and before he fell asleep he had reached a decision.

One morning, about three weeks after the battle, as the army remained encamped around Alesia, Sulpicius rose at dawn, unassisted, dressed and took his breakfast, and then made his way, alone, to Caesar's Praetorium. He told the guard standing before the entrance to the tent that he needed a word with the proconsul. The guard was appropriately deferential; Caesar was informed, and did the *legatus* of the Seventh Legion the particular honor of coming out in person, informally dressed in a legionary's rough tunic, to greet him warmly and invite him inside.

"I am utterly amazed," Caesar said, smiling, "to see you so well. The whole army's been talking about what happened to you. Why have you come all this way, alone, on foot? If you'd sent word, I'd have sent a sedan chair to bring you, or I suppose I would've come to you myself. Thought about it, actually, but my own doctors told me that your health would be too fragile for visitors. But what do they know?"

Sulpicius replied, enunciating his words perhaps just a little too carefully. "I have been a burden on my friends and fellow officers long enough, Caesar, and I find that my legs are ready to do their duty."

Once they were inside the tent and the guard had been dismissed, Caesar reclined on his couch, an obvious signal that he expected the conversation to be informal and friendly, and an equally clear indication that he considered Sulpicius a trusted friend.

Caesar was never one to linger over small talk of any kind, however, and he asked Sulpicius at once, "What brings you here, my friend? What is so urgent that a man just back from the gates of Hades has walked alone all this way to see me?"

Sulpicius had rehearsed over and over what he would say, but as so often happened, in the presence of this man he suddenly felt that everything he had meant to say was vapid and pointless. So he stammered at first, so tangled in his words and thoughts that Caesar decided to come to his rescue.

"Rufus, old friend, if you've come to ask for the hand of my daughter in marriage, I'm afraid it's out of my hands. She's not available any more. But I may have a niece or two to spare, if you're in the market."

It was never easy to know when Caesar's humor was intended to be kind, and when it was ironic, or even ghastly and cruel. Caesar's only daughter, Julia, as everyone knew, had been happily married to Pompey, and it had been precisely the bond between the two great statesmen created by this marriage that had allowed Caesar to turn his full attention on Gaul, without having to keep a constant watchful eye on the roads that led across the Alps from Rome. But Julia had died in childbirth two years before, and Caesar had been devastated by the loss of his only child, as Pompey had been by the loss of his young bride. Why, then, was he making such a callous joke about her now?

Sulpicius decided to cover his shock, and used the opportunity to calm himself down a bit with a touch of his own humor.

"No, no, I wouldn't inflict my mother on any innocent woman, let along a relative of yours. No way to repay a man to whom my family and I already owe so much."

Caesar did not reply, but his smile became, if not warm, at least slightly less enigmatic.

"No, actually what I came for, Caesar, was a matter concerning my centurion, Skaiva."

"Oh yes," Caesar replied, "the hostage, Mandubracius' son, the one who got so bored being a hostage he decided to try his hand at soldiering in our legions. Has he been a problem?"

"Quite the contrary," Sulpicius replied promptly. "He's probably the best staff officer I have, and he's saved my life on several occasions. He's quick to learn, extraordinarily observant, intelligent, but when the fighting gets close and physical he's a match for any man I've ever seen. He's also the best physician in the army, of which I am living proof. He saved my life when I should have died."

"I see," said Caesar, "so it's his hand in marriage you came to seek. Well, it's irregular, of course, but if you must . . ."

Sulpicius was now even more discomfited. There were all these rumors about Caesar's reputed sexual submission to King Nicomedes of Pontus twenty years ago, and allusions to the matter, even remote and unintentional, were known to annoy the Great Man beyond measure, but he was inordinately fond of teasing his officers by implying that they were all avid practitioners of the "Greek vice." One never knew what to do.

"Excuse me, sir, perhaps my praise of him did sound a bit over-blown, but I came here to ask for a favor, for him, precisely because in my view he has earned it." Sulpicius drew a breath—what he was about to say could be the end of his career. "I would like to ask you, as proconsul of Gaul, to enroll Skaiva as a Roman citizen."

Caesar raised an eyebrow.

"And further, I would like to ask that he be released from his service as centurion and allowed to return to Britain."

"As a Roman citizen? What would be the point of that, to make him a citizen of Rome and then send him off to be a barbarian king?"

"That would be precisely the point. Mandubracius is our friend now and protects our interests only because we are a useful counterweight against his enemies at home, and we are too far away to actually meddle in his affairs. If you don't return to Britain a third time, I doubt that we'll be hearing much from him in the future, as soon as he decides that we aren't coming back any time soon."

"Yes, that's a reasonable assessment. If I thought that cold, rainy island was really worth the effort, I'd have to go back at last one more time, any fool could see that. But then, I never really imagined Britannia as a Roman province. As you will recall, we discussed this in staff meetings many times. We went there because every hothead in Gaul who raised a rebellion against us seemed to have some connection with Britain, came from there or had been there, or had volunteers from there, whatever. We needed to put the fear of Roman eagles in British hearts to keep them on their side of the channel, and I think we did that. Vercingetorix had no British help, as far as I could see. What Mandubracius does now really doesn't interest me very much."

"Perhaps not, but client kings across the borders from our provinces have always been useful, and here is a future king, who spent several years in Gallia Narbonensis, and has now served in our army. He understands the Empire very well, at times, I think, better than I do. If he were a citizen, and returned to his people to show them in his own person how surrendering to Roman strength does not necessarily make you a captive or a slave—well, I'm not a statesman like you, Caesar, but to me it seems a good idea. Also, we show people in Gaul that we know how to reward loyalty and talent generously when they're combined in one man."

This time the smile on Caesar's face seemed almost warm. "I've been thinking about these matters, Rufus, ever since before Vercingetorix started his rebellion." He stood up from his couch and began to pace as he talked. "I don't need to tell the son of Publius Sulpicius Rufus, tribune of the plebs, a martyr to the cause of opposition to Sulla and all the extremist Conservatives, that the chief political problem of this Empire, even as it grows, and precisely because it has grown and most likely will grow further, is that it is still governed by a small group of elites who are interested only in their own aggrandizement. Their forefathers may have been great men, like my own, but this generation and the one that preceded it have shown over and over again that, given the choice between the common good and the interests of their own class, they will invariably choose the latter. This must change, or everything we've accomplished here, or that Pompey accomplished in the East ten years ago, will be lost, squandered away in our lifetime.

"But I grow tiresome, and here I am lecturing a man who knows all this as well as I do. Your father was a great man. It's too bad you were so young when he died, you never really knew him, did you? I've made it a point of honor to help his son bring honor to his name, and you've never disappointed me. You know, I suppose, that your patrician cousin Servius is standing for the consulship? He's sure to win, I hope he does, especially if Marcellus gets in."

The sudden change of topic took Sulpicius by surprise. It was, as he later reflected, a characteristic maneuver by Caesar, whose constant effort in almost every transaction was to keep the other person at least slightly off balance.

"I had heard of it," Sulpicius finally managed to say, embarrassed that he could think of nothing clever to add.

"Well, all this doesn't concern us just now. As for your young friend, Skaiva, I am happy to grant your request. When you return, you may address him as Publius Sulpicius Scaeva. I will have the necessary documents drawn up today. What he needs is a release from active duty, which I'll also provide, it's within my prerogative. Send him around this evening to pick up his documents, but consider it settled. I'd very much like to speak to this estimable young man of yours. Now, was there anything else?"

Caesar ushered Sulpicius out politely enough, even cordially, but without undue ceremony. Sulpicius found himself standing outside the Praetorium, more than slightly dazed, aware that he had gained what he had come to ask for, but unsure if he'd really won or lost.

He returned to his own quarters, took Skaiva aside, and told him what he had done. By now, he knew enough not to expect any great demonstration of feeling, positive or negative, and indeed Skaiva took the news with his usual impassivity. Sulpicius was unsure how his British friend would react to the change of name attendant upon being sponsored for citizenship by a Roman nobleman, but Skaiva was ready to become Publius Sulpicius Scaeva without protest. He put on his centurion's uniform over a clean tunic for his visit with Caesar, and made his way (alone, at his own request) to the Praetorium.

He wondered as he walked if the guard would demand that he hand over his sword before entering the general's tent, and pondered what he would do if such a request was made; but it was not. Evidently orders had been given.

This, Scaeva thought, was rash on Caesar's part. If I were a Gallic patriot, I could become a hero in all of Gaul and Britain by pulling my sword and plunging it into Caesar's heart. I would surely die myself, of course, but what is that to a Celtic warrior, to die in such glory?

But that is not why Skaiva/Scaeva was here today. The gods had other plans for him, and for Caesar.

He entered the tent when invited by the guard, and found Caesar, still dressed in his tunic, sitting at a desk.

"Come in, centurion," Caesar said, without looking up from whatever it was he was writing. "I shall finish this one sentence, and then I have a few questions for you."

Scaeva saluted and stood at attention.

"You may be seated, centurion," said Caesar, still not looking up. "Always makes me uncomfortable when everyone else is standing, and I'm seated."

Scaeva did as he had been ordered, but sat on the camp stool to which Caesar had gestured so stiffly that he might as well have been still at attention. Even so, however, he couldn't resist the temptation to take a good luck at this man, whose name made strong men tremble throughout Gaul, and even Britain. Scaeva had seen him before, to be sure, but only at a distance.

The man before him was tall for a Roman, and with his head slightly bent over his writing the bald crown of his head was obvious, though he combed his hair in such a way as almost to cover it, and seldom removed his plumed helmet in the presence of the legions. This touch of vanity puzzled Scaeva, as it seemed inconsistent with the casual way Caesar was now dressed, in a soldier's tunic hardly different from the one he himself was wearing under his armor. For that matter, he must have been aware that Scaeva could see his bald spot now, and yet he seemed utterly indifferent to it. So was he vain, this Gaius Julius Caesar, or was he not?

But old Segovax had taught his pupil Skaiva well: it is the small paradoxes that are the key to a man's soul. If Caesar were simply vain, that would be a fact worth noting, but of little intrinsic interest. Such a man does not know his own value, so he looks for it in other's eyes, and then tries to increase it by making the picture reflected in their eyes as pleasant as possible to look at. This was a man, though, who took care with his appearance in certain situations, but in others seemed indifferent. The solution was clear: it was a different sort of vanity, a calculating kind, on the part of a man who wanted to control how he was seen (not just how he looked) in every situation.

Scaeva's thoughts on all this were interrupted when Caesar finished his writing, laid down his pen, and looked up for the first time.

His eyes, seen at close quarters, were riveting. He had apparently made a point of showing Scaeva that he had important things to do, and that Scaeva, a mere centurion, was not worthy of too much attention. But now, his gaze was direct, penetrating, unwavering. Now that he had chosen to turn his attention to Scaeva, he seemed fully focused on him, undistracted by matters of grand strategy or imperial policy.

"As you know," Caesar began, "I spoke with your commander yesterday, and received from him not only a glowing account of your performance on his staff, but also a most extraordinary request. I will tell you honestly: if any *legatus* other than Publius Sulpicius Rufus had made such a request, I would have refused without a second thought, and probably considered replacing him as commander of one of my legions. But I have a very high opinion of this man, and what is more, I knew, admired, and respected his father. Do you know who his father was?"

"I know only that he never really knew his father, who died when he was scarcely more than an infant."

"Your Latin, by the way, is excellent," Caesar said in reply. "I can barely hear your accent, and I'm good at accents. I can talk to a man for two minutes and tell you within a ten-mile radius where he was born, and if he was born in Rome, I can almost tell you what street he grew up on."

Scaeva noted the digression, but of course he was hardly in a position to steer the conversation, so he merely nodded politely to acknowledge the compliment and waited to hear what Caesar really wanted to say. Apparently, the topic of Sulpicius's father was not it.

"I understand that you came here as a hostage, sent by your father, King Mandubracius, and yet at your own request you were made a supernumerary centurion. Your performance in that position has been excellent. Among your own people, however, you are the son of a king, someday to be king, a leader of warriors, who will be prepared to die to protect your life and your honor. How is it that a man born to be a king can accept the role of a staff centurion in a Roman army? It is beneath you, is it not?"

Scaeva replied, "I am indeed the subordinate of a man, who is a subordinate of yours, and you, for all your greatness, are not a king, so yes, I am not in the kind of position I would occupy in my father's army. But that 'army' consists of less than a thousand warriors, who are usually busy being farmers when there is no war afoot, and for all their warrior ethos and brave talk, all they know of fighting is to grab a sword, a spear, a club, even a rake or a shovel, and have at it. My father is king of a tribe that inhabits a territory I can ride around with a reasonably good horse in an afternoon. Across the hills to the north there is another such king, and to the east, another, and so on throughout the entire island, up to the northern end, where the painted Picts dwell. At any given moment about two-thirds of these British 'kings' are at war with each other, because one king's cattle fouled another king's pond, or someone's son seduced someone else's daughter, or one of them, drunk, called the other a pig. And for this they make war, though the war is hardly more than the brawls I sometimes saw in the tabernae when I was in Gallia Narbonensis."

He turned his head and looked at Caesar directly for the first time. "I have seen much and learned much serving in your army, Caesar, and I don't regret it."

For a moment the two men looked at each other. Scaeva, of course, was the first to drop his gaze to the floor.

"As part of my agreement with Sulpicius," Caesar resumed the conversation, "I agreed to release you from your service in our army, and you may return home, as you wish. This also means that you may claim the privileges of a veteran—if, that is, you will be somewhere where those privileges have any meaning. But I'm thinking that you may not wish to return home after all, to lead your armies into battle in the great cattle wars."

Scaeva was taken entirely by surprise. He had come prepared with arguments in favor of the course he planned to take, assuming that Caesar would not understand, not approve, or both. But this man knew what he was thinking, even though he'd shared his thoughts on this problem with no one, not even Sulpicius.

"As a Roman citizen, of course," Caesar continued, "you may go to any city or town in the Empire, to Rome itself, if you wish. You won't be the son of a king, to be sure, but you may find that being a citizen of Rome is worth at least as much. You will be, so far as I know, the first Briton to become a Roman citizen."

"What I most desire, Caesar, is to remain a soldier in your army."

"That is exactly what I hoped you would say. Your discharge can be torn up. See, here it is, I give it to you, and if you really wish, then tear it up now."

Without a moment's hesitation Scaeva tore the document in half, then again in half.

"I had prepared another document, then," Caesar went on, "which I was sure I would be needing. This is your promotion. You are no longer a centurion, but a military tribune."

"But sir, the Seventh already has its complement of six tribunes. I am deeply honored, but I am also . . . well, confused, to be honest."

"I'm afraid our mutual friend Sulpicius Rufus will be losing his best staff centurion, one way or another. I am detaching you from the Seventh. I shall be forming new legions, here, in Gaul. Yes, recruited from Gauls. It has occurred to me, you see, that a legion composed of Celtic fighting men, with their valor and loyalty, but subjected to Roman discipline, trained in our tactics, would be part of the most formidable army the world has ever seen. With such an army . . ."

But Caesar did not finish the sentence. Rather, much as he had done with Sulpicius earlier that same day, he ushered his new tribune, shocked and dazed at his own good fortune, out of his tent, not brusquely but firmly. His parting words were seemingly inconsequential.

"I hope, tribune, that we shall have occasion to talk again soon."

In fact, the two men would meet again. But it would be seven and a half years later, and a great deal happened in between.

5

Thapsus

April, 46 B.C.E.

North Africa, near modern Tunis

SALLUST RECEIVED THE SUMMONS from Caesar early in the morning, and made his way immediately to the Praetorium. Though it was April, and early, the North African sun was already scorching hot.

As was his custom, Caesar confined his social amenities to a courteous but brief nod of greeting, and then got straight to business.

"Sallust, thanks for coming so quickly. I've decided to make Numidia into a province. No more client kingdoms here, there's too much to lose. Juba betrayed us and I could have him crucified, but he's an ignorant savage and I can't blame him too much for giving in to Cato; smarter men than he were taken in by all that hot air. Have you ever heard what Cicero liked to say about Cato, by the way?"

"No, sir."

"Well, no, of course not, I don't suppose you've ever been to one of Cicero's dinner parties, have you? We'll have to do something about that when we all get home. Anyway, I'm told that he said something like this several times: 'Cato's a fine man, yes, but he gives speeches as though he were living in Plato's ideal city, and not standing knee-deep in the dung-heap of Romulus.'"

Sallust did not laugh, which seemed to disconcert Caesar.

"I meant no disrespect to the dead, Sallust, you needn't look so prim and proper. And the point is, he was right, wasn't he? About Cato, I mean. I couldn't bring myself to hate the man, though I was forced to destroy him. And it tells you something about him, the whole absurdity of it, that he couldn't even manage to kill himself properly. You and I, Crispus, if we were going to fall on our swords—and believe me, there were times at Alesia, or at Dyrrachium, when I was seriously thinking about how to go about this—we'd know where to put the point of the sword so as to die in a relatively short time. But here was Cato, falling on his sword like a great Roman general, but not knowing how to go about it. So he ended up ripping out his own guts, fainting, being patched up by a doctor, and then ripping his guts back out with his bare hands to finish the job when he woke up. Can you imagine what the pain must have been? I can't, not really. And for what? Did he suppose I was going to crucify him?"

Sallust finally spoke up: "That's exactly what he would have done to you, if he'd won and you'd lost. His famous *severitas*."

"But surely," Caesar replied, "he must have known I would have treated him at least as well as I treated his son-in-law Brutus."

"I must say, Caesar," Sallust objected, his usual reticence in Caesar's presence thrown aside for the moment, "that not everyone understands this policy of yours. I know you were displeased when the men went wild after the battle last month and gave the other side no quarter, but I think they were just afraid you'd let all our enemies go, like after Pharsalus, and all these brilliant victories would be for nothing, because the enemy lives on."

Caesar sighed. "I keep trying to explain this, but none of you seems to have grasped the point. We're not trying to conquer or destroy a foreign enemy this time, but our own people. Every man who dies in battle fighting against us leaves behind a brother, a son, parents, a wife, who will hate us to the end of their days, and who can blame them? And these are our neighbors, our friends, and in many cases our own families. And if the fallen are dead because I ordered them killed, not in battle but in cold blood, then everyone who loved them wishes me dead. More than that, any son of a father I ordered to be killed is obliged by his *pietas* to kill me. That's what Sulla never understood: his proscriptions cleared the Senate of his enemies, but filled the streets with more of them, all hating him and not only that, honor-bound to kill him.

"But that's not all. What about the men whose heads he cut off after the battle of the Colline Gate? Once he'd done a thing like that, he had no choice but to wipe out their whole families. But how do you do that in a city where everybody is everybody else's cousin? So if you think Sulla just happened to spit blood and drop dead one day because he drank too much, you're even more naive than your colleagues keep telling me you are."

Sallust had to give this some thought. The suggestion that his comrades on Caesar's staff were criticizing him behind his back made little impact. He had never fit in with them, these young aristocrats who fancied themselves great Populists, but sniggered at a man like Sallust, who was not related to any of them and failed to understand the private jokes, personal allusions and gossip that made up most of their conversation. It was not a matter of wealth or education: his father had seen to both of these, and nothing these other officers possessed or had learned was better than what he owned or knew, or even particularly different. But he had not spent his youth as they had, going to all the right homes for all the right dinner parties, and it showed. He often saw them suppressing their laughter, exchanging knowing looks, and was all the more annoyed because he really had no idea what he had done or said that amused them so much.

But this was something he no longer cared much about. While these little pricks had been on Caesar's staff, riding around Gaul and pretending to be soldiers, Sallust had put his career on the line for Caesar, and he'd been ejected from the Senate for Caesar's sake. He knew that Caesar understood this, and valued him above these privileged snots, who fought their battles safely behind the front lines: the only enemy soldiers they had ever seen at close range were already either dead or in chains.

No, what had really caught his interest in what Caesar had just said was the scarcely-veiled allusion to Sulla's murder.

Not that there was anything really new here: there had always been rumors, and it wasn't hard to understand the reasons. Just a year and a half after he'd voluntarily retired from public life to live quietly at his villa in Nola, Sulla dropped dead one day. The doctors had explained that this was the result of too much hard drinking, but hardly anyone believed that explanation: Sulla liked his wine, but he was no drunkard, and in fact his health and strength were legendary. He could have ended his retirement at any moment, and his veterans were still ready to fight for him. His so-called reforms needed to be repealed, urgently, but it would be unsafe to do so while Sulla was still alive, "retired" or not. And there was something in the way Caesar had referred to Sulla's sudden death, something that all but confirmed two decades of rumors. Sallust felt quite certain, now, that his commander either knew who had put Sulla out of the way, or perhaps, perhaps, had taken care of the problem himself. And if that were true, then Caesar was probably not the simple, honest soldier he made himself out to be.

It bore thinking about.

It was not, of course, that Sallust had any particular reservations about this murder, if indeed there had been a murder. On this point he had always agreed with Caesar: Publius Cornelius Sulla had been the most purely evil man Rome had ever produced. Both of them had suffered directly from the "medicine," as Sulla liked to put it, that he'd administered to the "sick" Republic. Caesar, thanks to family connections, managed to escape the dictator's displeasure alive, but he lost his home and his family fortune; Sallust grew up in a town infested with Sulla's veterans, whose victorious general had given them all farms carved out from the estates of local landowners, not least of whom was Sallust's own father. The soldiers had turned out to be poor farmers; most of them lost their farms within a few years, and many drifted away, doubtless to the capital; but those who remained near Amiternum became thieves, brigands, and not infrequently murderers for hire. Sallust's father had recovered from the financial blow, but their lovely town, nestled in the Sabine hills, had never been the same.

As these thoughts went through his head, punctuated by mental images of Sulla's old soldiers swaggering drunk around Amiternum, he looked at his commander's face and realized at once something essential. Sulla, who had died when Sallust was a boy, had been an object of hatred in his home as long as he could remember, but no one in Amiternum had ever even seen the man in person—other than the veterans, of course, but who talked to them? Sulla was an abstraction, a name that could be put to their frustration. But Caesar had known him very well. Sulla had ordered him, on pain of proscription, to divorce his wife, Cornelia, the daughter of Marius's colleague and friend, Cinna. Caesar had refused. His mother's relatives, close kin of the dictator, begged for his life and won a pardon of sorts, but the cost was high. After Sulla's retirement (and all-too-timely death), Caesar returned to Rome, but he was penniless. The villas he had planned to live in were gone, and there remained for him and his lovely young wife only the old family home in the Suburra.

"Do you know what the problem with Sulla really was?" Caesar asked suddenly, interrupting Sallust's train of thought with a disconcerting accuracy.

"He was a bloodthirsty tyrant," Sallust replied, "a *lykanthropos*, as Plato would have said, a werewolf. He said he was defending the old ways, the *mos maiorum*, but he trampled it."

"That's what most people think, those who never met him. He frightened me, you know, precisely because he absolutely believed in the things he said he was fighting for. That's what made him so ruthless."

Seeing puzzlement on Sallust's face, he explained, with the patience of a teacher. "There are two ways to become a killer: you can hate the other man so much that his death, preferably at your own hands, gives you pleasure. I hated Sulla that way, but I can't say I've ever hated anyone else so much. Or you can believe in an ideal, an idea of the good or a person who seems to embody it, so strongly that anyone who doesn't share it with you is an enemy of the good, an obstacle to be removed so that the good can triumph and evil can be destroyed. Sulla had that. Cato had it. Neither of them really enjoyed killing, but neither of them had the slightest hesitation about doing it when an ideal was at stake. Sulla had the chance to 'cleanse' Rome, so he took it. If Pompey had won at Pharsalus, Cato would have been another Sulla, but probably more thorough."

"So it's a good thing he died here," Sallust concluded.

"Yes and no, yes and no. He was a dangerous man, and he hated me since the first time we tangled in the Senate, over the execution of Catiline's people. It wasn't that I crossed him or offended him personally, it was just that he found my arguments dangerous. If I had just said, 'Let's not put these people to death, Catiline's really a nice guy, the Republic is a pile of manure anyway, who cares?', well then, he would have been satisfied that the enemy had shown himself in his true colors. He would have wanted me to be arrested and then strangled in the Tullianum with the other five, oh yes, but there would have been no great joy in it for him, only satisfaction. If you kill a mad dog, you don't hate the dog, you just know it has to be gotten rid of.

"But for Cato, what I did was really unforgivable: I made a case for sparing the lives of those men without casting the least doubt on their guilt, but rather by appealing to the *mos maiorum* itself. I really think that Cato himself, at some level, was almost convinced by my speech. But for a man like that, being 'almost' convinced of something is one short step from madness. When he rose to speak he was almost foaming at the mouth, and all the time he talked he never took his eyes off me.

"Of course he took the Senate with him. Passion always wins. I wasn't all that sorry to see Autronius Paetus and the others executed, you know; they were a sorry lot of bums, mouthing Populist slogans they were mostly too besotted to understand. But it was a horrible way to die, and what I especially hated was to see such a barbaric act performed in the majesty of Roman law. But you know, after all these years, I think I'm still about as proud of my speech that day in the Senate, these twenty years ago, as I am of anything else I've ever said, or written, or done."

Considering the victories that Caesar had won, and the position he now held as the undisputed sole master of the greatest Empire the world had ever seen, Sallust found this last statement hard to believe. A nearly forgotten speech from the very beginning of his career, when no one, himself included, could have imagined that he would become one of Rome's greatest.

"So no doubt you're asking yourself, Sallust, what's the great ideal that I've been willing to sacrifice so many lives for?"

Sallust had been thinking no such thing, but rather than correct Caesar's misapprehension, he merely nodded.

"If you're expecting a grand statement, my young friend, I'm afraid I'm going to disappoint you. Let me tell you, though, what it wasn't. I didn't cross the Rubicon because the Senate's insult to the dignity of the tribunes was unbearable. It wasn't because of their insult to me, demanding that I disband my army and submit to a ridiculous trial that would have been nothing but a spending match between myself and my enemies, to see who could bribe the most jurors."

"I was there, Caesar," said Sallust, "that day near Ravenna, whatever that place was called, when you came out of your tent, dressed in your best armor, to tell the men you were going to Rome and asking who would follow you. Surely you knew before you asked that question, that not a man of us would have thought of staying behind. You could have told the men that you were marching to Olympus to overthrow old Jupiter, and they would have cheered like mad and then fallen into marching order by cohort. They were ready to defend your honor against anyone."

"Yes, I know that. It bothered me then, and it still does, but that doesn't stop me from using it when I have to. As Sulla did."

Sallust winced at the comparison.

"But you see, I'm much more like him than you imagine, really. That's not something I would ever have imagined myself saying. But now that I'm pretty much in the same situation as he was, I understand him, and myself, a great deal better.

"The main difference between us, in fact, is that he believed in a Republic governed by the wisdom of the Senate, and he was prepared to kill anyone who threatened that ideal. He realized that the Senate had failed to defend itself adequately by merely killing the Gracchus brothers, first the one and then the other. The Senate slowed down the Gracchan movement, certainly, thinking that if you chop the snake's head off, it will die and the problem's solved. What they didn't realize is what they were really up against, in the persons of Tiberius and Gaius Gracchus, was not a snake, but a Hydra. It took about 20 years for this Hydra to grow another head, which was called Marius, and yet another, called Cinna, and yet another, called Carbo, and so on.

"So Sulla knew what he had to do. Did you ever wonder why he was so fond of the Hercules figure that he put on all his coins? Like Hercules, he chopped off all the heads of the Hydra at once and then singed the stumps by killing off their families, so no more heads would grow. And it almost worked."

"Why didn't it? Was the idea of the rights of the people too strong to kill off that way?"

Caesar rolled his eyes. "You know, Sallust, you really are so naïve, it would be sad if it weren't so funny. No, kings and tyrants and senates of various kinds have been very successful in killing off that idea for thousands of years. It can be done. How else would the Pharaohs have lasted so long? No, Sulla failed because he left three heads: one was Lepidus, the second was Sertorius, and I was the third. Lepidus he left because he misread the man, took him for one of his own, which is hardly surprising, since Lepidus fooled us all in the same way. Who would have expected that he would have started his consulship by trying to block a public funeral for Sulla, the man who had made him consul, and then reviving Cinna's whole program? Sertorius was just lucky enough to get away; he was a Sabine, like you, and Sulla didn't even know if he had any family to kill; besides, Spain was a long way to the west, while Sulla's imagination always tended the other direction. He would never have imagined that Sertorius would become such a problem.

"As for me, he left me alive because I was family, after all, as much his family as I was Cinna's, maybe more, it depends how you look at it. It was his fatal weakness, and he knew it. He didn't live to see Lepidus betray him, he was indifferent to Sertorius, but he knew I was going to be trouble. Do you know what he said about me?"

"Who doesn't, Caesar? 'In that Caesar there are a lot of Mariuses.'"

"Yes, and he was absolutely right. I'm the one head of the Hydra he didn't cut off, and now I'm about to destroy everything he accomplished. Which gives me the most incredible feeling of satisfaction."

"Is that the 'great idea,' then, that you were talking about, the one worth killing for?"

"Yes—and no. I didn't do all this just to piss on Sulla's grave"—the smile widened almost imperceptibly—"since I've already done that, to tell the truth. I was pretty drunk at the time, but anyway, no, I didn't do it to get back at my enemies, either. I didn't hate Cato, I didn't hate Pompey, neither of them had to die, and they wouldn't have, either, if they'd known how to behave when you've rolled the dice and lost everything you own on a bad bet. No, I've done all this because the Senate is just not able to rule the Republic, not the city of Rome itself, and certainly not the whole Empire. Which is exactly why I asked you here today, Sallust. I have a job for you."

It was then that Caesar had offered him the governorship, as proconsul (even though Sallust was not of consular rank) of the province he was about to create: Africa Nova.

"Do you know why this place is worth fighting for, Sallust? Seems like a wasteland, doesn't it? Especially to us Italians, we like trees and mountains and lots of water."

"It's very hot here, but the air is dry, sometimes it's almost invigorating." Sallust had not yet gotten used to the heat, to the feeling of never being quite clean because of the sweat trickling like a perennial fountain down his back, his sides, off his nose, down his legs.

"Have you ever noticed, Sallust, that the oldest civilizations in the world have arisen on the edge of deserts? Not in the desert itself, where no human being can long survive unless his mother was really a camel, but on the edge. You know, if you stand on the left bank of the Nile and look to the west, you can see the sands of the desert, but in that strip of land where the river keeps the desert at bay you can grow enough wheat to feed the whole Empire. So yes, to answer the question that's in everyone's mind but no one has the guts to ask it, that's why I went to Alexandria after Pharsalus, instead of coming straight back to the city to celebrate a triumph. It wasn't just to chase down Pompey. Dear gods, that was one of the worst moments of my life, when that slimy Egyptian eunuch pulled Pompey's head from a basket, thinking I'd be pleased. But it's all about food. We have a problem, and if we don't solve it, all the Conservatives and all the Populists will finally kill each other off and be eaten by the dogs.

"Did you know that Rome will soon have a thousand thousands of inhabitants—if it doesn't already, who can really count them? We don't even have a number in our language to count that many people. No other city in history has ever brought so many people to one place. Which is to say, no other city has ever had to deal with that much hunger, that much sewage and garbage, that much need for clean water.

"The rich and powerful, people like us, Sallust, you and me, we almost never think about these things. When we're hungry, we clap our hands and food appears, water, wine, whatever we need. If the slaves are slow in bringing it to us, they're beaten for it, precisely so that we don't have to think about it. When I want a bath, it's the same: I clap my hands, give a few orders, and everything I need appears as though I were a magician and could make things appear just by clapping my hands. And the world exists to give me my little comforts when and where I want them. All this to say nothing of the fact that we don't have to live in the smell of our own piss."

Sallust began to fidget uncomfortably. He did not much care for this line of thinking. But Caesar continued.

"What we never see, and don't want to see, is that none of this is really magic, nor is it the bounty of nature. Behind the curtains we never peek behind, hundreds and thousands of people are busy making sure that when I clap my hands, my dinner appears, and when I take a big old crap, it disappears. Have you ever thought, when you were putting on your shoes, how many people had to work how hard and how long to make these shoes and get them to where you can reach them when you're ready to go out? And multiply that by all the people in one city who actually have shoes.

"Now here's the problem: all these people and their families need to eat, need something to wear, need a roof over their heads when it rains. And add to them all the others who drift to the city, with no trade, nothing to offer but their bodies, whatever they may be worth, people whose choice is whether to starve to death out in a countryside that has no place for them, or in the city, where just maybe you can find something or steal something to keep alive another day.

"That's what the Gracchus brothers understood. After our great-grandfathers destroyed Carthage, the growth of the Empire brought all this wealth to the city, the city grew, and with it the population of people who needed to be fed every day. But here's the problem: in order to fight all these wars, farther and farther from home, we were taking most of the able-bodied young men from all of Italy and making soldiers of them.

And who's minding the farm in the meantime? Where's the food supposed to come from?

"And all this while, the rich men in the city are busy buying up failed farms as fast as they can, then driving up the price of grain to recover their investments as fast as they can. And so, by the time Tiberius Gracchus became tribune, in my grandfather's time, there were about 500 thousands of people in Rome, of whom at least 350 thousands didn't have enough to eat.

"So there you have it. You have to feed these people or they will starve to death, but before they starve, they will surely cut the throats of everyone left in this city who still has some food they can steal. Do you see any other choice?"

Sallust shook his head. In a sense, he had known all of this, but it was strange and very uncomfortable to have it all laid out so baldly. He himself had made many fiery speeches about the selfishness and haughtiness of the Conservatives in the Senate, but he had to admit he had never looked so clearly and coldly at the truth behind his own rhetoric.

"So the Gracchus brothers," Caesar continued, "realized that the city which had brought all these people here was responsible for feeding them, and began distributing grain to those threatened by starvation. This brought the price of grain on the market way down, and a lot of people in the Senate lost a lot of money. So what did they do?"

"Well," Sallust replied, feeling a bit like a schoolboy, not for the first time, "they murdered them, first Tiberius, and then, ten years later, Gaius."

"Yes, and then they left the grain distribution system pretty much the way the two Gracchi had set it up. They weren't stupid enough to think that they really had any other choice. The cat was out of the bag, so they punished the men who let it out, but they couldn't get the cat back in.

"And now the Empire is twice the size it was when Tiberius Gracchus became tribune, and the problem remains. Worse, because the whole agricultural produce of Italy and Sicily combined, with southern Gaul added in, is not enough to feed this one city. I think Gaul will end up paying for itself, but I'm not sure if that will happen in our lifetimes, and in the meantime, Rome still has to eat. Where to get the grain to feed it?"

"Egypt?" Sallust ventured.

"Of course," Caesar replied. "But Egypt is politically unstable and still rather far away. I thought I could make a good client king out of Cleopatra, but she hasn't the makings of a head of state. Scratch off the trappings of the Pharaohs she enjoys wearing, and underneath there's a

Macedonian peasant. Everything with her is personal. I . . . Well, anyway, here in Africa, on the other hand, is land almost as fertile as Egypt, likewise on the edge of the desert, which means a short, mild winter and a long, warm growing season. There's a reason why the Carthaginians chose this place, when they left Phoenicia, and why their city was nearly a match for Rome. There's wealth here."

"But we destroyed Carthage, we had to, one of the two cities had to fall."

"Yes, of course, and our great grandfathers expelled those people who had survived the long siege, tore the city down until one brick was not left upon another, and then called in priests to curse the soil and sow it with salt. The Greeks didn't even treat Troy that badly. That's how much we hated and feared the Carthaginians, the last enemy who truly frightened us. But you see, with Carthage gone there was nothing to keep the Numidians and all the others from running wild out here, constantly raiding one another's kingdoms, burning the fields and killing the farmers and shepherds, which means that most of this fertile land is sitting idle most of the time.

"Now the Numidians have done us all a great favor by choosing the wrong side in our civil war, and I've got a free hand to make Numidia into a province. And I think you realize what I want you to do here."

"Of course," said Sallust. "This new province must start feeding the city as soon as possible."

"Exactly. Now, what does it need to do this?"

"Political stability, good organization . . ."

"Yes," Caesar replied, "and more concretely?"

"Water, roads to bring the grain to market, a port city to ship it from."

"Exactly. All things that we Romans do better than anyone else: we build. Aqueducts, roads, docks. And soldiers posted around the province to make sure that the grain is grown, harvested, and sent to the port without undue disruption. These people need us as much as we need them, and I foresee a great future for the land that Hannibal once ruled."

"Hannibal was never king in Carthage," Sallust objected, and immediately regretted it.

"No matter." Caesar dismissed the pedantry with a flick of his hand. "Do you know, Sallust, why I chose you for governor? Many on my staff would have given their right arm to be governor here in your place."

"No," Sallust confessed. "I've done my duty as well as I know how, Caesar, but why you picked me over these others, I have no idea."

"As a soldier, Sallust, you're merely adequate, competent but not brilliant."

He wanted to protest, even stood up, but at once sat back down. His commander's judgement, though harsh and delivered with no tact at all, was unfortunately perfectly true.

"You're no coward," Caesar went on, "and no one's fool, but you're not a born commander. I had to save your ass, when the Tenth got a little unruly. I haven't forgotten that."

Neither had Sallust. He had been sent by Caesar, earlier that same year, a few months before the departure to Africa, to settle a nasty near-mutiny by Caesar's favorite legion, the Tenth, who had not been paid the premiums Caesar had (rather vaguely) promised them after Pharsalus. To make matters worse, most of them had served their time and were already well past their statutory date of discharge from the army. Full of himself, Sallust had stood before these men, veterans of so many of Caesar's victories, and suggested to them that they were being disloyal to their commander. He had been lucky to escape alive, while the Tenth had gone on a rampage, northward towards Rome, which ended only when Caesar confronted them, alone and unarmed, on the Campus Martius.

What happened then was already legend. The story went that Caesar appeared suddenly in their midst, in his dress uniform with his trademark scarlet cloak, and then mounted a makeshift platform to address them, as he had so many times before. This time, however, he began his remarks, not with the usual address, "Milites! Soldiers!", but with the formal address Roman politicians used when speaking to the populace at large: "Quirites!" As the story had it, the men were so ashamed to be addressed by Caesar as civilians that they dropped the mutiny on the spot, and even proposed a voluntary decimation, provided only that he would forgive them.

In reality, the scene had been played out rather differently, as Sallust knew, but the outcome was the same, and Caesar's mastery of the minds and hearts of his men was perhaps never more on display.

Caesar went on. "You fought well against Metellus Scipio, I'll give you that. If you hadn't, I would've been forced to replace you on my staff. Now, your performance gives me a pretext to let you do what you do best. That's always been your greatest value to me. If it hadn't been for you, and the provisions you organized, I and most of my army would have died of starvation three years ago in the mountains of northern Greece. And then you did a masterful job of organizing the expedition to Africa. You're not a great soldier, Sallust, but I've got a staff full of very fine soldiers—who aren't much good for anything else. That's why you're different from them: you see what has to be done and you do it. That's what I need in a governor here in Africa Nova. Unless I'm seriously mistaken, there'll be no fighting here after I leave: Labienus, Pompey's sons, and the remains of their legions have all taken off for Spain, and sooner or later I'll have to go after them.

"In the meantime, do what you do best. Put this province in order, do whatever it takes, and the first grain ship that arrives in Rome from Africa Nova will make you consul. You have my word. If you work as well as I know you can work, you will be consul before any of your 'friends' on my staff."

Sallust kept his half of this bargain. For a year he struggled with the natives and the unbelievably rapacious Roman merchants (who arrived in great numbers after news of Thapsus reached the capital) to begin making Utica into a proper capital city for a Roman province. Consistent with Caesar's wishes, he arranged for a Roman colony to be built over the ruins of Carthage, defying the century-old curses. Roads were built, garrisons were established, a few raiders who had attacked outlying farms were severely dealt with (that is, crucified, their bodies left to rot along the roadway). The first harvest, gathered not long after Caesar's departure, was barely adequate to feed the local population, but the next one was far more abundant, so that Sallust was able to send not one, but four well-laden grain ships to Rome. By sheer chance, the ships arrived in Ostia on the same day that Caesar, newly returned from his hard-won victory in Spain, finally celebrated his triumph; but Sallust, of course, had no way of knowing this.

Several more grain ships were sent. But there was no response from the capital. Sallust even began to think that he had been entirely forgotten, that Caesar meant to keep him in Africa forever. That idea was dispelled, however, when a ship finally arrived from Rome, bearing Sallust's designated successor, Titus Sextius, a man of undistinguished family who had served under Caesar as a legatus in Gaul, with no particular distinction.

The news that Sextius brought was conveyed more by his attitude than anything he had to say. Since neither man belonged to the senatorial elite, Sallust at first assumed that Sextius, whom he scarcely knew, would be easy to talk to. Instead, he watched the man grimace through his report on what he'd accomplished in the province, waiting in vain for a compliment, or some sign that the consulship Caesar had promised was already a matter of public knowledge. Sextius simply acknowledged the information he received with a bare minimum of formal politeness, declined Sallust's invitation to dinner with no explanation, and made it clear that Sallust was expected to leave on the same ship he himself had arrived on, as soon as possible the next day.

It did not bode well, but Sallust was prepared to write it down to a certain social awkwardness on Sextius's part. As soon as he arrived in Rome, however, he was quickly disabused of any such notion. He had no sooner stepped on the dock at the port city of Ostia, still a little queasy from the rough crossing, than a messenger had arrived, summoning him formally to answer charges at the permanent Extortion Court, the same court where Verres and his ilk, the whole long line of senatorial governors who had pillaged their provinces, had been brought to justice (or at least some of them had).

It was unbelievable: after all his efforts in Africa Nova, and the success of sending a total of seven grain ships to Rome less than 18 months after taking charge of his province, he was rewarded, not with a consulship, but with a criminal prosecution.

There was, of course, no truth to the accusations.

Almost all provincial governors appointed by the Senate in the past had used the resources of their provinces to provide the funds for increasingly expensive electoral campaigns. By that time, before Caesar crossed the Rubicon, there was no way to win an election in Rome without buying most of the votes outright; electoral strategy consisted in knowing exactly how many votes needed to be bought, in which tribes or centuries, to guarantee success, given that almost any candidate would enjoy a certain base among electors who would vote for him even without being paid for it.

And provincial governors certainly faced many temptations. Sallust had been approached by more than one wealthy merchant, anxious to acquire privileges and permissions, and ready to pay handsomely for them. But it was all quite pointless. Not only did Sallust not need a war chest for an electoral campaign (he'd been promised the consulship by Caesar himself, and by this time Caesar's was the only vote that counted), but he was already a wealthy man in his own right. He was only human, of course. There were other inducements that might have tempted him, but the men who wished to corrupt him hadn't been the sort of men who realize that there are any other inducements, or aren't in a position to offer them. He had rebuffed them all, and several he had threatened with prosecution for attempting to bribe a Roman governor.

Which, of course, was his mistake. In a corrupt system, it is always the occasional uncorrupted individual who is singled out for prosecution.

There was no chance to speak to Caesar personally; his letters went unanswered, and when he presumed so far as to knock at the door of the Suburra house, he was politely but firmly turned away. As a defendant accused of provincial extortion, he could not even attend the Senate, let alone stand for office, and so had not even the chance to present his case to Caesar in a more public way.

However, successive trials were postponed, and finally, just a month before the Ides of March, Sallust was informed that the charges against him had been dropped. The news was not as welcome as it might seem: for the last month, he had been preparing an eloquent defense, and imagined sweeping his enemies before him in a rhetorical display worthy of Cicero. But it would be not only foolish, but probably legally impossible, for the accused to appeal a dismissal of the case against him: if the ruling praetor saw no cause for trial, how could there be a trial?

That same day, a freedman arrived at the house of his father's cousins (where Sallust was staying, on the famous Via Appia), announcing himself with considerable self-importance as Caesar's financial agent. Caesar had a property in Praeneste that he wished to sell, and had ordered that Sallust receive the right of first refusal. The price was remarkably low. Suspiciously low. He hesitated whether to take the offer, wondering what the motive might be, but the freedman was insistent on an immediate answer. So he had said yes.

That is why the Ides of March found him far from Rome. It is also why he was so unsure how to react to what was either the attempted murder of the greatest man he had ever known, or the attempted assassination of a tyrant, the most dangerous man who had ever lived in that great city on the Tiber.

6

The Prosecutor Speaks

June 28, 44 B.C.E.

Rome, the Forum

JUST AS BRUTUS AND the others were approaching their appointed places before the Tribunal, there was a commotion behind them. Those who were sitting rose from their places as the first lictors came into view, bearing the fasces, the bundles of rods and axes that for many centuries had symbolized the sovereign power of the state. A consul was approaching, and all were curious to see which: the suffect consul Dolabella, who had been named by the Senate to take Caesar's place during his convalescence, or Antony, the only politician with direct access to Caesar since the Ides of March, who often spoke as though he might as well have been Caesar himself.

Cicero wasn't at all surprised; in fact, it would have been much more surprising if neither of the two consuls had appeared. He would also have been surprised if they had both appeared, since the two men notoriously hated each other. Antony's last public quarrel with the Great Man before the Ides of March had been over Caesar's announcement that he intended to resign his consulship shortly after the year began, in favor of Dolabella. Antony was upset for two reasons: first, that he was learning of Caesar's decision from a public announcement and had not been forewarned, and secondly, that of all the possible candidates for suffect consul, Caesar had chosen Dolabella. When Antony had refused to go to Africa and Spain with Caesar three years earlier, it had been because Caesar had pardoned Dolabella for what amounted to an attempted coup against Antony, and not only pardoned him, but appointed him to his staff for the campaigns in Africa and Spain, against Cato and Pompey's sons. It was characteristic of Antony that he had let everyone present see his surprise and anger at Caesar's announcement, and he hadn't waited for a private moment to complain. Caesar had smiled indulgently, as he always did when Antony lost his temper publicly, and changed the subject.

It made a great deal of difference to Cicero which of the two consuls, Antony or Dolabella, would be present for the opening of the trial. Antony had been an enemy ever since Cicero's consulship: Lentulus Sura, one of the five Catilinarians for whose summary execution Cicero took full responsibility, had been Antony's stepfather. Dolabella, on the other hand, was Cicero's own son-in-law, and though there had never been much warmth between them, and though Tullia had died a year ago, still, there was a bond there.

Theoretically, formally, the consul could only be present at any trial as a spectator, and had no formal role or judicial authority, no responsibility to be present or make any decisions. As a practical matter, when a consul was present, every move he made, every facial expression, every visible or audible reaction, was observed by all: the presiding praetor, the jurors, the defendants and their attorneys, the prosecutors, and all the spectators. A frown from a consul had caused more than one praetor to reverse a legal decision he had just handed down. Cicero had been both winner and loser in that transaction more than once in his career.

The uncertainty was relieved soon enough, when Antony came into view behind the last lictor. It was his gait that gave him away first, at this distance, as he walked along the Via Sacra, past the ancient Temple of Romulus. Even when perfectly sober he always walked almost on his toes, as though he were about to pitch forward on his face—which he did, often enough, when drunk. Privately, Cicero had laughed more than once at his own joke, that Antony's remarkably flat face bore the imprint of paving stones from one end of the Empire to the other. There was no denying that even now, in senatorial toga, he looked more like a gladiator than a Roman consul. Looks, in this case, were not perhaps entirely deceptive, Cicero thought to himself.

Antony was preceded by the statutory 12 lictors of a consul. This in itself was noteworthy. Caesar had been steadily increasing the number of his own lictors, from the 24 allowed a Dictator to 72 at his last public appearance before the Ides of March. No one had quite known what to make of this; some thought it a kind of joke, others were not amused. At first, Caesar had followed Sulla's precedent: his lictors carried fasces with axes even inside the *pomerium*, the ritual boundary of the city, marking off the sacred precinct where the bearing of arms in any but the most exceptional circumstances was *nefas*, a sacrilege, a crime against the gods. But then someone had delicately reminded Caesar that no dictator before Sulla had dared to have the axes within the pomerium. Sulla was not a model to which Caesar wished to be compared, so the axes had disappeared. But the number of lictors was not reduced.

As Master of the Horse, Antony probably enjoyed the right to have "dictatorial" lictors, though the learned authorities in such matters were divided in their opinions as to the appropriate number. Until he became consul on the first day of January that year, Antony had made a practice of making public appearances with exactly half the number of lictors attending Caesar. But upon assuming the consulship, Antony had had a sudden fit of unwonted *modestia*, and now strictly observed all the customary rights, privileges, and (perhaps most importantly) limitations of a consul.

Then, just a month before the Ides of March, Caesar had been named "Perpetual Dictator" by the Senate, and had named Marcus Aemilius Lepidus his Master of the Horse. And again, he had treated Antony's outbursts with amused tolerance.

Today, Antony was displaying his true character, thought Cicero, thumbing his nose at any rules which, at a given moment, were getting in his way. There were no more than the consular 12 lictors, to be sure: probably every man in the Forum had counted them carefully. But their fasces held the ax. Even more outrageous: Antony was not dressed in the senatorial toga, with the broad maroon stripe of senatorial rank, but in military uniform, breastplate and helmet gleaming, his sword in its sheath at his side.

So much for the *pomerium*, thought Cicero, and so much for the atmosphere of a court of law. Antony knew he was flouting law and custom by appearing in the Forum armed and in uniform. The whole idea of the Roman toga was that its bulk, and the folds around one or both arms, made it practically impossible to wield a weapon while wearing one. On the Ides of March, most of the conspirators had thrown off their togas as they began their attack; had Caesar himself done so, his self-defense might have been more effective, and his wounds less severe.

And there was an additional touch: Antony was wearing a flowing, bright scarlet cape—the trademark of Julius Caesar in battle, ostensibly worn to make sure his soldiers would always be able to see their commander, above all to show that he was right there with them, and not standing safely 15 ranks behind the front lines, or running away.

The symbolism of Antony's appearance was, as in almost all that Antony did, hopelessly confused. He often sent contradictory symbolic messages, and enjoyed the confusion he caused. It made him, at times, a dangerous opponent. Just when you started to laugh at his foolishness, you realized that his dagger was at your throat. But sometimes he was just a fool, no more than what he appeared to be.

The consul made his way to the seat of honor, in the first row behind the defendants and the prosecutors, and sat down, sweeping the red cloak behind him so that it could be seen from the other side of the Forum. Those who had chairs sat back down in them. The trial could begin.

It was only a moment before the *praeco* walked out from the Temple of Concord, whose imposing facade would be a suitable backdrop for this trial. He mounted the dais, and made his ritual call for attention, using language so archaic that even scholars interested in such matters argued among themselves as to the literal meaning of the formula. He then shifted into something much more like normal Latin, and began to call the parties: first the prosecutors, then the defendants and their attorneys.

"Quintus Pedius has brought this case. Is he present?"

"*Adsum*," said Pedius, rising, "I am present."

"The case has been brought against five men," the *praeco* continued. "Is Marcus Junius Brutus present?"

"*Adsum*."

"Who will speak on your behalf?"

"I call upon Marcus Tullius Cicero to stand beside me."

"Is Gaius Cassius Longinus present?"

"*Adsum*."

"Who will speak on your behalf?"

"I call upon Marcus Tullius Cicero to stand beside me."

The formula was repeated in this way three more times. In turn, Quintus Ligarius, Gaius Trebonius, and Gaius Servilius Casca rose and called upon Cicero to defend them.

In important cases it was customary for both prosecution and defense to be handled by a team of three or four men. Trials with multiple defendants, like this one, were so rare that some legal experts considered it highly improper, if not entirely illegal, to try these men all at once. But this was Caesar's Rome now, and the grumblings of traditionalists were not in fashion. There had been no lynching, no military trials with summary punishment administered immediately after a fifteen-minute trial before the commanding officer. There was ample precedent, in living memory, for proscription of the enemies of dictators, but Caesar had not changed his policy even after the Ides of March. The defendants could be grateful for that much, and no one was inclined to protest too vigorously at any real or imagined breach of legal procedure.

This was to be a duel of two advocates, in effect. Quintus Pedius would be speaking for the Dictator and all those who regarded him as Rome's savior, but there were so many things he could not say. The jurors, after all, were composed of men who might have been pro-Caesar, yes, of course, but their sympathies were hardly democratic. Populist demagoguery, a rhetorical attack on the privileged elite represented by the defendants, would not be outrageous enough to lose the case, no, but Pedius would lose the approval of his peers. Cicero would be speaking for all those who were still mourning the free Republic of old, but he, too, would be walking on a very dangerous tightrope. No one had been eager to join either one of them in a task that seemed unenviable in the one case, and very nearly suicidal in the other.

The parties having been duly summoned, the *praeco* continued his duties. "This case will now be heard by the praetor Lucius Antonius, and the panel of jurors selected according to law and the *mos maiorum*."

The moment having arrived and been duly announced, the praetor emerged from the Temple of Concord and climbed the steps onto the dais where his curule chair awaited him. The *iudices*, the panel of jurors, 51 of them, took their places to his right.

As Cicero looked over the jurors chosen (by lot, ostensibly, but who believes that?) to decide the case against Brutus, Cassius, and their three colleagues, he found several reasons for concern, and no one whose vote he knew he could count on. But this was hardly a surprise: Cicero could not honestly say that he had expected to argue his case before a friendly court. On the whole, the *iudices* could have been much, much worse; he had faced more hostile courts in his time, and won.

As presiding magistrate, the praetor would have been within his rights to lecture (or harangue) the parties on the rules of his court, but the younger Antony had clearly decided to forego this pleasure. Alternatively, he would be expected to give the prosecutor some sort of signal to start his case. Instead, he sat motionless. After a few moments, Cicero realized that he was waiting for something, and it had just dawned on him what that "something" might be when the elder Antony, the consul, rose from his own curule chair, in the place of honor, and moved to ascend the Rostra.

This was utterly irregular, unprecedented, but for just that reason, not really surprising. Anyone who thought that Antony would play strictly by the rules was not living in the real world. In another reality, not so many years ago, Cicero would have been on his feet already, using all the thunder of his famous voice, protesting the violation of procedure, of the Praetorian Edict, of the *mos maiorum*, the Way of the Elders. But he was not Cato, not a man unwilling or unable to bend to a changed reality, so he sat and waited to see what the consul would say. He was more than slightly curious to see if Antony was actually sober enough to address the court.

He was. Having reached the Rostra, Antony turned and faced down the Forum, ostensibly as though he meant to speak to the prosecutor, the defendants, and their attorney, but in fact speaking to the multitudes that waited within the reach of his voice. And his voice, even when he was sober, was at least as strong as Cicero's own.

"*Quirites!*" he began, omitting the courtesy address to the presiding magistrate and the judges. "My fellow citizens! I have asked the praetor, my brother, Lucius Antonius, to allow me to speak a few words at the beginning of this important and remarkable trial. I realize that the procedure is unusual, but the case is unusual, and the verdict reached here will have the gravest consequences for our Republic—and that means, now, the whole world.

"Some will say that the crime of laying violent hands on a magistrate, entrusted with a special sovereign power by the Senate and the people of Rome, is a crime so heinous, so dangerous in its immediate effects, and even more so as a precedent in these lawless times, that its perpetrators deserve no consideration."

Shouted agreement could be heard, even from a few senators, but above all from the *corona*.

"But it is not for such a Rome that Caesar himself fought and bled, alongside many of those present here today. Our Republic has risen to a greatness unexampled in the history of the civilized world precisely because we are a nation of law. When he was your praetor, in the consulship of Marcus Tullius Cicero"—he gave a kind of salute in Cicero's general direction—"and my uncle, Antonius Hybrida, Caesar himself argued that the law protecting Roman citizens against summary execution could not be set aside without undermining the very foundations of the Republic. 'If once we allow this sword to be drawn,' he said then, 'even by the best of consuls, who will sheathe it again?'

"This is the man some seem to think is a tyrant, deserving to die at the hands of men he trusted, whose lives he could have taken at a moment when few or none would have blamed him."

The *corona* roared. Antony raised his hand for silence, but it took some time before the shouting stopped.

"Those of us who love Caesar, who believe that he is indeed the Father of our Country, can give him no better tribute now than to allow our Roman court to do its duty according to law, free of violence and intimidation. The prosecutor, a man Caesar himself values and trusts very highly, will speak, and then, as our law and tradition commands, the defense will speak. I ask you, all of you, to allow this to go forward. Let us act as Roman citizens, not Greeks or barbarians, who scream for the defendant's blood one moment, and the next moment shed tears of pity for him and all his family. Let us hear with all due respect and attention what the defense has to say, and let the judges, able and honorable men chosen to represent the entire Roman people, give a reasonable and lawful verdict according to the evidence and the arguments that have been presented to them.

"The enemies of our Republic will never be able to say that we gave up these five senators to be crucified by an angry mob, or that we lacked confidence in our courts to see that justice be done.

"Speaking as consul, and thus as commanding officer of all our legions, I assure you that I will not allow any disturbances during this trial that may call the justice of its verdict into question, now or at some day in the future. May our children and grandchildren never have reason to be ashamed of what we do here!"

Without waiting for a reaction, Antony turned and descended from the dais, returning to his seat. The Forum, for a long moment, was as quiet as though it were midnight, rather than mid-day.

Cicero sat impassively, though he was aware that tens of thousands of eyes were on him, looking to see how he would react. He had to concede that Antony had spoken well. It was one thing to make the Forum roar, quite another to make it fall so silent that a cat's meow could be heard. Cicero himself had managed that only a handful of times, in all his long career of making speeches in this very place.

Now, finally, after this singular diversion from routine, the praetor gave the long-awaited signal. Pedius rose, moved to a position on the Rostra where he could address the judges directly, but could still be heard clearly by at least some of the spectators, and adjusted his toga. He looked at the ground for a moment, clearly gathering his thoughts, then lifted his head and began to speak.

"Gentlemen of the jury!

"Nothing that I or anyone else can say in this court will suffice to make any of us forget what happened, not so far from where I stand to-day, on the Ides of March. As long as we live, we will tell our children where we were and what we were doing when the news came to us that a group of Roman senators had drawn daggers, at a meeting of the Senate, and gravely wounded a man as beloved of his fellow citizens as perhaps no one before him. Some of us, indeed, were there on that day, and we need no one to tell us what our own eyes saw, or our hearts felt . . ."

7

A Restless Night

Late June, 44 B.C.E.

Rome

IT HAD BEEN A long, nearly sleepless night, again, like so many other nights since that awful day. Every so often, just as Calpurnia and the rest of the household had finally gone to sleep, Caesar would call out, again. And again, they would rush to his bed to find him thrashing, sweating, moaning, neither asleep nor awake. He seemed to be saying something, but the words were formless, "a-a-a" and the like. Sometimes, to her utter horror, he would howl like a wolf.

"Is he possessed?" she asked the doctor, who merely shook his head. She could see what he was thinking: "Stupid question, silly woman." But he was too smart to say it aloud, and he had proven too valuable to risk alienating him, just because she thought she knew what he must have been thinking. Might have been thinking. No matter.

How could she have found herself in such an absurd situation? How could the wife of the most powerful man in the most powerful city in the world be so completely at the mercy of incomprehensible events? This question went through her head at least ten times every day, but no good answer seemed to follow. It was, she told herself, a foolish question. If she had paid more attention during those interminable philosophical arguments her husband sometimes enjoyed after dinner, over wine, all these men trying to impress Caesar (and various other people, including the women reclining on the couches to the left and right) with their brilliant arguments, all decked out with quotations in Greek. But no, there was no answer to be found in philosophy, not to the questions that really mattered.

What if he had died, really? This barbarian doctor had said—and he was a man who treated mostly soldiers, the ones who weren't killed, of course, so he knew these things, how it is with stab wounds—that one more wound to the neck, chest, or belly would have finished him. And then there was the blow to his head, when he tangled himself in his toga and fell. It could all have ended, it would all be over, she would be the widow of Caesar, the tyrant, perhaps they would have needed or wanted to kill her, too.

Would it actually have been worse, to have it all over with? Death was horrible to contemplate, of course, but it happened, it was over, and then, as Catullus (that odious little man from Verona, more Gaul than Roman, how did he dare to imply that Clodia, the sister of Publius Clodius and wife of Metellus, would sink so low as to sleep with a nobody like him?)—yes, well, Catullus had a gift for a fine phrase, that you couldn't dispute, and he wrote that death was "one perpetual night's sleep." That was comforting, in a strange way.

When, Calpurnia wondered, would her head quit spinning like this, thoughts following thoughts in no order, but an incessant babbling in her head that kept her from properly feeling anything. Is that it, perhaps? The mind busying itself with nonsense to keep oneself from screaming at the horror of it?

It started the afternoon of the Ides of March, when they brought him in, on a litter, his hand dangling off one side, all covered in blood. So much blood! Could a man with a normal-sized body actually have so much blood in him? It didn't seem possible, he looked as though someone had come up and splashed him with a whole bucket of blood, and then another, and another.

And she had told him not to go that day, begged him, cried, and at one point he had even said he wouldn't go. But then that dreadful man, that Albinus, the man who dressed like a Senator and put on airs like a Senator and cursed like a drunken soldier—he had ruined it all and made a fool of her. And that prick Antony . . .

They didn't know, of course, no one but Antony, that she knew. The dream had nothing to do with it, there had been no dream, how could there be when she hadn't slept all night, knowing what she knew?

Because, you see, Antony had come to see her the day before.

"Calpurnia, there is something I have to tell you. You're Caesar's wife, and I trust your judgment to help me save his life and put those who wish him ill in a place where they can't harm him. I've always respected you."

This last statement just wasn't true, and she knew it. Antony wasn't the kind of man who respected a woman, any woman. Some he slept with, the rest he ignored if he could, tolerated if he couldn't. His wife Fulvia was hardly the sort of woman anyone would respect.

Still, Calpurnia felt that Antony really was loyal to Caesar, at heart, and so she heard him out and pretended not to notice the hypocrisy.

"A group of senators, including Brutus, Cassius, Albinus, and about 30 others, are planning to attack Caesar tomorrow, at the Senate meeting in the Theater of Pompey, and kill him."

"The Ides of March, after all." Calpurnia kept her voice and face under control, though it was not easy.

"Yes. It turns out that Spurinna, that old faker, is pretty well informed about some things, and I managed to discover what it was all about."

"Then why don't you simply arrest these men? Why doesn't Caesar do something, he's the one who pardoned them, that slimy Cassius and that holier-than-thou Brutus. Or that pig Albinus, all right, he didn't pardon him because Albinus was on his side all along, but still, the point is, why does my husband let people like that just walk around? If you see a poisonous snake on your path, and you've got your wits about you, you take a stick and kill it as quick as you can."

"It's not as simple as you think. These are men with connections, and there's the matter of proving their guilt in a trial, when they will be well—."

"It's every bit as simple as all that," she interrupted. "There's nothing complicated about it. You see a snake and you kill it."

Antony sighed. "Some time ago I came to Caesar with the information I had, but he wouldn't listen to me. He thinks the world of Brutus."

"Fatuous hypocrite."

"I couldn't agree more, but Caesar has a soft spot for the man and that's that."

Calpurnia made a face, but tried to hide it. She had heard the stories about Caesar and Brutus's mother, but like so many stories about her husband, it was better to pretend that one heard nothing and knew nothing.

"So here's what I've done," Antony continued. "I'm going to put a detachment of my best men in a hiding place near the room where the Senate will meet. I'll wait till they move, until I've actually seen a dagger, seen who's involved, then I'll give a signal, my men will arrest everyone who's carrying a dagger. That in itself is a desecration of the Senate and a serious crime. Then Caesar just won't be able any more, in the face of all this, to keep on protecting Brutus and his friends."

"So what do you want from me?"

Antony seemed unsure how to say what he wanted to say. Finally, he just said it. "The conspirators have made this plan for the Ides of March, because then the Senate will be meeting in Pompey's Theater, and the place suits them. Also, it may well be the last meeting Caesar attends before he leaves for Parthia. If it doesn't work out, they'll go back into hiding and make another plan, and it may be two years or three before they get their chance. Now for the moment I have information from the inside and I know exactly what the plan is, but that could change any moment. I need to catch them with dagger in hand, and I need it to happen tomorrow. Otherwise I can't guarantee that I can keep it under control. But lately Caesar's been more than usually quirky and odd, and he likes to put a feather up the Senate's ass sometimes. Call a meeting and not show up, that sort of shit." Antony had clearly abandoned his earlier efforts, rather painful to watch, to keep his natural vulgarity under control. "I can't let that happen tomorrow. What you can do is, you can help me persuade Caesar to go to that Senate meeting tomorrow."

Calpurnia thought for a moment. "Are you sure that you're ready for any contingency? You can keep him safe?"

"Of course," Antony replied, not even trying to hide his annoyance.

"Do you realize what you're asking me to do?" Calpurnia felt the panic rising. "Do you really? I'm being asked to help send my husband, whom I love more than my eyes, into a place of great danger, of which he knows nothing. So I'm asking you again: do you have a good plan? Can you handle any eventualities?"

"Yes, I know every detail of their plan, I've walked through it with my men. All I need to do to bring these shitheads to justice is to get Caesar to Pompey's Theater tomorrow. Can I count on you?"

"Yes."

And that had been that. Except that the next morning, after a sleepless night, when she came into his room and found him dressing to go out, she instantly realized that the plan was not going to work, Antony would fail and Caesar would die. And that was something she could not allow to happen.

Hence the dream gambit. She had indeed once dreamed that Caesar was on a boat, being rowed by some senators into a strange dark mist that hung over the water just a stone's throw from the pier. So that had been true, but this dream had actually occurred several years earlier, after Pharsalus, a few days after Caesar had told her he meant to pardon Brutus, Cassius, and the others and reinstall them in magistracies and the Senate.

What Calpurnia knew about her husband, which hardly anyone else knew, was that for all his Epicurean posturing, at heart he was deeply superstitious. He would smirk and wink at dinner parties whenever he talked about his family, the *gens Iulia*, being descended from Venus, and when he had been consul he had overcome Bibulus's religious obfuscations by simply ignoring them. Yes, all of that, but he was still a Roman. Which meant that the world in his imagination, at some level of his consciousness and quite independent of his intellectual convictions, was still populated by malevolent spirits, who had to be propitiated or warded off at every step. He was quite attentive to dreams, though when pressed about it, he denied that it was anything but curiosity. So Calpurnia had known what she was doing, trying to scare him with a prescient nightmare.

It would have worked, too, if Albinus and Antony had not engaged Caesar's other great weakness that he tried so hard to hide: his need for people to approve of him. Antony had shot her a look as they left that might have killed, if that were possible.

And then, two hours later, he was back with Caesar, barely clinging to life. She had screamed at Antony.

"Get out, you bastard! Get out of my house! This is your fault, you prick, you moron!"

And Antony, who had faced cavalry charges in more than one desperate battle without flinching, this time beat a hasty retreat. For all her fear and grief, Calpurnia could still smile, a little, when she remembered him slinking away. Surely he didn't really have a tail tucked between his legs, but somehow her memory had registered him that way.

The rest of that day had been a daze. The best doctor in the city, the Briton, Sulpicius Scaeva, the man Caesar had told her to get if he ever really needed a good doctor, had been summoned, and ordered to stay in the house without leaving for any reason, as long as it would take. He had used his skill to best advantage, he had saved Caesar's life, but neither he nor anyone else could say when Caesar might be himself again.

He was pitiful to look at. When the blood had been cleaned away, he was as pale as a corpse, and as the days went by, his body seemed to shrink and shrivel. He lay on his side most of the time, his knees curled

up almost to his chest, breathing but not otherwise moving unless someone moved him. He seemed somehow to be sleeping or waking at different times, but truth be told, the difference between the one state and the
other was difficult to tell. The doctor said that this was more the result of
the blow to his head than to the stab wounds, and only time would tell
whether and how he would recover.

What was going on out in the wider world all this time, Calpurnia
scarcely knew, and cared even less. Antony's plan had worked at least
this well, that the conspirators had all been either killed on the spot or
arrested. Since they were all senators, however, they were not put in
the Mamertine prison under the Forum, but were kept in house arrest.
Guards stood around Caesar's house, too, keeping the curious away. The
street outside, usually so busy, had never been so quiet.

The only other event of any interest to Calpurnia in those weeks
after the Ides of March had been the hasty departure of Cleopatra, who
had left Rome, vacating Caesar's guesthouse on the Via Ostiensis within
an hour after news of the attack on Caesar had been brought to her.
Doubtless she knew all there was to know about assassinations of rulers,
daggers, poison, plots. The news of her departure had not brought a smile
to Calpurnia's lips, but she took a moment to feel some satisfaction.

But the satisfaction was short-lived: in yet another display of her famous capriciousness, Cleopatra had been gone for ten days and then suddenly re-appeared in Rome. Or at least her entourage was here: Cleopatra
herself did not show her face. Whatever her reasons for returning, she
kept very quiet, and no one saw her or heard from her, though the whole
city was talking about her, again.

Calpurnia had missed her first opportunity to lay eyes on this woman, when Cleopatra had made a public but unannounced appearance,
ostensibly leading a delegation offering its congratulations to Caesar on
the occasion of his birthday. Calpurnia had stayed home that day, with a
slight fever and a cough, but she had been stunned speechless when she
heard of it. The audacity of this woman! playing out a public spectacle in
front of the man she had seduced, with every reasonable expectation that
his wife would be present.

Of course Calpurnia knew everything, or nearly everything, never
mind the sordid details, about Caesar's dalliance with the Queen of Egypt
while he was still trapped in Alexandria. Her sources were good, but they
had not told her everything. In her imagination, this exotic foreign queen
was a beautiful, dark-skinned, black-eyed seductress, this woman whom

Caesar himself could not resist. The first—and this was what Calpurnia found so hard to accept—who had seduced Caesar, rather than being seduced by him.

It was not, after all, her husband's infidelity as such that troubled Calpurnia so much. She knew him too well. He looked at a beautiful woman in much the same way as he had looked at Gaul, when he arrived in his new province the year after his consulship. A pretext would be found, the victim would be maneuvered into thinking that she herself had wanted it, had asked for it. And then, by the time she realized that she really did not want it, or was not quite sure whether she wanted it or not, or even thought that modesty required at least a show of demurral, it was too late, and resistance had become both futile and treacherous.

But as soon as the conquest was complete, it was a thing of no inherent interest, and Caesar's restless dark eyes were sweeping the room again.

One thing that Caesar had never done, though, was to mix politics and seduction. That would have seemed to him, not wrong, but pointless duplication of effort and dissipation of the intense mental focus he needed to complete a conquest, or a seduction. At least, not until Cleopatra.

That had been the dilemma of the years in Gaul. Calpurnia had missed her husband, but she also knew that so long as there were armies to fight and provinces to conquer, he had no time, no interest, no energy left over for more sexual conquests. On those rare occasions when he had come to the southern edge of his province for winter quarters, to Lucca or some other Tuscan or Umbrian town, she had found him hungry as a wolf, unable to keep his hands off her for days at a time. For that period of time, which might even stretch for a week, she was the center of his universe, the only person whose company he tolerated. She felt again, then, what she had felt the very first time she had found herself on the couch next to his at a dinner party: the power that emanated from him, the erotic hunger that was all the stronger because he had it strictly under the control of his will.

Three weeks after that first dinner party, the year after the Catilinarian affair and Caesar's praetorship, the Bona Dea scandal had broken out, and Caesar then seized the pretext of Pompeia's alleged adultery with Clodius to divorce her. Calpurnia had never known, never really dared to ask, if Caesar really believed the gossip, which was pure fantasy for anyone who knew the people involved: back then Clodius was dividing his time between his sister (or both of them, some said, but that was ridiculous, only the younger one was as perverse as her brother) and Fulvia, now Antony' wife (a fine match, that one, hard to say which of them was more assiduous in betraying the other, which would be piquant if only either of them cared about being betrayed).

How my mind does wander, Calpurnia thought, shaking her head as though to clear it of all those tangled gossamer threads of association.

It is odd, she thought, how my imagination goes wild as soon as Cleopatra appears on the horizon. Any other woman, surely, would be obsessed with the woman who had so notoriously seduced her husband, almost bringing him to death and disgrace before making him a figure of public ridicule. It should be different, I should be thinking every waking moment of every day about her, how much I hate her. But instead, as soon as I think of her, my mind runs and hides among the old clothing of my memories, long forgotten gossip and the sexual histories of Clodius and people like him, now long dead and rotting in their graves.

Caesar had never been a faithful husband, although (again, until Alexandria) he had been decently discreet about his affairs. That was all the easier because, although he enjoyed a good wine as much as anyone, he had an intense dislike of being drunk. Deep down, she knew, he was fully as amoral as Clodius, but unlike his flamboyant agent, Caesar avoided flaunting his contempt for the rules and laws that bound lesser men. And he hated the feeling of being out of control.

He never annoyed Calpurnia by talking about his erotic exploits to her or in her presence, but apart from that he made no effort to conceal what he was doing. Hypocrisy was not among Caesar's faults. For her part, she needed to know who was sharing his bed, to avoid public embarrassment, that was all.

When she wanted to feel him close, he was there, and it was good. She never supposed that she would be able to satisfy that voracious hunger herself. She did feel a certain relief when he had a war to fight, because then she knew that his virility was being channeled somewhere else, not through his loins.

Until that woman. Then Caesar, that Epicurean who could teach any Stoic to be abstemious when he had a mind to, lost his head completely, metaphorically, and very nearly literally as well. The victor of Pharsalus, rather than return home in triumph, the sole master of the known world, had gone off to Egypt and disappeared, for all practical purposes, in the sand. For the better part of a year.

But when he had finally come home, nothing was said about Alexandria, publicly or privately, no justification, no explanation, no apology.

None of which she would ordinarily have expected, anyway. He was himself again, voracious and insatiable in bed, but this time she had felt little pleasure. That woman, unlike any of the others Caesar had slept with in the 15 years of their marriage, managed to be there in bed with them, in her mind if not in his, and she could do no more than submit. He was disappointed, she could tell, but said nothing, and throughout the day, when he was at home, he was his usual genial self.

A chance remark, however, had suddenly revealed to her why this one silly woman had managed to make a fool of her husband. And the remark in question had not even pertained directly to Cleopatra. They had been guests of honor at a dinner party laid on in Caesar's honor by some senator or other, someone not nearly so abstemious with his wine as Caesar notoriously was, who had attempted to compliment his guest in a long-winded and embarrassingly florid speech by comparing him to Alexander. In his self-deprecating reply, Caesar had subjected the poor man's comparison to a withering, though speciously very polite analysis, and pointed out all the ways in which he had not matched Alexander.

"All of barbarian Gaul taken together could not have fielded more than a fraction of the Persian army Alexander faced at Gaugamela. Besides, at an age when I was barely elected praetor and had never led an army into battle, Alexander had already conquered half the world, the better half, and died of boredom in Babylon, having no one left this side of India that would be worthy of conquering. Now if I were to succeed where my erstwhile colleague Crassus so lamentably failed, six years ago, and bring into our Empire precisely those cities and people Alexander once conquered—oh, then, perhaps, I would allow myself to be compared to the great Macedonian. Perhaps."

And he had continued in this vein. In a moment, however, Calpurnia knew two things with absolute clarity: first, that Caesar meant to go to Parthia, indeed, everything he had done up to this point was just preparation to go and fight a great war over the same deserts and mountains where Alexander had fought. And secondly, Caesar had been fascinated by Cleopatra not because she was Egyptian, but because in reality she was Macedonian. He had wanted to sleep with the great-great-great (how many greats exactly?) granddaughter of Ptolemy Soter, Alexander's most trusted general.

That realization had made the whole affair more understandable, and thus more tolerable. Cleopatra as a woman had not given Caesar something in bed he couldn't get from his Roman wife, but in Cleopatra's womb was the seed of old Ptolemy, and Ptolemy was a man who had broken bread with Alexander himself, which meant that there was, so to speak, a connection. Caesar would never admit that such things mattered to him, but they did, and she knew that better than anyone.

That much, at least, she had learned from the only conversation she had ever had with Cleopatra, "the woman," as the wits of the city had it, "who made a woman of Caesar."

Calpurnia lay in bed as these and other thoughts went through her head, too exhausted after the sleepless night to rise, as she had always risen, just before dawn. Caesar was usually an early riser, also, though there were times when he worked all night and only went to bed for a few hours just as Calpurnia was rising. He slept as he ate: exactly when and as much as he wanted, not according to any schedule. Since their marriage, she had been amazed at how little sleep he seemed to need, most of the time. His slaves had informed her that before a major battle he would not sleep for two or three days, and then, when the battle was won and he was sure of his victory, he would retire to his tent and not emerge until the same hour of the next day. And yet she had seldom seen him actually looking tired.

Except, of course, for his attacks of the holy sickness, which mercifully occurred rather less often, on the average, than once a year. Then he would close himself up for several days, admitting no visitors, even close friends. Only then had Calpurnia ever seen him not fully in control of himself: pale, sweaty, scarcely able to speak above a whisper, often moaning in his fitful sleep. But this would last only a few days, until one morning he would emerge from his bedchamber, washed, shaven, and dressed with his usual care, cheerful as ever. It was one of the unspoken rules of the household that no one, Calpurnia herself very much included, ever alluded to these incidents in his presence. It was essential for everyone to act as though the lost days had never happened.

Apart from that he was seldom ill, which to Calpurnia seemed of a piece with his self-control, his dislike of being drunk, or giving way to an outburst of anger, or hilarity (he smiled very often, but seldom laughed), or for that matter—passion. As a lover he was . . . adept, that was the word, an odd one to use in this context, perhaps, but what else could you say? You felt the fire but it was under layers and layers of control, the rumble of distant thunder that tells you, on a summer afternoon, that a storm is raging somewhere, far away.

She wondered for a moment if he had been different in bed with Cleopatra.

The time had come, she suddenly realized, to get out of bed. The man she had been thinking about was lying in the next room, watched by slaves every hour of the day and night, weakened, shriveled, even though the doctor kept saying he was on the mend, the prognosis was good, still, to her eyes there was less of him every day. His face, which had hardly changed in the 15 years of their marriage, was now that of an old man, dried up, flabby at the neck, the flashing dark eyes now submerged in black hollows. When, that is, they were open at all, which was not often.

It was time to have a look at him, though she could hardly bear the sight of him, this shaking, foul smelling old man who had come to her house to die in her husband's bed.

At once Calpurnia felt ashamed for letting such a thought into her mind. She willed herself to think of something else. Caesar had been spared on the Ides of March because, she supposed, the gods still had some reason to want him alive, so they would surely not let him die in bed like this, reeking of his own waste, pathetic. By all the gods in heaven and hell, how he hated to be pathetic! It can't end like this, there must be a reason.

Her maid appeared silently, as though from nowhere, with dressing robe in hand, as soon as Calpurnia rose from her bed. Calpurnia's slaves knew that their mistress, though not unkind, did not care for slaves who talked, other than to answer a direct question, so the girl said nothing as she helped her mistress dress, first the *chiton*, then the *stola*. Calpurnia never left her bedroom without her *stola*, the garment of a married woman, though more fashionable women liked to complain that the *stola* was uncomplimentary and made a point of not wearing it, especially to fashionable parties. Undoubtedly, Calpurnia thought, the first senator's wife who arrived at a party and removed her cloak to reveal only a *chiton* underneath had made a great sensation, but the trick had grown old.

Once properly dressed, with her hair carefully arranged (but no flamboyance here, either) Calpurnia finally emerged from her bedroom, stepped out into the corridor and then into her husband's bedroom. She did not use the door that connected the two rooms privately; she had not used it since the Ides of March, somehow it did not seem right, and there was now no one, after all, to whom she had to explain her decision.

To her utter amazement, Caesar was sitting up in his bed, eyes open, his face somehow composed into its old, habitual half smile—though the marks of pain and wasting were still all too evident.

"It's quiet," he remarked in that oddly gentle voice he used now, on those rare occasions when he spoke, hardly above a whisper. "What's happening? This fool . . . seems to have . . . lost his voice."

Rather than answer the question, Calpurnia turned to the slave who was standing in the corner of the room. "How long as the master been awake? Why was I not informed that he was sitting up? Who sat him up? The doctor expressly forbade this."

"Mistress," the slave replied, cowering, "the master awoke only a moment ago, and sat up, yes, by himself entirely. I did not know what to do, please forgive my incompetence."

Allowing herself to be mollified by this show of submissiveness, Calpurnia dismissed the unfortunate slave with a gesture. "Go and fetch the doctor." Then she turned to her husband.

"Caesar, it is good to see that you are feeling better, but-"

"My dear wife, has everyone . . . in this house . . . gone deaf? . . . I have asked . . . a simple question, why is it so . . . quiet . . . and no one . . . seems able to . . . hear me."

This entire utterance, more words than he had spoken all together since the Ides of March, took much longer than normal, punctuated as it was by the effort to breathe. His voice was barely more than a whisper, with odd squeaking tones whenever he tried to speak louder.

"Husband, calm yourself, please," Calpurnia pleaded. "That doctor of yours has been very clear on the point, you are not to tire yourself."

He made a slight gesture with his left hand, ill-formed and weak, to be sure, but it was a gesture she knew well: the way he waved his hand as though to say, "Don't bother me with this nonsense!" He had once mortally offended a room full of Senators with just that gesture, not a week before the Ides of March.

Could it be, Calpurnia thought, that her husband, the man himself, Caesar, the idol and terror of the known world, had returned to his broken body? It seemed too good to be true. Which would mean, in Calpurnia's not inconsiderable experience, that it was almost certainly not true. But that gesture, and his words, so Caesar-like despite the weakness and odd squeakiness of his voice and the trouble he had to catch his breath . . .

"Caesar, do you remember . . . do you know why you're here, what happened to you?"

"Of course..I do . . . I've lost some blood . . . I think . . . but not my mind." At this he laughed at his own joke, suddenly, jarring, with a horsy laugh that Calpurnia had never heard from him before.

"Yes, Caesar, and that is why you must do exactly as the doctor says. Please, lie back down and do not trouble yourself, all is well in this house."

I do not sound, she thought to herself, like a loving wife who's welcoming her beloved husband back from the threshold of Hades. What's wrong with me?

Many women called their husbands by their first names, as one spoke to boys before they assumed the *toga virilis*; others, by pet names or diminutives. It was impossible, however, to call Caesar anything but "Caesar." She had known since their wedding day that she would never call him "Gaius," not even in bed. And "Caesarolus" or something like that? Unthinkable. Even that impudent little twit, Catullus, writing obscene invectives about a man he so loathed, for reasons he would never explain to anyone, had never called him anything but "Caesar." It was as though Caesar were an event, a phenomenon, something that could only be called what it was, and nothing else. He even spoke of himself as "Caesar" in the third person, not just when he was writing about his wars, but even in conversation. He would not say, "I do not wish it," but rather, almost always, "Caesar does not wish it."

Odd, that was, when one stopped to think about it. Rather as though the man who was speaking was merely reporting what he had been told by some invisible being of which he was the mere spokesman.

I am so tired, she thought, that my thoughts wander in the middle of a conversation, even now. He has been speaking again, and I have been thinking instead of listening.

".,and I noticed—even the . . . street windows . . . no, street vendors . . . are quiet."

"No doubt," she said, "they have all gone to the trial." And immediately regretted it. She should have been paying attention.

"What . . . trial?"

There was nothing to do now but brazen it out. It would have to be faced. Perhaps it would even do him good to know. Of course, she realized at once, as she had long suspected, that Antony was a liar: all the pronouncements about the trial that Antony had promulgated as "Caesar's orders," and here Caesar knew nothing of any trial.

"The men who tried to kill you," she explained, "those whom Antony's legionaries didn't kill on the spot. They're on trial."

"Is Cicero . . . defending them?"

So his mind, as it seemed, was back, as before. He had always been two steps ahead of everyone, his friends and his enemies, knowing what they would do before they knew it themselves, and ready to help them. Or cut them down, as the situation seemed to demand.

"Yes, Caesar. There are five of them, charged with treason, according to your statute."

"Who?"

"Quintus Ligarius, Gaius Trebonius, Gaius Servilius Casca, Gaius Cassius Longinus, and—she hesitated—"Marcus Junius Brutus."

"No!" Caesar shouted, with surprising strength, but the word came out as a shriek. But the shout had cost him dearly, the pain registered on his face. Still, he took two panting breaths and said again, "No!"

"Caesar, please!" Calpurnia rushed to him, tried to put her arms around him, both in a gesture of affection and an attempt to get him to lie back down. "I know you think much of him, thought much of him, but he tried to kill you!"

"No! . . . It is . . . a mistake . . . it . . . must be . . . stooped . . . stopped."

"Fetch the doctor!!" Calpurnia screamed at the closed door of the slave's quarters, adjacent to her husband's bedroom. "At once, or I'll have you all flogged!!"

She did not know how and whether to struggle with him. Aware of his wounds, which the doctor said were "mostly" healed, she did not want to open them up, but he was getting more and more agitated, and he seemed to want to stand, which the doctor had said would not be possible for another month at least.

After a moment, though, she felt the strength leave him, and he lay back. For a moment his eyes were closed, and she thought perhaps he was going to sleep now, but then he opened them again.

"Calpurnia." This in a whisper. "Please . . . believe me . . . Brutus . . . must not be . . . condoned . . . condemned."

"Even now, you impossible man," Calpurnia said with a completely unsuccessful attempt to cover the very real hurt and anger lurking under the pretense of irony, "you refuse to believe that your precious Brutus is a bastard." And again, she regretted what she had said as soon as it came out of her lips. She could have used any one of a hundred uncompliment-ary epithets for that piece of excrement that Caesar loved so much, and forgave over and over, but "bastard" was exceptionally poorly chosen. Or well chosen, that was the problem, wasn't it?

"He . . . did not stroke . . . strike . . . me."

"Of course not," she said, and stroked his head. "Of course not."

The doctor had warned her that if and when he did wake up from this long, long sleep, his mind might be altered. His memories would be confused, he might have visions, hear voices, fall into uncontrollable passions. So now it had happened, and what was she to do?

She was saved from her dilemma by the timely arrival of the physician, formally announced by the doorman: "Publius Sulpicius Scaeva."

He was, of course, a most curious individual. Reddish hair, blue eyes, tall as a giant, should be wearing trousers like his ancestors, but looking so incongruous wearing a toga. Still, he carried himself with such dignity that one didn't feel like laughing out loud. And here he was, a senator (by Caesar's personal appointment), and yet a physician. Absurd, that was, but under the circumstances Calpurnia was not inclined to dwell on that. It was a strange world they lived in, and the fact that her own husband was responsible for much of the strangeness did not prevent Calpurnia from wondering at it.

With that odd impassivity of his, neither friendly nor hostile, Scaeva merely nodded to Calpurnia and turned all his attention to Caesar. The man had lived under this roof for two months without leaving even once, tending his patient, but every time she saw him, it was like meeting a total stranger.

As she stood out in the corridor, waved away by the physician, she heard him call out a word she didn't recognize as either Latin or Greek, with his hand outstretched towards one of his acolytes, though he never took his eyes off his patient. The acolyte reached into a parcel he was carrying, pulled out a vial of something, and put it in the physician's outstretched hand. But she saw no more: another acolyte, an enormous man she instinctively identified as an ex-soldier (this made sense, the physician had made his reputation healing Caesar's soldiers from horrible wounds) took up a position in the doorway, his back towards her, blocking her view, almost certainly intentionally. But she had no strength or will to protest, even though as the wife of Caesar and mistress of this house she would surely have prevailed in any contest of wills.

Back in the quiet of her own bedroom, she could hear muffled voices from the next room, but no more shouting and no struggles, everything was apparently under control. she had time to think.

Issa, her beloved little white Melitaean dog, sprang up onto the couch and presented her head to be stroked by her mistress. Calpurnia was glad for the warmth. Dogs lead a simple life, she thought, with neither past nor future to haunt them or frighten them. Issa knows only that I am in distress, so she brings me comfort. No advice, no consolation, just the comfort of her presence.

Could it be true, after all, that that unspeakable little prig, that hypocrite, Brutus, was Caesar's son? The rumors were based on the undisputed fact that Caesar and Servilia had been, well, let's say "sweethearts" in their youth, and there was perhaps a physical possibility. Brutus's legal father, on the other hand, was a Junius Brutus of the old school, not a man likely to wed a wife already pregnant by someone else, or raise a son as his own who had been fathered by another man. But this taciturn, perpetually scowling old man, a poor match anyway for the lovely Servilia, had rather conveniently gotten himself tangled up with Lepidus's rebellion and killed (by Pompey, oddly enough) when their (?) son had been only eight years old. Servilia had later taken up with her old flame, Caesar (who was already married to Cornelia), and perhaps the close relations between Caesar and Brutus stemmed from this time. Many children regarded their mothers' lovers as alternative fathers, if they still lived with their mothers; there was nothing strange about it.

Calpurnia tried to add up the numbers in her head, but there were some essential facts she didn't know, and so many of the people involved were dead, so she gave it up. At least for now. There might come a time when it would be essential for her to know if Brutus was actually Caesar's son, or even if Caesar thought it possible, in which case it mattered little whether it was true or not.

Calpurnia sighed. If Caesar had actually fathered half the sons in Rome reputed to be his, it would be amazing that he could still walk without a cane. The irony was, he had had a daughter and a stillborn son with his first wife, Cornelia, Cinna's daughter, but neither of his subsequent two marriages, to the near-idiot Pompeia and then to herself, had been fruitful. For her part, Calpurnia had done everything she could possibly do to give Caesar a son. She knew, though he never really mentioned it, that he wanted a son, and she had seen how much he had doted on his daughter by Cornelia, Julia, and how devastated he had been by her death. But month after month had gone by, and now it was surely too late. Old mothers had feeble sons, everyone knew that.

The painful truth behind all this, she realized, was that Caesar had truly loved Cornelia, and her death in childbirth, preceded by the stillbirth of their infant son, had apparently left a scar on his heart that neither she nor any of his many paramours could even touch, let alone heal. There were times when she wondered if everything he had done, all this conquering of women, provinces, and now an entire Empire, had not been caused by his efforts to fill an enormous empty place that somehow could not be filled.

She herself could not fill this emptiness, try as she might. That was her pain, and she would carry it to her grave.

The tears were flowing freely now, falling on Issa's soft white fur, and the dog put its little paws on her chest and licked her face. Perhaps she really just liked the salt, but it was comforting to think that Issa wanted her to stop crying.

It was time to face the truth. Caesar had left home on the Ides of March knowing that he would be attacked. He left thinking he would not return. He had wanted to die, but since suicide was not an option, he was prepared to let others do it for him.

Thinking this, knowing that it might be true, was as much as she could bear.

8

The Trial, Day 2

June 29, 44 B.C.E.

Rome, the Forum

THE SECOND DAY OF the trial of the five conspirators had not begun auspiciously. June is usually a very dry month in Rome, especially as it gives way to the high summer months of July and August, when the heat drives the wealthy (and not only) out of the city, up into the mountains or down to the sea. But storm fronts sometimes blow in from the Mediterranean, and the resulting thunderstorms, when the warm wet air from the sea collides with cooler, drier air from the Apennines, can be violent.

The previous day, during the opening speech by Pedius, for the prosecution, scores of people had fainted in and around the Forum, overcome by the heat, and several of them had died. Some of the wealthy and powerful had even decided that the privilege of sitting close to the principals was not worth being baked alive, as the sun heated the dark blue-gray basalt paving stones to the temperature of bread ovens, or so it seemed. By the time Pedius had finished his opening speech, the crowd had still been enormous, but visibly less so than at the beginning.

This morning, by contrast, the sky was gray, and a thunderstorm had awoken much of the city just before dawn. To make matters worse, a lightning bolt had struck the Capitoline Temple, not exactly a rare occurrence (it was, after all, the highest point in the city), but always a bad omen. The College of Augurs met in emergency session and was prepared to declare the day, and perhaps the next ten days, *dies nefastus*, which would have the effect of suspending all public business, trials included.

But Antony had prevailed upon them to consult their books again (privately threatening them with even more than his usual tactlessness) and the decision had been made that since the lightning had struck on the right side of the temple, the auspices were good.

The storm had been as violent as the memorable one that had raged over Rome the night before the Ides of March, a coincidence that was not lost on anyone. The March storm had been followed by a comet, which appeared in the sky the night after the assassination attempt and remained visible for seven days, as Caesar's life hung in the balance. Spurinna, whose stock in public credibility had risen enormously, informed the public that the comet had been Caesar's pathway to Olympus, ready in case his soul had decided to depart his mortal body and take up a more fitting residence among the gods.

By mid-morning of the second day of the trial, however, the storm cleared, which had the effect of turning the city into a giant steam-bath, as the sun beat down on wet stones. Still, this didn't seem to diminish anyone's enthusiasm for the dramatic events in the Forum; the crowd that had assembled by midday was only a little smaller than the day before.

Pedius's speech the day before had taken many by surprise. The man was virtually unknown to the wider public; so much so, in fact, that the choice of such a relatively unknown senator to prosecute such important defendants accused of treason had provoked considerable commentary. There had been no lack of voices, gaining strength after it became known that Cicero would appear for the defense, that a minor player had been chosen with the intention that he would lose. It was to be the Gracchi brothers all over again: the people's champion had been murdered, and now the Senate would close ranks to see that none of its own were brought to justice for the crime. Not everyone was ready to believe this, but the mood in the *corona* had been nervous, even volatile, when Pedius rose to speak.

But he had spoken well. He had struck exactly the right balance, steered a safe course between Scylla and Charybdis, presenting the attack on Caesar as both a political murder committed by a small group of disaffected men who had attempted, for purely selfish reasons, to thwart the manifest will of the Roman people, and an act of lawlessness, daggers raised against a man whose person, as consul, was an embodiment of the majesty of Rome herself.

"How, in the name of the very *mos maiorum* these men claim to have been defending, the customs of our elders, can daggers be drawn in

the meeting place of the Senate, and thrust into the body of a sitting magistrate, a consul, without incurring the severest penalty the law provides?
If these men truly felt that Caesar's course was wrong, why did they not
exercise their liberty as senators and simply tell him what they thought
was wrong? Caesar is not Sulla, as they, of all people, should know. He
keeps no list of people who displease him, the proscribed, who can be
killed with impunity and their property taken by their murderers, with
the connivance of the law. On the contrary, three of these men were personally pardoned by Caesar for taking up arms against him; how can they
reasonably claim that they were oppressed by a tyrant? It would be laughable, this claim of theirs, had it not led to a tragedy, very nearly to the
greatest calamity to befall the Roman people since Hannibal destroyed
two consular armies at Cannae, more than 170 years ago.

"What did they mean to accomplish? Did they imagine that they
could strike this man down, walk out of the Senate with their bloody
daggers, and receive the acclamation of the Roman people? Who so
dearly loved the man they meant to kill? Did they imagine that they could
simply return to their homes, to their private affairs, wash their bloody
hands and discard their bloody clothing, and go on about their lives? Did
they imagine that the life they used to lead, pursuing their petty personal
interests and calling it 'politics', congratulating each other for their ef-
fectiveness in plundering provinces, competing for the honor of boasting
the largest fish pond in Rome—that all this would simply resume as it had
before Caesar came south and called them to account?"

This was a nice touch: a string of rhetorical questions, heavily laden
with irony, a weapon straight from Cicero's arsenal, now used to preempt
Cicero's forthcoming attack on the prosecution. The older among them
could remember how Cicero himself, almost 20 years earlier, had used
just such a string of questions to reduce the shameless, tireless, cynical
Catiline to sputtering, impotent fury, effectively sealing his fate in six
short sentences. "Just exactly how long, Catiline, will you abuse our patience?" Even those far too young to remember that speech had heard
that sentence from their elders.

Among the few senators not present in the Forum on the second
day to hear Pedius present his witnesses was Sallust. He and his son
were at home, in his town home, pleasantly situated north of the Forum,
between the Pincian and Quirinal hills, just outside the ancient Servian
walls of the city, in a district where such important families as the Luculli
had their ornamental gardens. Sallust's plan was to build such a garden

adjacent to his villa, and then, mostly to spite his aristocratic neighbors, open the gardens to the public.

No one noticed his absence among the senators present that day. This would not have surprised Sallust very much, had he known it. There had been a day when not being missed at an important public event would have been a personal disaster for him, but much had happened since he had arrived in this great city, an ambitious youth from the Sabine town of Amiternum, starting a career that he was sure would lead him someday to the very pinnacle of power.

He was a wealthy man now, though the simple fact was that he had been born to an affluent family and had never really lacked for much in his life. The land under the villa and the gardens he was planning had been given to him by Caesar, who had owned the property earlier but had never been much interested in it. The money to build the villa and the gardens had come from Sallust's own fortune, which was based on the land and money he inherited from his father, somewhat augmented by Caesar's generosity.

Sallust had attended the first day of the trial, goaded by Terentia, ostensibly to further Publius's education, and he had heard Pedius speak (he still counted the man among his friends, though they had not spoken for over a year). So his absence from the next day's events in the Forum was not the result of a mere lack of interest. Some part of him longed to be there even now, watching and listening. But the whole affair of the bungled assassination was exquisitely painful to him, and his sensitivity (and pride) won out over his curiosity. His presence would have been noted far more widely than his absence was. He was sorry he had come to the city at all. It had been, just as he'd told Terentia, an exercise in futility.

More than that, however, he still didn't really know how he felt about this trial, about the men on trial and what they had tried to do, and above all, about Caesar.

It wasn't that he had much personal sympathy for Brutus or Cassius, the privileged scions of old noble families, or the other three for that matter. Brutus, masquerading as a Stoic, who had made a fortune lending money to provincial cities to pay their tax bills, and then using his connections with provincial governors to extort payment. Cassius, who had suddenly converted to Epicureanism after Pharsalus, and used his brother's influence to get a pardon from Caesar. What was most galling about it was that after such an act of ordinary treachery, they had the cheek to present themselves as "liberators."

It was precisely the arrogance of such men, who viewed their own superiority as a fact of nature, that had brought Rome to this pitiable state. The Roman Senate, once an assemblage of the best and wisest heads in the Republic, had long since become an institution whose whole *raison d' être* was to protect the political and (especially) property rights of its members. It was the pettiness and avarice of such men, who prided themselves on their pedigrees, that had forced Caesar to cross the Rubicon.

Sallust allowed himself a smile at the heat of his own internal rhetoric, with phrases taken straight from his own speeches ringing in his head. He had believed all that, he had fought for the cause and sent men to their deaths for its sake; he had been prepared to surrender not only his life, but his honor, for Caesar, the only man who could take on the Senate and trample its arrogance in the dust. He had put all his talents and energy into supplying Caesar's army in Greece, and the fact that Caesar's army had arrived in Greece intact, and had not perished of hunger long before they ever had the chance to fight—that was his doing, Gaius Sallustius Crispus, no one else. Caesar knew that perfectly well, but in his published commentaries he had vouchsafed Sallust a single sentence, no more.

But Caesar had thought enough of Sallust's talents to make him praetor and take him to Africa, to fight Metellus Scipio, Labienus, Cato and the rest. He had stood side by side with Caesar, looking down at the bloody self-mutilated corpse of Cato, and he had seen the signs of emotions that Caesar was struggling to hide. It had been a formative moment in Sallust's life; by the time he had reflected on its meaning, he had fundamentally altered his attitude towards both these men.

Cicero

The excitement of the previous day had somewhat diminished. Pedius had spoken well the previous day, yes, better than anyone had expected, but Cicero's own task today, before the defense would begin, was not so much to rile up the *corona* as to convince the jury that the evidence did not allow for any doubts.

Witness after witness was called to describe the events of the Ides of March. It was hardly necessary. Who in Rome had not already heard all the stories, blow by blow? But Pedius plodded on: "Well then, whom did you see there? . . . Was he carrying a dagger? . . . Did you actually see him strike the consul? . . .". No one was really listening to this, and at several points the buzz of conversation in the Forum grew so loud that the praetor signaled the *praeco* to call for silence. The jury had to make at least a pretense of listening.

Things got more interesting somewhat later in the afternoon, however, when Pedius began calling witnesses to testify to the debt of gratitude that each of the conspirators had owed to Caesar.

"You were there with Caesar at Pharsalus on the afternoon after the battle?"

"Yes," replied the nervous witness, a junior officer whose name was given but immediately forgotten. "I was there in the officer's tent, with my colleagues."

"Can you tell us why Caesar was there with all of you, and not in the Praetorium?"

"After a battle Caesar never sits in his tent, he doesn't even change clothes. He always walks around, talks to the men. Everyone can see that he's dirty and bloody like the rest of us, I think that's what he wants us to see. He talks to the legionaries first, then to us junior officers, and he doesn't go to clean himself up and visit with the legion commanders until he's finished."

"So what happened that day, when Caesar was in your tent, talking to you and your colleagues?"

"We heard a noise outside, some kind of commotion, and we all ran out to see what was going on. My first thought was that maybe the Pompeians had had some reserves we didn't know about and were making an attack. I even grabbed my sword on the way out. But I could see a crowd was gathering by the camp gate, unarmed, it didn't look like anyone was attacking us, so I turned around to put my sword away. Caesar was standing right behind me." The witness paused, his eyes briefly flickered upwards in that particular way a person does when trying to remember something. The man was doing a passable job, he was visibly nervous but controlling it. It was obvious, of course, that he'd been well coached and given a script to perform.

"And then what?" Pedius prompted, smiling briefly at the nervous young officer, as though reassuring a nervous child.

"Well, I meant to go around him and put my sword away, but he just smiled and held out his hand, took my sword, leaned inside the tent, and tossed it on my bed. How he knew which bed was mine is more than I can figure." Despite his nervousness, or perhaps because of it, he smiled suddenly.

There was something like a collective chuckle. This was vintage Caesar: his ability to make everyone think he was the Great Man's special friend was legendary. He had a prodigious memory for small details, which he used deftly to turn the politician's standard "how's the wife and kids?" into a moment of personal contact. It would not be mentioned now, it was immaterial to the case, but in the campaigns that followed the victory at Pharsalus, this young officer fought like a lion, at peril of his life more than once. And that in large part because his general had once remembered which bed was his. That made it personal. It was all very well to fight for a cause, an idea, but when the swords come out, you fight to save your own life and the lives of those you care about the most.

Pedius gently brought the young man back to his task. "And then?"

"Then Caesar started walking up to see what was going on, and of course the crowd parted to let him through. I was right behind him."

(Of course you were, Cicero thought, ungraciously. Where else would you be to kiss his ass?)

"When we got near the gate, we saw three men, three senior officers to judge from their uniforms, on their horses. One of them was Marcus Junius Brutus."

"This man?" Pedius pointed.

The witness nodded. "I'd seen him before, in the Assembly, I knew who he was, I knew he'd commanded a legion against us. Of course we all realized he'd come to surrender. In fact we'd been talking about him, a little earlier, in the tent after the battle. Someone was wondering if he'd been killed, and someone else had said, 'If he had any balls he'd throw himself on his sword, the old-fashioned way, like his ancestors would have done. So I expect he's alive and well.'"

The witness clearly expected people to laugh at this, but hardly anyone did. The pause was awkward.

"Anyway, so here he was in person. He got down off his horse and walked towards Caesar. He was dirty and bloody like all of us, but he had defeat in his face, there's a look that every soldier knows, that you have on your face when you've lost. He wouldn't look up, wouldn't look Caesar in the face, just kept his eyes on the ground. And didn't say noth—anything. It got real quiet, everyone wanted to hear. Finally Brutus cleared his throat once or twice, and said in a funny, scratchy kind of voice, 'Caesar—', but Caesar didn't let him finish. 'Brutus, my old friend!' he said, Caesar did, and he went to him with his arms out. Brutus didn't even look up. Caesar just kept on talking to him like they were the best of friends, exactly as though Brutus had just come for a visit after being away for a while. And he put his arm around him and took him into the Praetorium. We didn't hear anything more."

Pedius thanked the witness, who was obviously relieved to have discharged his duty and almost scuttled off the platform where the witnesses stood, disappearing into the crowd.

The next witness was Gnaeus Domitius Calvinus, who had commanded the center of Caesar's line of battle at Pharsalus, and who, as a senior commander, had been present to hear the conversation between Brutus and Caesar after the battle, in the Praetorium. A few months after Pharsalus, Calvinus had been sent to deal with Pharnaces, an Armenian king who apparently supposed that the civil war in Rome gave him an opportunity to feel like a real king again. Calvinus had been humiliated and his army soundly thrashed in Armenia, but Caesar didn't seem to hold his failure against him. No one quite knew, perhaps least of all Calvinus himself, why Caesar considered him important, but that he did, no one doubted.

Calvinus was of consular rank and was greeted by the praetor and both attorneys with the appropriate dignity and respect. Cicero rose from his seat, not too fast and not too slow, and bowed, not too deeply, but not just a nod, either. There were advocates, even some good ones, mostly of the younger generation, who in such a situation, with a hostile witness or a defendant, would go out of their way to be rude, to show contempt, to send a message that "this person just does not deserve the rank he holds," but Cicero had never done this and never would. Twenty years earlier, when he was consul, he had personally escorted Lentulus Sura to the Tullianum to be garroted by the public executioner, because even though in his speeches he had called the man a traitor, an assassin, and a degenerate, and he was all of those things and more, still, Lentulus had once been consul. Decorum was important. It was a loathsome task but Cicero had done it without hesitation. There was no reason now to either flatter the estimable Calvinus or insult him. The speed of the standing up and the depth of the bow had been planned, and were executed exactly as planned.

Calvinus at first stood at the Rostra, as all the witnesses had done before, but as a man of consular rank he was allowed to sit, and a chair appropriate to his rank was provided.

Pedius began with polite formalities and then got to the point.

"You were present, I believe, at a conversation that took place on the day of the battle at Pharsalus, between the consul Gaius Julius Caesar and Marcus Junius Brutus, present here today as defendant?"

"Yes, I was."

"Can you tell us what transpired?"

Calvinus was, of course, a much more experienced speaker than the likable but forgettable young military tribune who had preceded him. He took his time preparing himself to answer.

"Caesar himself led Brutus into the Praetorium, as though he were a guest of honor. I was surprised, to say the least. I stood to go, because the situation was awkward, but Caesar motioned me with his hand to stay in my chair. So I did.

"The atmosphere was very odd, to say the least. Caesar was relaxed and friendly, Brutus was clearly in shock and said very, very little, just 'Yes' and 'No' sometimes, in a voice you could hardly hear. Caesar was talking about everything except the battle that we'd just won, and Brutus had just lost. I can't even remember about what, some of it was about their families, Caesar asked about Brutus's mother, I think, that sort of thing."

Some in the crowd reacted to this with a whispered remark to the person sitting next to them, or even a muffled laugh: Caesar's romance with Servilia was well known, even outside the Senate, so for Calvinus to mention her just at this moment was odd, even perhaps rude. But he resumed his testimony, unperturbed, as though he hadn't noticed anything remarkable about what he'd just said.

"Finally Caesar let the conversation lapse for a moment, and when Brutus didn't speak up, Caesar asked, in Greek, 'Son, what do you want from me now?' Or words to that effect, I'm sure he switched to Greek and I'm sure he called Brutus *teknon*."

This caused an even greater stir. Some of the Senate's liveliest gossips had long insisted that Brutus was actually Caesar's son, though the romance with Servilia had really begun some time after Brutus was born, so this was highly unlikely. Still, there had always been an obvious bond between Caesar and Brutus that seemed to require some explanation, all the more so as sons do not usually live easily with their mothers' lovers. Brutus had even shown a certain reluctance—strange, given his character, his convictions, and the fact that he was Cato's son-in-law—to throw in with Pompey after Caesar crossed the Rubicon.

"So what happened then?" Pedius prompted, as much to induce the crowd to quiet down as to instruct the witness to continue. Calvinus, like a good comic actor, waited exactly the right amount of time for the crowd noise to abate before he resumed his story and answered the question.

"Brutus began to weep. I saw his shoulders shake, his head hung even lower, then tears were falling on his lap, and finally he began to sob. It was pitiful—but I won't say pathetic, I've lost a battle myself and I'm sorry to say I know how it feels.

"Caesar went over to him and embraced him like a father embracing a weeping child, and then Brutus really began to weep.

"You see, I think Brutus was as puzzled as I was by the friendliness Caesar had been showing. I've known Caesar and served under him, proudly, for many years. He's the most . . ." Calvinus searched for the word, or pretended to, since he probably had chosen it very carefully several days ago—"magnanimous, yes, that's it, magnanimous man I've ever known. He fights like all the furies of hell, but when it's over and he's won, he's the first to stretch out a hand. He knew he had to put Vercingetorix in chains and send him to Rome to be displayed and then killed, but you could see that he didn't like it. I'll never forget the look on his face at Alesia, when Vercingetorix rode into the camp, dismounted, and then knelt in the dirt before Caesar. He really wanted to pick the man up and take him to the Praetorium for dinner, you could see that."

"I'm told, I don't know if it's true or not, but it easily could be, that on the night before his triumph, when Vercingetorix was to be strangled the next day as part of the festivities, Caesar actually went to the prison and offered him a chance to end his own life with a sword, like a man and a soldier, but Vercingetorix turned him down.

"Anyway, everyone knows that Caesar is never a vindictive man, he saw Sulla's proscriptions when he was a young man and never wanted to see anything like that again, so bloody punishment of his enemies was never an option, really.

"But there's another side to Caesar, there is something he finds unforgivable, and you'd better not forget it. He can't abide betrayal. When he subdued a new Gallic tribe he always made them a very generous offer and never treated them harshly; he explained to us many times that only in this way could he bring loyal children into the Empire, rather than angry and humiliated men who would just be waiting for the day when they could slaughter us to get revenge. The only exception to this *clementia* of his was in the case of towns or tribes or even individuals that had promised to be loyal and then revolted. When the Eburones revolted and slaughtered a whole legion after they'd promised to feed and quarter them, Caesar went in there like death himself, not a man left alive, and the women and children sold to the slave traders.

"You had to understand that, with Caesar. If you were insolent or even incompetent, he would just smile and let it go most of the time. But if you've been disloyal, or more specifically, if you promise loyalty and then betray him, he will crucify you—without showing anger or cruelty, but he will crucify you without blinking an eye.

"So what did Brutus expect, knowing the man at least as well as I do? Well, you'd have to ask him, if he cares to tell you, but my guess is that he felt then as though he'd betrayed Caesar personally, and he expected to be crucified, metaphorically if not literally. And I don't suppose Caesar's public friendliness did anything to make him less ashamed and afraid, since we all thought, I suppose, that Caesar might just be playing with him.

"So when Caesar called him *teknon*, the dam burst. Like any son who's betrayed his father and been forgiven."

Cicero showed no outward reaction to this, but inside, he cringed. Domitius Calvinus had just crucified Brutus, very cleverly and subtly, but effectively. He had played on that peculiarly Roman virtue called *pietas*, the loyalty and devotion a son owes to his father, a soldier owes to his commander, a citizen owes to his city, and sometimes, a man owes to a god. Cicero himself had used this powerful word in defense of sons whose attacks on an enemy could be construed as vengeance for a wrong done to their fathers. He'd never had it used against him before, but then again, he'd suspected it would be. He just hadn't anticipated exactly how and when it would be done. If the jury took its vote believing that Brutus had been *impius*, that he had betrayed his "father," literally or metaphorically, as Calvinus had not said directly but so obviously implied, then Brutus was a dead man, and all the others would probably go with him to meet the executioner. By tomorrow at the latest, Cicero realized, he would have to think of a way to turn that *pietas* around.

"So Caesar told him, as I recall, using that word *teknon* again, often, but shifting back to Latin, thank God, that nothing bad was going to happen to him. Everything could be put right and they would just put this unpleasant episode behind them. There had been a tragic falling out among family and friends, blood had been spilt, but it was over now and best forgotten. In a civil war, he said, really, all are equally guilty and all are equally innocent, even though one side has to win, and the other lose. 'I was sad, Brutus,' he said, 'when you decided to join the other side, but all the time I admired you for your courage.' And so on like that."

"What did you think of this?" asked Pedius. Calvinus seemed surprised and not entirely pleased with the question.

"Well, my first thought was, 'why did I fight and bleed and almost get killed for Caesar if the people on the other side are treated just as well or even better than we are?' And for a while I think I was pretty upset, and the truth is, a lot of other officers were, too. I didn't want proscriptions or anything like that, probably nobody did who remembers Sulla or remembers their fathers talking about Sulla, but I never expected to see the leaders of the other side walking away with a share in the spoils, so to speak.

"When I cooled down later, though, I realized what a master stroke this was. How necessary it was. We were all so happy that we'd won, jumping up and down and shouting, like always, but we also knew that we'd just killed ten thousand of our fellow citizens, that our friends and even family members were probably among the dead still lying out there unburied. I don't know about anyone else, but I woke up the next morning with the most awful feeling, thinking, 'OK, we won, now what?' And nothing. And at that moment I understood what Caesar had done with Brutus, with Cassius and all the rest. Pure statesmanship, I don't know what else to call it. How can you stop a civil war? Winning isn't enough, Sulla proved that. He killed a lot of his enemies but he couldn't kill them all, and as far as I'm concerned what we've been through all these years is really because of him. And Caesar understood that, understood that you have to win the war, and then you have to have peace that is something more than just an empty place between two wars."

Suddenly Calvinus stood up. This, it seemed, was not scripted, or if it was, Calvinus was at least as good a courtroom actor as Cicero was. His face was red, and his voice became at once louder and deeper as he thrust out his finger at the defendants.

"And that's what you tried to kill, you morons! you band of cretins! and the worst of it is, you failed to kill Caesar but you killed everything he accomplished, you killed the peace he tried to build! And for what?! Were you afraid that Caesar would take away your ornamental fish ponds? That some plebeian would fail to duck his head when you walked past in the Forum, in your scented togas? For what?!"

Calvinus kept on, but by this time a rising roar from the *corona* had drowned out the sound of his voice.

The praetor stood, alarmed, and glanced at his brother, who was sitting all this time in the place of honor, looking bored as he always managed to do on important occasions. But the consul, perhaps the only man in the Forum who did not seem to be either frightened or furious, continued to slouch in his seat and look bored, with only a wave of his arm to calm down his excitable younger brother.

When the noise failed to subside, however, and it seemed that the movement in the *corona* was becoming purposeful, Antony waved his hand again, in a gesture of annoyance, then stood and signaled the commander of his guard, who was prepared and knew what to do. A trumpet was blown and the legionaries standing around the edges of the corona assumed battle position. This quickly cooled down the hotter heads, and in a surprisingly short time it was possible to resume the trial.

Anything that Domitius Calvinus could say now would be anticlimactic, which both Pedius and Calvinus himself both understood without exchanging a word. Calvinus was thanked, respectfully escorted out of the witness area, and it was time for a new witness.

Pedius had accomplished his main task yesterday, then, and had every reason to be satisfied. Brutus was a disloyal "son" who had tried to kill his own "father." And he was a spoiled aristocrat who had tried to ruin everything the majority of the Roman people had wanted and fought for. And Brutus was the key: if Pedius could discredit him, the rest were as good as dead already. So now the task was at least a little easier, though each defendant played a somewhat different role in Pedius' concept of the case and would have to be handled just a little differently. With the help of two very different witnesses, he had discredited Brutus.

Cassius was the second most important, but for that very reason Pedius wanted to end with him. The remaining three defendants were of lesser social status, perhaps, but they represented somewhat different groups, each of which needed to hear a particular variant of the same underlying argument: "X is like me. X is scum and is about to be crucified. If I don't want to be crucified with him, I'd better shout all the louder to hang him high." But that was easy in a crowd. The problem was far more complicated for some members of the jury, who might feel themselves too easily identified with one of the defendants to risk a vote for acquittal.

Ligarius, for example, had fought against Caesar in North Africa, on the staff of Considius, the Pompeian officer in charge of Numidia. After Caesar's victory at Thapsus, Ligarius had considered it prudent to disappear into a voluntary exile, rather than place himself at Caesar's disposal, as so many others had done. Thanks to his brothers, who had chosen Caesar's side in the war, and to the eloquence of Cicero, who had defended him in a treason trial presided over by Caesar himself, Ligarius received a pardon and permission to return to Rome. Once he arrived, he made the obligatory show of gratitude and obeisance to Caesar, but within a few months he had joined Brutus and Cassius. He was not a man of strong character or intellect, not a man of principle, but a man who had risen higher than anyone in his family before him, mainly by sucking up to the likes of Considius, or Brutus, or Cassius, or whoever seemed to him at any given moment to represent the "right" people to be seen with. Not every *novus homo* was like Cicero; many were desperately eager to be accepted at the right houses, ready to do almost anything just to be seen in the forum talking with someone of consular rank.

Trebonius and Casca, on the other hand, were Caesar's own men. Casca had been chosen to strike the first blow exactly for that reason. The plan was to surround Caesar in such a way that neither he nor anyone else would realize that it was happening until it was too late. But Caesar was not a stupid man, and there might come a moment when he realized that there were no friendly faces in sight. Better, then, to have the first approach within striking distance made by a man who had fought under Caesar's command. But Casca had approached from behind and struck a glancing blow that surprised and angered Caesar more than it hurt him.

As for Trebonius, he had begun plotting to kill Caesar even before the fateful meeting at Brutus' house, and some even whispered that he'd approached Antony a year before the Ides of March with the suggestion that the two of them should kill their commander. Why Antony had not told anyone else of this at the time was still an open question. But this was all gossip, and Antony was the kind of man who attracted lurid stories like rotten meat attracts flies. About half of them were probably true, but who could say which half?

It was not clear to anyone, at least not yet, why these two men, along with Albinus and several others who had fought for Caesar, had joined with Brutus and Cassius in the attack on Caesar. Some imagined that they felt resentment against Caesar for allowing pardoned Pompeians not only to escape with their lives and their fortunes intact, but even to hold offices as high or higher than those given to loyal Caesarians. Others argued that some of Caesar's men had fought less for Caesar than for a cause, the radical reform of the government and the abolition of the Senate's prerogatives as the final arbiter of state policy, and felt betrayed by Caesar's refusal to go far enough in his reforms.

Either of these motives might have accounted for a plot among Caesar's officers to kill their commander, but neither could explain why they would conspire with their Conservative enemies. "The enemy of my enemy is my friend," some said, but this was a truism that just didn't explain why such men as Brutus and Albinus, who were indeed cousins but had nothing else in common, would make common cause against Caesar, a man to whom they both owed a great deal. It was a topic for discussion throughout the city, from the seedy *tabernae* in the Suburra to the posh *triclinia* of the senatorial homes on the Palatine. And it was the main thing on Cicero's mind just now, as he listened to Pedius's witnesses and mentally prepared himself to present his own case.

Scaeva

There can be no doubt, Scaeva reminded himself over and over as he listened to the second day of the trial, that nothing in this life happens without any purpose at all. Everything is just as it should be, even if we may not be able to understand the divine reasoning. This he had learned from old Segovax, when he was still Skaiva, son of Mandubracius, king of the Trinovantes; and his study of the Stoic masters, which had begun soon after he had arrived in Rome with Caesar, led him to the same conclusion. There is no good or evil, the Stoics said, except in your soul; the world outside of you is such as it is because it cannot be otherwise. So he could not say that what was now unfolding in the Roman Forum was something wrong or evil, because it had happened as it must.

One lesson he had learned, however, was that accepting this certainty, that things happened as they must, did not always relieve the pain he felt. He was now watching men he knew, and in many cases liked and respected, trying to tear each other apart, and the fate of the world as he knew it rested in the balance. He had come to believe, ever since his days in the camp of Sulpicius Rufus, in Gaul, that the gods had ordained Rome to impose order on a chaotic world, and this conviction had lead him to actions that had made it impossible for him ever to return home. He had not only risked his own life many times, he had taken many lives in battle, including many Gallic lives, out of this conviction, that he was serving the ends of Providence.

How, then, watching this trial, could he not lose faith in the wisdom of his decision? How was it possible that the great Republic he had served so faithfully, in defiance of his people and his family, had come to such a moment? Could he have been mistaken? The thought was unbearable. But it had come to his mind, and once there it could not be wished away.

Soon, in all likelihood, he would have his turn to testify at this trial. He had been in Pompey's Theater that day, and he had done his duty. When the rest of the Senate had fled, Scaeva (prominent among the Celts whom Caesar had coopted to the Senate, indeed the only Briton) had flung aside his toga and stood beside the Dictator; he had even been wounded, and had parried at least one dagger thrust meant for Caesar. More importantly, perhaps, he had been summoned later that same day to Caesar's house, where his medical skills were sorely needed, and since that time he had scarcely left.

To Caesar's adoring public, then, Scaeva was a hero, the savior of their savior. Pedius fully expected Scaeva's testimony to destroy whatever remained of Cicero's arguments in favor of his clients. For all but one of the defendants, that might even be the case, which did not trouble Scaeva in the least. They had made their choice. One of the defendants, however, had made a different choice, and there were only three men who knew that, one of whom could not speak and the other certainly would not.

The choice to speak of this matter or let it pass in silence lay with Scaeva. And it was not an easy choice.

Scaeva thought he knew the answer to the question that was occupying the entire city. He knew why the conspiracy against Caesar was composed in roughly equal numbers of men who had fought on opposite sides at Pharsalus, Thapsus, and Munda. But he had not come to this answer easily.

His earlier reading of the situation had been accurate to a point: there would be an attack on Caesar, and it would take place when the Senate met in the Theater of Pompey on the Ides of March. He had been there to save Caesar because he was sure this would happen. And yes, his judgement had been correct and his presence in the right place at the right time, armed with a dagger he had smuggled into the meeting, had been crucial in preventing a tragedy of cosmic proportions. It had come as a shock to him, however, to see those particular men with daggers in their hands that day. He had thought of little else since that day.

9

The Ides of March, Revisited

March 15, 44 B.C.E.

Rome, Pompey's Theater

SCAEVA WAS FIGHTING HARD to get close enough to Caesar to protect him. He had already struck at several senators unlucky enough to stand between him and his goal, daggers in hand, men he hadn't recognized. Then, still three steps from Caesar's side, he saw Cassius thrust his dagger under Caesar's ribs, on the right, near the liver, giving him the first really dangerous wound he received that day. Caesar dropped the stylus he had been using to defend himself (not without good effect), and staggered back, opening himself to attack from his left.

Scaeva reached Caesar's side just in time to parry a powerful and surely fatal thrust from Albinus, who, experienced soldier that he was, immediately turned his attention to the enemy at hand. The seriously wounded Caesar could be finished off later; first, Albinus knew, he would have to deal with Scaeva.

The Roman legionary, going into battle with a stabbing sword in the right hand and a shield in the left, was trained to use the shield aggressively to push the enemy back, keep him off balance, ideally to trip him up; then the sword thrust was made either over the top of the shield or from the right side, mid-high or low, depending on what part of his body the off-balance enemy was not protecting. Only an inexperienced soldier would expose his own body to make a thrust, which meant that many battles were initially mostly pushing matches, shield against shield, until the moment when one side or the other lost their nerve, broke and ran.

With a dagger, on the other hand, you could not let your enemy get too close at any time, until you saw an opening. Slashing was done to keep the enemy away, but the death wound that ended the fight was almost always an upward thrust into the abdomen. Scaeva knew this, but Albinus, like the other senators with him, did not. This went far to explain why Caesar was still alive after several dagger thrusts into his body. No fatal wound had been delivered—at least, not yet.

Albinus was strong and determined, but there came a moment when he slashed at Scaeva with his dagger just a little too hard; Scaeva dodged expertly, the blow missed, and Albinus lost his balance for a moment. It was enough. Scaeva's dagger thrust was as swift and deadly as a cobra's strike, and Albinus crumpled to the floor.

Scaeva spun around towards Caesar, alarmed that his struggle with Albinus had taken him too far from Caesar. He was just in time to see the fatal blow about to be struck.

Caesar, bleeding profusely now and already pale as a ghost, had his arm on Brutus's shoulder, supporting himself and making no attempt to defend himself. Brutus's dagger was out, and Caesar had seen it, seen death about to come to him at the hands of someone he loved. He spoke.

"*Kai su, teknon? Kai su?*"

Scaeva knew this was Greek, but it was not until later, when there was time to reflect, that he realized what had been said.

"You, too, son? You, too?"

He would also wonder why Caesar, at this particular moment, facing imminent death, had spoken in a foreign language, rather than his native Latin. At the time, however, he could see that this Greek sentence had reached something in Brutus. There was a moment's hesitation.

Brutus did not turn his eyes away from Caesar, but the dagger remained poised. It was not withdrawn, but neither was it plunged into Caesar's belly. Scaeva stared at it, transfixed, knowing that there was nothing he could do in the blink of an eye that remained before Caesar died—or not.

The river was about to fork.

Brutus's hesitation was momentary, but it was enough. The world had not stood still all this time. Two of Antony's legionaries, who by that time had fought their way to Caesar, grabbed Brutus from behind and wrestled him to the ground. He did not resist.

Caesar, however, stumbled backwards, tripped over his toga, and fell, hard, with a sickening crack as his head struck the base of Pompey's portrait bust.

The fight was over. And Scaeva's life nearly ended with it. The legionaries did not know who he was, had not seen the fighting, and here was this man, his toga thrown aside, all covered with blood and holding a dagger, standing only a few steps away from Caesar. They were in no mood to ask any questions, and the number of toga-clad bodies lying on the floor was proof of that.

Scaeva made no effort to fight them, but he did not surrender, either, or protest that he was on their side. He felt a great calm, an almost complete indifference to what would happen next. Caesar had been saved, and Scaeva felt quite certain just now that he had already performed the great task that the gods had given him, for the sake of which they had made him a Roman and sent him to this place.

It was this calm detachment, perhaps, that saved his life. The legionaries hesitated before thrusting their swords into his belly, and in the quiet that suddenly fell, Antony's voice could be heard. It was the voice of command, the voice of a man used to giving orders that would be obeyed without question.

"Soldiers, stand down! This man saved Caesar!"

Of what happened later Scaeva remembered little. He realized suddenly that he was bleeding from several wounds, including a very deep slash to his upper left arm given him by Albinus. In the heat of battle he had felt nothing, as usual, but now a wave of pain and weakness overcame him, and he sat heavily where he stood. He did not know who it was who picked him up, where they took him, who treated his wounds.

He slept for several hours, till early evening. As soon as he awoke, however, the picture of Albinus about to kill Caesar came into his mind, and he realized that there was something very odd about the presence of Albinus with Cassius and Brutus. Although he had been sure that Caesar would be attacked that day (the signs were all in place, even the warnings of old Spurinna), he had not known which of the two groups of men who might feel they had reason to attack Caesar would actually be making the attempt that day. In other words, he would not have been surprised to see Albinus there, or Trebonius, or Casca; even in Celtic Britain mutinies of this sort were not unknown. He would not have been surprised, either, to see Brutus, or Cassius, or Ligarius; he had never believed that Caesar's famous *clementia* would actually be enough to buy the loyalty of men who hated everything Caesar stood for. It was seeing them all together that he could not make himself understand.

It was just at this moment, however, as Scaeva contemplated the oddness of the whole conspiracy, that messengers arrived with an urgent summons. Caesar was dying, and his services as a field doctor whom Caesar trusted absolutely were necessary. Forgetting in a moment his own pain and perplexity, Scaeva dressed, took his medical kit, and followed the messengers back to Caesar's house in the Suburra.

He arrived to find utter chaos. No one was guarding the door, while from inside he could hear women shrieking and men shouting. He rushed inside, stopped by no one, and followed the noise to what must have been Caesar's bedroom. From the doorway he could see immediately what was going on. Caesar was on the floor, thrashing violently, and white foam was gushing from his mouth.

"It's the holy disease!" cried the Greek doctor in attendance, "the falling sickness! I've seen it before! We have to put a spoon in his mouth to keep him from—." But he didn't finish his sentence, and shoved a fist in his mouth, appalled at having blurted out the truth that everyone in this house knew, but no one ever dared mention aloud.

"Absolutely not!" Scaeva snapped from the doorway. "It will do more harm than good. Help me move him. He needs to be lying on his side so that the foam in his mouth doesn't strangle him. Then we'll try to keep him from hurting himself until it passes."

Several of the men standing around, slaves and soldiers mingled, did as Scaeva commanded, and the seizure passed in a few moments. But Caesar didn't regain consciousness, and it was clear that his fever was rising.

"It's the blow to his head," Scaeva told them. "Sometimes it happens this way. There is some small bleeding inside his head, and when the blood gathers, little by little, it puts pressure on the brain until it squeezes the life out of him. There is no other way, I must open his skull."

There was a shocked silence, but no one protested.

Scaeva stood, placed his hands over his face for a brief moment, took a deep breath and let it out, then set to work.

What he was about to do was something he had seen done in his youth. Sometimes it worked, at least as often it failed, but it was always a shock to contemplate. Still, the problem of blood accumulating in the head after a blow occurred often enough in battle that he always kept the special drill he needed for this operation in a separate pouch inside his medicine chest. He dug it out now and unwrapped it.

At the sight of it, Calpurnia paled, but rather than protest, she left the room. Though none of the Romans present knew what to call this thing, the Greek doctor knew. This instrument, which resembled the drills carpenters use to bore holes in wood or stone, was used to bore holes in the skull. Although he had never done this himself, the Greek knew what was going to happen next. He turned to the group of men standing around.

"This will be very hard to watch. You should all probably leave."

Without looking at anyone directly, Scaeva stated in a strained voice, "I will need two or three strong men to help me." None of the soldiers had the courage to leave, though none of them really wanted to stay, either.

Scaeva first took a razor from his kit and shaved a patch of hair on the left side of Caesar's head, about the size of a silver denarius, a finger's width in front of the ear and a finger's width above it, on the opposite side of Caesar's head from the gash left when his head had struck the base of Pompey's statue. Neither he, nor any of his teachers, nor the medical books he had read, could explain why the blood collected inside the skull in this way, opposite to the blow, but he had seen this so many times he now chose the site automatically.

Then he asked two of the soldiers who were standing by to hold Caesar's arms and legs, gently but firmly, and another, the strongest of them, to hold his head.

"I doubt very much that he will awaken, but if he does, he will be in great pain and may thrash about. You must hold him or the struggle will surely kill him."

The Greek doctor, who had retreated to the corner, was also pressed into service. He was told to get a large jug of water, and then wait for the order to pour some water onto the wound to wash away the blood.

Again Scaeva closed his eyes, covered his face with his hands, breathed in through his nose and out through his mouth. Then he picked up a small, sharp knife from his bag, which he used to slice the skin in the spot he had chosen. He pushed the sides of the wound he had just made to the sides, exposing the skull. Without a moment's pause, he then picked up the drill. He placed the point very carefully, then began to drill with as much speed as he could. It was essential, once the drilling began, to finish quickly, before too much blood was lost and too much pain was inflicted. But it was also essential to drill carefully, deep enough to penetrate the skull but absolutely no further.

It seemed to all of them that this took hours, but in fact it was not so very long. Three times Scaeva told the Greek doctor to pour some water, but even then he did not stop turning the drill, until suddenly there was a spurt of much darker blood around the drill bit. Scaeva immediately stopped drilling and removed the bit from the wound. Caesar groaned, but did not awaken.

Scaeva grabbed a clean cloth, but waited to apply it until the flow of dark blood began to slow. Then he reached into his bag for a metal disk, with the same diameter as the drill bit; he pressed it into the wound, then folded the skin back over the wound, pressed a cloth onto the wound, and tied another tightly around Caesar's head to hold the bandage in place.

The next few hours passed in waiting. Scaeva explained: "We have released the pressure from his head. But he has lost a great deal of blood. We must change the bandage every time it gets soaked through. If he does not bleed to death, he will live. We must also watch to see if too much pus appears, in which case either he will die, or we will have to do this again."

"Shouldn't we give him some extract of apple seed to stop bleeding?" said the doctor. "I've already administered some, and the bleeding from the dagger wounds has slowed."

"No," replied Scaeva. "It's good that you did what you did, that he didn't die at once from the bleeding. But now, in his condition. I doubt that he could swallow, and if we put something in his mouth and he did not swallow it, it could pass into his lungs and kill him. No, now it is all in the hands of the gods."

In fact, it was two full days before Caesar finally stirred, opened his eyes, and asked for something to drink. Scaeva, who for all that time had done no more than nap on a blanket next to Caesar's bed, gave him a drink of boiled water, ordered the servant to call him if anything should go wrong, and finally went to sleep.

Though he remained preoccupied with his patient for many days to come, there were still moments when his mind returned to the puzzle of Albinus's participation in the attack on Caesar. It was Cicero, finally, who helped him reach an understanding of this bizarre conspiracy.

The two men, unlikely friends to say the least, met one evening at Cicero's house, about a month after the attack on Caesar, not long after Cicero had agreed to defend the five surviving conspirators. As for Caesar, he was by no means in good health yet, but the crisis was over, and Scaeva finally felt able to accept Cicero's invitation, to relax at least for one evening, at Cicero's Esquiline house. In his own modest home he had no slaves to prepare his dinner, and the opportunity to eat something without having to cook it himself was more than welcome.

After they had eaten a modest supper, Cicero didn't wait for Scaeva to ask the question that was on his mind that evening. "You are no doubt curious, Scaeva, my friend, why I was not there in the Senate on the Ides of March with a dagger in my hand. When it first happened, in fact, I was outraged to find that the 'liberators' didn't invite me to their little banquet. Things would have gone differently, I venture to say, if they had."

"Is that why they didn't include you?"

"I really don't know, but I suspect so, yes. If I'd been part of the plan, this would have been a tyrannicide. Just as Harmodius and Aristogeiton murdered the son of Pisistratus and made room for the people of Athens to assume the government of their own city, so Brutus, Cassius, and I would have raised our daggers to remove a tyrant and restore the Republic. We would have done it with sorrow for the man we all liked and admired, and some of us even loved, but we would have done it with determination, to remove this man before he did the one thing we can never, ever allow to happen, so long as one genuine Roman still lives. We could not have allowed him to assume the crown that Brutus's ancestor, Junius Brutus, took from the head of Tarquinius, figuratively if not literally. The Republic, no matter how well or ill it is governed at any given moment, ceases to exist when it is no longer a public thing."

"I'm not sure I understand," Scaeva answered.

"Rome is not and has never been a democracy, like Athens in the days of Pericles and Socrates," Cicero replied. "But for more than four millennia now it has been a republic, a *res publica*, a "public thing," not a *res privata*, the possession of a single man, whether he is called "king" or "tyrant" or whatever. We cannot allow all important decisions to be made in the Forum, as the Athenians did, because the mass of men are foolish and selfish, and they make poor decisions. But neither can we allow one man to say that he is the master of the state, as the *paterfamilias* is master of his home and all who live in it. Then all are slaves, and as Plato demonstrates, in such a case even the tyrant is a slave, too."

"This makes sense to me, in a way. I had already grasped this strength of the Roman people, but you have put it very clearly. It seems obvious now."

Cicero smiled. "That seems to happen to me a great deal. I make a point based on what I have read and experienced, and given long thought, and then everyone says, 'Well, yes, when you say it like that it seems obvious.' I think my reputation as a philosopher would rise much higher if I would give up the orator's habit of trying to make things clear." He allowed himself a slight chuckle before he resumed.

"At any rate, Scaeva, look at these men who raised their daggers on the Ides of March. There was no political program behind it, not for all of them or even most of them, because there was not a single thing they could agree on except for one: Caesar had to die. If I had led the conspiracy, as I said, it would have been a tyrannicide. If someone had killed Sulla before he suddenly decided to retire, it would have been tyrannicide and we would have all joined in erecting a bronze statue of the assassin in the Forum.

"Look at Sulla, then. He was the champion of the Conservatives, the senatorial aristocracy, so it's obvious that the other factions would hate him. But can you find anyone on either side of the political divide who will say a kind word about Sulla today? Pompey was Sulla's creation, in some ways his creature, to be painfully honest, but did you ever hear Pompey even mention Sulla's name? I've championed the cause of the Senate, as I understand it, for all of my public life, but I detested Sulla and his memory, and not only because Marius was my countryman and a relative of my wife."

Scaeva gave a slight frown of puzzlement.

"My first wife, Terentia," Cicero explained.

Scaeva sighed. "In Britain, we have many kings, and the family relations of these kings can be very complicated and yet inordinately important. In Rome, it seems, you are all kings, and no one can understand your politics without knowing who is related to whom, by blood or by marriage."

Cicero laughed. "Your point is well taken. That's why it was so hard for me, as a *novus homo*, to make a career in this city. I was not related to anyone important. When I gave a good speech, they all applauded, and they even voted for me and commanded their clients to vote for me in the Assembly. But they would never think of inviting me to join them for dinner. They still don't. Even Brutus, for example, he comes to my philosophical gatherings in Tusculum, yes, but he never invites me to his dinner parties."

"Does that still bother you?"

"Not any more. No. In fact, I'm glad to be free of that, to be able to invite to my home only people I really want to talk to, who may have interesting things to say, like you, Scaeva. You are the man of the hour, of course, I'm sure they're still drinking your health in every *taberna* in the city, but you're a Celt, a foreigner, and who knows if you are not wearing trousers under your toga, but don't expect to dine in any houses on the Palatine, you know."

"I don't," said Scaeva, "it matters nothing to me."

"I've enjoyed your friendship, Scaeva, and I'm glad to be just far enough from the best social circles that I've been able to talk to you and get to know your mind."

"That is mutual," Scaeva replied, "but I am a little unsettled by the valedictory tone you are using. Do you expect to lose my friendship?"

"I don't know what will happen," Cicero replied, "now that I've taken on this case. I'm sure of one thing, though: it will be my last case. It will cost me many friends, and it is more than possible that it will cost me my life. But I won't insult you, Scaeva, by explaining why I took the case, knowing what it might cost me. You may be the only man in Rome who can understand my reasons. My brother Quintus certainly doesn't."

The two men sat in silence for a moment, each lost in his own thoughts.

Cicero finally broke the silence. "You will testify against us, I know that. I also know that you will tell the plain truth. And you must know that I will have to discredit you somehow. As much as I like and respect you, my duty is to my clients, and you are a threat to them. I regret that very much."

"There is no need," said Scaeva. "I would expect nothing else from you, Cicero. I would be disappointed if you went easy on me for the sake of our friendship. But there are some aspects of my testimony that may surprise you. I can tell you nothing more now, it would not be right."

Again there was a moment of silence.

"But Cicero," said Scaeva, "you started to tell me why these men who really hated each other were able to make common cause to strike at Caesar."

"Oh yes," said Cicero, relieved at the change of subject. "I wandered from the topic, forgive me. I suppose I could say something about my age, but the truth is, I've always been easy to distract. Anyway, what brought things to a head were the rumors that Caesar was toying with the idea of having himself crowned king. Yes, of course, he kept on making public demonstrations that he had no such intentions, but how else to understand this new title he invented for himself, this Perpetual Dictator abomination? Once you have simply assumed unchallenged sovereign power in this way, what does it matter if you actually, physically, have a crown on your head? 'King,' *rex*, it's just a word. What Caesar held (holds, rather, if and when he recovers his health) is kingship, *regnum*, in every way except in name. No colleague to check him, no term of office that would leave him open to prosecution for abuse of power, and one by one he has even begun to assume the signs of kingship: he started wearing the maroon toga, he appeared inside the *pomerium* with 24 lictors rather than the 12 allowed by law to a consul, and there was that moment when he failed to stand when approached by a delegation of senators. He later tried to pass this off as absent-mindedness, but I was there. I saw the look on his face as he chose very deliberately not to rise from his seat."

"This is surely a small thing after all, whether a man sits or stands, or how many bodyguards he has with him."

"Yes, these seem small things when I mention them now, but in the context of so many other small things pointing in the same direction, it all becomes clear. The tyrants of the Greek cities, Pisistratus or Jason of Pherai, never appeared in public without their bodyguards. Our Roman lictors, to be sure, are appointed by law, but the rules that govern how many they shall be, and whom and when they attend, have all been devised in such a way as to prevent them from becoming a tyrant's bodyguard. When Caesar acts as though he and he alone will decide what the lictors do, then he is saying, 'I am greater than the law, the law limits others but it does not limit me.' In this way he could accustom us to the idea that his power does not come from the law, rather the law comes from his power. That there is no one in this great city or beyond its walls who can stand up and say, 'Caesar, this cannot be done.' And at that point, with or without a crown on his head, Caesar is a king.

"For the Pompeians, then, this was the fulfillment of their worst fears, the reason they had fought Caesar in the first place. That is obvious. But for many Caesarians, too, Caesar's flirtation with kingship was a shock, even a kind of betrayal. This was not what they'd fought for. If Caesar had told them before he crossed the Rubicon that he meant to be crowned king, I wonder how many would have followed him. Perhaps not too many. They had fought to put an end to the misgovernment of the Senate, and yes, to avenge a series of insults to a commander they had come to love and admire. And they expected to be rewarded generously for the blood they shed in his cause, yes, that too. But you see, once all the senatorial armies had been crushed, then the job they signed on to do had been done. Making Caesar king was not that job."

Scaeva shook his head. "I understand your reasoning, Cicero, and I'm beginning to understand theirs. I don't share, however, your antipathy to kings, on principle. Does not nature itself show us that the strongest individual must rule, or else all will die? If the wolves in a pack do not know which of them is the greatest, they will tear each other to pieces."

"That may be true of wild animals, Scaeva, and it may even be true of barbarians, but—oh, I am sorry!"

Scaeva laughed. "I am not ashamed of who I was or who I am, Cicero, I am not offended by the word 'barbarian.' Continue. You wanted to say, I think, that Romans are not wolves or barbarians and cannot be governed in the same way."

"Well, yes, exactly that."

"But who is more civilized than Plato, who writes in his *Republic* that no government could be finer than the absolute monarchy of a man possessed of true wisdom, founded on the knowledge of what is truly good? The only real argument against monarchy, in my view, is that birth to a royal family does not guarantee that a king will possess that wisdom. If we could solve that problem and make the wisest and best man in the state the absolute ruler of all, then who would want to live in any other state?"

"Are you claiming that Caesar is such a man?" Cicero protested. "Plato's philosopher-king? Is that why you are so peculiarly devoted to him? To be perfectly honest, I've often wondered about that."

Scaeva paused some time before he answered.

"I'm not sure that he is possessed of a wisdom superior to that of all other men, though on the other hand I'm also not sure, if you asked me to point out a man wiser than he, to whom I would point. The gods have given him every gift that a king should possess, and who else has enjoyed so much of their favor? What skill can do, Caesar has done, but he has never lacked for those divine favors some men call 'luck.' And if the gods seem to be telling us that Caesar is to be king, what will come of our resisting?"

"But Caesar follows Epicurus, which is to say, as you know, he doesn't even believe in the gods!"

"That's as may be, but what is more important is that the gods obviously believe in him. Have you ever wondered why I stood with him, alone, on the Ides of March?"

"Well yes, now that you mention it. I've always supposed that you were told to be there, though as usual we can only guess who told you.

Antony knew what was about to happen, and you would not have been necessary if he had planned things just a little better than he did. You were his second line of defense, I suppose, the only senator he could trust to keep quiet and perhaps the only one physically and mentally up to the job."

"No, it was not Antony. I knew there would be an attack on Caesar that day because the signs all pointed that way, and once I saw that it had begun, and no one else was there to stop it, it was clear what I had to do."

"'Signs,' you say? What, did you have a vision? a dream? a message from an oracle? I'm no atheist, Scaeva, as you know, no Epicurean, but on the other hand I don't believe the gods are carnival magicians. I wrote an essay on that, you know."

"I read it, Cicero, and in fact I agree with almost all of it. No, there were no dreams involved. I simply knew. Your Roman augurs try to read the future from the flight of birds, others from the entrails of slaughtered animals, but the signs I read are people. I saw that the gods mean to crown Caesar, even if he refuses to crown himself. And I knew that some, many even, would never be able to accept that, even at the cost of tearing down the Empire you and your ancestors have built. As for the Ides of March, well, the Senate was called that day to the Theater of Pompey, and if I were an assassin with political motives I could not choose a more fitting place for what you have called tyrannicide. And once I had reasoned this far, the sureness I felt within me was indeed a sign from the gods. From my British gods, I hasten to add. I am still a Briton at heart, even though I wear the toga and sit in the Senate."

"At least you wear that toga, Scaeva, not like some of those Gauls Caesar made into senators. Trousers in the Senate house! I never thought I'd live to see that. Not that I can object to Caesar making you a senator, of course. There are native-born Romans in the Senate, many of them, whose intelligence and sense of personal honor are no match for yours. But I have to admit I'm glad you dress like a Roman and talk like a Roman."

"That is high praise coming from you, I shall always try to be worthy of it."

The conversation drifted into other topics from that point, and neither man felt obliged to return to the problem of Caesar. It was very late when Scaeva rose and went home, later still before he fell asleep, pondering what he had heard.

The problem of what to do with his knowledge of what Brutus had really done—or rather, not done—on the Ides of March continued to occupy his thoughts for the days and weeks that followed until the trial actually began. He had said nothing to Cicero, who had avoided anything that might be understood as an attempt to influence his testimony, or even to find out in advance what he would say.

There was nothing to indicate that Brutus himself had told Cicero what Scaeva would have reluctantly declined to tell him. This was hardly surprising. To begin with, Brutus might feel ashamed of what many would take for cowardice. He might also have felt that he must share the fate of the men with whom he had conspired, without making any effort at all to distance himself from them. There were those who found Brutus something of a hypocrite, but Scaeva was not among them. He was sure that Brutus would willingly go to his death at the hands of the executioners rather than plead for any special consideration, the more so as he was probably ashamed of his lack of resolution.

He also said nothing to Pedius, who, to Scaeva's relief, did not ask him directly for a detailed account of his testimony. Cicero would not have made that mistake, in Pedius's place, but how many advocates were really a match for Cicero? Pedius was nervous and even frightened, anyone could see that, despite the strength of his case and the power wielded by those who had chosen him for this task. But either he did not know that Brutus had stayed his hand, or he knew, and didn't want the jury or anyone else to know. Certainly he had focused his main attack directly on Brutus.

The dilemma was excruciating. If Scaeva were to testify that Brutus had relented, had not struck a blow because he had held his hand of his own accord, then he would save him from a painful and humiliating death by public strangulation. But he would bring upon him another humiliation, one that Brutus himself clearly did not wish to endure. It would be quite another matter if Brutus were to claim that he had drawn no blood; then Scaeva's role would be simply to confirm the factual truth of this claim. But Brutus evidently wished everyone to think that he was one of the assassins, even one of the ringleaders, only prevented by sheer force from giving Caesar his death wound. This is how he wished to be remembered, and he would hardly thank the man who caused him to be remembered in a much less glorious light.

From Scaeva's point of view, of course, not using his dagger had been Brutus's noblest act. He had not wanted, finally, the murder of a friend and benefactor to be the culminating point of his life. Perhaps he had even recognized the will of the gods, as Scaeva himself had seen the divine will at work in the life and career of Caesar. If he had killed Caesar, Brutus would have been a martyr to the cause of a dying Republic, a greater martyr even than his father-in-law, Cato. He would have been true to his Stoic principles, not allowing personal attachment to take precedence over his duty. But he would have murdered a man who had shown him only kindness, and more, a man whom the gods had clearly chosen to transform Rome from an overgrown Italian city into the capital of a new world order. He would have murdered the world's last best chance for peace, not the peace that is merely the empty time between two wars, but a lasting peace that would enable the mass of men, perhaps for the first time ever, to go about their lives free of the fear of war.

That, at least, is what Scaeva wanted to believe. And he wanted to believe that Brutus had understood this, somehow, at the last minute, seen it in Caesar's eyes, understood that the kindness one human being shows to another is the highest principle of them all, and held his hand. And if neither Brutus nor Scaeva revealed the truth, no one would ever know it.

When, on the second day of the trial, Scaeva took the place designated for witnesses to give their testimony, he still did not know what he would do. He could only trust that the gods would tell him, finally, when the moment came, what to say, or what not to say.

Pedius

Pedius, as planned, asked only one question. "What did you see, and what did you do, on the Ides of March past?"

Scaeva told his story, clearly and simply, without undue elaboration, in his lightly accented but nearly impeccable Latin. He explained his reasons for coming armed to the meeting of the Senate without appeal to any metaphysical powers; he merely remarked that he was afraid someone would make an attempt on Caesar's life and came prepared to defend him, even though he knew he was breaking the law by bringing a weapon to a meeting of the Senate.

"We can only be glad you decided to break the law this time, Sulpicius Scaeva, since so many others broke the same law that day, for much lower purposes than yours."

This remark by Pedius won a general shout of approval from the *corona*. One particularly loud voice was heard over the noise: "Too bad he didn't kill all the bastards that day and have done with it!" Another shout of approval. Cassius looked scornful; Ligarius, Trebonius, and Casca seemed very uneasy; only Brutus acted as though he had heard nothing, his gaze seemingly fixed on some abstract point in the distance.

Scaeva completed his story by stating simply that two legionaries had seized Brutus from behind before he'd been able to strike. Pedius glanced at him to see if he would say more, but Scaeva merely shook his head slightly. He had made his decision. There was nothing more to be said. Pedius turned to the Praetor.

"I think, Lucius Antonius, that we have learned what we can about the events of the fateful Ides of March. I cannot conceive of what my opponent can possibly say in defense of his clients, knowing what we all know, but it is always a pleasure to hear the eloquence of Cicero, perhaps especially in a hopeless case."

There was some laughter at this sally, and even Cicero smiled. Inwardly he said, Pedius, if only you knew just how hopeless it is.

"There is little I can add," Pedius continued. "I shall not presume to add or detract from anything said here today, or even to comment on it further. The law is clear: whoso lays violent hands upon a Roman magistrate, thereby violates the majesty of the Senate and the People of Rome, and for that the penalty is death.

"You have heard witnesses today who have told you in great detail how these men brought arms to a meeting of the Senate, concealed in their document boxes, in shameless defiance of the laws and the *mos maiorum*, and when they had contrived to surround Caesar and push those not engaged in their plot too far away to interfere, they drew their weapons like so many hired assassins and struck. And were it not for the courage of the witness, Publius Sulpicius Scaeva, and the foresight of the consul Marcus Antonius, who sent guards to the Theater of Pompey, and surely above all the beneficence of the gods who have always kept Rome safe in the moments of greatest need, Caesar would surely have died that day.

"Not a word has been spoken to express even the slightest doubt that these five men were there, armed, and they actually wounded Caesar. No one here today believes for a moment, I think, that any of these men will rise to say, 'No, I wasn't there.'

"Now many a Roman jury, in this place, has been called upon to decide a case in which the law, its meaning and its application, is not entirely clear, or when different laws seem in a particular case to contradict each other. Many a jury has been asked to decide cases when the facts are in dispute. And there have even been cases when the law seemed ambiguous and the facts hard to ascertain.

"You may be grateful, *iudices*, that none of these things is true of the case before you. The law is clear, and the facts are manifest, no one disputes them in any significant respect. I am sure, then, that when you consider the gravity of the offense, the fact that the victim was a man in whom the Senate and the People of Rome have placed all their trust, and the manifest guilt of these men under a law whose terms are plain and clear, you will bring us the only verdict the entire city is waiting to hear: 'Guilty!'"

Pedius turned sharply on his heel and returned to his place. The *corona* erupted in a roar of applause, which washed over the court in waves. As the noise subsided, the Praetor turned to Cicero and beckoned. "Marcus Tullius, you may speak!"

Ordinarily, of course, even for a major trial that was expected to last for two or three days, the closing speech for the prosecution would have been followed on the same day by a response from the defense. But Cicero now asked to be allowed to postpone his opening speech, pleading the muggy afternoon heat in the Forum and the danger of more senators being overcome, and the Praetor, though clearly displeased, agreed.

In a lesser man, the delay might have been taken for a sign of weakness: Pedius had been far more eloquent than expected, the crowd had liked him, and the atmosphere when he finished was hardly favorable to the defendants. The prosecution testimony on the second day had not gone well, either. Pedius went after the Caesarian conspirators, Casca and Trebonius, with even greater effect, calling up witnesses who had fought alongside these men, but had not been inclined to join them in killing Caesar. The mood by the end of the day had been ugly, and no one was really surprised that even the courtroom magician himself, the "optimus omnium patronus," as Catullus had so wittily called him, "everybody's favorite lawyer," Marcus Tullius Cicero, was not eager to begin his defense in an atmosphere that threatened lynch.

But Cicero had spoken in such circumstances before, and no one was better than he at the art of changing the atmosphere around a client. And yes, there were times before when he had found it expedient to delay his remarks until the jury had had time to cool down. But he had sought the delay for more or less exactly the reason he had stated. He had seen many red faces in the jury, and emotion was only part of it. Ahenobarbus, for example, had looked as though he would drop dead at any moment, and that was a swing vote on this jury. His personal history during the civil war read rather like that of Brutus and Cassius—so much so, in fact, that his absence on the Ides of March had been commented. That is why Cicero made the tactical decision to ask for a delay, so that he could begin presenting his case the next day.

10

The Trial, Day 3

June 30, 44 B.C.

Rome, the Forum

As HE SAT WAITING for the praetor to appear to open the third day of the trial, Cicero thought over the speech he had prepared, briefly running through it one more time in his head. As usual, he had labored especially long over the first sentence. At the first lecture on rhetoric that Cicero attended in Rhodes, in his youth, his teacher Apollonius remarked, "You can never win with your first sentence, but you can certainly lose with it." Years of practice had confirmed the wisdom of that adage.

What do you do when you know, and everyone knows, that your clients are guilty?

This was not, of course, the first time that Cicero had defended someone who had actually performed the criminal deed with which he was charged. Eight years ago, to choose only the most notorious example, he had defended Titus Annius Milo, who never even tried to deny the truth of the charge that he had killed Clodius Pulcher, by his own hand.

It was not a case Cicero liked to remember, for several reasons. On the one hand, there were few men he had ever hated as much as he hated Clodius, so defending his murderer should have been a pleasure. But Milo was himself an unpleasant man, frightening even, and his account of how he and his "friends" had met Clodius and his "friends" on the Appian Way, a meeting which had ended with Clodius expiring on the street, had been chilling. In the end, Cicero had prepared a speech for Milo, but never delivered it, since riots had broken out; the lead defender had withdrawn in fear, and when Cicero tried to speak, even his fabled ability to tame an unruly crowd with his voice had not sufficed for him to make himself heard. He had finally resorted to publishing the speech he meant to give. As for Milo, he left that night for Massilia and that was that. At last report, he was still alive and living a comfortable life in the great port city of the province of southern Gaul.

A noise in the crowd, which seemed to begin in one place and spread, like the ripples in a pond when you've thrown a stone in the middle, interrupted Cicero's mental rehearsal of his speech. At first it seemed that someone important had arrived, but then the sound died back down.

In so many ways, Cicero thought, this day will end badly no matter what I say. It's not Antony I fear, certainly not Caesar, who, the rumors would have it, is out of his mind anyway, no threat to anyone. It's the crowds, the urban mob—yes, all right, the dungheap of Romulus. No, that's not a good metaphor any more, if it ever was: this may be a stinking, dirty mass, but it's a living thing, perhaps more alive now than ever before. Caesar has unchained a beast, riding its fury to victory over his enemies, but nothing indicates that he or anyone else really knows how to keep this beast from tearing us all apart.

Precisely as Plato had predicted in the *Republic*: the demagogues rouse the beast, the *demos*, stoke its fury, but lose control over it, until a man appears, the *tyrannos*, who is strong enough to put it back in its cage. But when he does, the last traces of freedom in the city are gone: all who are left alive become the slaves of this one man, who is the slave of his own appetites.

He looked around at the guards, who formed a single line separating the seething human mass of the *corona* from the court itself and the special seating area for senators. How long would they hold, he wondered, if the mob decided to storm the Rostra and lynch the defendants? To the count of ten, maybe, maybe not that long. And if riots were to break out, as they had after Milo was allowed to leave the city in voluntary exile, how many legions would it take to restore order? Would the legionaries actually pull their swords and slash at people very like themselves, perhaps their own friends and family, in order to defend people like him?

Brutus suddenly turned to him, interrupting his gloomy speculations.

"We haven't a chance, have we?" he said, in much the same voice he would have used to say, "My, it's hot today, isn't it?"

"It's by far not the worst jury we could have gotten."

"It's not the jury," Brutus replied, "it's *them*. All they're waiting for is the verdict: if it's guilty, they'll wait a few days, perhaps, to see us strangled, but if we're found innocent, they'll tear us to pieces themselves, and the jury as well, and you, and at least half of these noble senators, don't you think? Maybe all of them."

Was there anything to be gained by dissembling? "Actually, I was just thinking the same thing, or at least I had reached very nearly the same conclusion, perhaps by a longer road."

"So we will die today, perhaps tomorrow, the day after at the latest, and it will not be a pleasant death, one way or the other. But you could still save yourself. If the jury votes to condemn us, the crowd will let the law have its way with us, and you can go home. It wouldn't be your first defeat, would it? Milo comes to mind. In any event, you will have done your duty by us, but unfortunately you were not able to save us. Who could reproach you? All you have to do is—"

Cicero broke in with more anger than he had realized he was feeling. "And I could have avoided the whole problem by not taking your case in the first place. Do you think I'm that big a fool, that I didn't know what I was facing? If I win, the crowd will kill us all. If I lose, it will be the greatest failure of my life, the one case for which I shall be remembered for hundreds of years to come. But to refuse the case would be an act of cowardice that would also be remembered. One way or the other, either my life ends, or it loses all meaning. And you did this to me."

"I'm sorry. Truly. But tell me the truth: if I hadn't sent for you, hadn't asked you to defend us, wouldn't that have been for you the final insult? The *novus homo* from Arpinum, put in his place at last by the patrician Marcus Junius Brutus?"

"Yes, yes, yes, I've thought of that, too." It hurt to admit this, but it was undeniably true. "We neither of us actually had any good choices, did we?"

"Depends on what you expect. What a 'good' choice would be. We will all die anyway, so what does it matter if it's today, or in a week, a month, a year. You've said that yourself, in your *Tusculan Disputations*. Fine piece of work, that, by the way. I just can't make it out, why you resist acknowledging that you're a Stoic at heart."

"Because I'm not a Stoic."

"Oh, yes, you are. But no matter. My point is, if being a philosopher means anything at all, it means that you spend your life preparing to die. My time has come, I'm quite sure of that. I knew it the night Cassius came to my house and told me what he had in mind. He was asking me to help him murder a man who has never been anything but kind to me, a man who was more a father to me in my childhood than that old man Junius Brutus ever was."

"I thought you put no stock in all that gossip. I never did."

"You mean about him sleeping with my mother? That he's really my father? No, I don't believe that. Well, yes, of course, he did sleep with my mother, I know that, but only later, when my father was dead and I was already in the world. But all my father ever did for me was to put his seed inside my mother's belly. I was eight when Pompey killed him at Mutina."

"I've wondered, you know, how you could have seen your way fit to support the man who killed your father. It's hardly a model of *pietas*. No one could have blamed you for taking Caesar's side. I have friends who did so for less reason."

"You're thinking of Caelius Rufus, I suppose."

Cicero didn't answer, and after a moment Brutus continued.

"I had more reason than you know. When I was ten years old and needed a man to tell me how to be a man, or really *show* me how to be a man, that was Caesar. My uncle tried, he even adopted me later, as I think you know, but it was never the same. Caesar filled the house when he was there.

"One day he walked into the room just as I was about to hit a slave who'd tripped over a chair and dropped my supper on the floor. He grabbed my wrist in mid-air and held me, so hard, I can still feel his fingers. I was furious. How could he humiliate me like that in front of a slave? But I was helpless, and his strength frightened me so much I couldn't speak. When he spoke to me, though, he was neither kind nor angry, just reasonable, like a teacher with a dull student. He asked me, 'If you beat a slave, what happens? What do you get?' And I said, 'Well he won't do that again, will he?' And then he explained to me, that yes, the slave would be more careful in the future, to avoid that beating. But he would hate me all the time while he was serving me, and if the day ever came when he could pay me back for that beating without anyone knowing about it, he would do it. We can't make slaves love us, but the house where the slaves hate the master is not a happy house. I've never forgotten that lesson.

"But after Pharsalus I had to think about it all over again. After Pharsalus I was the slave who dropped the master's dinner, and the master . . .

refrained from beating me. And I was grateful. But it didn't stop me from trying to kill him, did it? Does that make me worse than a slave?"

"Better, I should think," Cicero replied. "You did what you had to do for a higher good, something that took precedence over both the wrongs that Pompey did your family, and the favors Caesar did you personally. A slave has no principles but his own survival and comfort, he's petted when he does well and beaten when he does poorly and that's all he knows."

"A higher good . . .".

Their conversation was interrupted by the bustle that preceded the appearance of the *praeco*, and then the praetor, on the podium. The formalities were quickly performed, and then the moment came for Cicero to speak. He mounted the Rostra, as he had so many times before, slowly and deliberately. This had always been his advice to inexperienced speakers: "You must take your place as though it were your own place. Never let yourself be hurried. Let them feel that you are in control of the place, of yourself, that you and you alone will decide when to speak."

When he reached his place on the Rostra, then, Cicero bowed his head for a moment, as though gathering his thoughts (though in reality he was simply counting to ten, slowly, in his head), before he lifted his head, scanned the crowd with his eyes, willing them to quiet, and finally opened his mouth to release the words he had prepared, resting his eyes on the jury and turning his body slightly to face them squarely, as though deliberately turning away from both the assembled senators and the corona.

"Gentlemen of the jury!"

He had considered the placement of the word *iudices* in that all-important first sentence for some time. It was not his practice, as nearly everyone knew, to begin with the vocative, addressing the intended audience directly; the word usually occurred as an insertion after the first phrase or clause. It was a formal necessity in a trial, just as one had to say "*Quirites*" when speaking to the citizen body, or "Conscript fathers" when addressing the Senate. Odd, when you thought about it: no one really knew why you had to say "Quirites" and not just "citizens," just as no one really knew why the "fathers" of the Senate were "conscript" (or was it "fathers and conscripts," as some people liked to say?).

But *iudices*, "gentlemen of the jury," was quite an ordinary word, no special meaning here, at least until today. That was the whole point of this trial, that it was a pretext for solving a whole range of political problems of far greater importance than the fate of these five men, noble as they were. Everyone knew what was at stake. Still, the appearances of a criminal trial had to be preserved, though Antony, in his extraordinary address at the opening, two days before, had already trampled on convention.

What Cicero needed, however, if he had a ghost of a chance, was for the jury, the "*iudices*," to think of themselves as the embodiment, for this moment, of the Civil Law, the *ius civile*, and not as politicians. They were not an Athenian jury listening to a demagogue, who would know how to make them laugh, or cry, or scream with rage, but Roman senators and equestrians, men who knew the law and (mostly, most of the time) lived according to it. Not that appeals to emotion were pointless. Far from it. Cicero knew as well as any, and better than most, how to stamp his foot and wave his fist, when the moment was right. But you couldn't start with that, not even in Athens. Only once, during his own consulship, that day in early November almost twenty years ago, when Catiline had had the nerve to appear in the Senate as though nothing were out of the ordinary, had Cicero begun an important speech on a high note. It worked then, but he never did it again. There are certain tricks you can only use once.

So he had decided to put the vocative, *iudices*, in the place where no one expected it, precisely to call attention to this word, which usually passed as a formula. He was playing off against the expectation of his listeners that the speech would open in "Ciceronian" style, with an elegant, almost musical sentence, flowing and rhythmic.

Playing with expectations was a tricky business. The Athenian orators, Aeschines, Demosthenes, Lysias, began most of their speeches by claiming not to be eloquent, to have no experience in making speeches, to be simple men who could only use simple words to express simple ideas. It was very clever, turning the eloquence of the opponent into a weapon against him, making him look like someone dangerous and dishonest, the more so, the more persuaded they had been by him. But the Athenians could get away with this maneuver precisely because they wrote most of their speeches for others, their clients, to deliver. If Demosthenes himself had stood up and said, "I am a simple man of simple words, I just don't know how to make great speeches," it would have been ludicrous.

So Cicero could not allow himself to use the "simple man of simple words" gambit, though of course neither could he say, "Greetings, mortals! I am the god of oratory, prepare to be enchanted!" His advice to beginners was always the same: "Know what your audience expects to hear. Don't give them exactly that, ever, because they will simply go to sleep on you. But you can't just disregard those expectations, either; they'll either be hopelessly confused, or they'll take you for an idiot, or even worse, they'll think you think they're idiots. You have to know when to soothe them, and when to surprise them."

So here he was, surprising them with the very first word: "*Iudices!*"

He paused for a moment, letting the effect work for a moment before he resumed. This was an essential skill for delivery: knowing just how often, and how long, to pause for effect. If the pauses were too short and too few, the audience would drown in a sea of words; if they were too many or too long, no one would remember, when the sentence ended, how it had begun. "You can't let them drown, and you can't let them float. You have to make them swim, and then you show them the shore they need to swim to." It was a good metaphor, which he often used in conversation, though it had always seemed too facetious to use in one of his essays on rhetoric.

So he drew another breath, never dropping his gaze from the jury, and continued.

"It is no easy matter, here, in the presence of nearly the entire Senate, and so distinguished a representation of equestrians, and so many Roman citizens gathered in the Forum that the streets of our great city must be nearly empty, to bear in mind that we have come here to this place today, not to settle matters of public policy, not to celebrate a triumph or mourn a defeat, not to declare war or make peace, but to hear a case at law.

"Yesterday, my worthy opponent, Quintus Pedius, ever so eloquently made the case before you that these five men—in league with others, who for various reasons are not present on the defendants' bench today—attempted to assassinate a Roman magistrate, which is an offense against the majesty of the Roman people and as such is punishable by death. The matter seems so simple, that one might well have wondered if there was really any need for further deliberation. Perhaps I am wasting my time, and yours, as though I were arguing that the sun shines at midnight and not at noon, when the time has come to mete out punishment to the guilty."

At this there was a growing murmur from the *corona*, a wave of noise, but Cicero, who was taking a calculated risk here, was pleased to note that no one in the jury was nodding.

"If this were Athens, judges, and not Rome, if you were all shopkeepers and farmers chosen by lot to reach a verdict, with no understanding of the law, unknowingly at the mercy of whatever demagogue might know how to rouse your passions, or soothe them, at his will, then no doubt these five men would not be here today; their bodies would be on public display, their necks showing the traces of the hangman's garrote."

Another risky move, but again, it seemed to have paid off. Some of the judges were clearly discomfited by the unsightly images he had deliberately conjured up in their heads. Cicero, like any great speaker, was adept at reading the faces, even the movements of his listeners, how they frowned or smiled, sat straight or slouched, spoke to each other or kept quiet, were calm or fidgety. He had them, at least some of them, enough of them to start with, about where he wanted them. They needed to feel how difficult their situation actually was, and then, just as they despaired, he would show them a way out.

"But if the Republic created by our forebears, by Junius Brutus and Collatinus and the entire Senate that drove out the Tarquins and resolved never to let another king rule this city, means anything at all, it means that the law is our monarch. If the Greeks gave the world so much that is wise and beautiful, still, they never understood that civilized life without the preeminence of law over the desires of men, of one man, of a few, or of many, cannot thrive or even survive. Sooner or later the beast will bite off the slender bonds of mere culture and run wild through the city, ripping apart those who try to resist, hunting down those who try to hide.

"What we Romans know, and will teach the whole world, is that only the firm hand of law can tame the beast, transform the wolf into a watchdog, and allow us to live free of fear. And that is the one freedom without which all other freedoms are just so many empty words.

"That is why we are here today, because no case is ever so simple that the law does not allow both sides to speak, and honorable men to decide which of them is right.

"Quintus Pedius produced his witnesses yesterday, to tell us all precisely what we already knew. Who in this city can pretend to have any doubts? On the Ides of March, a group of senators, among whom were these five men, drew daggers at a meeting of the Senate and attacked one of the sitting consuls, C. Julius Caesar, gravely wounding him, and would have killed him if they had not been prevented. Doubtless, if Pedius had been given another day, he would have produced witnesses to swear before the court that the Appian Way runs south and east from Rome to Brundisium, or that cocks have been known to crow at dawn."

It never hurts to elicit a laugh at your opponent's expense. You can't seem to be mean. It can't appear that your sole purpose in speaking is to ridicule and humiliate your opponent. The tactic does not work nearly so well if the opponent has shown that he knows how to laugh at himself; indeed, one can appear like an incompetent gladiator, who hits so hard against his opponent's shield that the sword arm bounces back and wounds the attacker. Cicero himself knew how to avoid slashing his own face: if an opponent made fun of him, and many of them tried, he would laugh as hard as anyone present, as though he were thoroughly enjoying the good joke. It also meant, of course, that he was not wounded by it, and that was the best possible outcome.

He had initially underestimated Pedius, and the quality of his speech the day before had come as an unpleasant surprise. But he had seen the Achilles' heel: like many ambitious young men, Pedius took himself far too seriously. The laughter angered him, and he showed it. A serious mistake.

"No doubt you have all been wondering, 'What will Cicero say?' From the most elegant homes in this city to the lowest taverns, that question no doubt took up a good part of the evening. 'What will Cicero say?'

"What shall I say? What indeed? Perhaps I should have been walking the streets last night in disguise, looking for ideas, or at least for a few good phrases. Perhaps it was a waste of my time, to sit in my house alone and ponder the state of our Republic, how it grew from a small town whose walls could all be seen from the place where I now stand, to the capital city of an Empire that stretches from one end of the known world to the other, from the cold, dark forests of Gaul to the sun-baked sands of Egypt, on either side of the sea that occupies the very middle of the earth.

"So let me tell you, here and now, what I shall not say.

"I shall not say that these men were not present in the Theater of Pompey on the Ides of March this year, or that they did not have daggers in their hands, or that they did not strike Gaius Caesar with the intent to kill him.

"I shall not say, as many doubtless expect me to say, that my clients, in raising their hands against Gaius Julius Caesar, were merely fulfilling the role the gods have given to the Senate of Rome, to allow no king to rule our city, that Brutus here was simply . . . being a Brutus."

This, predictably, caused another wave of noise to rise from the *corona* and roll over the Forum. Cicero waited patiently for it to subside.

"I shall not say these things, for the simple reason that Gaius Caesar on many occasions, publicly and privately, refused to even consider the possibility of becoming king. He refused, even when the priests consulted the old books and proclaimed that only a Roman king can defeat the

Parthians. He refused the crown offered him during the Lupercalia, three times, and we were all witnesses of that."

Here the merest of glances at Antony, the man who, as everyone remembered, had actually approached Caesar with a diadem in his hand.

"Some may say, I am sure, that Caesar was being unduly modest, or even disingenuous, hiding his true inclinations. But I know the man, I have known him for many years, sometimes on the same side of the growing division in our Republic, sometimes, regrettably, on opposite sides. He is above all an honest man, not a man who said whatever he thought the people in front of him wanted him to say, and then said the exact opposite to the next group of people he met. If he said he did not want to be king, I believe him."

The uncomplimentary allusion to Pompey would perhaps have been lost on the *corona*, but those who counted, the men in the jury, also knew very well that Pompey was a man who always said "Yes" to your face and then did exactly what he wanted as soon as you were gone. Cicero had never viewed Pompey as anything more than the lesser of two evils, a fact which most of those present knew well. It was useful to remind them of it now. He could not let himself be seen, just at this moment, as an unrepentant Conservative.

"Now if I were a schoolboy learning rhetoric, and the master had given me an assignment similar to the task to face today, I might be tempted to make such an argument. I would talk about Harmodius and Aristogeiton, the Athenian tyrannicides, I would trot out all my reading in the philosophers who discuss the ethics of tyrannicide. I would ask, 'what is a tyrant?', and I would answer, 'a man who seizes power in the state by force, usurping the legitimate authorities,' and then I might complete the syllogism by saying, 'Caesar seized power in Rome, overthrowing the rule of the Senate and suspending elections of magistrates by the people, therefore he is a tyrant, and, since that is so, tyrannicide would be morally and legally defensible.'"

The murmuring grew into a roar of disapproval, and the moment was touchy; tension had appeared on the faces of many jurors. This line of argument clearly made them very uncomfortable, especially those who privately thought exactly this way. Cicero could only hope that his clients, sitting behind him where he could not see them, had the good sense not to show any particular reaction. He had coached them the day before, mainly to sit very quietly, as though paying careful attention to everything he said, but without showing any particular reaction, positive or negative. He had warned them that there would be moments when such passivity would be difficult, but for many reasons he hadn't told them what exactly he would say. They hadn't asked.

Cicero began shaking his head and waving his arm, as a man who has been seriously misunderstood. When the level of noise subsided to the point where he thought the jurors could hear him, he continued.

"But I am not a schoolboy, and this is not Greece, where the palm of victory is always given to those who make the cleverest arguments, regardless of the truth. I have already said that I do not believe Caesar wished to be king, and though the Greeks may find it useful to draw a distinction between a king and a tyrant, we Romans do not. If I say that Caesar does not wish and never wished to be king, I have said that he does not wish and never wished to be the sole ruler of this Empire, and it would be a tautology to say that he is not, in word or deed, a tyrant."

On the last nine words of this sentence, which he had crafted so carefully, he raised his voice to its full carrying power. This speech as a whole was not addressed to the *corona*, that was true, even obvious, but Cicero was not foolish enough to suppose that they could be ignored. They did not need to hear everything he said. They would understand little, and of that little, there was a great deal they would surely not like. But he had to give them, from time to time, something they liked, as a boy surrounded by a pack of barking dogs might throw a bone or a scrap of food, hoping the dogs would turn their attention away long enough to let him escape.

The trick seemed to have had the desired effect. The murmuring continued, but there were now some shouts of approval, and the level of hostile noise went down somewhat. The beast was far from tamed, but it was at least temporarily mollified.

"It may seem otiose," he resumed, deliberately using the recondite word "otiose" to make it clear that he had no intention of pandering to the crowd he had just managed to (partially) appease, "to rehearse here and now events that we all remember, indeed too well. It will not be possible otherwise, however, to understand the argument I will make on behalf of these five men, that they should not be made sacrificial victims to expiate the guilt of us all.

"I have no doubt that generations to come will ponder the sequence of events that led to the outbreak of civil war, five years and six months ago. Where to begin? Which is to say, where shall we place the cause of this conflict, which left hardly a home in all of Italy untouched by grief?

Was Sulla to blame? or Marius? the Gracchus brothers, or those who slew them? Who can say? This is not the time and place to speak of such things, better left to our children and their children to determine. In the midst of events, as we have been and still are, no one can see where it will end, and that, judges, makes it nearly impossible to determine where it began.

"Towards the end of December, in the consulship of Lucius Aemilius Lepidus Paullus and Gaius Claudius Marcellus, the Senate formally ordered Gaius Julius Caesar to disband his legions and report to Rome, unarmed, thereby implicitly refusing his request to be allowed to stand for the consulship *in absentia* during the next year. Various were the reasons given by Caesar for his request, various were the reasons that led the Senate to first accept it, then reject it. Be that as it may, the decision of the Senate, as I think we all understood at the time, was a decision for war. If the Senate in those days included any senators who actually believed that Caesar would meekly submit, having at his back the legions that had conquered Gaul, they were surely few in number. I was there, most of you were there, there is little use pretending that the Senate did not declare war on Caesar, even if the words were not spoken, the consuls were not ordered to make ready for war. It was not necessary to do so; the consuls, together with Pompey, then dictator in all but name, were already doing so.

"What we did not know, and should have known—for who among us did not read with interest the commentaries Caesar wrote on his conquest of Gaul?—is that Caesar would not wait for the spring, for his legions to gather, before he moved. In the middle of January, when winter rains were still falling and the mountain roads were still blocked by snow, Caesar crossed the border of his province, in defiance of an order he considered illegal, and Rome was at war—with itself.

"Is there anyone here who does not remember?"

11

The Rubicon

January, 49 B.C.E.

Rome

ON A COLD, RAINY morning, 17 days into the ill-fated consulship of the elder Marcellus and Lentulus Crus, a messenger arrived at Cicero's remarkably modest home on the slopes of the Caelian Hill.

The home had been carefully chosen. Fifteen years ago, when he had bought it, other, even more fashionable properties had been available, but Cicero knew what he wanted: a pleasant but not extravagant residence, from which he could walk to the Forum, but situated on the opposite slope of the hill, facing the Servian wall, away from the center of the city. Near the center, but not at the center. It was an apt metaphor, he often thought, for his position in the social and political life of this city.

His aged father, now dead, had urged him to buy a more "suitable" residence on the Palatine Hill, three years after his consulship. Crassus, for reasons Cicero had never fully understood, had made him a very reasonable offer to sell an impressive residence, so in the end he had given way to his father's arguments and his wife's pleading. But he had not sold the Caelian house to do it, and in recent years he'd preferred to spend most of his time in his first town home. This location was perfect. No small part of its charm, to be perfectly honest, was that Terentia refused to leave the Palatine villa, ever. Her husband was an infrequent, unwilling, and probably unwelcome guest there.

The message bore the seal of Pompey, and a very short text: a summons, not to the Senate this time, but to Pompey's home on the Esquiline

Hill. The messenger, a centurion, then informed Cicero that an escort of soldiers was outside. The matter must have been exceptionally urgent, so he dressed hastily and left with his escort.

The trip didn't take long, and the way was simple, along and just inside the Servian wall. The streets were largely empty, but the hour was still early and there was no reason to find the quiet remarkable, especially in this area, where there were very few shops or workshops of any kind. From here, if one wished to buy something, or to amuse oneself of an evening, it was better to go south and west to the Aventine, or north and west into the Suburra. That was something Cicero never did if he could avoid it; the noise and smells generated by so much humanity milling about in such a confined space were precisely what drove him to his country estates, especially Tusculum, as often and for as long as possible.

Over the years, Cicero had been in Pompey's house on the Esquiline no more than three or four times. He'd been Pompey's champion for almost 20 years, through many difficult periods, but in all that time he'd never seen the slightest indication of any personal affection from this man, or even any personal interest. Pompey had his friends, but Cicero was never among them, though there had been times when he wanted to be. The year after his consulship, he had expected Pompey to say something, anything, to indicate that he understood the importance of Cicero's suppression of Catiline, which occurred while Pompey was still off in the East, adding new provinces to the Empire. But in the Senate, when asked directly what he thought about the events of the previous year, Pompey had managed to grunt a few words to the effect that Cicero had "done well," using the tone and the language a general uses when he has decided that a lackluster but acceptable performance by a subordinate is not going to be punished, this time. When Clodius had attacked Cicero, several years later, by bringing the bill that would lead to a year in exile, Pompey had done nothing. When the act was repealed and Cicero had come home, it had been necessary to thank Pompey, but the truth was, there was really nothing to thank him for. He had, at best, declined to hinder those who were trying to have Cicero recalled, just as he had declined to hinder Clodius a year earlier. Thanking him publicly was not one of the moments Cicero liked to remember from his career.

Now Pompey was the man of the hour. He was not consul or proconsul, but he was the man everyone looked to whenever any important decision was to be made. The actual consuls, Marcellus and Lentulus Crus, simply took their orders from him as though it were the most natural thing in the world. There had been talk, when the crisis with Caesar seemed to have grown inevitable, of naming him dictator, but he had brushed the idea aside, and it was a mark of his real power that no one even mentioned the topic again.

To be sure, Pompey had used Cicero in a last effort to resolve matters with Caesar, but even then there had been little personal contact: Cicero wrote letters to Caesar, received answers, sent them with his comments to Pompey, and then waited for the latter to tell him how to respond. It had been most unsatisfactory, the more so, as his own advice and comments had been completely ignored. What became manifestly clear from the whole correspondence was that Caesar was negotiating in good faith, ready to make compromises to avoid confrontation, in contrast to Pompey, who was only pretending to negotiate, while all the time trying in every way to provoke Caesar into making the first hostile move.

Cicero had to admit, at least privately, that Caesar's position was not unreasonable, under the circumstances. True, in an ideal republic he should have obeyed the Senate's orders, disbanded his legions, and come to Rome as a private citizen, if he wished to stand for the consulship, for which he was legally eligible: the mandatory interval of ten years had gone by, so there was nothing in custom or law that would prevent this. But Caesar's enemies had already prepared prosecutions against him on many charges, and that meant, not so much that they had prepared evidence and marshaled arguments against him, but that they had fixed the courts to make sure that Caesar would be facing, not a trial, but an officially sanctioned lynch. No one on either side of the increasingly savage debates had much doubt about that.

According to Quintus Cicero, who had better sources close to Pompey than his brother Marcus did, Pompey was most pleased with himself. He had maneuvered his way out of the arrangements previously made with Caesar, and positioned himself as the champion of the Senate, the law, the *mos maiorum*, which meant that Caesar could either submit (in which case Pompey would simply sit quietly and allow his former father-in-law's many enemies to devour him) or take arms against Rome itself. In that event, he would finish like Lepidus, Sertorius, Catiline: an outlaw, who would do best to fall in battle or commit suicide, since otherwise he would die miserably on a cross, with the same common people whose cause he affected to champion watching him die and laughing at his agony.

Cicero had long realized what Pompey was driving at, why he needed to force Caesar to make the first overt move, which in turn explained why he found it . . . say, inconvenient to make any concrete preparations for a military response just at this moment. Caesar was now in winter camp at Ravenna, the southernmost city in his province, with a single legion. By the time he could bring enough legions across the Alps to make up a respectable army (and assuming they would all follow him into civil war and certain destruction, which seemed highly unlikely), it would be summer, or even autumn, and by that time, if Caesar was still in defiance of the Senate's orders and was openly gathering troops, there would be time to declare him *hostis*, a public enemy, and then raise an army of Pompey's own loyal veterans, who would flock to his legionary eagles as soon as he raised them. It couldn't be done now, however, because Caesar, though technically in violation of an order, hadn't yet broken any law. The smart thing to do, then, was to provoke him into revealing his intention to fight in a such an obvious and public way that a forceful response would seem to result, not from Pompey's personal ambition, but from prudent public policy.

But Pompey was not a reader. His public persona was always that of a gruff, no-nonsense soldier, with no time for trifles, and even privately he was not much given to reading. He had not read Caesar's many, ample reports from his Gallic campaign, which had been widely circulated around the city; when asked, he had merely said that his father-in-law seemed to be in control of the situation, though, he had intimated, he would have handled things differently himself.

But Cicero had read the commentaries from Gaul, all of them, as they became available. And he knew what Pompey apparently did not: Caesar had won most of his battles in Gaul before the first blow was struck, by managing to appear suddenly when the enemy was quite sure he was still far away, putting them off balance and forcing them to fight when and where he wanted the fight to take place.

Pompey, to be sure, had never lost a battle. But anyone who looked closer at the records, as Cicero had, would soon realize that Pompey had never really faced an enemy who challenged him both strategically and tactically. There was some truth to the bitter accusation made almost a decade earlier by old Lucullus, whom Pompey had replaced as general in charge of the campaign against Mithridates, King of Pontus: that this "Pompeius Magnus," Pompey the Great, was a great vulture, swooping in at just the right moment to devour victims already killed by others.

For some time, Cicero had watched with growing despair as the Republic had been reduced to a plaything over which two bullies, so to speak, were about to have it out. It actually made little difference now, which of them won. His young friend, Caelius Rufus, had spelled it out last September in a letter, with remarkable clarity: there would be war within a year, at the very latest, Rufus wrote, and the winner would take everything. He had also ventured some unpleasantly blunt but remarkably apt advice: "When it's just politics, among civilians, I follow my conscience, but when the swords come out, I'm going to look for the winner."

In fact, Cicero had only just arrived in Rome the previous November from his year and a half as governor of Cilicia, in Asia Minor, a task he had neither sought nor welcomed, but had not refused. Caelius had kept him informed of doings in the capital during his absence, in letters filled with delightful malice. Still, he had assumed, wrongly, that his young friend and former client had been exaggerating in his description of the looming crisis. Caelius was like that, a man of strong emotions, inclined to see things in very bright or very dark colors. But when he returned and saw things for himself, Cicero quickly realized that any hope for some kind of a peaceful resolution had dwindled to the merest of flickers. His epistolary efforts to mediate had produced no results so far, and now this peremptory summons from Pompey did not bode well.

It looked even worse when he arrived with his military escort at Pompey's house, to find his host already dressed in his uniform, surrounded, not by senators in togas like himself, but by officers.

When he finally managed to make his presence known to Pompey, his fears and suppositions were confirmed.

"Caesar has crossed the Rubicon in force and is marching on Rome."

"I thought he had only one legion with him in Ravenna," Cicero protested.

"That's what we all thought. Apparently he brought up more forces without our knowing about it, though I can't think how the devil he did it. At any rate, I've got nothing in the field to put against him right now. I'm headed south, and I'm ordering—no, strongly suggesting—that the Senate follow my lead. But I haven't got the time to go to the Senate myself and explain it all to that gaggle of geese in togas, too late for that. So here's what I need from you. I've instructed the consuls to convene the Senate today, as soon as possible, and I want you to use all your eloquence to convince them that they've got to leave the city now, today if possible, tomorrow at the latest. And I'll need a declaration that Gaius Julius Caesar is now *hostis*, an enemy of the state, and that I am empowered to take command of all Rome's armies to defeat and destroy him."

"But how can we do that?" Cicero objected. "The consuls are the commanders-in-chief, you're a private citizen, the declaration of martial law only empowers consuls-"

Pompey exploded in the way only generals can allow themselves to explode. "There's a war on, you jackass, and I don't have the time for all this legal shit! I don't give a donkey fart how you do it, just do it!"

Cicero stepped back—and immediately regretted it. No doubt he looked as though he were thoroughly intimidated by this profane outburst, but he was not. Pompey thought of Cicero, obviously, as the purest of civilians and thus a man of no real character. He had misjudged, but this was pretty much to be expected. Whatever his actual merits, Pompey was no judge of character.

"I shall do what my duty requires in this extraordinary situation." Without waiting for a reply, he turned his back on Pompey and walked out with all the dignity he could muster.

"But can I count on you?" Pompey called out from behind him.

Cicero did not reply.

There had been a time when he would have imagined this meeting with Pompey very differently. After Cicero returned in triumph from his exile, cheered on the streets in every Italian town he passed through on his way to Rome, he had seen an opportunity to drive a wedge between Pompey and Caesar, with some help from Crassus. He had been heavily engaged in making sure that Pompey (after all, a protégé of Sulla) would awaken from his peculiar infatuation with Caesar and assert himself as the natural leader of the Conservatives. But then, just a year after his return, in the consulship of Lentulus Marcellinus and Marcius Phillipus, Caesar had come as far south as Lucca in Tuscany, near the southern boundary of his province, and invited his disaffected partners to a meeting.

More than half the Senate went north with Pompey and Crassus. Cicero did not. There were those naive enough to believe that Pompey was going to Lucca to put the upstart Caesar in his place. But Cicero knew better. By that time he had come to realize how important Pompey's marriage to Caesar's daughter Julia actually was. For all his Conservative credentials, Pompey was not by birth a member of the inner elite of the Senate, and the fact that he had begun his career as Sulla's protégé in fact argued more against him than for him, especially since he'd commanded armies for Sulla without ever having held the magisterial office that law and tradition required. Realizing that Sulla was deeply hated, personally, on both sides of the political division in the Senate, Pompey made common cause with Crassus, his colleague in his first consulship, to begin the process of dismantling the more unpopular of Sulla's "reforms." It had been naive of him to suppose that this would win him friends in the Senate: the Populists still didn't trust him, while the Conservatives, though most of them hated Sulla for the bloodshed which made them all feel implicated in murder, didn't want to see his legislation repealed.

Throughout his career, in fact, Pompey had vacillated between fawning servility towards the inner circle of the Senate and unabashed bullying. The marriage to Caesar's daughter had brought patrician blood into his family line, just as, ironically, it brought him a measure of popularity on the streets. And those same senators who had once snubbed him repeatedly, publicly and privately, now stood meekly in line "to kiss his plebeian ass," as Caelius Rufus had put it, salty as always.

To Cicero's disgust, it had become increasingly clear that Pompey, at this point, had everything he ever really wanted. The harder Cicero tried to get closer to him, hoping to play on their shared status as the scions of Italian (not native Roman) aristocracy, the more Pompey avoided him. Instead of joining forces with Cicero to save the Senate and the Roman people essentially from themselves, as the times so clearly demanded, Pompey had contented himself with resurrecting the almost forgotten *agnomen* Magnus, "Great," that Sulla had conferred on him after his return from the campaigns in Sicily and Africa.

It said much about Pompey, Cicero reflected bitterly, that he had never grasped the irony of Sulla's name for him, never understood how ridiculous he had been made to seem then, as a young man, strutting around calling himself "Magnus" while the senators all laughed up their sleeves. Now no one was laughing; but it was fear, not respect, that kept their faces straight, and the fear was not even so much fear of Pompey's own power, but of Caesar's. The meeting at Lucca had made it perfectly clear to everyone, or nearly everyone, which of these two men actually knew exactly what he wanted and exactly how to get it. In a letter to Atticus, written in October of that year, Cicero had freely confessed: "You ask me why I defended that scum Vatinius, of all people. The answer, I'm afraid, is very simple. I'm beaten. It's time to furl my sails and turn downwind. The game is over and I lost. May the gods help us all."

Even a few years later, when the death of Julia in childbirth, and then the death of Crassus in Syria had converted the relatively stable "triumvirate" into a very unstable rivalry between Pompey and Caesar, Cicero had seen little point in getting himself involved. Caelius Rufus was after all not far from the truth: one of these two men was going to destroy the Republic and become king, in fact if not in name, and it really mattered little which one.

Now the crisis he had seen coming all this time was at hand. And he had no idea what to do. How do you play out the game when the dice are loaded and you've already lost all your money?

He returned home to find another messenger waiting for him, this time with an official summons to attend an extraordinary meeting of the Senate. He didn't even bother to go inside, but read the message in the street and set out immediately for the Temple of Concord in the Forum, where the meeting had been called. Along the way he met up with a number of senators, whose anxious faces betrayed the fact that they, too, had either heard the news or surmised it from the summons itself. The merest of courtesies were exchanged; no one was anxious to talk.

The streets were still quiet, but now it was no longer the quiet of an early morning; rather, people were gathering in larger and larger numbers, whispering in small groups, or, which was more unsettling, simply standing and watching as the senators walked by, or rode by in their elaborate covered sedan chairs.

Cicero was in his fifty-seventh year, which made him something of a senior in the Senate. Both his rank and his age entitled him to the comfort of being carried to the Senate in such a chair, especially when his knees hurt, as they usually did in the damp, dark chilliness of January in Rome. But he had never liked the ostentation—or at least that's what he said. The truth was (as he admitted to himself, to Quintus, to Atticus, but to no one else) that he enjoyed the feeling of walking through the streets of Rome in his senatorial toga, with the broad maroon stripe, often surrounded by a cloud of clients and retainers, and having people in the streets stop and point him out to others.

This time, there was no such pleasure, and it might have been a good time to travel more or less anonymously. But now it was a matter of pride.

The meeting was dominated by an atmosphere of tension, augmented by the palpable absence of the usual murmuring background: on any ordinary day, some senators would be transacting business while others delivered their speeches. But this was no ordinary day. Fortunately, the meeting was mercifully brief. Pompey's fears that the Senate would carry on a long debate proved to be groundless, and Cicero was relieved of any need to either practice his storied eloquence, or withhold it in defiance of Pompey's orders. The consul Marcellus presented a motion to declare

Caesar *hostis*, an enemy of the state. Those who would surely have voted against such a motion on an ordinary day were not present today. Cicero remained silent, so in the absence of dissent the resolution was considered to have passed. The same occurred with the resolution conferring an extraordinary command on Pompey. Surely most of the senators, like Cicero, knew that such a resolution was quite illegal, but they also knew that voting against it, at this stage of affairs, would be pointless at best, dangerous at worst.

Cicero maintained his silence throughout the meeting, and spoke to no one when the Senate was adjourned by the consuls. He made his way home quickly.

The streets by now were full of people, and the level of conversation had risen. Some of those who looked at Cicero as he passed by were overtly hostile. But this was nothing new. He was, after all, the man who brought Catiline down, and the city was still full of men who thought that Catiline had been Rome's last best hope. Now, however, the hostile looks took on a new meaning, and Cicero recalled Caelius's warning: "Don't be fooled by Caesar's manners. Even if he wanted to restrain his people, he couldn't. There's too much bad blood."

Caelius was with Caesar now; Pompey was fleeing Rome and ordering senators to follow him. There was no point hoping any longer that this moment could be avoided. His silence in the Senate had not been a lack of conviction or courage: it had been the only possible course. There was nothing left to say.

By that evening Pompey himself was gone, headed south with a substantial cavalry escort, and by midday the next day much of the Senate was gone as well. Some of them had put on their armor and set out to follow Pompey; others merely pretended to do so, and veered off to their own country estates as soon as they felt sure no one was watching; and some made no pretense at all of doing anything other than simply running for their lives.

Cato, obstinate as always, dressed in his conspicuously modest, ancient-looking uniform, set out from the city at dawn, southward, to join Pompey. It was a mark of the ferocity with which he hated Caesar that this utterly inflexible man, who would never admit to having changed his mind about anything in his entire life, was ready to place himself under the command of a man who had changed sides so many times since Sulla's day that some cynics were placing bets that even now Pompey would eventually turn up in Caesar's camp.

Against the advice of those few friends who were still in the city and still willing to be seen talking with him, Cicero did not leave the city for one of his country villas, not even his favorite retreat in Tusculum, from which, on a clear day, Rome could be seen in the distance.

Caesar's advance guard entered the city two days after Pompey's departure. But contrary to what Pompey had presumed, Caesar did not have an entire army with him, but only one legion, the 13th. Given the fighting quality of these men, it was a formidable force, but it was not the overwhelming force that Pompey, confused and ill-informed, had felt it prudent to flee. Cicero recognized, again, the master's hand.

The invitation (far too polite to call a summons) to visit Caesar at his home in the Suburra came by messenger within a few hours of Caesar's own arrival in the city. A guard of four very tough-looking legionaries had been thoughtfully provided to escort Cicero through the streets of Rome, which had lately grown so unfriendly to him. He was grateful for the gesture, and not for the first time he felt a rush of warmth towards this strange man: Caesar seemed bent on destroying everything he believed in, but somehow Cicero found it impossible to hate him.

His goodwill towards Caesar began to evaporate, however, as he walked down the street with his escort. Like any politician, Cicero was keenly sensitive to how things look. And right now, he looked like a man who had been arrested and was being taken to trial before the praetor, by force, since he could not be trusted to come freely, on his own responsibility. With an ironic distance of which he would not have been capable even five years earlier, Cicero found himself wondering, idly, how true this picture might be.

The welcome he received at Caesar's home, which was surrounded by soldiers and as bustling with activity as a Praetorium, was cordial. This in itself was not an answer to the question of Caesar's intentions towards Cicero. Caesar was always, habitually, perpetually, unnervingly cordial. If he meant to kill you, Cicero thought, he would take you by the hand first, smile, inquire about the family and their health, and then express his deep regret that unfortunately your head was about to fall on the ground. There was a purity about his ruthlessness: there was no malice in it, nor any pleasure, for that matter. What had to be done, he did. That was all, no need to be unpleasant about it.

There was a story about this aspect of Caesar's character, widely repeated, and Cicero was inclined to believe that it was true. As a young man, the story went, Caesar had been on a ship that was captured by pirates (this in the days before Pompey had cleared the seas of pirates), and been held for ransom. When the pirate leader informed him how much ransom had been demanded, Caesar laughed and said, "You are a bigger fool than you look. I'm worth at least twice that much." All the time while negotiations were being carried out and the ransom paid, Caesar had done his best to charm his hosts, drinking with them, throwing dice, exchanging ribald stories. His hosts had even let him go sightseeing around the island of Crete, taking his word of honor that he would not try to flee. Once the ransom was paid and he was freed, however, he called on his connections, raised a small naval force, and within a few weeks captured these same pirates.

He crucified the lot of them, on the spot. But because he bore them no ill will, after they had hung on their crosses for a day, he ordered their legs to be broken, so that they would die within an hour at the most, and not linger there for two or three days, like Spartacus and his men. The bodies were left dangling there until the birds had eaten them, a message to any other pirates who might be in the vicinity. The thing had to be done, so he did it.

Caesar began the conversation, as he had begun the war, with a sudden and unexpected move.

"Cicero, old friend! Did you think you'd been arrested? Thought of it too late, you know, I should have sent bearers for you with a sedan chair, rather than having you marched through the streets like a common criminal. Probably thought I was waiting for you to cut your head off, eh?"

Taken completely aback by the uncanny similarity of all this to what he had actually been thinking, Cicero found himself, uncharacteristically, at a loss for words. He finally managed to stammer out a denial. "No, no, no such thought ever crossed my mind."

Caesar smiled. "Well then, are you and your brother safe and well? There's been no unpleasantness? I was quite worried, you know, when I was informed that you were still in the city. Was it really prudent to stay?"

"Some would say that it was not, but I could not see that I had anything to fear."

Caesar sighed. "This really is a very extraordinary situation I find myself in. Not the worst I could have imagined, by any means, but not precisely what I had in mind. What troubles me the most, you know, is that the whole situation, and my own role in it, is so redolent of Sulla. And that's not a comparison I enjoy. But where are my manners? Would you care for some wine?"

"That would be quite nice, thank you." He appreciated the memory and tact Caesar exhibited by not offering food: all his life, Cicero had been told by his doctors that for the sake of his overly delicate stomach he should take no food before sunset, and then only simple food in small portions. This was one of the reasons he had always avoided invitations to the elaborate dinner parties of which the senatorial class as a whole was so notoriously fond. His own philosophical gatherings were noted for the restraint of their menu.

Caesar sent a slave to bring two cups of Falernian. "You can't imagine," he said, inviting Cicero to join him in sitting, "how hard it was in Gaul to live on the local wine. Awful stuff. The first thing I did when I got home an hour ago was have the slaves open an amphora of Falernian."

"Couldn't you have had some brought to you? There were plenty of couriers moving back and forth."

"Appearances, you know. What would Cato have said? 'The proconsul, known for his profligacy, is now using the resources of the mandate given him by the Senate to supply himself in elegant wines.'"

The imitation of Cato's manner of speaking was remarkable. Cicero laughed, almost in spite of himself. He and Cato were usually, though not always, on the same side of things in the Senate, from day to day, but the man was insufferable. And his intransigence had led directly to this moment: in convincing the Senate not to accept Caesar's really quite reasonable final offer, Cato had precipitated this war, in full knowledge of what he was doing, and quite visibly pleased with himself.

When the wine arrived, the conversation resumed in a somewhat different way. Caesar, as seemed appropriate, began.

"Have you given any thought, Cicero, as to what you will do, now that the swords have come out, despite all our efforts, yours and mine, to stop it?

"Caesar, I hardly think of hardly anything else. That doesn't mean, though, that I've reached any real clarity."

"It would be a dream come true, old friend, if you would put aside these differences that have kept us on opposite sides for so many years, in spite of my respect for you personally, and, I venture to hope, yours for me."

Cicero nodded. "Of course. There is hardly anyone in the Senate with whom I have not quarreled a time or two. I respect your honor and your intelligence. But please don't ask me to condone civil war. It's more than I can do. It's exactly what I've spent my life trying to prevent, even at the cost of switching sides from time to time, as the situation seemed to demand."

Caesar sighed. "You pay me a great compliment, Cicero, by your candor. You realize that I respect your position, even if you finally decide to join Pompey. Which, of course, I hope you won't do."

"Pompey has disappointed me, failed me, even betrayed me more times than I can count," Cicero replied. "I would have chosen a different champion, perhaps, if I could, but there were none available."

"Yourself, perhaps?"

Cicero laughed. "I would have made your task much easier, wouldn't I? You know, though, I even won a battle or two in Cilicia."

"So I heard, Imperator."

As so often when he talked with this man, Cicero wondered if he was being mocked. How could a successful siege of a mountain fort held by a rabble of brigands compare to what Caesar had done? But he continued. "Well, I've no illusions as to my military skill. Neither does Pompey. As he left, he was handing out legions to senators like so many loaves of bread, but somehow he passed me over."

"More than one of those senators will be happy to trade places with you rather soon, I expect. But no matter. You still haven't answered my question: what do you mean to do?"

"When you convene the Senate, as I assume you will, I shall be there. I cannot help you, but neither shall I go out of my way to hinder you."

"That is good enough for me. For now. Not as much as I hoped, I suppose, but rather more than I feared. Regardless of your generalship, Cicero, which I think we can say is more untested than actually proven deficient, you are a formidable opponent. And now, if you'll excuse me, there are pressing matters that I must attend to."

"Of course."

"I shall remedy my oversight this time, and send you home in a proper sedan chair. And please be assured that you are not under any kind of house arrest and may come and go as you please. Even if that means heading south."

By the time Cicero left the room, Caesar was already busy.

The contrast between this conversation and the unpleasant interview with Pompey a few days ago could not have been more stark. Cicero thought this over on his way home, and later that evening, he talked with Quintus, who had served with Caesar as a legate in Gaul. When his unit had been suddenly surrounded at the beginning of Vercingetorix's rebellion, Caesar had personally led the attack that lifted the siege. Quintus had been embarrassed to have been caught in a situation where he needed to be saved, but Caesar had never mentioned it again.

"He's going to win," Quintus asserted, as usual absolutely sure of himself just when no one else really knew what was going on. "He's already won. He took an incredible gamble, marching in here with only one legion to back him up, but he knew it would work. And it did. Pompey will never regain the initiative. I saw how Caesar did it in Gaul. Like a good swordsman in the arena, you know, jab high, jab low, jab low again, jab high, then feint high and slash low, and the son a bitch is dead before he hits the sand."

Cicero did his best not to show his distaste for the metaphor. He'd never understood his brother's taste for bloody gladiatorial combat, but after all these years he knew there was no point in discussing it.

"You may be right, brother, you may be right. I'm inclined to agree. Pompey was a great general in his day, but it's been 15 years since he last led an army into battle, and his veterans are old men now. Caesar's fresh off a string of spectacular victories, leading the same men he'll be taking against Pompey. I don't know what odds the bookmakers are giving on the Aventine, but if I were a betting men and had a lot of cash, I think I know where I'd put my money."

"Don't worry, big brother, I've put up 2,000 sesterces that Caesar will win it all. I know a fellow—"

"You what?!"

"Oh, don't worry, it's all my money, you won't lose anything."

"Quintus, you've a wife and son to think about, and hard times are coming!"

"That's exactly why I wanted to make some easy money, don't you know? They're giving 6 to 1 that Pompey will finish Caesar by the end of the summer. 12,000 denarii is a good pile of money, more than enough for a nice house in the city, maybe the bitch will get off my back at last."

The conversation was getting out of control. Quintus was married, unfortunately, to Pomponia, Atticus's sister, and Cicero had spent much of the last ten years trying to convince his brother to be a better husband to her. Without much success. But tonight was not the time for yet another fraternal quarrel on that topic.

"Never mind, Quintus, never mind. You're quite right, it's your business, perhaps you've made a very clever deal. You know how to make money much better than I do."

This was only partly true, of course. Quintus did have a knack for meeting "interesting" people with "interesting" ideas, and with his characteristic impulsiveness he was quick to invest in all sorts of schemes. Naturally, most of them didn't work out, and Quintus would lose his money, but from time to time he did in fact pick a winner, so that in a month's time he would regain everything he had lost in the previous two years. Cicero was far more cautious with his money, investing the inheritance he had gotten from his father in properties like the Caelian house they were now sitting in, or villas in places like Tusculum or Pompeii. He very seldom accepted money from his legal practice, as befits a Roman senator, but he was not averse to receiving testamentary legacies from grateful clients. As the years passed, the amount of money that came to him from the estates of deceased former clients was growing steadily. Cicero was by no means the wealthiest man in the Senate, but he was far from being the poorest.

But right now the decision he had to make was far more important and more difficult than any business decision.

Cicero and his brother sat up late into the night, talking. They were joined later by Tiro, Cicero's freedman and confidante.

"You have three choices, Cicero." It was not really proper, of course, for a freedman to address his patron, his former master, in such a familiar way, but the relationship between Cicero and Tiro had always been unusual. And this was precisely what Tiro had always been able to do that Cicero valued so highly: to break a difficult matter down into a manageable number of options and then briefly describe the pro's and con's of each possible choice. Quintus had never really approved of Cicero's liberality towards his slave, now freedman, but by this time he, too, had come to appreciate the Greek's calm, reasonable approach to difficult, complicated problems.

"First," Tiro ticked off on his fingers, "you can join Pompey. Caesar has given you liberty to do so, and for all his faults he's not a liar or a cheat. Or, you can join Caesar's party. You have his trust and his respect, as he has demonstrated. Pompey, for his part, has given you no reason to love him or trust him. And thirdly, you can do nothing at all. You can say that you find equal portions of right and wrong on both sides, you are above faction, you cannot participate in a civil war. Pompey and Caesar are forcing you to decide which of them you think should be king, in fact if not in name, and your choice is: neither. Now, if you choose Caesar, and Pompey wins, your life is almost surely forfeit. The Conservatives, if they win, will use proscription on a scale that will make Sulla seem mild by comparison. If you choose Pompey, and Caesar wins, there is a chance of the same, but I doubt it. Caesar hates Sulla's memory too much to wish to be compared to him. Still, you will have almost no real influence in whatever form of government Caesar decides to erect on the rubble of the Republic he will have destroyed."

Quintus broke in. "But what if we choose the right side, you know, the winners? All you're talking about is what if we lose." Quintus was not a man who liked to think about what would happen if he lost (even though he so often did).

"If you choose Caesar's side," Tiro replied, not looking at Quintus, but at his *patronus*, "and he wins, then you will be safe, but I doubt that you or anyone else, for that matter, will be able to tell Caesar what he can or cannot do. He will be grateful and generous, that is certain, but he will not be anxious to share, or even temper, the power he will have acquired. No man since Alexander will ever have been as great as he, and he knows it.

"If you choose Pompey, and he wins, your position will still not be a strong one. He will know that you have stayed in Rome, that you met with Caesar. He has never been more than reasonably polite to you, though no one can say why that is. You should not imagine, I think, that his victory over Caesar will mean that the Republic will be restored to its ancient glory. Pompey, too, wishes to be a king, though he is far more easily manipulated than is Caesar, and is surrounded by men who know exactly how to make him do what they want. You would not be one of those men, no matter what you do."

"So what would you do, in my place?" asked Cicero.

"In your place, Cicero, I would take the third option. If you remain in Rome, neutral, then Caesar will not be unkind to you if he wins, and Pompey will not be much more unkind to you than he would be if you had actually fought for him. You stand to lose only a little, at worst, and you will not risk the worst."

There was a long silence. Cicero finally lifted his head from a long contemplation of the triclinium floor.

"You're a wise and prudent man, Tiro, as I've always said of you. What you advise is wise, yes, and prudent. But I cannot do it. At the greatest crisis the Republic has ever faced, after I've spent my entire life trying to save the Senate, as an institution and as a class, from its own foolishness and selfishness, which has brought us to this moment, can

I now sit back and watch while others decide what will become of the greatest city in the world and its Empire?"

Seeing the slight smile playing around Tiro's mouth, he suddenly became aware of the rhetorical flourish, and stopped.

"Perhaps this isn't the moment for my fireworks, Tiro, I can see by the expression on your face. I can fool 10,000 people with my tricks, but not one man, and especially not you."

Quintus interrupted. "I've never understood why you let your own ex-slave twist you around his finger. What you were saying makes sense. If you disappear now, withdraw into your precious philosophy, why, then, what was the point of it all? You'll be forgotten, or worse, you'll be re-membered as a man who made a lot of noise, but when the swords came out he ran and hid. Take a side, by all the gods of Hell, either side, I'm not sure I really care which, and let's go down fighting, one way or the other!" By this time he was standing, shouting, red in the face—in other words, playing his part as Quintus.

Cicero did what he always did when Quintus lost control this way: he sat and looked at his brother, impassive and silent. It took some time before Quintus stopped pacing around the room and sat down. Then Cicero spoke, as calmly as if he were presiding at one of his philosophical evenings in Tusculum.

"My own estimation of the situation, Tiro, is rather grimmer than yours. One of these two men, Pompey or Caesar, will crush the other and take uncontested, sole power, essentially regal power. That's been inevitable, really, since Crassus died. When there were three of them, any two of them could keep the third one from getting too powerful and upsetting the balance. Pompey, Crassus, Caesar—every possible combination of two against one occurred at some time, from the year before Caesar's consulship to the moment Crassus left for Parthia and didn't come back. A wise man once told me—oddly enough, you know, it was the elder Marcus Antonius, the father of our good friend, he was a weak man, yes, a poor general and almost as corrupt as his son, but he wasn't a stupid man, really, and he took a liking to me after I thumbed my nose at Sulla and defended Sextus Roscius. Wonder what he'd think of his son now, if he were still alive?

"Well, anyway, what he told me was, at any given moment the Senate will have three factions, grouped around the three most important men in the city. No matter what people say and how they group and re-group themselves, how they quarrel about matters of state and what have you, all the threads of influence in the Senate lead to one of these three centers. Things get crazy, he said, not when one of those three gets too strong, but rather when one of them gets too weak or just disappears, which happens. Then blood will flow until a third one appears, restoring the equilibrium, like a juggler who drops one of his apples and can't get the rhythm back until he gets another one.

"So when Crassus and Pompey, who were always circling each other and sniffing like a couple of stray dogs, decided they could each get what they wanted if they joined forces instead of fighting each other, it was obvious they'd need to co-opt a third. And Caesar, back then, remember, he was the heir of an old patrician line, yes, but he was still very young and the *gens Iulia* had fallen on hard times. He was just a cipher at first, just put in there to keep Pompey and Crassus from tearing each other's throats out. Which we all expected to happen as soon as Caesar left for Gaul, where, we were sure, either he'd be killed soon enough, or he'd make such a mess of things that the Senate would have to recall him. Who'd have thought it would turn out the way it did?"

No one answered the question. After a moment Cicero, with a visible effort, brought himself back to the present.

"So I have to choose between them. Maybe I should play it like Crassus would, become the third man in a new triumvirate, stop this insanity before we kill off all our armies fighting each other and let the provinces wander away like so many stray cattle."

"Too late for that," Quintus grunted.

"Yes, brother, this time you're absolutely right. Even six months ago I might have pulled it off, if I'd wanted, but not now. You know, I was talking once to that British Gaul, what's his name? the doctor? Oh, yes, Scaeva, Sulpicius Rufus's friend, and he told me that among his people, if a warrior draws his sword and sheathes it again without drawing blood, he's disgraced. It sounded awfully barbaric at the time, and Scaeva himself called it foolishness, but you know, here we are. The swords are out, and I can't see them going back in their sheathes until they've been blooded. So that means my sword has to come out, too, doesn't it?"

No one answered.

Cicero sighed. "Neither of these two men will voluntarily give up power once they've gotten it. They won't do what Sulla did, put things right, as he saw it, and then just walk away. He was a bloody tyrant, Sulla, he's as soon kill you as look at you, and he did a lot of harm, but the man had character, you had to give him that, even if you hated him."

Quintus nodded, reluctantly, and Tiro smiled.

"Now, the Senate loses, no matter who wins. But Caesar, if he wins, he's the champion of the people against the Senate, and he'll have no reason, really, not to dismantle it, metaphorically if not literally. And he's a very thorough man when it comes to dismantling things, he'll do what he sets out to do or he'll pull a lot of people down with him. Pompey just isn't so thorough: he's vain and wants power, but he's lazy and easily manipulated. If Caesar wins, and I survive the fighting, I'll be treated with respect, but . . ."

"You'll have about as much authority as a flea on a camel's ass," Quintus finished his sentence.

Cicero laughed. "Well put, brother, well put, tactful as always. If Pompey wins, then I don't think I'll be much better off, at least at first. But I can imagine Pompey, after he's governed Rome like a king for, say, half a year, just sitting in the Senate and grunting 'enigmatically' from time to time, not taking sides on anything until the decision's really already been made and it becomes clear whether or not it was the right decision. That's when there's a little room, not much, but a little, to push things the right direction."

"It sounds," said Tiro, "like you've made up your mind."

"I have," Cicero replied.

The next day, the two brothers set off, south down the Appian Way to Brundisium, accompanied by Tiro and a few retainers. Their departure was immediately reported to Caesar, who grimaced, but said nothing. No orders were given, no effort was made to stop them. They reached Pompey's camp in two days, and were greeted, as they both expected, with no particular enthusiasm.

12

The Trial Continues

June 30, 44 B.C.E.

Rome

IT WOULD LATER SEEM providential: just at the very moment in his speech when Cicero took his audience back in time to remember Caesar's unexpected arrival in the city, this same Caesar, against every reasonable expectation, arrived in the Forum.

It began with a distant roar that seemed to rise from a point far to the rear of the *corona*, and rolled towards the Rostra like a wave, gathering strength. There was a general commotion, but gradually it became possible to hear what people were shouting: "Caesar! It's Caesar!"

No one had seen Caesar or heard his voice in public since the Ides of March. Only the immediate family, Scaeva the doctor, and Antony were allowed to see him, and only the doctor ever sat with him for longer than it took to say a few words. For three months now, Antony would go to Caesar's house from time to time, and then emerge from his brief meetings to announce the Dictator's will in important issues of state. The grumbling in the Senate was more and more overt: no one knew for certain, no one could prove, that these "decisions" Antony was bringing to the Senate were actually the will of Caesar.

The news that Gaius Julius Caesar had finally succumbed to his wounds had been expected every day since the Ides of March. There were rumors around the city that he was dying, or even that he was already dead, but his death was being concealed by Antony for his own purposes—though no one could explain what those purposes would be. Others whispered that Caesar's mind was unhinged, or that his heart was broken by Brutus's treachery and he would never show his face in public again. Certainly he had not been expected to appear at this trial, and it would be hard to say who looked more surprised, Pedius or Cicero. The praetor stood, as did the entire jury, and the crowd began to ebb away from the Rostra, in the direction where Caesar's arrival seemed to be imminent.

By now it was clear to those in the Forum itself that indeed Caesar must be on his way. The top of his sedan chair could be seen, though the curtains were drawn and no one could see who was inside. The burly lictors, all 72 of them, were doing their job, using the fasces to push the crowd back, keep the curious away from the sedan chair, and make a path for the bearers. The crowd parted to let the procession pass and then immediately filled in behind it.

A chant had begun and was building. "CAE-SAR! CAE-SAR!! CAE-SAR!!!"

The only person in the Forum who did not seem to show the slightest interest in what was happening was Brutus. His gaze remained fixed on some distant point, perhaps the Capitoline Temple itself, founded at the highest point of the seven hills by Brutus's most illustrious ancestor, M. Junius Brutus, the scourge of the Tarquins and the founder of the Republic. Pedius glanced at him, now, and wondered why the man seemed so detached.

As the procession reached the center of the Forum, the crowd was parted by the lictors, and finally Caesar, dressed in the maroon toga he was entitled to wear as Perpetual Dictator, emerged slowly from the sedan chair, accompanied by a slave who supported him. His always thin face now looked almost cadaverous, and he was pale as a ghost. To those who knew him well he looked ever so much older than before, his hair now so much grayer and even thinner than it had been; his efforts to conceal his baldness, which that had been the butt of so many jokes, had now been abandoned completely. But he was very much alive. The adulation of the crowd seemed to have pumped blood into his veins, and his steps, feeble at first, grew a little stronger as he walked. But his gait was awkward, stumbling, disturbing to watch.

Caesar approached the Praetor's tribunal. The younger Antony nervously shifted from foot to foot, unsure how to behave.

"Gaius Julius!" He did his best to make himself heard above the roaring of the crowd, but only those standing nearest could actually hear him. He raised his hand and shouted the louder, "Gaius Julius!"

Finally the noise seemed to diminish enough to allow him to continue, and he spoke, in a voice no longer shouting, but still audible in the Forum.

"I am sure that I speak for all present, Caesar, when I express my joy and my deep satisfaction to see you well enough to join us today. None of us were expecting your arrival."

He paused. The crowd fell silent. Caesar leaned and whispered something into the ear of the slave who had been helping him walk. The slave listened, nodded, then spoke in a loud and crystal clear voice, with only a trace of a Gallic accent.

"My master wishes to apologize that he cannot yet speak for himself, and begs the Praetor and the honorable judges for permission to address the court through me. He is aware that the procedure is irregular, but the circumstances are extraordinary, and the Praetor's discretion in such matters is sufficiently broad to allow it."

It was typical of Caesar to display, at such moments, a cavalier disregard for the rules by which things were done in Rome. He often seemed like a child playing at draughts, who grew petulant at the way things were going in the game, and then showed his displeasure by upending the board and sending the playing pieces flying in every direction. But he always did so with that mildly benevolent half-smile that almost never left his face. Cicero had seen this so many times before, and he was disquieted to see a trace of that mischievous-brat smile on Caesar's ravaged face even now. He was about to do something outrageous, and there was no way to stop it.

"My master," the slave said again, after listening to another whispered message, "begs the Praetor's permission to give testimony for the defense."

There was a moment of stunned silence, then a rising murmur of conversation that turned into a roar.

Lucius Antonius was sweating profusely. He was, like his famous elder brother, a drunkard, but unlike his brother, there was not much more to him than that. He was out of his depth now, barely able to manage such a trial under the best circumstances, and here he was, confronted with a situation for which his limited knowledge of the law left him ill prepared. And not a cup of wine in sight to calm his nerves.

His consternation was nothing, however, compared to what Pedius was feeling. He had never been allowed to speak to Caesar during the evidence-gathering phase of the trial, after the indictment, when the five conspirators had been charged. Whatever he had needed had been supplied by the consul Antony, who had brought him written answers to all his questions, with the assurance that Caesar had dictated them or approved them. Whether this was literally true or not, Pedius did not know, nor did he want to know. He had no idea why Caesar was here now or what he meant to say on behalf of the defendants, but whatever it was, nothing good could come of it. The case of a lifetime, the case that would raise him from relative obscurity to fame (and very likely fortune), was almost certainly about to go completely wrong.

Pedius glanced at the Praetor and saw immediately that the man had no idea what to do, and, for a long moment, he was sure that Lucius Antonius was about to turn and run from the Forum. It would have been comical in a different situation.

Fortunately for his reputation and his career, the Praetor managed to maintain control of his legs (and his sphincters) and found his voice.

"Caesar, I am sure I speak for all present when I express once again my great joy to see you here, after so long a time when the Senate and the People of Rome have not . . .". His voice trailed off when he saw Caesar's impatient gesture. Evidently the strategy he had chosen, to buy some time with flattery, was not going to work. All eyes—including of course Caesar's—were on him now.

He turned to Pedius. "I presume that the prosecutor has no objection to the appearance of a new witness."

Pedius was trapped. There was nothing to be gained by objecting, though there was everything to lose by allowing this to go forward. He said nothing, shook his head, and sat down.

The Praetor turned to Cicero. "There being no objection, you may present your new witness."

Cicero's consternation was scarcely less than that of Pedius. In his rise to the position he now enjoyed, as the preeminent advocate of his day, Cicero had made it a point never to allow himself to be surprised in a trial. That had not always been possible, but nothing in all those years of trying cases in the Forum had prepared him for something like this. The Praetor had asked him to "present his witness," but Caesar was in no meaningful sense "his" witness. Still, he could hardly refuse.

The urgent question he needed to answer within a heartbeat or two was whether or not to ask for a recess, to try to find out in advance what Caesar's testimony was going to be, so as to be better prepared to either make good use of it, or (which seemed far more likely) to mitigate the damage. But it didn't take him long to realize that nothing was to be gained by a delay. So he walked over to where Caesar stood, supported on the arm of his slave.

Caesar's gaze, despite his evident physical frailty, was as direct and compelling as ever.

"Cicero, my old friend," he said, leaning close to him and speaking in a hoarse whisper so as not to be overheard, "I know I should've let you know I was coming, but the matter is urgent and I was afraid I would be too late if I took the time for the formalness . . . formalities. I hope you can forgive me for springing such a surprise on you."

"Caesar," Cicero said, deciding instantly not to stand too much on his dignity, "I just wish I had at least an inkling of what it is you want to say. I don't even know what to ask you."

"Never mind," said Caesar, "I can interrogate myself."

Cicero smiled, without answering, and gestured toward the witness's stand.

When Caesar stood in the place Cicero had indicated, still leaning on the slave's supporting arm, the crowd grew very silent. The slave leaned over to hear what his master was saying, then straightened and spoke. "My master wishes to inform the Praetor and the honorable judges that there is one among the defendants who is not guilty of any violence against him."

The murmuring in the Forum rose again to a level that made it impossible to continue.

There were two men listening, however, who already knew what Caesar was about to say.

For Scaeva, the realization that Caesar was about to tell the court what Brutus had done on the Ides of March—or rather, had not done—was an enormous relief. He was freed from the sense of guilt he was feeling for deciding, a few moments ago, not to save Brutus's life.

Brutus, on the other hand, as soon as he had seen Caesar tottering into the Forum, had also known immediately what was about to happen. He kept his gaze fixed firmly on a distant point and showed no sign of outward interest in what was happening in the Forum, but his feelings were in an indescribable turmoil.

His mind went back to the Ides of March.

13

The Ides of March, Once Again

March 15, 44 B.C.E.

Rome

THERE HAD BEEN SO much shouting and confusion, a fair amount of blood spattered about from Caesar's neck wound, but Brutus had been in battle more than once and the sight of blood did not frighten or sicken him. For that matter, the shouting and pushing were also familiar enough.

He had drawn his dagger as soon as Casca had attacked, but he had made no particular effort to be among the first to strike. It was not hesitation, certainly not cowardice, though yes, he knew very well that Caesar with a stylus could be as dangerous as many a man with a sword. No, Brutus knew somehow that it would all depend on him, that the killing blow had to come from him and no one else. The others could have the honor of drawing the tyrant's blood, but the act of tyrannicide itself could only be performed by himself, by Marcus Junius Brutus, a direct descendant of the scourge of the Tarquins.

He wondered, briefly, if Caesar had always known, somehow, that Brutus would be the one to kill him. His Stoic teachers had always said that Destiny was ineluctable, the Cosmos would go its way no matter what you and I thought or desired. It was Destiny that Caesar would overthrow the *libera res publica* with the intention of becoming king, but it was also Destiny that he, Brutus, would now, just now, strike the blow that would stop him.

His contemplation, along with the blessed serenity it brought him in the midst of all this passion and confusion, was interrupted by his awareness that something was not going as planned. There was fighting going on in other places around him, not just in the area where Caesar, a few paces in front of him, now bleeding profusely, was thrashing around at his circling attackers. In one direction towards the entrance, he could even see the glint of swords.

Cassius's gladiators had obviously failed, somehow, and soldiers were coming to rescue Caesar. Senators in togas with only daggers in their hands would not stand long, if they stood to fight at all. The moment had come to act. Brutus turned back towards Caesar, who, at just that moment, lunged through the men around him with a roar and came towards Brutus, his arms outstretched as though begging for help, the bloody stylus dropped.

Before Brutus could strike, however, two things happened in the blink of an eye.

First, Albinus pushed aside two or three of his co-conspirators and walked up to Caesar, pulling his arm back to aim a deadly blow between the ribs on his left side, towards the heart.

Second, just as Albinus was about to strike, someone lunged at him, and a desperate fight began, in which Caesar himself was not directly involved. The hapless conspirators nearby stood in confusion, seeming not to know whether to defend Albinus or renew the attack on Caesar; some were already aware of the presence of soldiers, coming from a different direction, and there was panic in their eyes. Some dropped their daggers. All this while, Albinus was fighting for his life against the British doctor-turned-senator, Scaeva, that peculiar man, whom Brutus despised and admired in the most confusing way.

In a moment of incredible violence, though, it was over, and Albinus lay twitching on the floor.

By that time, however, Caesar had reached Brutus. He placed his bloody hands on Brutus's shoulders, holding himself up. For a horrible moment Brutus thought he actually meant to embrace him, but then Caesar glanced down and saw the knife in Brutus's hand. He raised his eyes, those deep, black, expressive eyes that could hypnotize a legion in the midst of a melee, and spoke in Greek:

Kai su, teknon? Kai su?

The moment had come, the *kairos*, as the Greeks called it, when there is no more time to decide, when not acting is an irrevocable decision.

What had stayed his arm? To this day, Brutus did not really know, though he thought of little else.

It was not fear. He wasn't the least afraid of dying, not now, as witness the fact that here he stood, among the accused, ready to accept a painful, public death at the hands of the public executioner rather than step away from his fellow conspirators—none of whom, as far as he knew, had actually seen the moment when he had held back the blow that would have killed Caesar. No, Brutus was a Roman, a senator, a patrician of the most distinguished lineage, he feared dishonor far more than death.

Was it compassion? Was Caesar his friend? It was not an easy question to answer. Brutus had resolutely and consistently stood with Cato, his uncle who became his father-in-law, and that meant opposing every move Caesar made, almost by reflex. But Brutus had never shared or even really understood Cato's visceral hatred of Caesar, which caused him to attack Caesar publicly and privately with the same relentlessness his famous great-grandfather had shown in demanding the destruction of Carthage. By the end, Brutus had come to agree, though reluctantly, with the opinion of Cato that Cicero had voiced at Tusculum that day, provoking a quarrel: Cato had allowed his feelings to cloud his judgement, and his obsession made him politically ineffective. It was a hard thing for one Stoic to think of another, harder yet when it involved someone whom he liked and respected, who was a member of his family and ultimately his father-in-law. This last was a bond no Roman could take lightly. Even Pompey would never have drawn his sword against Caesar if Julia had not died in childbirth. Still, the truth was hard to avoid, and the events of the last few years had proven Cato wrong.

But none of this could explain why Brutus felt as though there were some bond between himself and Caesar, despite all their differences. And he knew that Caesar felt it, also, perhaps much more strongly. In the Senate, he would sometimes feel Caesar's eyes upon him, and when they spoke privately, there was a certain warmth. Brutus felt it, though he couldn't explain it.

The inescapable fact that Caesar had been his mother's lover, the rumors that Caesar was actually his father—Brutus had never wanted to think about these things, and he seldom did. But the Greek word *teknon* that Caesar had used, "my son . . .". Had this stayed his hand? Had he recoiled at the last moment from committing the most grievous of all sins for a Roman: patricide, the killing of a father by a son, the ultimate *impietas*?

Had that single word transformed the noble tyrannicide Brutus had been planning into a patricide?

Or had it been something else, the memory of Pharsalus? That horrible day, when Pompey lost a battle he should have won, and Brutus found himself in Caesar's tent that same evening, in shock, searching for the right way to ask for pardon. He had been received by Caesar as though he had come to the house of a dear friend, and not to the tent of a victorious enemy. In fact, yes, the posture had been much the same as it was now: Caesar put his hands upon his shoulders and looked into his eyes. Only the situation was reversed: now pardon was his, Brutus's, to give or to withhold.

The symmetry seemed far more than accidental. As a Stoic, indeed, Brutus could not be convinced that anything was truly an accident. Mercy, *clementia*, had been wanted in both cases, though neither Brutus, at Pharsalus, nor Caesar, in the Aula of Pompey's Theater, had actually asked for it. Brutus and Caesar had each presented themselves at a crucial moment, helpless, to allow the other to give life or take it.

Both had given.

Caesar had placed his arms on Brutus's shoulders and looked into his eyes, both times, once as conqueror, once as victim. Should the man who had made *clementia* his personal motto, who had made such a point of not following the bloody examples set by Marius and Sulla, or before them, the senators who had assassinated the Gracchi brothers—should this man not receive the *clementia* he had modeled for the world?

What Brutus knew was this: the moment Caesar put his arms on Brutus's shoulders and said, "*Kai su, teknon?*," his own soul stayed his arm. Whatever it was, deep within him, that had withheld the blow, neither his arm nor his mind had been strong enough to prevail.

And then Scaeva had spoken to him, so unexpectedly, when the legionaries had already bound him. But it should have come as no surprise, really, that Scaeva had been there. Brutus had talked to him many times, especially at Cicero's philosophical gatherings, and found him intriguing, for all his barbarian mannerisms. The man said so many things that seemed lifted from the pages of Posidonius, despite the Druid trappings. This "Teaching" he talked of, was it not after all the *logos*?

They had always disagreed so completely about Caesar. Scaeva saw him as a man singled out by destiny to turn the world away from the path to mutual destruction. Cicero and Brutus alike, along with all the other people who frequented the Tusculan meetings, saw him as a tyrant, a man who had kidnapped the majesty of the Republic, aspiring to the crown Brutus's own famous ancestor had declared no Roman would ever wear.

But this moment, on the Ides of March, there was no time for philosophical discussion. It was the overwhelming feeling of wrongness, a feeling he still could not fully explain, that saved Caesar's life.

If he had been able to explain that feeling of wrongness to himself, he might later have been able to explain it to others, to Cassius and the other surviving conspirators, to Cicero, his defender. But he knew that if his explanation was feeble, they would put it down to cowardice and weakness of will, like the boy who deliberately shoots his arrow high to miss the deer that his father has spent half the day stalking for him. So he would finally decide to go willingly to his death with his fellow conspirators, taking his dilemma with him. He took no role in Cicero's deliberations about the line of defense.

As he listened to Caesar's slave telling the story, three and a half months later, he knew it would not be so easy.

14

The Trial Concludes

Late June, 44 B.C.E.

Rome

THE STORY WAS TOLD simply, in Caesar's best style, with no words wasted
and no explicit judgements expressed. By the time it was over, all eyes
were on Brutus. Cicero had not actually asked "his" witness a single
question.

The Praetor gestured to Pedius. "As *delator*, you may ask any questions of this witness as may seem appropriate to you."

Pedius rose to his feet, slowly, with only a glimmer of an idea what
he might say in this impossible situation. How to interrogate a Perpetual
Dictator who was also the victim of the alleged crime and had now given
testimony in favor of the one defendant Pedius most needed and wanted
to destroy?

"Caesar," he began, and then cleared his throat, "we all appreciate
the effort you have made to come here today and help us clear up this
very painful matter. I wonder if you would help us now to understand the
meaning of what you have told us."

Caesar smiled and nodded. Pedius had known the man long enough
not to be especially reassured by the smile.

"You've told us that you saw Brutus standing behind your attackers
and went to him, put your arms on his shoulders. He was armed, but did
not strike, nor did he resist when the legionaries who came to your rescue
seized him. In your opinion, had Brutus come armed to a meeting of the
Senate in order to defend you from an attack?"

Caesar spoke only one word to the slave, who simply stated, "No."

Pedius waited to see if Caesar would elaborate, but nothing was forthcoming. His heart was beating so hard that he was sure the bystanders could hear it, but he went on.

"Do you know why Brutus did not strike?"

Again a short answer, with no comments: "*Nescio*. I don't know."

"Does it not seem likely that he failed to strike simply because he was forcibly prevented from doing so by the legionaries who happened to arrive just at that moment?"

"He had plenty of time to kill me if he had desired," the slave replied in Caesar's name, after a somewhat longer whispered conversation. "My arms were on his shoulders, I could not protect my belly. I knew, and I believe he knew, that whether I lived or died at that moment was entirely up to him. As you can see, I am alive."

Was Caesar really that good a judge of character, that he exposed his belly to Brutus's dagger knowing that Brutus would not be able do the deed? It takes something not every man has in him, to look a man in the eyes, a man you know and do not hate, and then put a knife in his belly. But Pedius put the question aside, to think about later. Now there was no time.

"Perhaps he lost his nerve."

"You will have to ask him." When the slave had spoken this answer, Caesar pulled him back down and spoke again. The slave listened, then resumed. "I do not know what purpose these questions serve. The facts are plain. I am alive today because Brutus could have killed me and did not do so. What was in his mind at the time neither I nor anyone else knows, except for him, and it matters little. I grow weary and wish to go home."

Pedius, defeated and even a little frightened, said merely, "Thank you, Caesar, you have made the matter very clear for us." He sat down.

The Praetor looked at Cicero nervously. "Are you finished with this witness?"

No, Cicero wanted to say, I certainly am not. But he had not won his position as Rome's greatest advocate by making stupid tactical moves, so he merely nodded.

The Praetor, obviously relieved (he was wondering, in fact, if this was actually the very first time that Cicero had ever been caught in public at a loss for words), rose from his seat and spoke. All who were sitting rose with him. "Caesar," he said, "we can only express our joy and our gratitude that you have risen from your bed of pain to bring us such important information. May the gods speed you to health, so that you can resume the great task they have given you." He might have gone on in this vein, but the look on Caesar's face put an end to his speech.

Caesar and his slave made their way back to where the lictors were standing, and got back into the sedan chair that had brought them. The lictors formed up, the bearers picked up the sedan chair, and the procession left the Forum as it had entered.

The cheering was deafening, and it took some time after the maroon sedan chair had disappeared before Lucius Antonius could reasonably give the signal for the trial to continue.

Before Cicero could resume his interrupted speech, however, Brutus suddenly rose from his place and spoke directly to the court.

"I wish to speak for myself," he said to the Praetor, not looking in Cicero's direction, "and in light of the information we heard a few moments ago, there seems little point in going on with the trial until the matter of my involvement is cleared up."

"This is highly irregular," said Lucius Antonius. After what had happened with Caesar's intervention, he felt it absolutely necessary to assert his authority now. "It is a Greek custom for defendants to speak on their own behalf, but our Roman way is different, and it is the task of the advocate to speak to the court. You know that as well as I, Marcus Junius."

The scolding had little effect. Brutus did not reply, but remained standing, gazing directly at the Praetor, as if waiting patiently for permission to speak. His message seemed clear: what you just said is so completely beside the point that I will not even trouble to answer it.

Cicero looked on in disbelief. This was very like one of those awful dreams, he thought, in which everything goes wrong and you haven't the least idea what to do about it. All he could do was watch, wondering if there was anything short of a direct divine intervention that would surprise him now.

And it was not only these five men's lives that were at stake. The whole idea of the Republic, for all its faults, was that no man, no matter how powerful, was above the law. There may be exigencies when the strict observance of an ancient law might be so inconvenient that the survival of the state depended on its suspension, but it could never just be set aside, Athenian style, for no other reason than this, that no one wanted to bother with it.

So it was not merely the prospect of losing his most important case that so upset Cicero. After all, he expected to lose anyway It was the feeling that things had come undone, and it would take more than his eloquence to put them right.

The impasse between Antonius and Brutus ended when the former turned to Cicero and asked for his opinion. There was indeed nothing to say in reply. Cicero merely shrugged and sat down. He had no intention of making the Praetor's task any easier. His own task had by now become impossible anyway: between Caesar and Brutus, with their utter disregard for forensic decorum, he had been left, rather literally, speechless.

Pedius spoke up. "Let the defendant speak. But let him be aware that I have questions for him that he will have to answer when he finishes, whatever speech he means to give."

"Very well," said Antonius. "Marcus Junius, you may address the judges."

The *corona*, which had become increasingly restless, was clearly divided between those who wanted to hear what Brutus had to say, and those who did not. Loud arguments had erupted in many places, and some of these rapidly developed into shoving matches. Antonius, alarmed at the level of disorder in the Forum, summoned an attendant and ordered him to fetch his brother, the consul.

Brutus strode to the Rostra and took his position. He waited for the noise to subside, showing no impatience. This took some time, but finally it grew quiet enough for him to speak.

Theoretically he was speaking to the jury, the panel of *iudices* who would be voting to acquit or condemn him. Rather than turn to them, however, Brutus faced out into the Forum, and he began his address as though he were speaking to the Comitia, the electoral assembly, addressing the citizens directly:

"Quirites! Hear me! Whether you believe that I deserve your praise or your blame, show yourselves true Romans and hear me out!

"What Caesar has said this day is true, every word. Everything happened exactly as he said. I could have killed him. I did not. Before I die, I wish to explain why I did not.

"Caesar also spoke truly when he said that he could not look into my soul and see what I was thinking or feeling at the time. Only I know that. Every one of us is the only person who knows what is in his own heart.

"So yes, to answer the question Pedius asked and Caesar would not answer, I was not there to save Caesar. I came to kill him. I believed, and still believe, that for all his many virtues, Caesar has tried to destroy our Republic and make himself a tyrant, or king." He raised his voice nearly to a shout to be heard over the angry sounds coming from the crowd. "Tyrannicide is not merely the right of a citizen, it is the duty of a citizen. The nature of tyranny is such that it will not yield to arguments, and the only recourse of citizens who love their city is to strike the tyrant down. That is what I came there to do on the Ides of March."

This elicited an angry roar, and Brutus was forced to wait before he could resume speaking. Again, he waited patiently, showing no emotion, until finally his impassivity seemed to have made an impression, and the shouting died down, at least to an extent that made it possible for him to continue his impromptu speech.

"You may ask: why, then, if I believed I was there to do my duty as a Roman citizen, did I hold my hand? And secondly, why, if I did not strike Caesar and thus did not violate the *lex Iulia de maiestate*, have I kept silent and stood trial here with the others? Even my able *patronus*, Marcus Tullius Cicero, knew nothing of this until Caesar came here a few moments ago.

"I am truly sorry, Marcus Tullius, that by my silence I placed you in this very awkward position, but I believed, and still believe, that I should stand trial for tyrannicide, and be found guilty or innocent on the basis of what I meant to do.

"For our law says that if a man kills another man, but had no intention to do so, he still does wrong and must be punished. So it is only reasonable that if a man means to commit murder but does not do so, then he must be punished as though he had actually committed the act he meant to commit. The will to commit a crime is itself a crime."

There are flaws in this argument, Cicero thought. I really thought Brutus was better at dialectic than this. A schoolboy should realize that the argument from lack of intention was not reversible.

Brutus continued. "I cannot explain why I held my hand that day. Perhaps some day the gods will open my mind and I will understand. Perhaps it was they who stayed my hand, as Athena stopped Achilles from killing Agamemnon, grabbing him by the hair."

Unbelievable, Cicero thought, though he tried his best to keep a stern Roman face. This was a Roman court, and here was Brutus, on trial for his life, calmly citing Greek mythology, and even calling Minerva by her Greek name. Inwardly, Cicero cringed. In their many philosophical discussions, he and Brutus would switch to Greek rather often, since it was, after all, a far more philosophical language than Latin. But the first rule of rhetoric is to remember to whom you are speaking. You can quote Ennius in the Forum Romanum, but not Homer.

"Regardless of the reasons," Brutus continued, "I ask to be judged along with these men, exactly as though I had struck that blow. If these men are guilty, I am guilty. If they are innocent, if they are found to have acted nobly, in the best interests of our city, then I can ask for nothing more than to be counted among them. I have nothing more to say."

He returned to his place with the other defendants. It had grown very quiet. Even for those present in the Forum that day who hated Brutus and the entire class he represented, it was almost impossible not to feel some respect, however grudging, for a man who was offered an easy escape from a capital trial and refused to take it.

The Praetor turned to Cicero. "You may now resume."

Cicero

Cicero stood slowly. It seemed silly, under the circumstances, to go through the whole "taking control of the Rostra" routine one more time. But he still needed a moment to think.

His carefully crafted and thoroughly rehearsed speech, the speech for which his entire life had prepared him, had been rendered mostly pointless within less time than it had taken him to wash and dress that morning. He really did not know what to say now, even how to begin again, or what he really could hope to accomplish. A different *patronus* might have been pleased to learn that one of his clients was not, after all, guilty of attempted political murder, and to have that information from, of all places, the mouth of the intended victim. If five men had been facing certain conviction and execution, and now only four, that was a victory of sorts, even if only partial.

But Cicero had built his entire defense strategy around the manifest and admitted guilt of his clients. Brutus, by his act of *devotio*, had restored the situation as well as it could be, but his own mind was reeling with the implications of what had just happened. What could be going on in the minds of the jurors?

So he would have to improvise. It was not the first time, of course. There was that day, in November of his consulship, when the city was full of rumors of brewing revolution that Cicero knew to be true, when Catiline had the nerve to appear in the Senate, unperturbed, as though it were the most normal thing in the world for him to be sitting there, among men he had marked for murder. Cicero had stood then, setting aside the rules of precedence, and uttered the most passionate speech of his career, entirely improvised. And when he had finished, Catiline was the most despised man in Rome, a bugbear still used to frighten naughty children.

So he began again, as though it were not the resumption of an interrupted speech, but an entirely new one. "*Iudices!* Gentlemen of the jury!

"Has there ever been such a trial? Who among us could ever have imagined such a thing? We have seen in our lifetime so many extraordinary things, things our fathers could scarcely have imagined, but are we not, all of us, in a state of disbelief?

"There has never been a trial in which five men stood together before the court, accused of a capital crime. To be sure, five of Catiline's men went together to their deaths for treason, as many of us remember very well, but that was a public emergency, one which gave us no time to deliberate and employ all the resources of our law. And what of the men, senators all, who decided that the good of the city required the death of first one Gracchus, and then, ten years later, another? All Rome knew who had killed the Gracchus brothers, but no one came forward to prosecute them.

"And now, we have all witnessed a public trial in which witnesses appear without being called, and defendants accuse themselves before their advocate has even opened his mouth to speak.

"Gentlemen of the jury: if I were to complain that there are no precedents for this trial, that would be to belabor the obvious, and to insult your intelligence and your knowledge of the law. We all knew before this trial began that it would be like no other before it. Certainly I knew, when I agreed to represent these five men, that the task I would face would be the most difficult of my life. I can hardly complain, then, that the events of these last moments have done me any great harm. If a task is impossible, can it become any *more* impossible? If a man is alone and unarmed at night on a dark street, surrounded by ten armed assassins, does the appearance of an eleventh actually make his situation any worse? I think not.

"The advocate who speaks for a man accused of murder can defend his client in one of two ways. The easiest way is always to prove that the defendant did not do the deed at all: someone else killed the victim. I began my career as an advocate with such a case, when Sextus Roscius was accused, falsely, of murdering his own father. I succeeded then in convincing the jury that the truth was quite different from the lurid picture painted by those who were prosecuting Roscius—entirely for their own purposes, as it turned out. Truth and justice finally prevailed, and we were witnesses to a most satisfactory demonstration of the greatness of our laws and customs.

"But the case before you today is very different. I cannot argue that all of these men, or any of them, did not actually commit the acts for which they have been brought here. Nor have they asked me to do so. None of them has ever denied that he was there that day, in the Theater of Pompey, with the avowed common purpose of taking a life. Four of them actually struck blows, and even though we now know that the fifth defendant did not draw blood that day, he, by his own request, stands accused of the same act, which he meant to commit along with all the others. Yes, others also struck blows that day, men who are not on trial for their lives today, for the obvious reason that they were themselves killed in the course of committing their crime—if it was indeed a crime. It may even be that some who struck blows on the Ides of March managed to escape undetected in the confusion. But that does not concern us now, it does not change the situation of these five men.

"So my defense, the only line open to me in this situation, is to concede that blows were struck with the intention to kill, but that these acts, individually or jointly, do not fall within the definition of the crime for which they have been accused, under the *lex Iulia de maiestate*."

Inwardly, Cicero breathed a small sigh of relief. He had managed to recover his prepared speech, or most of it. It would go easier now, with a little extra effort to cover the situation Brutus had created.

"This law states," he resumed, that "whoso offers violence to any lawful magistrate of the Roman people shall be deemed to have offended the majesty of the Roman people, and his life and property shall be forfeit."

"That these five men laid violent hands on Gaius Julius Caesar on the Ides of March last, or meant to do so, is a plain fact. We are not going to hear a line of witnesses who will claim that one or another of them was not there, was in some other place at the time, or never had a dagger in his hand. They were all there, all armed, all meaning to kill. So how can we claim that their lives and property are not forfeit under the law?

"All this is to assume, however, that on the Ides of March last, Gaius Julius Caesar was indeed a lawful magistrate of the Roman people. He certainly claimed to be so, having named himself consul for the fifth time, over and above his title, *Dictator Perpetuus*."

Much of crowd was clearly displeased with the direction this seemed to be going, and the murmuring was growing louder.

"We are not here, gentlemen of the jury, to pass judgement on the law promulgated by none other than the Praetor presiding here today, Lucius Antonius, according to which Caesar was given the power to nominate half of all the magistrates, without election. That law, as extraordinary as it was, may have been justified by the extreme situation in which we found ourselves, after five years of civil war. We may all have different opinions on that point, but we are not called here to decide on it. What I wish to remind you now, gentlemen, is that even this most remarkable law made no provision allowing a man to name himself consul, without even a pretense of putting that important matter to the will of the people.

"According to law and custom, a man who has been consul may stand for election again after an interval of ten years has passed. Of all men, Gaius Caesar knows this law best. So when he became consul for the second time, it was in accordance with the ancient law: ten years had passed since his first consulship.

"But when he made himself consul for the third time, only two years after the second consulship, and then again the very next year, this time without a colleague, he could no longer say in good conscience that he was observing the ancient laws and customs of the Roman people.

"Our ancestors, foreseeing the possibility of emergencies that would require the temporary exercise of supreme authority by a single person, allowed the Senate to choose a dictator, and some of our most illustrious men of state have held that office. So when the Senate named Caesar "Dictator," this was within the law. But a Dictator named in accordance with our ancient law, like Cincinnatus or Fabius, was given his extraordinary authority for only so long as the emergency lasted, and in no case longer than six months. We can all remember hearing, as children, the edifying example of Cincinnatus, who accepted the dictatorship from the Senate to save the Roman army from annihilation at the hands of the Aequi and the Sabines, and then, as soon as he had won the battle, returned to his plowing only two weeks after he had left it.

"There is nothing in our law that would justify the giving of sole authority to a Dictator for life. What does it really matter whether such a man actually wears a crown or not? Our ancestors limited the dictatorship to six months precisely so that no dictator would ever become a king. These men took up arms against Caesar on the Ides of March for the same reason that many of us here today, myself included, stood with Pompey at

Pharsalus, or with Cato at Utica. They could see no other way to remove a man who, they believed, meant to be king, in fact if not in name."

These were very dangerous waters, and the angry voices reaching him from the corona confirmed it. It was a calculated risk, to speak the word *rex*, king, at this moment and in this place. Cicero could not push the attack on Caesar any further now, without provoking the crowd to a dangerous fury. But he needed to make an important point with the senators sitting in front of him, and he could see from their faces that he had made it. It was time to back away from the conclusion that was surely in all their minds just now: that Caesar had indeed, whatever his motives, shown a fine contempt for law and precedent. Even the Dictator's friends knew that.

After pausing for a long moment to let the crowd quiet just a little, he resumed.

"It may well be true, of course, that the extraordinary crisis we have been facing these six years, or even much longer, required the extraordinary and unprecedented measures that Caesar has used, not, as he says, to destroy the Republic, but to restore it. Caesar's victories alone are perhaps enough to show us that the gods are not displeased with him, and those who expected Caesar to be struck down by Jupiter's thunderbolt have been proven very wrong. The signs of divine favor are clear, and who are we mere mortals to argue?"

It was not easy for Cicero to force this argument through his lips. It went contrary to everything he believed about the gods, and about the Republic. But it was a necessary expedient. There were greater things at stake here than his pride, much more to be lost than self-esteem.

"I remember well when Caesar was praetor-elect, during my consulship, and the Senate was debating the fate of five supporters of Catiline, whom I had arrested. He made the most eloquent argument that day for *clementia*, for mercy, one which I could not help but admire, even though I was, as you all know very well, on the other side. He did so without ever once suggesting or implying that he was not appalled by the enormity of the treason those five men had contemplated. His case would surely have won the day, if Marcus Porcius Cato had not followed with a speech that was equally as eloquent in arguing for condemnation. Caesar argued that the Roman state could not afford to kill its citizens if there were any other way to solve the problem of their crime. It would be, he argued, the worst possible precedent. 'If this consul,' he argued, referring of course to me, 'shall once draw that sword, even in the best of causes, I greatly fear that we will never be able to sheathe it again, not until a great deal of innocent blood has been shed, and the moral core of our Republic has been completely compromised.'

"Would he not say that again, in this case? Not long ago, we saw him come here, despite his pain, not to condemn his attackers, but to argue for clemency for one of them. His own example, not just today, but so many times in recent memory, has been most clear on that point. We know, we have all heard him say it on many occasions, how deeply he despised the cruel example of Sulla, who made the very stones upon which we stand right now run red with the blood of Roman citizens.

"Those who were with him say that Caesar wept when he saw the head of Pompey, presented to him by the odious Egyptians who had killed him to curry Caesar's favor. Pompey would have shown no mercy to Caesar, had he been the victor at Pharsalus, but Caesar's magnanimity is beyond all doubt. We have all seen it, most of us have felt it very personally.

"Let no one think, then, that in condemning these men, he is paying a tribute to Caesar, so miraculously spared on the Ides of March. Caesar would not wish any such tribute—even though, ironically enough, the law under which they are being prosecuted bears his name.

"And that law itself reflects Caesar's own hatred of bloodshed. For the penalty prescribed by that law, in the form in which he wrote it, is exile, not death. Indeed, the penalty of death by strangulation at the hands of the public executioner is not the penalty laid down by the *lex Iulia de maiestate*, the Julian Law of Treason, but rather the penalty prescribed by the *lex Cornelia de maiestate*, an act of that same Sulla whose memory Caesar loathes will all his being.

"Gentlemen of the jury: I am not asking you today to find that these men were right to make a personal attack on Caesar. Rather, I am asking you to act in accordance with Caesar's own example, which we have all seen. Do not shed citizen blood if there is any way to avoid it. These are not common assassins, who tried to kill an innocent victim in order to rob him. They are senators who acted in their belief—a belief with which I do not ask you to concur—that their action was necessary for the common good. If you punish them with all the severity for which the prosecutor has asked, in violation of our laws and customs, and contrary to the spirit of civic amity that Caesar himself has championed all his life, you will have done no service to Caesar, and a great disservice to this city and all its people.

"I cannot believe that you will wish to be remembered for such an act. The law is about justice, not revenge. Let justice be done. That is all I ask for today. That is my entire defense. I can say no more."

The Forum was remarkably quiet as Cicero returned to his place.

The speech had been, in the end, a long one, but that was hardly surprising, since in effect he had delivered two speeches. Cicero was not in fact the most long-winded orator in the city, but he was not known for brevity, either. His decision to abandon his prepared speech half-way through and start a new one had been a tactical gamble, but the silence in the Forum seemed to say that it had paid off. People were thinking about what he had said, and he had left them a way to agree with him about the verdict without seeming to be disloyal to Caesar. And Caesar's own appeal had made this course seem even prudent.

The Praetor rose and turned towards the panel of jurymen. The time had come to poll the jury. He stated the formula, upon which the jury would vote: "If you find that these men here before you, on the Ides of March last, offered unlawful personal violence to a magistrate of the Roman people, then you must condemn them to death. If you do not so find, you must absolve them."

He continued, though it was common practice for the Praetor merely to recite the formula and ask the jurors to vote. "The law does not allow you to alter this formula, to give any other verdict than 'I condemn' or 'I absolve,' nor can you assign a different penalty. You cannot say, 'I condemn them, but for a lesser crime, not treason, one that would bear a lesser penalty.'"

Cicero realized that Lucius Antonius was not really saying these things for the jurors, who surely already knew it, but for the *corona*. The clemency for which Cicero (and Caesar, too) had so eloquently pled could be granted by the judges in only one way: a majority of them would have to mark their voting tablets "*Absolvo*." Had he chosen to do so, the Praetor could have refined the formula to allow them to vote for a lesser crime, and spare their lives while not absolving them of guilt for their action. But he had not done so. He'd also failed to present the jury with a separate formula for each man, so they would all be acquitted or they would all be condemned.

Cicero had not expected that the formula would be other than the simple one the Praetor had announced; Lucius Antonius was neither intellectually nor politically capable of refining the formula in such a way as to leave the jury a graceful exit. The defendants, all five of them, would leave here either to their homes or to their deaths: there was no other choice available now.

The time had come for the vote. The jurors marked their wax tablets by erasing one of two letters already inscribed there: A for "*absolvo*" or C for "*condemno*." The voting was done openly, but no one could see, or would ever know, who had voted which way—unless, of course the jurors were unanimous, but that seldom happened.

There had been a rising hum of conversation as the judges marked their ballots, which rose to a crescendo as one of the assistants laid the tablets before the Praetor in two stacks, A and C. To judge from the height of the two stacks of tablets that were rising before him, it was obvious that the vote would be very close. This was more than Cicero had expected: he would have felt some moral satisfaction if there had been at least a few tablets in the "*absolvo*" stack, but with that formula he had no reason for optimism. So the even stacks were a pleasant surprise.

A few moments later, however, when Cicero saw the look on the Praetor's face, he felt a surge of impossible hope. Antonius was as white as a ghost, and that could only mean—

The Praetor rose from the curule chair and motioned for silence. The crowd fell quiet.

"The judges have voted in accordance with the law, and a majority of them have voted to acquit the defendants of the charge—-"

Everything word that Antony said after the word "acquit" was lost in a roar.

It was not, however, entirely a roar of outrage. Cicero had managed to split the *corona*, not by any means in half, but certainly into two camps: those who would settle for nothing but the defendants' blood, and those who had been convinced by Cicero's argument that Caesar himself, had the decision been left to him, would have pardoned the defendants. And there were those in the crowd as well who felt that Brutus, Cassius and the others had been in the right, that Caesar was a tyrant and needed to be removed. These last had so far found it prudent to keep quiet. Now they could show their satisfaction.

It was to be expected that such an enormous crowd in the grip of such strong, conflicting emotions would not remain peaceful for long. The soldiers who were keeping the *corona* at bay, away from the Rostra, were hard put to it, but they were holding their own.

The defendants—all but Brutus, who was still lost in a world inhabited only by himself—were hugging each other, and Cicero; they were all laughing, weeping, unable to believe that they would not be leaving this place for the Carcer, the ancient underground dungeon whose entrance was not a hundred paces from the place they now stood, to await the garrote. Cicero, in his own way as stunned by the verdict as Antonius had been when he announced it, returned their hugs and their smiles, but his feelings were a tumult that would be hard to describe.

The only coherent thought he could maintain in all this chaos was, "What now?" And for the moment, he had no answer.

It would be a long and dangerous trip home, a long night for sure, and who knew what the morning would bring? Looking at his clients—or again, the four of them—he thought again how foolish they were, thinking that this verdict actually solved all their problems, and everything would now go back to normal. In the same way, they had imagined that it would be enough to kill one man, Caesar, to bring the moribund Republic back to life. But how could anything, ever, be normal again in this city?

Calpurnia

Caesar arrived home before Cicero had even finished his speech, so exhausted from the exertion that he was only semi-conscious.

Calpurnia had been in an unspeakable state, swinging back and forth between fury at her husband for never, ever listening to her advice, and a frantic worry that something would happen to him again, as it had the very last time she had let him leave home without her.

As soon as the sedan chair returned, however, she set to work to get him settled in, then took her place on the settee that had become a permanent fixture of his bedroom. It had been placed there for the doctor, but now he appeared only occasionally, and Calpurnia spent much of her time on this couch.

Caesar slept comfortably, not moaning or tossing in his sleep as he had done so often in the months that had gone by since that awful day. For some days and nights after the attack, he had lain very still, so corpse-like that the doctor had put a feather under his nose more than once, just to be sure he was still breathing. But then, as he had slowly come back to life, he had been very restless, feverish, mostly incoherent. Some of his organs had been damaged, Scaeva said, and he had lost much blood. And the blow to his head was no less dangerous, its effects harder to predict as the days and weeks and months went by. Nothing more could be done now than to keep him as comfortable as possible, encourage him to sleep, and allow his body to heal itself.

When, as occasionally happened in those first weeks, he had become agitated to the point that there was some danger of reopening the wounds, Scaeva gave him *pharmaka* that quieted him and made him sleep for a very long time.

At Scaeva's insistence, the bandages on Caesar's wounds had been changed often, and the wounds rinsed with water that had been boiled. These were not common practices in the treatment of wounds, but Scaeva was highly regarded, and the other doctors Calpurnia had summoned deferred to him.

All this Calpurnia had watched in silence from a distance. At first, Scaeva had politely asked her to leave during his ministrations to her wounded husband, but she had refused, firmly, as befits a Roman *matrona*, and it was Scaeva who backed down in the end. Physicians are valuable in their own way, even though most of the Greek ones are slaves, and some leeway must be given them, but when the *matrona* of the house says no in that particular voice, the matter is settled. The fact that this Briton was not actually a slave, and was even a senator, did not really change the situation, as far as Calpurnia was concerned.

As Caesar's wounds had slowly healed, the fever subsided, and from time to time he would say a few sensible words, though often in the mumbling, unintelligible voice of a man who talks in his sleep. Until the day had come when he opened his eyes and spoke more or less clearly; and in less than an hour's time, he was on his way to the Forum, ignoring the doctor's advice and her vehement protests. Now he was back, and Calpurnia was afraid that everything he had gained in the last few weeks had been lost.

After Caesar had slept a while, though, he awoke suddenly, and when he saw that Calpurnia was sitting by the bed, he asked her to come and lie beside him. She did not hesitate.

He whispered. "There is something I want to tell you, and I want you right here beside me when I tell you."

Not without misgivings, Calpurnia composed herself next to him on the bed, being careful not to disturb the bandages. It was an awkward moment, but a fine one, too, to feel the warmth of him next to her again.

"I want to tell you about Cleopatra."

In an instant the warmth of the moment was lost. Calpurnia stiffened. "I don't think I really want to hear this."

"But you must. When a man is dying, Calpurnia, when you think it is all up, a thousand thoughts go through your head. And if you survive, you find that some of those thoughts remain. You're changed by them. I am still Gaius Julius Caesar, oh yes, but I'm not the man who left his house—was it a month ago? or yesterday? or a year ago? I really couldn't say, you know."

"It was in March. Now we are at the end of June."

"Yes, well. Anyway, I'm not that man. I'm going to tell Cleopatra to go home. And I want to thank you for not having her poisoned while she was here."

"The thought had crossed my mind, Caesar, don't think it didn't."

He laughed, but it hurt him and he winced. "You know I value you for many things, Calpurnia, but your honesty is very high on the list. I'm surrounded by men who tell me only what they think I want to hear and make me guess what they're really thinking, but you, since the day I met you, you always say exactly what you think."

Not always, Caesar, she thought to herself. Not always. But most of the time, yes.

Caesar continued. "This dalliance with Cleopatra . . . Do you know what it was really all about?"

"It wasn't about a middle-aged man having wild sex with an exotic young girl, if that's what you mean. I know it wasn't that. I've always supposed she was your Roxana. You know, playing a role in this whole obsession of yours with Alexander, may he howl forever in Hades. Though I can't say why he's so important to you; you've done so much more than Alexander."

Caesar pondered this for a moment. "It won't be certain, you know, whether I really have achieved more than he did until after I'm dead. If I build something that lasts after my death, something that's not immediately torn apart by vulture politicians, the way Alexander's empire was divided up among Ptolemy and Seleucus and all the Diadochoi. You know, when I was lying here thinking I was about to die, I used to worry that the whole lot of them would get into a cat fight over my body until Antony would grab it and embalm it, the way Ptolemy stole Alexander's body and put it on display in Alexandria. I saw it, you know, I can say that I've looked upon the face of Alexander. But it was just a dead body, after all."

"Was that before . . . or . . . after . . . ?" But Calpurnia regretted the question and didn't finish it.

"I think everyone expected me to seduce Cleopatra and add her to my harem, as Alexander did Roxana, yes. And I know Cleopatra expected to seduce me. It was the only weapon she had, you know, the only hope she had of surviving, and the only way she knew to get me on her side."

"What was she like, really? In bed, I mean." Calpurnia wasn't at all sure she really wanted to hear the answer, but she also knew that Caesar would tell her the truth if she asked it, and if she didn't ask it she would never know. And the not knowing would be a worm in her heart. So better to have it out.

"Much like Roxana, I suppose, now that you mention it. A tigress, dangerous, a little mad, but it was something of an act, all planned and rehearsed. I've read, you know, that Roxana brought a dagger to her bridal chamber and planned to kill Alexander with it, but he found it and took it away. And then he pleased her so much that she never thought again of killing him. No, Cleopatra brought no dagger. She knew many tricks that amused me for a moment, but I grew weary of the pretense."

"You stayed so long in Alexandria, though, which made everyone think you were utterly infatuated with her, and the whole adventure nearly got you killed when you had much more pressing things to do here, in Rome, after Pharsalus, than frisking about in Cleopatra's bedchamber."

"That's where you're wrong, Calpurnia, sorry, but there's nothing more important than Egypt. Not really."

"Why?"

Caesar sighed. "No one here really understands. If this Empire is to last, it needs all its parts. After all these years of war, and I mean Marius and Sulla, too, maybe especially them, so much of the farmland of Italy has gone to seed. It's been ruined, or it's in the hands of people who don't have any idea how to farm it. There are probably a thousand thousands of people living here in Rome now, and how many of them are actually producing food? What are we to eat? That's the question we should be asking ourselves every morning before we do anything else, and what have we done but ignore it?

"Egypt has the Nile, and the Nile makes fertile land that grows wheat, far more than the Egyptians need to feed themselves. We need their grain, and we need it to be *our* grain. They need us to keep them from cutting each other's throats, even if they don't know it.

He trailed off. "But I am so tired." And after a moment he was asleep.

It was not the way that Calpurnia had wanted this conversation to end. But it would have to do.

She lay awake well into the night, lying beside her sleeping husband and thinking.

So it had been political, after all. She had always supposed that it was, to be honest. After all these years of marriage she knew her husband to be the consummate political animal: nothing he did was apolitical. Every smile he gave or didn't give, in private or public, all planned for a purpose, and the purpose was political. She had been a political choice as his third wife, and he had been a political choice for her, too, the horse she bet on—and won, finally, beyond her dreams. The love that had developed between them had truly taken them both somewhat by surprise.

He drove her mad with his politics. But she would never stop loving him, never love another man. Over the last fifteen years he had been away from her home and her bed more often than he had been present. She was not the only Roman wife in that situation, of course, and she knew well what others did to amuse themselves. Opportunities were not difficult to find, even now, when she was no longer in the very bloom of youth. But it was unthinkable, for another man to lie in Caesar's bed.

She wondered if he'd told her the truth about Cleopatra. Or no, what she wondered was, had Caesar's analysis of his own motives been correct? She knew him to be as ruthlessly honest as she herself was, with others and with himself. A man of a thousand talents, but lying wasn't one of them. He was a politician, yes, and political life doesn't often allow for complete personal candor. But he knew how to sidestep a question he didn't want to answer, how to deliver facts in such a way that they were interpreted the way he wanted them to be interpreted. But he didn't lie, not in public, and certainly not in private. He had told her that Cleopatra was not, after all, the grand passion everyone thought she was, and if he said so, to her, he must have thought it was true.

Was it?

For all his genius, there were things Caesar did not see. He had never believed her that Brutus shouldn't be trusted, probably because he just assumed that she hated Brutus because she was jealous of Servilia, the ex-lover from long ago. He hadn't realized that Antony was not to be trusted, either, and it remained to be seen whether or not he had grasped that fact even now. No, it wasn't that. She'd seen the look in Brutus's eyes and knew what it meant, and as for Antony, she could read him like a book. Caesar, who was in so many respects the most astute judge of character she had ever known, was oddly blind and foolish whenever either Brutus or Antony was involved. And the only way she had found to open his eyes was to let him walk into a terrible trap that almost cost him his life.

So was he also wrong about Cleopatra? Was his judgement clouded here, too? Was he unaware of his own motives in carrying on this tawdry and notorious affair with her?

And now, when she was again in his cubiculum, watching him sleep, that old question came back to her again. She wondered why it was that she thought of Cleopatra now, again, when there seemed to be so many other things to be thinking about just now. But it was impossible not to wonder, as she watched Caesar sleep, if Cleopatra had ever done the same, ever lain on her side watching him sleep, adoring him as Calpurnia did, even now. It was an exquisitely painful thought, but she could not help exploring it, as one explores a bad tooth with the tongue, no matter how much it hurts.

No, she hadn't tried to poison Cleopatra, though yes, the thought had crossed her mind. But she'd done something that he knew nothing about. One winters' night, earlier that year, three months before the Ides of March, she had gone to see the Queen of Egypt.

15

The She-Wolf and the Viper

January 15, 44 B.C.E.

Ostia, the seaport of Rome

CALPURNIA HAD DEBATED WITH herself, her closest friends, and yes, her Greek maid, Diotima, how to approach this meeting: formally, informally, to invite, to request a meeting, to appear suddenly, to confront the Queen publicly, or visit her privately. In the end she chose the last of these: she would go to Caesar's country house just west of the City, on the road to Ostia, a pleasant villa where he never stayed, though for some reason he never wanted to part with it. She would go with only a small retinue for safety's sake, and corner the woman in her own "palace," which the Egyptian (this was Calpurnia's kindest and most repeatable name for Cleopatra) had claimed for her own. It was a dangerous choice, in so many ways, but when she considered all the alternative scenarios, this was the most effective for her purpose, and the level of risk was not negligible, but acceptable. If Caesar found out, he would be displeased, and Calpurnia knew what that would mean: her husband would be ever so polite, ever so cordial, just a tiny bit sarcastic at times, and very distant. She also knew that he would not, could not, make a scene, even if he wanted to. Just once she'd seen him really angry, in a rage, and that was something she never wanted to see again. But he couldn't afford a rage just now, even if outside the house he was Perpetual Dictator and all that. Calpurnia knew exactly what Caesar needed from her, which meant she knew exactly what she was worth to him, which meant she knew exactly how far she could go.

A confrontation with the Witch Queen (another name, meant to evoke Medea, of course) was close to that limit, but not beyond it.

So she went one evening, rather late but well before the third watch, attended by two legionaries as bodyguards and three female slaves: in other words, enough of a retinue to keep her safe on the streets and protect her dignity, but not enough to draw unwanted attention. There'd been a chilly drizzle all day, which showed no signs of abating after dark. This was good, since it meant fewer inquisitive people on the streets and an excuse to travel in a covered sedan chair, wrapped in a cloak for even more privacy. It wasn't the first such nighttime expedition she had made, after all. But she didn't usually do this when Caesar was at home, and his irregular sleeping habits made it all rather awkward. One never knew, exactly, when he would retire and when he would be awake. And there were those times when he would indicate that he wished her to share his bed that night; these were all the more precious for being relatively infrequent. So she'd ordered her servants to be on the alert for her signal (which, she warned them, might not come at all), and make all preparations in the utmost quiet, so as to disturb no one with the bustle of their departure.

This particular night, in mid-January, it all went remarkably well: Caesar had risen before dawn to write, had put in a rather full day of meetings, drank a little more wine than usual with his supper, and retired early. He was not a lover of winter, generally, with its short days of feeble or no sunshine.

Calpurnia and her retainers arrived in due time at the Ostia house, where everyone in Rome knew Cleopatra was staying. If things were as all the gossips liked to report, the party would be in full swing, with revelers already lying face down in the gutter, dead drunk. But either the gossips were wrong, or the revelers had taken a day off to rest: the house was quiet and dark. Calpurnia hesitated for a moment, wondering if it wouldn't be best to just turn around and go quietly home. But she was Caesar's wife and felt it her duty not to hesitate or show any fear, so she shook off her doubts and ordered one of the legionaries to knock at the street gate and announce her.

The staff inside was slow to answer. Calpurnia was about to order the soldier to knock again, louder, when she heard the noise of bolts and chains being removed. A burly Egyptian, naked to the waist and with a bare curved sword in his hand, opened the door and said, with the accent of a bad comic actor, "Hoo ees there?"

The legionary, much to his credit, did not pay the barbarian the compliment of reaching for his own weapon. Instead, he spoke with the loud voice and exaggerated pronunciation that one always uses to speak to foreigners. "Go and inform your mistress that Calpurnia, wife of Gaius Julius Caesar, *Imperator, Dictator Perpetuus,* wishes to speak with her." When the man seemed to hesitate, the soldier took a half step forward and said, "Now!"

There was a moment's tense confrontation, but the Egyptian blinked first. "You weel pleeze to wayut here."

Without waiting to be instructed, the soldier responded, "The wife of Caesar does not wait in the street for anyone. We will come in, we will wait in the atrium of this house until your mistress sees fit to appear, which for her sake should be soon. Stand aside." At this, the second legionary stepped forward, and the Egyptian backed up. He was a fierce-looking man, but he was no fool. He turned on his heel and ran into the atrium, shooing away the servants who had begun to gather.

Calpurnia, preceded by the two soldiers and followed by her maids, stepped into the house.

It was an odd sensation, to be in her husband's house, and have it look and feel so very strange. No matter how it had looked when Caesar bought it (the gods only knew why), it was now exactly the sort of place occupied by a foreigner with a great deal of money and no sense of class whatsoever. It was impossible for her to imagine Caesar setting foot in such a place, or for that matter, having anything at all to do with a person who would be content to live here. But then again, there was no indication that Caesar had actually come to see Cleopatra even once during her stay in Rome. And when he had dallied with her, in Alexandria, it had all taken place in the setting of a genuine royal palace, built at a time when most Romans, senators included, were living in round houses made of bent poles. So perhaps it would be better to withhold judgement, at least for the moment.

It took some time for Cleopatra to appear, but when she did, Calpurnia was nothing less than shocked at her appearance. The shock was odd in itself, since she had fully expected Cleopatra to be, yes, shocking. But this person was nothing like the exotic witch Queen, the Pharaoness Medea, of her imagination, fueled by so much gossip. To begin with, she was clearly older than everyone had said, not at all the nubile nymph of Calpurnia's morbid daydreaming. Her skin, to be sure, was remarkably smooth, and her figure was more slender than that of a self-respecting

Roman matron; but Calpurnia could see around the eyes and the throat those signs that no cosmetics can ever actually hide. This was a woman nearer 30 than 20, at least ten years older than she was said to be.

And secondly, even more shocking: she was not beautiful. She was not even particularly attractive. Yes, yes, Calpurnia thought, women always think they know what men find attractive and they're usually wrong, but really. Cleopatra dressed like an Egyptian, wore her hair like an Egyptian, but her face and her complexion were 100% Macedonian. In fact, she was rather horse-faced, the nose not only over-long, but also oddly protruding, and her teeth seemed to be trying to push their way out of her mouth. Calpurnia had imagined an olive-skinned, dark-haired, slinky Oriental beauty seducing her husband, and here was a woman who, if you'd bought her at the slave market, you'd put her to work in the fields or in the kitchen at best, where no one would see her.

Calpurnia was baffled, but she also tasted success, at least tactical success. Her reluctant hostess seemed unsure whether to play the offended monarch or the gracious Queen, and her perplexity was amusing, and gratifying. But suddenly Cleopatra seemed to have decided on a course of action, and with that decision she regained her composure. The change was startling.

"To what," Cleopatra asked, in a voice with just the right mixture of formality and graciousness, "do I owe the pleasure of this entirely unexpected visit? I am afraid that the hospitality of this house may seem deficient for such an important guest, given the late hour and the fact that somehow, someone in my household completely failed to inform me that I should be expecting your visit."

Her voice was yet another shock. To begin with, she spoke impeccable Latin, without a trace of an accent. Calpurnia had been fully prepared to speak Greek, assuming (correctly) that this was the language Cleopatra and Caesar had used to converse. She had no idea, no one had ever mentioned, that Cleopatra had engaged tutors and learned to speak Latin with impressive fluency, threatening them daily with floggings if a single Roman ever said anything to her about her accent. No such floggings had proven necessary; Cleopatra, it turned out, had a natural flair for languages.

On top of that, the timbre of her voice was truly remarkable. It was somewhat lower than what one expected from a young woman, but not low enough to be grotesque. And there was no mistaking the royal quality: it was the voice of someone who was used to giving commands and having them instantly obeyed, without any of the characteristic arrogance or shrillness of people, women or men, who give orders without being completely sure of their position.

All this went through Calpurnia's head in a moment, as she thought furiously, deciding which of the various openings she had prepared would be most appropriate for the situation as it had actually unfolded. And almost immediately she realized that none of them were right. She would have to improvise.

"Cleopatra." She exhaled, then took a long breath before continuing. "Your Majesty. I have thought of a thousand things that I might say or do when I finally met you. I so regret missing your performance"—the word was an insult, and was taken as such, though there was only the twitch of an eyebrow to show it—"at Caesar's birthday. So now, here I am, face to face with a woman who seduced my husband and very nearly got him killed in the hour of his greatest triumph. And yet, I have to admit that as I look at you, I can't think of a single thing to say."

"If I were in your place," Cleopatra answered with a very slight smile, "I would be doing everything I could to poison your wine. Indeed, in some ways I really am in your place, and I really have thought of having a little something extra poured into your wine."

"You are Caesar's whore, not his wife, so you're not in my place at all." She regretted the ill-chosen word as soon as she said it. That was exactly the sort of crude vocabulary she expected to hear from Cleopatra, but she had let herself be provoked. And the conversation had scarcely even begun.

Cleopatra played it perfectly. She smiled slightly, and then replied, "I suppose you are right, please accept my apologies for my presumptuousness."

But Calpurnia, though she had had a moment's lapse, was not one to be bested so quickly and easily, even by a Queen. Especially by a Queen. She replied, smoothly and with a kind of sweetness that might have been mistaken for friendliness, "Oh, please, it is I who should apologize for being so crude. You must think I'm one of those awful Romans, all dressed up in fine clothes and talking like the cowherd's wife. I do hope," she continued, shifting effortlessly to Greek, "that you can forgive the indelicate word. It is not an easy situation for me, but believe it or not, I really didn't come here to insult you. Or to poison you."

Cleopatra allowed herself a little laugh that sounded genuine enough, and seemed to relax a bit. "You know," she said, following Calpurnia's lead into Greek, "it is something of a relief to find myself in the same room with you, and not to have to begin with both of us pretending not to know what we both know. To be quite honest, I had been expecting you, in a way, for some time, and I, too, was not sure what I would say."

There was a moment's silence, which Calpurnia finally broke. "I was Caesar's third wife," she began, "and I knew perfectly well when I married him what I could expect. And he never tried to convince me that it would be otherwise. That is Caesar, he keeps much to himself, but he is not a liar. If I had asked him, 'Did you sleep with Terentia?' or whoever, he would have said yes or no, and of course I would believe him, because it is just unthinkable that he would in fact sleep with Terentia and then tell me that he didn't. We just had this understanding, though I don't exactly remember discussing it with him, somehow it was always understood. I just don't ask, and he tries his best to make sure that I am not humiliated, publicly or privately. So I really don't know how many women he's slept with during our marriage, nor do I care to know. I know he doesn't sleep with slaves or whores, we have a sort of understanding about that sort of thing. The main thing is, again, he makes a point of not humiliating me. Until Alexandria. And that's what I don't understand."

For the first time, really, Cleopatra allowed herself to look at Calpurnia without searching for a vulnerability to exploit.

"I don't understand it, either," she said, startling herself with her own candor. "I thought I did, at first, but then I realized that I had no idea what was going on. I thought I'd seduced him. I had to do it, you know, my life, very literally, depended on it. There was the matter of my brother."

"I've heard the story," Calpurnia said, "though I wouldn't bet much on the accuracy of what I've been told."

"So I won't lecture you on Egyptian history or the House of Ptolemy. But here I was, with three choices: I could either kill my brother, or let him kill me, or marry him. One of those three, and just at the moment Caesar arrived in Alexandria chasing Pompey, it looked like the first choice wasn't going to be available. So I could either marry my brother or wait until he had me killed, that was it. And then Caesar appeared, and my dear brother had made a really stupid mistake: he ordered his men to kill Pompey, and put his head in a basket, which he then presented to Caesar, expecting him to jump for joy."

"My husband had a very complicated and strange relationship with Pompey." Even as she spoke, Calpurnia had no idea why she felt this need to explain her husband to his lover. "I know he was devastated that he had to go with war with him, and devastated that the very last time he looked on Pompey's face, it was his head in a basket. Your brother made about the worst mistake he could have made in that situation."

"And I'm so grateful to him for that," Cleopatra continued, "because it gave me a third option. If I could get Caesar on my side, I could use him to remove my brother without my having to kill him myself. But I had a problem, which is that I'd just lost the war with my brother and I had nothing to bargain with. Except my body. But I'd heard of Caesar's reputation with women, so I thought I had a chance to win that way. I did. So I didn't have to choose between killing my brother and marrying him."

"Why on earth would you marry your own brother? Now my husband had a friend, Clodius, who slept with two of his sisters, but he didn't try to marry them, and anyway, he was a nasty little man."

"Sex had nothing to do with it, Calpurnia, believe me. The idea of having sex with my brother, let alone children, made me sick. But you see, when Alexander took Egypt from the Persians, he expected it to be a province, governed by a satrap, like all the Persian provinces. And he left it as a satrapy to Ptolemy, my ancestor. But after Alexander died, and his empire went to pieces, Ptolemy had to govern Egypt himself, so he made himself over from satrap to Pharaoh."

"I see," Calpurnia replied. "And the Pharaohs always married their sisters. Yes. And all the little girls in all the world go to bed at night and dream of being queens. They really have no idea."

Cleopatra was silent for a moment. "You are not at all the person I expected to meet, Calpurnia, when I finally met Caesar's famous wife. Shall we sit down and talk, finally? We've been standing here like a pair of gladiators, but I for one have lost any desire to kill or be killed. I'll have some wine brought out."

This is not at all what I expected, Calpurnia thought. Fully aware of the strangeness of the whole situation, still, she found herself grateful for the suggestion to just sit and talk, over some wine. She briefly considered whether or not it was wise to drink wine in Cleopatra's house, but then she was overcome by the feeling that she may have misjudged this woman.

When they were seated, and the wine was brought, the two women sat for a moment and sipped from their cups. The wine was quite good. The silence seemed to both of them awkward and companionable, in roughly equal parts.

Calpurnia spoke first. "Is that all you really wanted from him, to get rid of your brother?"

"At first, yes. But soon, I began to dream other dreams."

"I can imagine," said Calpurnia. "When Caesar divorced his second wife and asked me to marry him, just like that, no courtship, no engagement, well, every sensible friend I had in the world told me not to be so stupid. Now my father said, and I remember it so well, 'That man will take you as high as a mortal woman can go, and you will pay for it with utter misery. It's for you to decide if the trip is worth the fare.' I didn't think very long. So what dreams did you have? Did he promise to make you Queen of Rome or something?"

Cleopatra looked at her for a moment, and it almost seemed for a moment as though the two gladiators were going to return to the arena. But then she laughed and replied, "I think you know the answer to that question without my having to answer it. No, he promised nothing. He seemed to care about me, to want to make me happy, but he never spoke of any future together, nothing beyond the question, 'What shall we do tomorrow?' I made plans, but I had the sense to keep them to myself, and he never asked. He seemed to be perfectly happy to be exactly where he was, at that moment, but somehow I knew after a few weeks that one day he would leave and that would be that.

"By that time my dear brother had gone to join the gods, Egyptian or Greek, I'm not sure, but anyway my immediate problems had been solved. The larger problem I still had to solve, now that Caesar had made me Queen, was what to do with the kingdom I was supposed to be ruling. Egypt has such a glorious past, it is such a terribly ancient country, but for about 600 years it has mostly been a province in someone else's empire, not a nation. I could keep on being a granddaughter of Ptolemy pretending to be Pharaoness, but what would be the point? Anyone can see that eventually the Romans will take over Egypt. They need the grain our farms produce along the Nile. I finally realized that it was not me, not Cleopatra, that Caesar wanted, it was Egypt, the breadbasket of the empire he was going to have to govern once Pompey was disposed of."

"I don't think," said Calpurnia, "that you've got that quite right. There is something else he saw in you, something he wanted, for himself, not for Rome."

"Don't insult me, Calpurnia, by asking me to believe that he loved my pretty face. I have mirrors in my bedchamber."

"No, Cleopatra, it was not your pretty face, nor Egypt per se. He saw Alexander in you, and that's what he couldn't resist."

"What do you mean?"

"Caesar is a man with enormous needs, no, I'll be frank and call things by their proper names, he has a sexual appetite that I can't fill. No one can. I don't think you can, either, and from what you say, I think you've already realized that. But that's just one part of him, this Eros that fills him with a desire to conquer and possess women, even if only for a moment. I know, I was conquered and possessed, one of many, but the only one who somehow knew how to remain a province in his personal Empire. The rest try to be all-in-all for him, and he discards them, one after another, politely but firmly. Because really, it's not about Eros, finally. He wants to be Alexander, and to be more than Alexander was, to fight and win the Last War. You see, some part of him believes in that philosophy of his, which teaches that we all just live a while and then we die, so there's no point in worrying about anything more than getting as much out of each day as that day has to offer. You've already said that, that's the Epicurean in him. But another part of him, probably the stronger part, doesn't want to believe that life has no meaning other than just being alive until you die. Sometimes I think that part of him wants to be a god."

Cleopatra laughed. "You surely don't believe that. He makes so much fun of religion and religious people, I can remember laughing until it hurt."

"Yes, yes, that's all true, but if you don't realize that, in some way, he also longs to be a god, you don't understand Caesar. If he really believed all that Epicurean stuff, why would he go and conquer Gaul, and then fight a civil war, and become the greatest man in Rome, and probably in the world? It's all a paradox. He will say, 'You have to just accept that life is meaningless and make the best of it,' then he will go on to fight another war, conquer another province, govern the world."

"There were these moments when I thought that he and I together could overcome the Parthians," Cleopatra replied after some thought, "put Alexander's empire back together for the first time since he drank himself to death in Babylon. If you were right about Caesar's fascination with Alexander, he should have wanted that as much or more than I did. But it wasn't long after I told him about my idea that he left. I was just hoping that if we had a child together . . .".

Cleopatra broke off, suddenly aware that she had probably crossed the line again, and the good feelings that seemed to have surrounded them would burst like a bubble. But Calpurnia surprised her again.

"With another man, the child might have done it. But not with Caesar."

"But what man does not want a son?"

Calpurnia smiled a little sadly. "Caesar has only fathered one child, his daughter Julia, whose mother was his first wife, Cornelia. He is reputed to be the father of half the men in the Senate, I think, because the truth is he probably did sleep with all their mothers. But I don't think any of them are actually his sons. It suits him for people to think so, sometimes, but I really don't think he can father a child. Not now, maybe not ever, maybe the virtuous Cornelia wasn't so virtuous after all, who knows?"

Cleopatra bristled. "Aren't you just saying that because you haven't borne him any children?"

Calpurnia sighed. "I suppose it's just possible that I'm the one who's barren. But I don't think so. Neither do the doctors. No one wants to say it aloud, 'Caesar's sterile,' but I'm afraid it's true."

"He is Caesarion's father, I'm sure of that."

"Cleopatra, please, tell that to someone, anyone else, who will believe it. I know what I know. So does he. He will never acknowledge your child because he knows beyond a shadow of a doubt it isn't his."

Cleopatra looked away. "The moment no one still believes that Caesarion might actually be Caesar's son, he is as good as dead, and so am I. Thank you, really, for trying to tell me what in fact I already know, but it is something I can't allow anyone else to know, ever. This is the first and last time I will face that truth squarely, and from this moment on I will deny it as though my life depended on it. Which it does. If I had actually conceived Caesarion by another father, of course I would have had to dispose of that man, and of everyone who knew of his existence, and if in spite of all my precautions the truth were to be made known, not only would my son and I surely die, but all those other deaths would have been for nothing, and I would go to the Land of the Dead with innocent blood on my hands. But that is all just hypothetical, Caesarion is named after his father and I will go to my grave, if I must, insisting that this is true."

Calpurnia stood up. "I want to thank you, truly, for this whole conversation. You have nothing to fear from me, and I hope I have nothing to fear from you. I came here hating you, not for sharing Caesar's bed, because then I would have to hate half the women in this city, but for trying to steal his heart and perhaps even succeeding. Now I understand you. I could even wish that I had a heart that would let me embrace you as a sister and tell you how sorry I am, but I don't. I can't do that, and I think you probably wouldn't want me to, anyway. My people and I will see ourselves out."

She headed towards the entrance hall of the atrium, where her retinue was waiting, but turned back at the entrance to the triclinium and spoke again to Cleopatra, who was sitting, motionless, silent, head down.

"I would advise you, for your own safety, to leave Rome as soon as you can. I am not the only enemy you have here, so even if I am not your enemy, there are still people here who do not wish you well."

She turned and left, expecting no reply and receiving none.

16

After the Verdict

June 30, 44 B.C.E.

Rome

NO ONE HAD SUPPOSED, least of all the newly acquitted tyrannicides, that the journey home from the Forum would be an easy one. None of them had even really imagined that they could possibly be acquitted, since they all knew perfectly well that they were guilty, and they also knew that no one in this city, even those who wished them well, believed in their chances of acquittal. The possibility that they would be able to go home, just like that, and resume their lives, had been so remote that none of them had really given the matter much thought. They had parted from their families that very morning with the certain conviction that they would never see them again, and yet, here they were, alive, free, with a life to live. But how to do that, when you've already said goodbye to your life?

A detail of guards appeared, the same soldiers who had held the *corona* at bay during the trial, now under orders from the consul Antony to escort the five defendants and their advocate to their respective homes. They formed a kind of rectangle with a wedge at the front, placed the six men in the center, deployed their javelins and shields, and began to march. The mood of the crowd was still mixed: some smiled, waved, called out congratulations; others called out much less pleasant words of greeting, glowered at them, muttered to each other.

They left the Forum to the southwest, with the Cattle Market on their right and the Circus Maximus on their left. It seemed an odd route, since most of the men under escort, including Cicero, lived east or north

260

of the Forum, on the Caelian and Esquiline hills, but it enabled the small procession to avoid the throng milling in the Forum, and effectively blocking the passage along the Via Sacra and off to the east.

Cicero noted with growing alarm that the further they progressed towards the Aventine, a rowdy tenement district roughly governed by gangs of professional criminals, the crowd actually grew thicker, not thinner, and the proportion of friendly to unfriendly faces was clearly shifting in favor of the latter. Cassius, by the look on his face, had noticed the same. Brutus, who had not shared in the jubilation after the verdict, and in fact had still not spoken to anyone or shown the slightest emotion, was staring off into space, lost in another world. The other three former defendants were still slapping each other on the back, laughing, oblivious to the increasingly hostile atmosphere just outside the row of spears and shields protecting them.

Then the first stone struck.

It came seemingly out of the air, perhaps from a rooftop, and struck Casca straight on the forehead. He fell hard, as though he'd been struck in the head with an ax. The soldiers stopped and faced outward, trying to see where the stone had come from, and if there were any other threats. It did not take long to get an answer: two or three more stones followed, and the angry muttering of the crowd turned into a roar.

The commander of the guard ordered the soldiers to make the *testudo*, the "tortoise," a maneuver used in battle to protect an infantry formation from attacks by archers or slingers; it is done by raising and interlocking the shields over the men's heads. It may have seemed a sensible response, and would have been, had this been a battlefield: no enemy is going to use slings and arrows when their own infantry is engaged. But this was a riot on a city street, and the *testudo* had a serious disadvantage in this setting: it protected the men's heads from above, but by the same token it left the midsection unprotected. If the angry men who surrounded them had meant to kill the soldiers, it would all have been over very quickly. But it was the men inside, the five defendants and their advocate, that the crowd wanted dead. Several of the legionaries holding their shields aloft were tripped, dragged aside, and pinned to the ground, but no weapons were drawn, and no blood was shed in the process.

What the embattled legionaries did not know was that the men attacking them were not merely outraged citizens eager to administer a rough justice that the court had not seen fit to provide. Despite all appearances, this was not a lynch mob. This attack had been planned for

some time, in the event of an acquittal. The attackers were themselves soldiers, and they'd been given an assignment and a plan to execute. Among
their orders was to incapacitate the guards without harming them, and to
seize the five defendants. They had also been ordered to take Cicero, and
remove him as quickly and quietly as possible to a place of safety, which
had been prepared in a nearby tenement building.

When the first missile had struck Casca, bloodying his head and
knocking him unconscious, Cicero had been quite sure that his last
hour had come. This came as no surprise: he, too, had left his house that
morning rather sure that he would not be returning to it, regardless of
the verdict. Cicero feared them, in his head and in his gut: the crowd,
the urban mob, the great mass of drifters and criminals who swelled the
capital's population without adding anything to its power and greatness,
who adored Caesar beyond all measure. They would not easily forgive
Cicero's defense of the five defendants, regardless of the verdict. In fact,
he was quite sure that his own life would be in even greater danger if his
clients were acquitted, and this realization had tempered his joy when the
verdict was announced. Now it was happening just as he had supposed it
would. In a few moments he would die. He was desperately afraid, a fear
that resided in his belly and took all the strength from his limbs; but he
was even more afraid of dying like this, giving these men the satisfaction
of seeing the great Marcus Tullius Cicero cowering before them, soiling
his underclothes.

But it didn't happen that way at all.

Cicero was grabbed from behind by strong arms and entirely surrounded by sweaty men, armed but not in uniform; he noticed, however,
that his attackers were mostly facing outward, not towards him. They
were hardly gentle as they pushed him along, but neither were they especially rough. Through their arms, though, he caught sight of momentary
images on either side: Brutus and the others being knocked down, pummeled, kicked, all this in an overwhelming roar of collective rage. But he
was in some strange cocoon, being swept away from this place, obviously
being kept on his feet instead of being knocked to the ground, protected
instead of being thrashed. It made no sense to him at all. But there was
absolutely nothing he could do, except wait to see how it would all play
out. For the moment, he was only aware that there was now a struggle
going on around him again, that blows were falling on him from several
sides. The protective cocoon was holding, it seemed, but there was no

apparent reason to believe that this handful of armed men guarding him, whoever they were, could possibly prevail over the rage of the mob.

Cicero prepared himself to die.

Sallust

When Antony announced the verdict, Publius turned to his father, perplexed.

"How could they not convict them, Father? They didn't even say they didn't do it."

"The jury didn't want to convict them, son. Half of them are related to Brutus or Cassius or one of the others, by blood or by marriage, and they are either in the Senate or hope to be in the Senate someday. And who knows, perhaps they will. You're right, though, it looked to me as though they weren't going to have much of a choice. But then Caesar himself suddenly appeared to plead for Brutus, and Cicero used that opening very cleverly to give the jury a way to get out of it, saving their social position without offending Caesar. It was a remarkable performance."

"I thought you didn't like Cicero."

"I seldom agree with him, that's true, but I can't help admiring him. And there are moments when I realize the two of us have rather a lot in common, despite our political differences."

"What do you mean, Father?"

"Oh, never mind, Publius, I'm just thinking out loud and making very little sense. The important thing is, never underestimate your enemy. The Senate is full of privileged fools, and Cicero has been their champion for over 20 years now, for reasons only he can understand. But he's not one of them, not really, even though he's *consularis,* an ex-consul. I don't fully understand his motives, his thinking, but it would a mistake to think that he's just a windbag."

"So what will happen now?"

Sallust looked around the Forum, which, despite the departure of the court and the defendants with their escort, was still crowded and still buzzing with conversation. The mood was ugly, and Sallust suddenly felt very strongly that he and his young son needed to be in a safe place, not here.

"I'm afraid, son, that this isn't over yet. And if I'm right, then I really think you and I need to get home as soon as we can."

Before they had gone very far, however, there was a sudden bustle at the opposite end of the Forum, and a murmur that grew steadily louder. Everyone in the Forum began to turn and look, craning their necks to see what was going on. Sallust heard what other men were saying long before he could see anything for himself. "It's Antony! It's the consul!"

Before long the fasces carried by the lictors came into view, and behind them strode Antony, in a civilian toga this time, not in armor.

"Why has the consul come back to the Forum after the trial, Father?"

"I don't know, son, but I suppose he feels the need to comment on the verdict. There's just no telling what he will say, with him you never know what he'll do next."

The lictors cleared a path for the consul through the center of the Forum to the Rostra, and Antony then climbed the steps to the speaker's platform. The crowd at first roared its approval of his appearance, but when he waved for silence, the noise began to subside.

"My friends!" he called.

It was, Sallust thought, a very odd way to start a speech, unprecedented, really, but that was Antony. The man had that particular kind of arrogance, carried himself as though rules and conventions were made for other, lesser men to follow, not for him.

"My friends!

"I've not come here to ask for your votes this time, just for your attention. Please hear me out."

He waited for a moment, and the crowd grew quiet enough that he could continue without having to shout.

"The court has spoken, and that's it. That's our law. We're not Greeks, we don't just set aside the law any time it doesn't suit us. Everything was done to make sure this trial, the one that just finished here, was a fair one, and I suppose it was, though I won't pretend to understand why it ended the way it did."

This brought a noisy reaction, but when he raised his hand, the angry murmur again subsided.

"I don't think that Caesar is angry, in fact it seems to me that this verdict was exactly what he wanted. And as far as I'm concerned—and I'm just a simple soldier, not a politician, I mostly don't know what all these people are really up to—anyway, for me, if Caesar says it's fine with him, then it's fine with me. Let them go home."

There were cries from the crowd: "No! No!"

"Let them go home! Let them try to live with themselves, knowing they tried to kill the greatest man this Republic has ever produced. I wouldn't want to be in their place, not for all the gold in Asia. Even though they're not in jail right now, waiting to meet the public executioner, they're not truly free men, they can't sleep comfortably in their fine senatorial beds, with their fine senatorial wives. Surely they have a conscience.

"I wish them well. I wish I never had to look at their faces again, in the Senate or in the streets, but I suppose I'll just have to get used to it. We all will. That is the law, and we Romans follow the law—well, most of the time, anyway. I can't help but think of the Gracchus brothers, how they tried to help the people, your grandfathers and grandmothers, and were murdered by senators for their pains. No trial, just daggers, and then, though everyone knew what had been done and who had done it—the arrogant bastards didn't even try to hide—the Senate just went back to its business, everything went back to the way it was before. So I suppose" (Antony's voice was rising, and his face grew red) "that the law is not always the law, not if you have the broad maroon stripe on your toga, then you can just kill the elected magistrates of the Roman people, wipe the blood off your hands, and go back to your fishponds, your fancy dinners, and back to the Senate. As if the blood of the Gracchus brothers was worth nothing! As if the blood that Sulla spilled on these streets was worth nothing!"

Sallust quickly sensed where this was going. Antony had not really come to calm the crowd, but to turn them into a mob. He would say nothing that could be used against him later, but he was choosing his words perfectly to ignite a fire that would not be quenched until the crowd was satisfied. And they wanted six men dead: the five men who had drawn their daggers on Caesar, along with their advocate. Antony had played all the right notes, and the dance was on. If he had meant to say anything more, it hardly mattered: the roar was deafening, and there was a general movement out of the Forum. The lictors formed a cordon around the consul, but the crowd flowed around it like water around the pontoons of a bridge. Sallust caught a glimpse of Antony's face. The man could never hide his emotions, especially not now. Antony was not at all frightened or angry to find himself in the middle of a riot. He was radiantly triumphant.

It was more than time to get Publius out of this place, but the crowd was getting thicker and noisier: there was really no place to run or hide. They were swept along, south and east from the Forum, to the Aqueduct of Appius, then along it southwest into the Aventine. There was nothing to do but go along.

Sallust was puzzled, though, at the direction they were taking. If the crowd meant to catch up with the defendants and murder them, why were they headed to the Aventine, when Brutus, Cassius, Cicero and the rest all lived to the north and east from here, around the Caelian and Esquiline hills? Yet the crowd never seemed to waver, as though they knew exactly where they were going.

It wasn't long, in fact, before the mob overtook the small column of soldiers that had escorted the defendants out of the Forum a quarter of an hour earlier. The legionaries formed the *testudo* to protect against the stones that had begun to rain down on them from the rooftops, but they were quickly knocked off their feet and immobilized. Then the crowd set to work. Wooden benches were taken from the merchants' stalls, broken into pieces, and the pieces used as clubs. Sallust watched in horror as Brutus, not resisting in the slightest, was clubbed to the ground and pummeled; it took only a blink of the eye, and all were on the ground.

Then the cry went up from somewhere in the back of the crowd: "Crucify them!"

With so many strong men in a blood-red passion, it was hardly surprising that some roof beams were quickly found and lashed into X's. And then the condemned were in turn lashed to the beams, which were lifted up and propped against the walls of the building.

All five men were bloody and disfigured from the clubbing. Their clothing had long since been ripped from their bodies, and so they hung there, naked and helpless, as the crowd howled its rage, vilified them, spat at them, pelted them with vegetables taken from the grocers' stalls. They were saved from the pain and disgrace of it all only by the fact that they were already dead, their empty eyes staring at nothing.

Sallust stared at the wreckage of everything he had once thought he believed in, and found himself rooted to the spot, unable to move, even though the crowd had thinned behind them, and they were no longer trapped. It was Publius who took the hem of his father's toga and pulled him away.

"Let's just go home, Father. Let's just go home." Speechless, Sallust obeyed his son.

Several hours later, safe in his home just north of the Quirinal hill, clear across the city from the horrible scenes he had just witnessed, Sallust took a few sips from a cup of wine, nibbled on a few olives, and tried to make some sense of what had happened.

And there were several things that seemed to make no sense at all.

There was no need to ask why Antony had spoken in just the way he did, that was obvious. He had known exactly what he was doing, and it was clear from his face how pleased with himself he really was. The man never could hide his feelings, and this was the only failing that kept him from being the most dangerous man in Rome.

Why, Sallust wondered, had the squad sent to escort the defendants home taken such a circuitous route from the Forum, heading more south than east, around the Palatine Hill and the Circus Maximus, into the dangerous Aventine, instead of heading east and then north, the straightest and safest road to their destination?

Why had the crowd, roused to a passion and intent on murder, headed straight for the Aventine, circling the Circus Maximus from the other side, as though they had known exactly where to cut the escort off and push them further into the Aventine?

Why was Cicero not among the five bodies hung on makeshift crosses?

How did exactly the right number of roof beams just happen to be lying in the right place at the right time?

There was no escaping the conclusion. None of this had been fortuitous. Someone had planned it all, and had planned it in such a way as to make what happened look like a spontaneous eruption of popular fury, and not what it actually was: a political murder.

Of course, in a city as huge as Rome had become, at least ten times as large as the Athens of Pericles had been at its heyday, such eruptions were bound to happen from time to time. Everyone, even the most rabid Populists, lived in fear of the moment when this great, heaving mass of desperate people—slaves, freedmen, and theoretically free citizens who were barely surviving on the food the City was providing—realized that even an army could not really stop them, once they decided to vent their rage on the wealthy and powerful. But this, Sallust now realized, had not been that moment. It had been carefully engineered to look like it, but it was something else entirely.

Who, then, had done this thing, and why?

17

Recovery

Summer, 44 B.C.E.

Rome

THE SUMMONS HAD COME in the late afternoon on the last day of the trial, while Scaeva was still busy with Caesar, his most important patient, so that his first impulse had been to send the messenger away with a blunt suggestion to find another physician. Caesar had exhausted himself with his ill-advised outing to the Forum, and was now lying in bed, feverish and weak. But he was not delirious, not even particularly groggy. That characteristic half-smile of his was flickering across Caesar's face again, and he seemed content with his day's work.

The patient had even insisted on spending a few moments alone with his wife, in his bed, which was ill-advised, but with this patient, how do you say no?

And something else was back, it seemed: Caesar's almost preternatural hearing, his apparently mysterious ability to hear things whispered in the next room, or two rooms away, when it was something that mattered. Scaeva had often wondered how he did it, and wondered, too, at the boyish delight Caesar seemed to take in it, as though it were a magician's trick he had learned to perform to entertain his guests. It was not a laughing matter, though: Scaeva was sure that it had something to do with Caesar's extraordinary gifts as a general, the ability to know what the enemy would do long before they had actually done it. So far as Scaeva knew, Caesar had never been taken entirely by surprise, ever; or if he had, he had covered his surprise so skillfully that everything always seemed to unfold exactly as Caesar had planned.

In other words, it was not a supernatural gift of hearing, but an almost inerrant intuition, which told Caesar what people meant to do, long before they actually did it.

So Scaeva was not surprised that Caesar somehow knew, already, before the messenger had arrived at his door, that Cicero had been severely beaten, and carried to his home unconscious. And he also somehow knew (despite all the best efforts of Calpurnia and the entire household not to upset him just now with bad news) that a riot had broken out, and that Brutus and his four co-defendants had all been killed. This Scaeva had learned from no one else but Caesar himself, from his sickbed, just moments before the messenger's arrival had been announced. "They're all dead, of course. All five. Brutus, too." This Caesar had whispered with a strange sigh, not grief, exactly, but a terrible weariness of soul. Then he had closed his eyes and seemed to be asleep.

So when Scaeva returned to Caesar's bedchamber, he was not really surprised to find his patient propped up in bed, fully alert.

"You should go to Cicero and tend to him, Scaeva, at once. I appreciate your attentiveness, but at this moment you're more needed there than here. I couldn't save Brutus, but I need Cicero alive and well. You will do me the greatest favor if you can manage to bring him back from the gates of Hades, as you did me. My people can tend to me. Caesar is weary but he needs only food and rest, not a matter that needs a physician's attention."

Scaeva was not so sure that it was wise to leave Caesar to the ministrations of slaves just now, but he also knew that there were times when one could discuss things with this man, and there were other times. When Caesar began speaking of himself in the third person, the signal was clear: no questions, no debates, no hesitation. Scaeva bowed and left, taking his bag as he went out the door to find the messenger, who was still outside, waiting. Somehow he was not all that surprised, when he stepped outside the door, to find that the messenger was not a solitary runner, but was attended by a sedan chair, four bearers, and a small squad of armed guards.

What he found when he arrived at Cicero's home on the Caelian hill was not encouraging. The patient was unconscious, unresponsive, pale, the limbs as flaccid as a dead man's arm. But when Scaeva jerked a bit of hair from his chest, Cicero flinched, and when Scaeva opened his patient's eyelids, he found, to his relief, that the pupils were dilated evenly.

There would be no need for trepanation this time. Cicero had been struck a sharp blow to the back of his head, yes, he was not responsive to questions or simple commands, and there was a surface wound which had bled rather profusely. But the skull was intact, and his automatic reactions to pain and light indicated that his brain was not injured.

Cicero was still breathing, so things had gone, so far, about as well as could be expected. The next days and weeks were a blur of activity, which turned into months. Scaeva hardly slept, or ate, as he shuttled back and forth between Caesar's house in the Suburra and Cicero's Palatine villa, in the stifling heat, when anybody who could manage it left the city and headed for the sea or the mountains. Caesar was sleeping long and well now, despite the tension and excitement, and he awoke every day calm, collected, observant but somehow detached. In a word, he was himself. He began first to suggest, then finally to order, that Scaeva devote all his attention to Cicero.

Here, however, the problems Scaeva faced were of a very different nature. Cicero mended well, as far as his physical wounds were concerned, but it took almost a month, to the hottest part of the Roman summer, before Cicero could be convinced to stand and leave his bedroom. By that time, his self-imposed confinement and inactivity had left him emaciated and barely able to walk. What was worse: the great voice that had rung through the Forum and the Senate house on so many occasions was no longer capable of much more power than something between whispering and mumbling. When spoken to, he often failed to react; when he did answer, he mostly confined himself to monosyllables, or, if he made the effort to begin a sentence, his voice would trail off, leaving the sentence unfinished.

It was perhaps just as well that Cicero could barely walk more than ten paces unassisted, since just now it would have been unwise for him to leave his house: even if his door had not been guarded by a small squad of soldiers, day and night, it was unlikely that he would have survived the first encounter with the bands of looters who still roamed the streets. It was something like the worst days of Sulla's proscriptions, but in many ways even worse. The battles of the civil war had been fought far from Rome: Pharsalus in Greece, Thapsus in North Africa, Munda in Spain. That had been Caesar's intention from the start: to keep the fighting as far from the capital as possible, and until now he had succeeded. He had not been forced to draw Roman blood on Roman soil. With Sulla it had been different: after a nasty, bloody fight just outside the city walls, at the

Caudine Gate, Sulla had entered Rome, armed, with blood on his hands and his face and his clothes, and the proscriptions had begun immediately. That was exactly what Caesar had tried so hard to avoid: he was not averse to bloodshed, when it was necessary, but the idea of Roman gutters running red brought back the worst memories of his life.

None of the remaining conspirators survived long enough to stand trial, and most were killed before the corpses of Cicero's five clients were even cold. Some of those who were sought out by the lynch mobs had actually been part of the conspiracy, but had somehow escaped being identified, until the verdict. Then it was their turn to be dragged from their sedan chairs or their homes and beaten to death. But this was not the end of it: as the summer went on, it seemed that anyone who had ever exchanged words with Antony, in the Senate or in the baths, was in imminent danger. Some fled, but many did not flee far enough.

Scaeva himself had been threatened on the streets several times by gangs of roving youth, but his escorting legionaries, though in civilian dress, had dealt with the situation quickly and efficiently. Oddly, this happened without the need for bloodshed. It was enough for the centurion in charge to call out, "Caesar's physician, let him pass!", and the surly gang would stand aside until they had gone by. There could be no mystery, of course, what would happen to the next passer-by who came across these angry young men, if his bodyguards did not know the password.

It was more than a month after the trial and its bloody aftermath before squads of Antony's legionaries began to patrol the streets. No one knew exactly who had died, or even how many, but there was scarcely a house in the Palatine or Esquiline districts that did not show at least some signs of mourning. Scaeva was called upon several times with urgent requests to attend to seriously wounded patients, but at Caesar's express command he refused every such summons, and tended to Cicero with the same day-and-night diligence that he had previously shown to Caesar himself.

One evening, shortly after the patrols had begun to bring some order in the city, Scaeva was awakened well after midnight by one of Cicero's slaves. The summer heat was at its height, and for all the time Scaeva had spent in Italy, far from the damp and cool of Britain, August was a month he still loathed. His sleep was always uneasy, and he especially hated the feeling of awakening, as now, soaked with sweat. His dreams were troubled, and at the slave's touch he jumped as though he had been struck.

"Sir," the slave said, "I am most sorry to have awakened you, but there is a man at the door who says that he must see you in a matter of urgency."

"Tell him," replied Scaeva, instantly awake, "that unfortunately I am not at liberty to leave this house for the time being, so long as my patient requires my attention."

"He does not wish to take you away, sir, but only to talk to you, and it is about your patient, our master, that he wishes to speak." Seeing that Scaeva seemed perplexed by his persistence, he added. "Sir, I would not dare to speak to you in this way, but this man is known to me and to this house. He can be trusted, and he has only the interests of my master, your patient, at heart."

"Bring him into the *aula*, then, but be sure to stand where you can see me at all times."

They walked together from the bedroom Scaeva had been using in Cicero's house, next door to his patient's own bedroom, through the dark and empty house to the main hall, the *aula*. Only the flickering light from the slave's oil lamp relieved the gloom.

The mysterious guest was cloaked and hooded, so that his face could not be seen. Without introducing himself, he spoke first: "I suggest that we retire to the *triclinium* now, so as not to awaken the household." Scaeva concurred, but he gestured with his head to the attending slave, to make sure that he would not be left alone in the dark house with this odd night visitor.

The hooded man walked towards the *triclinium*, despite the feeble light, with a sure step, leading the way, as though he knew exactly where he was going. When they reached the formal dining room, he turned, threw back his hood, and introduced himself.

"I am Titus Pomponius Atticus. We've never met, of course, but you may have heard my name, as I've certainly heard yours; and I've even seen your face, though I doubt you've ever seen mine. I've been Cicero's friend and confidant for over 30 years."

"I know all this, Titus Pomponius Atticus. Cicero speaks of you often. What brings you here in the dead of the night, with all this secrecy?"

"I wasn't sure what, or who, I would find here, and a daytime visit would actually be more dangerous for me than coming by night. I know the streets, and more, I know a number of people on the streets, to be honest. I don't fear thieves and robbers, I do fear gangs of assassins with a kill list in their hands."

"So why do you come to me? The household knows you, they would surely have taken you to see Cicero, if you had asked."

"It isn't Cicero I came to see, but you. By all accounts, my friend is not himself, and I should learn little from him, if his mind is not right, and upset myself for no reason. You are his physician. I would like you to tell me, in all confidence and candor, what has happened to him, and as far as you can know, what will happen."

Scaeva pondered this for a moment. The situation was unusual, and in uncertain times, "unusual" most often means "dangerous." But there was something about this man that seemed entirely genuine. Without letting down his guard, Scaeva decided to answer at least some of his questions.

"He will live, he suffered no serious injury in the scuffle that occurred when he and his clients were attacked."

Atticus dropped his head for a moment, and his shoulders slumped.

"I'm relieved. I feared the worst. I wasn't just dropping a name when I said that Cicero is my friend. No man alive knows his heart and mind better than I do, even though we've spent more years apart than together, I in Athens, he in Rome."

Scaeva searched his face for a long moment; then, liking what he saw, he continued. "His mind, I think, is mostly unaffected."

"The servants in the house have gotten word to me that their Master is not himself, speaks little, barely ever leaves his bedroom, walks like a man drunk."

Scaeva sighed. "They've never seen what I've seen in all my years as a physician, so they're misled by superficial similarities to what they know. The words are there, in his mind, but the will to speak them is missing. He has not gone mad, not in the ordinary sense of that, but his mind is like a ship becalmed, unable to catch the wind and sail on to some destination."

"I'm afraid I don't quite understand you. Has he or has he not lost his mind?"

Scaeva took a moment to decide how to answer.

"What you call the 'mind' or the 'soul' is not a single thing, not an object that can be lost or found. There is the part of the soul that thinks, which the Greeks call *nous*, and the part that feels, which the Greeks call *thymos*, and in my native language we call *ghost*."

Atticus seemed startled by the guttural sound of this last word, but Scaeva continued as though he hadn't noticed.

"This is the part of the soul where one wishes to live, or not, to act, or not to act. When it is weak, the body may be ready to rise and go about its business, but the mind gives the body no direction, fails to perform its task of assigning purpose to motion or activity. The *thymos* is the part of the soul that feels anger, or fear, or joy, reacts with pleasure or displeasure to events, makes the soul feel the desire to participate in some action, or revulsion against that action."

"I take your point. But you should be aware, Scaeva, that I've always been a follower of Epicurus. It won't be easy to convince me that this *thymos* you speak of can be anything but a physical entity. Did Cicero take a blow to the head, or the heart, that might have upset the workings of his *thymos*?"

"As I said, the physical injuries that Cicero suffered are relatively minor, hardly more than if he had tripped over a doorway. But the experience of succeeding so brilliantly at the trial, only to see the clients he had saved from death at the hand of the public executioner being pummeled and crucified by a mob—this was a different kind of blow than the blow of a fist, or a club, but in its own way much more devastating."

"Cicero is a man who has suffered much in his life, and there have been many times when sadness has overwhelmed him. Surely he will shake this off soon, he's always done so in the past."

"This is not sadness, not really. He does not feel sorrow now, not even despair, really. He feels nothing. He feels no desire, no need, to do anything at all, even to eat or, excuse me, to relieve himself. For days at a time he speaks to no one, lies in bed, as unmoving as though he were dead, his face to the wall."

"Will he get better, then?" Atticus seemed to be bracing himself for an unfavorable answer.

"That's not easy to say," Scaeva replied. "Much depends on him, on his heart, his will to overcome. He must emerge from the darkness of his bedroom, both literally, physically, and metaphorically, that is, from the dark place to which his soul has retreated. Some men, after fate has dealt them a great misfortune, will work like Heracles and overcome; others will wish they were dead, and soon Death will hear their prayers and come for them. Quite often such men will take their own lives. If you know him as you say you do, you may know better than I what will become of him. Or not."

Atticus looked away. "I've been with him in the worst moments, when his daughter died, or when Clodius drove him into exile. I've seen him when he thought he was finished, and I thought he was finished, too. He isn't a stone-faced Stoic, he feels it, and what he feels, he says. But I've also seen what happens later, when he wakes up one morning and realizes that there is still work to be done, as much as he would prefer not to be doing it. Once he has grieved for what he has lost, he puts his grief away."

Atticus paused for a moment, consumed by the power of so many memories. Then he continued.

"What I would like to know now is this: is there anything, anything at all, that we, any of us, you or I or anyone else, can do to bring my friend out from this dark place?"

"I wish I knew," Scaeva replied. "If I did, as a physician, I would do whatever I could. Every day I think, how to get Cicero to hear me, how to call his soul out of the darkness. At some moment, let us all hope, something will awaken his *thymos*, make him feel that he still has work to do, as you've said has happened in the past. I shall not rest, I promise you, until I find some way to do this."

"Thank you," Atticus said, rising to take his leave. "I've learned from you what I came to find out. I can show myself out. Please excuse me for disturbing your rest."

Scaeva returned to his quarters, but for some time sleep did not return.

Most people assume, he thought, that the physician's work is done when the patient either lives or dies. And sometimes that's true, sometimes it's enough to sew up the wounds, wash and salve them, then you've won. But sometimes it's not, and then, it's often just not enough to stave off death.

His thoughts returned to the moment when he knew that Caesar would live, contrary to what everyone had believed, himself included.

It had been a hard night, and a hard day after the assassination attempt. Caesar had alternated between periods of such complete inactivity that Scaeva had several times placed a feather under his nose, expecting the worst, and periods when he moaned and tossed with such intensity that Scaeva needed help to restrain him, so that his thrashing would not re-open the wounds. In that situation, Scaeva had ordered a chair to be brought so that he could sit by the bedside; but as the next night went on, Caesar grew calmer and seemed to be sleeping almost normally, until, lulled by the dark, the quiet, and the even breathing of his patient, Scaeva had dosed off in his chair.

He had awoken suddenly, as though he were a sentry who had fallen asleep at his post and awoke with terrible fear that he had been discovered and was in for a lashing, if not more. Instead, the first thing he saw was Caesar, still lying on his back but with his head turned in his direction, looking at him with that familiar penetrating gaze.

"So I'm not dead, then, right?"

Scaeva managed to stammer a response. "No, Caesar, you're not."

"What a relief! For a moment, I was sure I had died and this was the afterlife, and there I was thinking, what a fool I've been to believe old Epicurus!"

And with that, he laughed soundlessly, turned his head back to the ceiling, and fell back asleep.

This was in itself one of the most frightening moments, of course. Any experienced physician knows that dying patients often rally for one last moment of lucidity before the soul departs the body. But Caesar's breathing had been steady, perfectly normal, almost snoring, such that it had not even been necessary to fetch the feather.

Not that the going was easy after that. Caesar had been too close to death for too long to expect that he would sleep a few days and then rise from his bed, ready to return to the Senate. He was weak, unable to walk more than a few steps without stopping to rest, often speaking in a whisper because speaking aloud required too much breath; and when he did speak above a whisper, his voice was high-pitched and hard to listen to. And there were days when he was groggy, listless, muttering to himself, such that it was nearly impossible to determine if he was speaking sensibly or not. Still, almost every day, for at least a few hours, he would sit in bed and converse with Calpurnia, with Scaeva, and occasionally with Antony, who would visit every few days. No one was allowed to stay in the room during the conversations with the consul, but Scaeva learned that periodically, after one of these meetings, Antony would inform the Senate that Caesar desired this or that. Whether or not these "wishes" were in fact what Caesar told Antony—well, who knew? Most of the time, Caesar's conversation with others in these moments of lucidity was desultory and inconsequential.

Now with Cicero, the course had been very different, but that was normal with a hard blow to the head: everyone reacted differently. It could take a year, even more, before anyone would know whether Cicero would ever be Cicero again.

At least the timing was, if not perfect, at least not as bad as it might have been. Cicero now needed Scaeva's full attention, while Caesar could be tended by his household, with only the occasional visit to make sure that things were progressing.

18

Four Conversations

Late summer, 44 B.C.E.

Rome

THE MESSENGER, BEARING A summons from Caesar, came on the very last day of August, a hot and sultry day that gave as yet no sign of approaching autumn. It was entirely unexpected, and not a little unsettling. Sallust re-read the letter, just delivered by a dusty, sweaty, weary messenger on horseback, who said that he would wait for a reply. The fact that he made no move to dismount suggested that he was not expecting to wait long.

"C. Julius Caesar, Imperator, sends his respects to C. Sallustius Crispus. If you are well, that is good. I am well.

"There are things that I must learn from you, and from you directly, not by letter or by proxy. Please come to Rome at your earliest convenience. Do not go to the Regia, but come to my house in the Suburra. This is a private matter, and I would be most grateful for your utmost discretion.

"Farewell."

Sallust looked up at the messenger. "Kindly inform Caesar that I shall come to Rome as soon as I've made the necessary arrangements."

The messenger said nothing, but nodded once, and then turned his horse's head to the north, towards the road that led to Rome. To be sure, he spared the horse the effort of galloping away in a cloud of dust, but even so, it was not long before he was well on his way, out of sight.

Sallust turned back to the doorway of his house. Terentia and Publius were both there, their constant bickering at least temporarily forgotten, looking anxious. A cluster of slaves was just visible behind them, their curiosity evident in their eyes, despite the habitual impassivity of a household slave's face.

Sallust saw the questions in his wife's eyes, too. There was no need for her to say anything. "I am summoned to Rome, to speak with Caesar, privately."

"Dear gods!" said Terentia, and for a moment it seemed as though she would faint.

"Publius!" Sallust seemed not to notice his wife's distress, but turned his gaze to his son, who despite his age looked at that moment as though he wanted to hide behind his mother. "Close your mouth, please. You're the son of a Roman senator, and one day, if the gods are willing and you do what needs to be done, you will be a senator yourself. Don't stand there looking like a stable boy who's been kicked by a horse."

Abashed, Publius closed his mouth with an audible snap, straightened his shoulders, and did his best to look senatorial.

But Sallust had not meant his rebuke for Publius, and Terentia had received the message. She composed herself, with an effort, and did not speak until she was sure she could control her voice.

"Do you know why?" she asked, in a reasonably calm voice.

"The letter is most enigmatic," Sallust replied. "Vintage Caesar, an odd mix of formality and friendliness, not a word wasted, and he lets me know what he wants but no idea on earth why he wants it. I'm to come to the house in the Suburra and keep it quiet. That's either very good or very bad, and who's to say which? The only person who knows the answer to that is neither a god nor a ghost, so divination won't help. At least not yet." Sallust smiled sardonically, as though pleased with himself for keeping his sense of humor in the face of catastrophe.

He had, in fact, no idea at all why he'd received such a summons. Years had passed since Caesar had even acknowledged his existence, the four long years Sallust had spent living the quiet life of a country gentleman, trying to convince himself that the ambition of his youth had been misdirected. Caesar had moved mountains to have the extortion case set aside, and then he had quite obviously scratched Sallust's name from his list of friends. Sallust had even written several long letters, full of his best commentary on the political situation, and a little advice, knowing that Caesar was a man with no patience for fawning or begging.

But there had been no reaction at all. Sallust was not in favor, nor in disfavor: to all appearances, he had ceased to exist in Caesar's mind.

And now, suddenly, like a thunderbolt from a clear blue sky, this peculiar summons.

He left the next morning, much as he had left home a few months earlier, to attend the trial. This time, however, he left Publius at home. There might well be lessons to be learned on this trip, but not for a boy who still had several years to manhood. His farewell to Terentia and Publius was casual, even cheerful, though he could not help wondering if he would ever see them again. But the look in Terentia's eyes told him that she was playing the same scene. Sallust felt a rush of gratitude to her, and right behind the gratitude, a rush of love. But he turned, mounted his horse, and rode off, waving without turning back. If this was to be their last sight of him on this earth, let it be of a man unafraid.

He had decided to travel alone, on horseback, though Terentia had complained, predictably, that Roman senators did not ride to the city on horseback, unless they were in armor. But bearers could only walk, and needed more stops than a horse did, and Sallust felt strongly (though he could not explain it) that it would be best to have this over and done, whatever it was.

He arrived in Rome, then, just after sundown that same day, dusty, weary, and more than a little saddlesore. It took some little while to find a place to stable the horse, outside the city; inside the gates, the darkening streets were already clogged with carts and men carrying merchandise into the city, where such traffic was now forbidden during the day, thanks to an edict from Caesar. Sallust finally made his way to his city house, awakened the sleeping servants with his banging at the door, ate some bread and fish, and fell asleep almost immediately after he retired to his bedroom.

The next morning he bathed, took out his toga with the broad maroon stripe of a senator from the chest where he kept it, dressed, and left for the Suburra, refusing to allow any of the manservants to accompany him. All these details took careful planning and thoughtful decisions. If he appeared at Caesar's house in country clothes, looking like a merchant's son (which of course was exactly what he was), he would be received as a suppliant, though in this situation he really had no idea what it was he should be begging for. If he arrived as a senator, carried by six slaves in a sedan chair, he would be received as a merchant's son putting on airs. As it was, he showed a certain *severitas* by arriving alone, on foot, but maintained his senatorial *dignitas* by wearing the toga befitting his rank.

As he put it on, he remembered how he'd explained to his son, Publius, just a few months ago, that he had no desire to be a senator, and that the two thin stripes of an equestrian were fine for him. He could not now explain, even to himself, why he'd changed his mind.

As it turned out, it was a good choice. Caesar's servants were suitably deferential, showing him immediately to the *triclinium*, and Caesar, when he appeared to greet his guest, smiled just enough to show that he was pleased: too broad a smile would be ironic, too little would be ominous. After all this time, Sallust knew his old commander just that well, and immediately felt the muscles in his face, back, and gut relax, ever so slightly. But only slightly. The Great Man's genius lay exactly in his ability to prevent you from seeing into his mind.

Caesar's greeting was disarming. "Sallust! It's good to see you, my old friend. You've been absent from this house for far too long."

What Sallust thought in response was, Well now, why is that? What he said, of course, was something else. "No one regrets that more than I."

"Come," Caesar said, "let's walk in the peristyle." He took Sallust's arm, affectionately, and led him out through the door of the triclinium into the peristyle, the covered portico surrounding a pleasant garden courtyard.

Caesar's Suburra house was ostentatiously unostentatious: located in a rather rough neighborhood where no other senators cared to live, it was outwardly little different from the houses of the merchants, tradesmen, and shopkeepers who lived nearby. Inside, however, it was arranged and decorated with the understated elegance that only a true aristocrat can manage. The floor mosaics were simple, but exquisite.

The peristyle, especially, was a work of art, meticulously done, with flowers and shrubs tastefully arranged in symmetrical patterns, while the inward-facing walls of the surrounding portico were decorated with murals, in which the artist had worked very hard to give the illusion that there were no walls, that one was looking out into a pleasant meadow with hills and forests in the background. One had to admire how the whole peristyle blended the natural and the artistic in such a way that there didn't seem to be any tension between them, or even any clear boundaries between the one and the other. So patrician, really, this brilliant, understated art inside a modest home in an old, decaying neighborhood.

For a moment, they walked together in companionable silence.

For anyone who had known Caesar personally before the Ides of March, the effects of the ordeal he had been through were painfully obvious. His stride, previously so confident and vigorous, a large part of his remarkably ability to enter a room, or even the Forum, and immediately draw the attention of everyone present, was changed. He walked slowly and deliberately, clearly paying attention to every detail of the whole process of picking up his feet and putting them down. Just as clearly, he was trying to conceal all this. The effect was odd, disconcerting, and at the same time strangely appealing.

Finally, apparently feeling that he had allowed enough time to establish an atmosphere of confidence, Caesar asked the question he had brought Sallust here to answer. He stopped.

"Ever since last March, old friend, I've been asking myself one question. Why Albinus, Casca, Trebonius, and at least a dozen other old comrades of ours? The other group, Brutus, Cassius and their lot, that was to be anticipated, it came as no great surprise. A disappointment, yes, but not really a surprise. I can understand how they felt. Sulla spared my life, and if the bastard hadn't croaked when he did, I would cheerfully have cut his throat myself. No, it's the men who fought and bled for me, and then tried to kill me, they're the ones who visit my dreams at night. And I can't find the answer."

"But I hadn't seen or spoken with any of them for a year or more before . . . before it happened." Sallust felt a moment of intense anxiety. "I wasn't one of them, you know that."

"Yes, of course I do, and that's exactly why I thought you're the one who might be able to help me work this all out. You were there with me at Pharsalus, at Thapsus, every step of the way, and now you're living two day's hard ride from the Senate, forgotten by everyone. I could understand, Sallust, if you were to decide that I haven't been fair to you, and if someone had come to you and said . . .".

"I would never have joined in such a plot against you," Sallust interjected, not wanting to hear the rest. "No one could have persuaded me to do that."

"Don't be disingenuous, Sallust, it doesn't suit you. I can't pretend to know what's been going on with you since your, well, retirement, shall we call it? But you did a fine job in Africa, and came back to find yourself in a nasty mess you didn't deserve. I got you off the hook, my friend, but I threw you back in the water without so much as a 'Thank you and good luck.' They would have eaten you alive, you know, one way or another, if you had stayed in the City, and you were a bleeding fish in a sea of sharks."

"I never thanked you, either."

Caesar waved his hand in dismissal. "That's exactly what I didn't call you here to do, Sallust, is make amends for a decision I made two years ago. What I want to know is this: why would a man like Albinus, or Trebonius, be willing to make common cause with men who'd been on the other side of more than one battle in a civil war, just for the privilege of sticking a dagger in me? Because, you see, if I can't answer that question, there's every chance I'll make the same damned mistake again, and again. Either I did something wrong, that turned them against me, or they were the wrong men from the beginning, and I didn't see it. Either way, my mistake. I can't go forward till I know."

"They were good men, Caesar, all of them. I fought alongside them, as you did. When you know a man that way, there's nothing like it. I don't know my own brothers as well as I know them."

"Then what turned them? What did I do?"

Sallust stopped walking. He stared at the ground for a long moment, gathering his thoughts and his courage, before he decided to speak his mind. The question Caesar had just asked was one he had put to himself, at least a hundred times since the Ides of March.

"You're asking the wrong question, Caesar. Forgive my bluntness, but I want to answer your questions as truthfully as I can. Before you can know why they turned against you, first you need to understand why they fought for you. Why they turned on you later, I can't say, they weren't my friends any more, I hadn't seen them for a few years, and I just don't know what was in their minds. But I can tell you why they fought, why *we* fought, and if you know that, surely you can figure out why they were disillusioned enough to try to kill you."

For the first time in all the years Sallust had spent with or near this man, he saw what looked like puzzlement on Caesar's face. Well, he thought, I've actually managed to surprise the Great Man, for once. I may not survive it, but I may as well enjoy it. He continued.

"This is the greatest city the world has ever seen, but it has become more than just a city, more than Athens, or Sparta, or Babylon, or Alexandria. The legions have given Rome an empire that puts Alexander to shame, but who fills these legions? It's been hundreds of years since the Roman army was composed entirely of men born within these walls. The legions are filled with men like me, and more and more often commanded by us, by men whose fathers were important in their home cities, but were not Romans, not senators, certainly not patricians, like you."

"I've never made a fuss about that, Sallust, really. I live in the Suburra, and"—

"That's all very well," Sallust dared to interrupt, "but still, let's be honest: you belong to an ancient family that claims lineage from a goddess, and no matter how hard you try to be a man of the people, there's that goddess. You know what I'm saying, I think, perfectly well. If you weren't descended from Aeneas, would you be where you are today? I think not. Even people who hate the wealthy, the few, won't follow a leader they think is just one of them. You could take on the Senate, and win, because you were as well-born as the best of them, and smarter than all of them, at the same time. Take away one of those two, and you would not be Caesar."

Caesar smiled slightly. "Go on. I see I was right about you, that's always gratifying."

"But this Rome," Sallust went on, "this city above all others, the only city fit and able to rule the world and put an end, finally, to the petty bickering of kings and tribal chieftains, was being ruled by a small group of people, your kind of people. They take their power and privilege so much for granted that they've become incapable of seeing any value in Rome higher than their own status and wealth. They may know the technical, legal differences between a slave or a freedman and an Italian like me, but they don't feel the difference, and there are these moments when they let you know that. And that's what we fought for, those of us who aren't well-born Roman nobles. For Caesar, the goddess-born Roman who really saw beyond the petty interests of his own class, who understood what Rome could be for all of us."

"What do you mean?"

Sallust paused before he answered. "My grandfather fought in the Social War, did you know that? On the other side, of course. Do you know what he was fighting for? Not for freedom from Rome, but for the freedom to be part of this Republic, the Republic we Italians have fought and bled and died for from the pillars of Hercules to the deserts of Mesopotamia. My grandfather didn't want to see Rome fall, he wanted to see Rome open its arms to the men who'd shed their blood to make it great. They were happy to lay down their arms when another man named Caesar stopped the whole war by making them all Roman citizens."

"My father's first cousin," Caesar replied.

"Exactly. Now, you see, the problem of the Italian allies, my own people, was largely solved by your cousin. But the problem actually grew larger as the empire grew larger, more wars, more soldiers. And more senators getting filthy rich, buying up the land from poor farmers whose sons were off in the army. A wealthy elite whose numbers were constantly shrinking, in their villas, and outside, a growing population of desperate people with no resources and no hope, and in between, fewer and fewer people like my father, and me, people who aren't poor, but don't belong to the senatorial class, at least not by birth."

"I know all this, Sallust. Spare me the lecture, please. I think I've done as much as a man could do to change things in Rome, and I still don't know why my own men turned on me."

Sallust looked away. "I was never a great commander, Caesar, you know that, you've told me that yourself, and I won't pretend it was otherwise. But I was in battle more than once, and close enough to the real fighting to have blood on my face and my sword when it was over. Do you know, when the enemy is coming at you, everyone shouting and screaming, the noise of iron weapons is all so loud you can't hear yourself think, and you feel that any breath you take could be your last—at that moment, you don't remember what the war is about, not really. It's not for someone else's city, or really even your own, that you find the guts to stand up to an enemy. Sorry, but every soldier, in his heart, knows it's true. You stand there and fight because you can't run away from your friends, that's all. It's the only thing that could possibly keep a sane man standing in line at that moment. The man next to you, in the rank in front of you and behind you, the one who'll step up to take your place when the centurion blows his whistle, or the one whose place you'll take next.

"There are two reasons why you've been one of the greatest generals this world has ever seen, or is likely to ever see again. The first is, your ability to know what your enemy is going to do before he knows it himself. The second is, you make every man in the ranks think that you know him personally and count him as a friend; for them, you are that man, the one they'd rather die than let down. You walk down the ranks and call men by their names. I've seen them, the way they look when you've said something to them, something that makes them feel you know them.

"And I was there the day we crossed the Rubicon. It was a terrible thing to see, awful, frightening, beautiful. No one else could have led those men across the boundary of your province into a civil war. Well, no one but Sulla, and he did it by making his men, good Roman soldiers, into pirates, promising them plunder to fight for him, when hardly one of them really knew what the fight with Marius was all about, or cared.

You were different. If you'd said, that day, 'Let's march down to Hades and bring all the dead back to life,' they would have shouted just the same, and they would have gone.

"But when all the battles were over, they looked, and here were the same faces in the Senate, as haughty as ever, as rich as ever, as if they'd never lost a battle. And there was Caesar, no longer on his horse, with his scarlet cape, sharing life and death with his men, close enough to the front line to smell the enemy's sweat, but here's Caesar in a maroon toga, disappearing into the Senate House.

"And I believe, though I don't know, can't possibly know, that Albinus and the others said to themselves something like this: 'Is this really what we were fighting for? We thought we were going to change the rules of the game, but all we did was to make Caesar the winner of that same old game. Which hasn't changed a bit.' It was enough to turn them, I think. To be perfectly honest—"

"Please do, Sallust, that's exactly what I want from you".

"—they felt betrayed. Used and discarded, like an old slave who's sold to a poor man in the city when he's too old to work in the field any more."

"But they knew I was leaving soon to fight the Parthians," Caesar objected. "We'd be back in camp again, like the old days."

"But that's just it, Caesar. You drove your enemies from the field, then put most of them right back in the Senate, and then you were just so obviously bored with all that, ready to go fight. And for what, exactly, were we—they—going to fight and die, this time? No one cares about Crassus that much, you know, and Parthia is a long way away, too far, really. Even if you took it, what would you do with it? It's exactly the Parthian campaign that told your old soldiers, or at least some of them, that they had fought for a man who in the end didn't want a better Rome. He only wanted to be a greater conqueror than Alexander."

"Sallust, Sallust, you're contradicting yourself, surely you see that. A moment ago, you were arguing, oh so eloquently, that men don't fight for causes, they fight for each other, and you were kind enough to suggest that I have some talent at making men fight for me. Now you're telling me that they wanted something more from me than just winning battles."

The smile on Caesar's face was not the half-smile that everyone who knew the man well feared so much. It was oddly warm and direct, completely at odds with his pointed, critical words. Sallust began to reply, but Caesar held up a hand to cut him off, and continued.

"I had thought, I suppose, that there were two possible reasons for Albinus and the others to make this odd alliance with Cassius and Brutus: one, that they had simply been bought, or two, that they were angry with me for not putting up proscription lists to get rid of the people they had learned to hate so much. The second alternative makes no sense to me at all: why join Brutus to kill Caesar because you're mad at Caesar for not killing Brutus? Now Albinus and Trebonius are no mental giants, believe me, but I can't see them giving their hands to someone when they would be ever so much happier just cutting off those same hands.

"But the only third alternative I could think of was that they were just bored, tired of sitting in camp here, no more battles to fight. I was sure that the Parthian campaign would quiet them down, give them something to do, something to think about, besides being bored and annoyed by the sight of Brutus being carried to the Senate by litter bearers.

"Now you've given me something to think about. I'm not convinced you're right, of course, but there may something to what you say."

Sallust shrugged. "Who am I to tell Caesar anything?"

"You mentioned the Rubicon. Do you know what I felt that day?"

Sallust shook his head.

"It was . . . indescribable. I knew at once that we were going to win: with that kind of power, who could stop us? You're right, those men would have marched right up to the Palace of Hades himself if I'd given the order. There is nothing like that, the feeling of power that comes from command of an army, when the army is yours, completely yours. But at the same time I wished I were somewhere else, not here, not doing this thing. Because I never realized before that moment how a general leading an army is like a man riding an elephant into battle. Once the elephant charges, you can't really stop him. And I mean no one can really stop him, not the man who is facing him in the enemy ranks, and not the man who's riding him, either. The best you can do with that kind of brute force is just to point it in a certain direction and set it into motion, but what happens then is pretty much out of your hands.

"Once we crossed the Rubicon, and the men's blood was up, Pompey couldn't stop them. And neither could I. All I could do was try to arrange for them to be in the right place and pointed in the right direction when they started killing. Pompey had, at that moment, I don't know, maybe twice as many men under arms as I did, maybe even more, when I crossed the Rubicon. But I had an army, even though it was only one legion, and he didn't. He knew that, he was a great general, that's why he abandoned Rome, abandoned Italy, made me chase him across the Adriatic. It almost worked. He almost forced me to stretch myself too far. It was a near thing."

Caesar turned to Sallust and put his arm on his shoulder.

"I haven't forgotten all the work you did, by the way, getting the army across in one piece, and supplies. Pompey would have finished me off at Dyrrachium without you."

"I'm a merchant's son after all, Caesar," Sallust replied. "I know how to move people and goods from here to there. I wasn't much of a field commander, though, was I?"

Caesar laughed. "I had plenty of good soldiers, Sallust, and they would all have died over there without you, and me along with them. Shall I tell you why you're not a great general?"

"I'm not sure I want to hear it," Sallust replied with a rueful smile, "but yes, I still think about it. I wish I could tell my son how I led my men into battle, and won. But I can't."

"Really, I've already told you the answer. You couldn't deal with the wild beast that we call the 'army.' You expected the men to do their duty because it was their duty, because that is what soldiers do. Except, of course, that you've already said it yourself: when the swords come out, men fight for completely different reasons, and all the political reasons everyone talks about before and after the battle don't mean much. They fight and kill out of fear, or they fight and kill out of anger, one of those two. No other feeling is strong enough, except, maybe, for shame. But even so, none of these alone is enough. If soldiers are afraid, but not angry, then they are as likely to run as they are to fight—unless they're afraid of being slaughtered when the line breaks, or they're too ashamed to show their backs to the enemy. If men are angry, but not afraid, they'll do stupid things in the heat of battle, and a good general on the other side will cut them to pieces."

Caesar paused for a moment before he resumed; his arm dropped, and his gaze shifted away from Sallust's face. He seemed far away.

"When the 13th Legion crossed the Rubicon, they were all of these: afraid of what would happen to them if they lost, angry at being treated like outlaws by the Senate, and ashamed not to follow me when I rode across the river. Now none of that happened by accident: I worked hard for years to make sure that when the time came, they would be in this frame of mind: scared, angry, and ashamed to hold back when I was watching. That's what you couldn't do, Sallust. You're a thinking man, you don't realize that most men, 99 out of a hundred, or 999 out of a thousand, I couldn't say—anyway, they don't do what they *think* is right, they do what their belly tells them to do. You kept trying to get into their heads, and what you needed was to get into their guts."

Sallust could only nod. He felt nauseous. And at once he realized that his nausea was the best possible proof that Caesar was right. It all starts in the belly, after all.

"Now the whole problem is this," Caesar continued, "it's always been this: an army needs a fire in its belly in order to fight. The city, Rome or any other, needs an army, otherwise it will be devoured by some other city with a better army. But the army by its very nature is a beast, all feeling, no reason; and the moment it has a will of its own, a purpose of its own, other than just surviving the next battle in the next war, then it becomes a very dangerous beast indeed. Do you know why Hannibal lost against us?"

The sudden change of topic was unnerving, but Sallust was equal to the task, and replied without blinking. "Old Scipio, the elder Africanus, as my father told me, went to Spain and fought against Hannibal's brothers, and there he learned to fight like a Carthaginian. So at Zama, he out-Hannibaled Hannibal."

"Well put, Sallust, your father was right, as far as he went. But there was more to it. Hannibal was a professional soldier, with an army that had followed him for over ten years, never lost a battle, inflicted the worst defeats the Roman army has ever suffered. And that made him at least as dangerous to Carthage as he was to Rome. Do you know what he would have done if he'd won at Zama? He would've marched straight to Carthage and cleaned house. Sulla would've looked like a puppy dog by comparison. The Carthaginian Senate was glad to have him fighting in Italy all those years, far away from home and too busy to make trouble for them; they would've been terrified if he'd taken Rome and marched home victorious, and they were not happy to have him back on African shores. That was Scipio's real genius, Sallust: Hannibal lost the minute he left Italy, because the Carthaginians by that time were more afraid of their own general than they were of the Romans. So now you see the position I found myself in after Munda. I was riding an elephant, and it's damned hard to get off a rampaging elephant without getting trampled. I have to take that army to Parthia, or it will become so dangerous that neither I nor anyone else could possibly control it."

"But you can't just leave," Sallust interjected, "without putting the city in order beforehand; otherwise, while you're gone, the Senate will go back to playing the old games, and you will have to cross another Rubicon."

"I couldn't have put it any better myself. That's it, exactly. What I didn't realize was that during the year that went by after Munda, before I could get things well enough organized to leave for Parthia, the beast got so angry, not at the Senate, but at me."

"Because, you see," Sallust again interrupted, "this anger you were talking about, the anger that pushed your men over the Rubicon behind you, was their own anger, not yours. It was the anger of men who'd fought so long and hard for this city, but it's a city that rich senators treat as their private estate. You managed to focus their anger on your personal enemies, because you'd earned the army's trust. But then, for a year after Munda, they saw you coming to terms with these same senators, they began to see you as one of 'them,' not one of 'us.' They'd fought in Gaul, they'd fought in Greece, Africa, and Spain, they'd made you the greatest man in the greatest city the world has ever seen, and still they were just the *plebs urbana*, city plebs, one cut above slaves or livestock. So going to Parthia became, for them, a symbol of the pointlessness of all their sacrifice."

"I don't think the men in the ranks would agree with you, Sallust."

"No, of course not, they'd still follow you anywhere, or at least I think so. Remember when you stopped that mutiny after you got home from Egypt, just by going out to the camp and giving the men exactly what they had been demanding, which made them so ashamed they followed you right to Africa, and on to Spain. When you addressed them as 'citizens' instead of 'soldiers,' I swear, every man there looked like a boy who'd just been slapped by his father. No, I'm talking about the officers, 'your' senators, Albinus and Trebonius and the rest. They were angry men, they thought you would clean house in the Senate, give them their dignity back—and you didn't."

"Rome can't be governed by the Senate any more," Caesar replied, showing just a touch of impatience. "That much any fool can see, but the sticking point is, it can't be governed without the Senate, either."

It seemed odd, even disturbing, to hear Caesar trying to justify himself. It wasn't his way.

"In the end, Sallust, I'm going to have to deal with Parthia, if not now, then soon. Now of course, I admit, it's not just the army that will be happier once it has another war to fight. I know that I'm a great general, as great as Alexander, if not greater. But I thought, right up to the Ides of March, that I was as great a statesman as I am a general. And in that, I thought, I would beat Alexander, because he knew how to conquer an empire, but had no idea at all how to govern it, once he had it. Now it turns out, I don't, either."

Caesar's shoulders slumped, slightly but perceptibly, and for a moment he looked much, much older. Then he shook himself like a man awakening from a bad dream.

"Sallust," he said, his tone of voice back to normal, "you have a house in the city, don't you?"

"Yes, I own a villa just outside the city walls, to the north and west."

"It would be good if you could stay there for a while. You are a most excellent writer and I enjoy your conversation. You can be of use to me. Stay close, will you?"

"You never answered my letters, Caesar, I had assumed you had little use for my writing."

"I read them all, Sallust, all your essays. Most of it is pretty useless stuff, to be quite honest, but you have your moments. I want someone to tell my story. I've told as much of it myself as I reasonably can, now Caesar need a Callisthenes."

"But Callisthenes ended up being executed by Alexander, before he could even start writing his history of the conquest of Persia."

This was met by Caesar's trademark half-smile. "That's a risk, Sallust, that you'll just have to take. Or go home to Praeneste, it's your choice."

Cleopatra

Cleopatra was almost asleep, or perhaps she had just fallen asleep, when she was awakened by her eunuch, touching her shoulder.

Not for the first time, she grabbed the dagger she kept concealed by the bed and put it to the man's throat long before she was awake enough to realize who he was. He had been through this before, though, and showed no sign of being startled or afraid; but even so he thought to himself, as he did every time this happened, that one day it would all end very suddenly.

"Mistress," he said, with his voice carefully controlled, "there is a man outside who wishes to speak to you."

"I have no desire to speak with some man who comes to me in the night. Send him away."

"He seems a man of consequence, mistress, and he is accompanied by soldiers, though he wears a cloak and his head is hidden under the hood. He said to tell you that the password—"

"We have no password, you fool, what nonsense is this?"

"—the password is 'the jewels are in the rug.'"

Cleopatra's eyes opened very wide. "Show him in," she said, after a moment, in a muffled voice, almost childlike, very unlike the voice her servants and her subjects were used to hearing, in public.

After the eunuch had left to bring in the unexpected nighttime visitor, Cleopatra looked around, wishing she had had some advance notice, then perhaps she would have arranged things differently. But what to do?

For half a year now, she had been living here in her ship, tied up at a private slip along the Tiber, downstream from the bridges of Rome, about halfway to the port in Ostia. It was not far, in fact, from Caesar's Ostia house, where she had been staying as Caesar's guest before the Ides of March had changed everything. It was a quiet spot. At first, she had worried about the possibility of being attacked out here, but it was only a day before a group of six or seven tough-looking men had appeared. They were, she assumed (correctly, as it happened), a squad of Caesar's soldiers, out of uniform but armed, sent to protect her. But by whom, exactly? There had actually been a day, during the riots that broke out after the trial, when a large group of thugs had appeared in the area, carrying torches and clubs, and looking as though they meant trouble. In a flash, though, legionary short swords had appeared, and after two or three of the mob had ended up bleeding and dying on the quayside, the rest had vanished.

The idea of living on her own ship, rather than taking up residence in the nearby villa Caesar had put at her disposal during her first two trips to Rome, seemed prudent. She was close enough to the city to be in touch with things, at Caesar's disposal, even though, till this moment, it had seemed increasingly unlikely that he even knew she was there, let alone that he would some day send for her, and their son. But she could still escape at a moment's notice, down the Tiber and out to sea before any pursuit could be organized. The ship was furnished and decorated with an opulence that, though it fell far short of her standards, was enough to impress these half-barbarian Romans.

Now, however, it suddenly seemed to her incredibly shabby. What was it about Caesar that you never really knew what was going on?

And now, here he was in her sleeping quarters, again, after all this time, the two of them, alone. Here she was, tongue-tied, alternating between angry and abashed and elated, and he . . . he was Caesar, smiling and looking at her, giving not the slightest outward sign of what he was thinking or feeling. It was as though this long, long time of separation had never happened, as though he had been away for a day or two.

Except, she suddenly realized, it was not like that at all. This was Caesar, the man she knew, and yet it was not. The lines in his face were edged more deeply, his hair was mostly gray, and he walked so slowly, stooping slightly. But his eyes still had that intensity, as though they were not mortal eyes at all.

She remembered, with aching clarity, the first time she had laid eyes on this man in Alexandria, almost four years ago.

She had hit on a scheme to reach him, even though the streets were full of soldiers and spies belonging to her odious little brother, Ptolemy, who was also her husband, and her life would not be worth a wooden obol if she'd been caught. She sent Caesar a modest gift, a carpet from Persia, and then at the last moment she traded places with one of the servant girls who accompanied the gift. This is what gave rise to the ludicrous story, still repeated by the uncritical, that she had wrapped herself up in the carpet and had herself unrolled at Caesar's feet. The reality had been far less amusing (or far more amusing, depending on your point of view): she had presented herself that evening at the door to Caesar's bedchamber, still in the guise of a maidservant, assuming that her sexual services would be desired, only to be dismissed with the merest glance. Just as he was closing the door in her face, she had called out, in Greek, in desperation, "Wait! If you send me away, I will be put to death. Please have mercy on me!" Why she had expected this to work, she had no idea, but it had been a lucky stroke: Caesar had paused, opened the door again, and beckoned for her to come in. The man was a conqueror of nations, slaughterer of tens of thousands in a single day, with a soft spot for a helpless slave girl, and this was only one of the paradoxes.

This had given Cleopatra her opening. At some length, she had convinced Caesar of her true identity, presented her case against her loathsome worm of a brother, Ptolemy, and found Caesar surprisingly amenable to her case; he was, as it turned out, still raging inwardly over the humiliating death and mutilation of Pompey, at the instigation of Ptolemy's advisor, that slimy Pothinus.

She spent that night, as she had hoped, in Caesar's bed. He was assertive without being brutal, attentive without being subservient, gave as well or better than he got; in a word, he was the kind of lover women always think they want.

And yet, at the core of it, she knew he was not completely satisfied. It baffled her at first, then it rankled, and then it caused her more and more pain, even, finally, despair.

She knew perfectly well that she was not the kind of beauty some modern-day Praxiteles would have tried to carve into a marble Artemis, or Aphrodite. She could count the flaws: the nose too long and too crooked, the jaw too long, the teeth not quite straight enough or white enough. But she also knew that when she wanted to get a man's attention, she could. She knew how to move, how to put a certain quality in her voice that made men want to bury themselves in her flesh. And once she was in bed with the man of her choice (and she seldom failed to gain her target, once she'd identified him), she knew how to excite him, how to bring him to the edge and hold him there, how to leave him breathless, exhausted . . . and unable to ever find another woman who pleased him even half so much. And in the process, she knew that he would do anything she wanted to please her. She knew how to use her own pleasure to increase his, which increased hers, so that the intensity of her pleasure would help her forget, for that moment, all the things that made her life seem so precarious and, at times, awful.

And now, four years later, she remembered how she had felt when she finally had in her arms, in bed, the master of the known world, the greatest conqueror since Alexander, the man who had enough power in his right hand to put dear brother Ptolemy into a well-deserved grave, and seat her on the throne of the pharaohs.

And what was even more astounding, he had agreed quite willingly to do all that she asked. In the end, Ptolemy had lost a civil war, and his overfed adolescent body had been found in the bulrushes by some fishermen, half rotten, half eaten. In the process, Caesar and his rather small squad of soldiers had fought several small but exceptionally nasty battles, which Cleopatra had watched with fascination. Caesar in danger was completely unruffled, and he always won. Always. When it was all over, everyone fully expected him to announce that Egypt was to become a Roman province; but instead, he kept his promise, and put Cleopatra on the throne of a nominally independent Egypt, along with a yet younger brother, also named Ptolemy, as co-regent. The child was devoted to his powerful big sister, and posed no threat at all: Cleopatra often seemed to forget that he was even there, and she was not alone in that. For all practical purposes, Caesar made her Pharaoh.

But she had never seen that particular look she longed to see in Caesar's eyes, the look that told her she had become a goddess for him. He would look contented, yes, lying next to her in bed, but it was not the look of a man who had encountered the divine. It was the look of a man who had just enjoyed a very nice meal, thank you, and though to be quite honest the food had been a little short of perfection, still, he was far too courteous to mention any of these trivial faults, and just kept saying how delightful the "meal" had been.

And that wasn't the worst of it.

Many men had tried to pleasure her in bed. It was part of her technique, her "witchcraft," to let them think they were succeeding. Underneath her thrashing, moaning, and cries of feigned ecstasy, she was always in complete control. The goal was to make his manhood entirely subject to her will. That was why she always searched the man's eyes for the look of adoration, and when she saw it (and she had never failed before), she felt a keen pleasure, far greater than anything a penis could ever give her.

Until, that is, she met Caesar, the man whom she needed to enthrall more than any other. Not only was some part of him held back from her (as she herself, with other men, had always held back some part of herself, the most important part), but he had managed to break through her defenses in a way and to an extent she could not have imagined. He always seemed to know exactly what she wanted, when she wanted it, when to be gentle and when not to be, when to move fast and when to go slow, until she was no longer in control, she was a wax tablet on which he could write whatever he wanted. And yet he didn't seem to want to write anything at all.

And so, after only a few days and nights, she found herself exactly in that position she had meant for him to be in: she was his, only his, all his. She had become insatiable, and she couldn't even tell if her passion came from her desire to bewitch this man, or from something far more ordinary and even demeaning: her need to feel him.

The siege her brother laid, trying to catch Caesar and Cleopatra in Alexandria, was a near thing, which would have cost both of them their heads, but she had passed through it in a daze, barely noticing the danger in the air. Then there was the long trip down the Nile, in her royal barge. Caesar had agreed so readily, but what was he thinking, really? She knew what the gossips were saying in Rome, even now, four years later: that she had cast a spell over Caesar, who had momentarily forgotten that he still had work to do, preferring to float down the river with her, drunk with love. She knew it was rather the other way around: he enjoyed himself, yes, but she was the one who was besotted, not he.

And then she'd discovered that she was pregnant. There had been a time, before Caesar, when she might reasonably have wondered who the father was, but if she was truly two months along when the tell-tale signs of her pregnancy began to appear, or even close to that, there was only one other candidate, and he would tell no one. In the months prior to Caesar's arrival in Alexandria, she had been under virtual house arrest, thanks to her loathsome brother/husband, with no time or inclination for honing her erotic talents, except for that one, and he was already out of anyone's reach. There was no real doubt in her mind: the father was Caesar. Or if he wasn't, no one could prove he wasn't, which made it true for all practical purposes. That nighttime conversation with Calpurnia had shaken her in this certainty, yes, but only for a time. Perhaps Caesar had deliberately misled his wife about his alleged infertility.

That was why she had not resorted to the foul-tasting drugs her servants had procured for her on a few previous occasions when something like this had happened. This baby had a brilliant future, and so, of course, did its mother, the Queen of Egypt. Or could it be something more? She was almost afraid to think about it.

But by the time the baby was born, Caesar was gone, off to Pontus, and then, finally, back to Rome. She had named her son Ptolemy Caesar, to be sure that everyone knew who his father was, sure that the aura of that name would keep people from even thinking that the child was, after all, a bastard. Well, there was no need to put too fine a point on the matter.

By this time little Caesar, Caesarion, as she called him in private, was almost four, and his features, his bearing, and most of all his character, a paradoxical but perfect mixture of detachment and passion, seemed to make his real parentage perfectly clear, to her if not to anyone else. But even though she had brought Caesarion to Rome to meet his father, Caesar had avoided ever laying eyes on him. Every time she had proposed a meeting, Caesar had looked her straight in the eyes, smiled slightly, and said . . . nothing. He never once replied to anything she said on that subject, ever.

This was baffling, but then, rumor had it that Caesar had several illegitimate sons, including, irony of ironies, both of the two Brutuses that had tried to kill him. And he had never addressed these rumors, never denied them, never confirmed them. In this, then, he was consistent, though it wasn't easy for Cleopatra to understand his reasons for this. Perhaps he'd never acknowledged paternity, but he'd sponsored the careers of all the men reputed to be his sons, and the lengths to which he had gone to protect Junius Brutus were truly remarkable. There were those who reported, in fact, that when Brutus had approached him with dagger in hand, Caesar had said, in Greek, "You, too, my son?" And then, of course, as by now everyone knew, Brutus had dropped his dagger. Well, no, not dropped it, but he hadn't used it, either.

So why, then, did he seem so utterly, utterly indifferent to Caesarion? Was it because her son was only half a Roman? This, from the man who enrolled Gauls in the Senate?

All of this, and more, went through her head at the speed of a lightning bolt, from the moment she set eyes on him, appearing so typically without the slightest notice, smiling at her as though no time had passed and nothing had happened since the last time he'd appeared in her bedchamber.

Had he come to say that he was ready to acknowledge Caesarion as his son and heir? Could his close encounter with death have softened his heart?

But Cleopatra refrained from asking the question that almost burst from her lips. Worse, she immediately discarded all of the various clever or powerful or poetic things she had rehearsed saying when and if she ever saw him again, in private. Instead, she fell back on the utterly banal:

"Caesar, it's so good to see you again."

"It's good to see you, my dear."

Cleopatra's heart sank at the distinctly paternal tone of this affection.

"And," he continued, "please accept my apologies for this melodramatic late-night appearance, all in disguise, no warning. But that's a consequence of being an Important Man, you know, the loss of freedom. I can't go anywhere or do anything, any more, without a great deal of fuss. You're a Queen, you have the same problem. And this is a meeting I wanted to have without any fuss. Odd, isn't it? The first time we met, you had to sneak into my quarters pretending to be someone else, and now, the roles are reversed."

Cleopatra smiled, and for just a moment, their eyes met. Her heart skipped a beat.

"Cleopatra, my love, I've come to talk to you about your future, and your son."

"He's your son, too, Caesar, surely you know that."

"Be that as it may, for now at least, he's your son. And I wish him the best, for that reason alone, if for no other. That's why I'm here, to discuss what, and how, and when." He sighed, and for a long moment seemed to be lost in thought, before he resumed. "I really do wish you hadn't given him my name, though, it makes everything so . . . awkward."

"Aren't you called Caesar because your father was named Caesar? I've never understood these Roman names. Your parents chose the name 'Gaius,' but no one ever calls you that; your friends call you 'Caesar,' and the rest call you "Gaius Julius" in public. I named my—*our* son the way a Roman should be named, a given name and a family name, together. He is a Caesar, after all."

Caesar laughed, or rather chuckled, really, the kind of laugh a father gives when his children are being adorably childish. "Well, to be perfectly correct, you should have named him 'Ptolemy Julius Caesar,' or no, that's not quite right either, just pick any good Roman first name except Gaius, say Marcus or Lucius or Sextus, and then add Julius Caesar—hmm— Ptolemaeus. Something like that."

It was as near to an acknowledgement of paternity as Cleopatra had ever heard from him, or, as it turned out, would ever hear.

"But I do have plans for him, Cleopatra, and for you, if you're interested."

"Of course I'm interested, Caesar. Really, sometimes you are the most exasperating man. Why do you think I've been lingering here, tied up at a dirty dock in a dirty river on this scow, instead of staying home and tending to my own business, and my own subjects?"

"You're the only one who can really answer that question, Cleopatra. I've no idea what goes on in that beautiful head of yours, never have."

It was a lie, and they both knew it, but there was no need to spoil the moment.

"Do you know what my plans were," Caesar continued, "before I very nearly got myself killed?"

"It was common knowledge, Caesar, everyone knew that you were about to leave to fight the Parthians. I liked the idea."

"Of course you did. You knew that I would stop in Alexandria on my way out, right? And on my way back, too, if I survived. But I won't insult you by implying that you think only of the bedroom. You must have realized, also, that I couldn't possibly leave the East without making some more permanent arrangements, and that you would be a part of those arrangements."

Now it was Cleopatra who smiled ever so slightly, but said nothing in reply.

"Now that I am back on my feet, it's time to do something about the East. But you see, I can't just pick up my plans where I left them. One thing I've learned from what almost happened to me is that Rome, as it exists today, cannot govern both itself and its whole empire. It's too much. We have a republic that was made up, several hundred years ago, of citizen-farmer-soldiers, where the senators were just as much farmers as the soldiers they led into battle. The Senate, you know, has no real power: its resolutions are not laws, and a senator as such cannot give orders that anyone has to obey. Yet for hundreds of years now it has been a private club where all the decisions are made, and nothing happens without the Senate's knowledge and approval. Rome can't stand the very idea of kings, and I have more than half a dozen nasty scars on my body to prove it, when I wasn't quite vigorous enough in denying that I wanted to be king."

"It's all so foolish, don't you realize that?" It wasn't the first time she'd expressed her frustration with the arcane rules of Roman politics. "It's Agamemnon's war council without Agamemnon. Nothing can be done that way."

"And yet it's been remarkably successful so far, don't you see that? Still, you're quite right, it can't go on like this, not when this city rules most of the world, from Syria to Britain. The constant bickering and squabbling in the Senate, worse, the need for cash to bribe your way into office, the need for provinces to plunder to get that cash, and all so that one group of senators can say to another, 'We can piss higher than you.' No, it has to change, any rational man can see that, but Rome is a city, not a 'rational man.' This is going to be much harder than I thought. I can't leave the city right now, not until I've made this incredible mass of human beings into some sort of a rational being, able to do its work."

"So you are going to forget about the Parthians?"

"No, but I can't do it all myself. I'm going to stay here and govern this city, and Antony, in my name, will take down the Parthians. I'm sending him in my place. It's the perfect solution for him, he's a good soldier but a terrible politician, no use to me here, but perfectly capable of fixing the problems poor old Crassus created for us by getting himself and his army massacred out there in the desert. Then, when he's brought back the eagles Crassus lost, restored our honor, and perhaps added a few more provinces to the East, I will make him Regent of the Eastern Provinces."

"You mean satrap?" Cleopatra was genuinely puzzled: what Caesar was proposing was fascinating, but the only word that came to mind was "bizarre." It was neither a Greek nor a Roman solution, but typical Caesar, so outrageous that you couldn't even find arguments against it.

She continued. "So you are going to be the King of Kings, like Cyrus or Xerxes, and all your various lands will be ruled in your name by satraps?"

"You can use that term if you like, Cleopatra, but please don't use it in public. Romans, as I've just been painfully reminded, are so touchy about names. I'm going to have to rule like a king, but 'king' is a word that I must never use nor allow anyone to use in my presence."

"So where do I fit in to all this?" Cleopatra asked. "I can see no place for me in this scheme of yours."

"That all depends on you, Cleopatra. But think of it this way, just between us: Antony will be King of the East. Who will be his Queen?"

"Antony has a wife, doesn't he? I think so. Whoever she is, I pity her, the man is such an ass. Anyway, she'll be his Queen, won't she?"

"You don't really know Rome, Cleopatra, and you certainly don't know Fulvia. She won't be anyone's Queen, any more than Calpurnia would be. We Romans have other expectations of our wives. And anyway, I seem to recall that you were never much concerned about such things, about men already having wives. If you want to be Queen of the East," he went on, talking right over her angry protest, "you will be Queen, and poor Fulvia doesn't stand a chance. Antony is not the sort of man who would hesitate for more than a heartbeat to change wives."

This was stunning, in its way, but Cleopatra in an instant realized what it was that Caesar meant for her to do. And she also realized that there was really no need to talk about it any further. He was passing her off to Antony, really, but in such a way that he and she were going to do this thing together, with Antony as their unsuspecting victim. What Cleopatra didn't know was that Caesar had done very much the same thing before, with remarkable success: the successive partners of his ex-wives and ex-girlfriends were all brought into Caesar's camp in this peculiar way. But that knowledge, if she'd possessed it, wouldn't have done much for her ego.

"I never cared much for this Antony friend of yours, Caesar. A drunken lout, was all I could see in him. Perhaps he's more interesting when he's sober. If he's ever sober."

"Don't underestimate him, Cleopatra. He's twice as smart and twice as dangerous when he's drunk as most men are when they're completely sober. If I ever manage to catch him completely sober, and live to tell of it, I'll give you a full report."

He stood, suddenly. "I really must be going, Cleopatra. I've kept you up half the night already, and though you may be still quite young enough for such foolishness, I am not. Good night." And he was gone, before she could say any more than just "Good night" in return.

She did not sleep that night until nearly dawn.

Cicero

The messenger who arrived at Cicero's door the next morning, a few days after Sallust's visit to the Suburra house, was just polite enough not to be surly. He delivered the letter from Caesar and explained that he would wait for a reply. The servant who answered the door took the letter, bowed very correctly, and closed the door in the man's face. Then he went inside to give the letter to his master's secretary, who in turn took it to Cicero.

The voice he heard in reply from the master of the house had not yet ceased to distress everyone in the household. Prudent slaves who are fortunate enough to work in the house learn very quickly, of course, to give every outward sign of attachment to the family, but in this house the attachment was, if not completely genuine, at least not entirely feigned. Cicero treated his slaves fairly, took care of them when they were ill, and often freed them after many years of service: Tiro was not the only example of this. So now Cleitophon (an educated Greek of Athenian descent, who had been highly recommended by the estimable Tiro to take his place as Cicero's secretary) was not really feigning his distress at the sound of his master's voice, so altered, barely audible, barely intelligible.

The invitation for Cicero to dine at Caesar's house was couched as an invitation, not a summons, but even so it was not to be declined. It was not even a matter of prudence or subservience, not now, not as it had been a year or so ago, not long after Caesar's return from the East, when Cicero had dined at the Great Man's house. That dinner had been memorable for the quality of the conversation, seasoned, as it were, by the tension Cicero always felt in the presence of this peculiar man. Now, however, there was an additional element: gratitude. Without the expert services of Caesar's own physician, the Briton—what was his name? Cicero was finding it increasingly hard to remember names. He knew the man well, but his name? Oh yes, Scaeva, apparently the nearest Roman equivalent to his barbarian name. A most interesting man, a pity only that they hadn't met when I was still . . . Cicero.

With difficulty he brought his mind back to the present.

It would not be easy to hold his own this time, for obvious reasons. He was still avoiding contact with all but the closest of his friends. But after what had happened that awful day, could there be, anyway, any possibility of resuming some semblance of an ordinary life? What to discuss? What was there to gain by going, or lose by not going? Cicero's inclination was to retire to his bedroom, go to bed, ignore the invitation, come what may.

But the invitation from Caesar unsettled Cicero, and this unsettling was more than he had felt, inside, since the day of the trial and its aftermath. But no, it could be declined, surely, since Caesar was not usually a spiteful man. He was acutely aware of his own greatness, yes, forget that at your peril, but it was a measure of Caesar's innate sense of *noblesse oblige* that he never wanted to seem petty. There would be no punishment, Cicero knew instinctively, if he politely refused. On the other hand, the invitation, if declined, would not be repeated, and then, whatever there might be that Cicero could learn, he would never learn.

At which point Cicero realized, suddenly, that there were indeed things he wanted to learn, though he could give no reasonable account of what these things might be, or why he needed to know them. He wanted to go eat at Caesar's table with the same desperate intensity he wanted not to go, not to see this man ever again.

In the end, then, curiosity won the day. Cicero told his slave to tell the messenger waiting outside that Cicero was grateful for the kind invitation and would be pleased to be Caesar's guest at the appointed day and time. Fortunately, the slave had no need to have the message spelled out in any detail. He had learned to grasp the gist of what his master had in mind from a few words ("I'll go, tell them thanks") and flesh them out with the necessary verbiage, all socially and grammatically correct.

The invitation was for the early evening of the next day, so Cicero set out as evening fell, properly but not ostentatiously attended, for Caesar's house, traveling in a litter with six bearers. It was the first time he had set foot outside the door of his Esquiline home since the day his anonymous protectors had carried him there. This dinner was to take place in the Regia, the official residence of the Pontifex Maximus, right in the Forum. Cicero would have felt uneasy in the Suburra, and Caesar, of course, knew that perfectly well.

For Cicero, one of the things that was so infuriating about Caesar was precisely the fact that it was so impossible to actually hate him. He was the living embodiment of everything Cicero had feared and fought against in his political life, but as a human being he was . . . indescribable. In the deepest recesses of his mind, Cicero still wondered, occasionally, if he would have joined the conspiracy to kill Caesar, if he'd been invited. And if he had been there, would he actually have been able to look Caesar in the eye and thrust a dagger into his belly?

There had been no chance, of course, to discuss all this with Brutus, after all the drama of the last day of the trial. If there had been such a conversation, Cicero would probably have told Brutus that in his place, he would probably have done the same as his client, his arm would refuse to do what his mind told it to do. Philosophers do not make good killers. Cold comfort for both of them. He wondered, idly, if Socrates would have been capable of tyrannicide, given both the necessity and the opportunity. Worth thinking about, some fine day.

The summer evening was pleasant. A brief rainstorm had rolled in from the sea in the late afternoon, cooling the air, the first hint that summer was about to give way to autumn, the season when Italy is perhaps at its most beautiful.

Cicero was met at the door of the Regia by Caesar himself, standing with a welcoming smile on his face just behind the burly slave who opened the door. Unconventional, as always, in a way that seemed to be almost democratic and yet thoroughly patrician, all at the same time.

The meal was simple, but exquisite. The quail were seasoned with spices that Cicero could not quite make out, but the choice, whatever it was, was perfect. An excellent Falernian was served, in a quantity sufficient to complement the meal, but not enough to addle anyone's thinking. Neither of these men were drunkards on any occasion, and on this particular occasion no one wanted his wits duller than usual.

The conversation during dinner moved easily from topic to topic. Caesar had a gift for finding some topic of conversation with almost everyone he met, but he was famous, too, for have no patience for idle chatter. Catullus, the fiery poet from Verona who had vilified Caesar, often obscenely, and had his poetry published by Cicero (whom he brilliantly skewered with an elaborate poetic compliment that was a complete parody of Cicero's own style), was discussed at some length, without embarrassment: Caesar was a man who enjoyed a joke at his own expense. Or was this, Cicero wondered, all part of the role Caesar had decided to play? Caesar hadn't lost his poise even when two dozen senators were trying to kill him. He would play to his dying breath, Cicero thought, the role of a man exceptional in every conceivable respect, including that quality the Greek called *sophrosyne*, for which the closest Latin equivalent was *moderatio*, self-control, the ability to perceive, automatically and exactly, how much of anything was too much. Taking personal offense at real or imagined slights was beneath the dignity of a man like Caesar, so he would never allow himself to be seen doing it.

When the food was cleared away and the wine cups discreetly filled for the last time, Caesar allowed the literary talk to lapse naturally, then turned to Cicero.

"Cicero, my friend . . . I hope I can still call you that?"

A slight smile, a slight nod. Caesar continued.

"There are things of great importance that I wish to discuss with you. There is so much of value in that head of yours, Cicero, and I have great need of it, just now."

"There is really nothing, now, that I can do." Cicero's struggle to control his voice and complete this sentence was obvious, and painful to watch.

"On the contrary, my old friend, there is very much you can do. You were already 'Father of the Country' almost twenty years ago, but now is the moment when this country needs a father more than ever."

Cicero pointed a finger at Caesar, then at himself, followed by a gesture of negation.

"You mean to say, I think, that I am *Pater Patriae* now, not you. Am I right?"

A nod.

"I was given the title by the Senate, yes, just as you were after you crushed Catiline's project, whatever it really was, but as for me, I still don't honestly know if I saved the country or destroyed it. I can lead an army into battle, and if the god of war is not determined to destroy me, I will win. Even if I lose, I win. But I've learned from recent events that I have no talent for *ta politika*. I'm not a statesman. I don't mean 'politician,' I'm not bad at that, after all it's much like war, just without quite as much blood. I mean 'statesman.' By which I mean someone who can do for this city and its Empire what Scaeva has done for me, and for you. Rome is a great city, the greatest, far beyond any other, but it has fallen ill. We need someone who can look at the symptoms, name the disease, and tell us how to cure it, before it is too late. That someone is not me, Cicero, but you."

"How, in the name of all the gods, do you expect me to do that?"

"I don't expect you to stand at the Rostra and give great speeches that will move the Senate and the people to do what needs to be done. There is a kind of providence, you know, in the fact that your . . . injuries have removed you from doing what you have always done better than anyone else could do. The same providence, I suppose, that kept me from going off to Parthia at exactly the wrong moment."

"But what would Epicurus say? 'Providence,' indeed!"

"Well," Caesar replied, with a grimace that might have been a wink, "he wouldn't like it much, would he? But there you have it. I'm a soldier, really, not a philosopher. I think you know what I mean, Cicero, you've fought a few battles yourself, in Cilicia, and from what I hear you did very well. Now tell me, on the night before each battle, did you have a plan all worked out?"

A nod.

"And did the battle ever go just as you planned it, down to the last detail?"

A smile that clearly said, No, of course not.

"I always went into a battle with three plans, a main idea and two variants in case something went seriously wrong, and at least half the time I still ended up making a fourth plan in the saddle, when the whole thing just went balls up."

Cicero grimaced.

"Oh, sorry for the language, Cicero, you see? I am so much more the soldier than the statesman."

"Oh, it's not that, no. War's just a shitty business." Cicero suddenly smiled to hear the casual obscenity leave his own mouth.

Caesar laughed. "I couldn't have put it any better."

"Speeches are the same, you know," Cicero resumed. "You write for days, then you stand up and improvise anyway."

"Yes, that happens to me, also. I write a beautiful speech, polish it, learn it off by heart, and then when I stand up to speak, I end up saying something completely different. Tell me, when you publish your speeches later, do you publish the version you wrote, or the version you actually spoke."

"Neither." A croaking laugh, stifled. How long had it been since he had last laughed? "I write what I should have said."

A laugh in response. "You publish what you should have said, which is neither what you planned to say nor what you actually said, right?"

A nod.

"So that's my point about philosophy. Philosophers are like generals who go into a battle with only one, brilliant plan, or like orators who come to the Senate with a brilliant speech in their heads, which they deliver word for word as they wrote it."

Cicero thought at once of Cato, but decided not to mention him, at least not just now. For that matter, Brutus had the same flaw, as a speaker: he gave lectures, not speeches. But that was another name that should probably not be mentioned just now.

"As for providence," Caesar continued, "show me a soldier who doesn't believe in it, and I'll show you a soldier who's never actually been in a battle. The trick is, to see when providence, or the gods, or whatever, has given you one more fleeting chance to save yourself, and then you take it, and you win. That is exactly what I meant, Epicurus be damned. Well, of course, that would make him even angrier with me, wouldn't it? How can you be damned if your philosophy won't allow you to believe in damnation?"

This got an appreciative laugh from Cicero, and this time it came a little easier.

"But to get to the point.

"I'm not going to live forever. If I were under any illusions before on that point, I'm certainly not now. And I don't want to be Alexander. I don't want to conquer most of the known world, and then have it fall all to pieces when I die, before my body is even cold. If all of this blood and money spent in fighting a civil war is not to be for nothing, then I have to be sure that the republic will survive me.

"Cicero, it's always distressed me that you and I have mostly been at odds with each other in political matters. It distresses me all the more because I sense that, at some level well below the surface of the bickering factions, we see the same problems and we share the knowledge that things just can't continue as they are. What I did was to smash a broken system, like tearing down the remnants of a bridge that has already failed, and is just roiling the water without serving any useful purpose. You and

I may not agree that this was the time and this was the way to go about it, but I think you would not disagree with me that this 'bridge' was about to fail, catastrophically. And that would be a catastrophe, not just for the likes of us, for the Senate, not just for Rome itself, but for most of the world, which would instantly devolve into the chaos our great-grandfathers set out to deal with, after Carthage was finally defeated.

"The fish pond people." It seemed a complete non-sequitur, but Caesar caught it immediately.

"Exactly. Most of the Senate consisted of men who thought about little else but exotic carp for their ornamental fish ponds, while people were starving in the Suburra, or the Aventine. The more people and the more land we came to rule, the larger the sphere of our responsibility, and yet all the important decisions were being made by people who could not see past the walls around their gardens.

"Now I come along, with an army behind me that no one could defeat, and I kick over the game board, scatter the pieces, so that no one can seriously think about picking them up and starting the same old game all over again. Sorry to change metaphors, again, but you can follow me perfectly well, I think."

"Yes."

"Now, let us imagine for a moment that Brutus had done what he was supposed to do, and opened my belly. I'm dead. What happens now? Could you possibly think that those men had a ghost of an idea what they would do after they performed their 'tyrannicide'? Because I'm pretty sure, myself, that they had no idea at all. They would have gone home, cleaned themselves up, put on a nice dinner, congratulated themselves for a good day's work. And the next day they would have gone to the Senate, and taken things up just where they left them when I crossed the Rubicon, more than five years ago, as though all of this had never happened. But it did happen. The army, my army, would have reacted very quickly. It might have taken a few days for the word to get out to all the men, but sooner or later the army would appear outside the city and demand the heads of the men who killed Caesar. And that's assuming that they would not already have been lynched by angry mobs. Within a few days, ten at the very most and probably not that long, they would either be dead or they would have run for their lives. And my dear friend Antony, waving my bloody toga here and there, would have whipped up such a frenzy, in the city and in the army, that he would just step right into my place. So the Senate would find that they had just traded the egomaniac Caesar for the drunken maniac, Antony."

Cicero could not suppress a laugh.

"I don't want this to happen," Caesar went on, "or anything like it, Cicero. I don't want it all to be for nothing, and I don't want Antony or someone like him taking over when I'm gone. Something more lasting has to be built. It's not enough to tear down the old bridge, we have to build a new one."

By this time Cicero was completely overwhelmed by emotions that seemed to batter each other like waves against a breakwater. So much of what this man was saying was repugnant to every political value Cicero had spent his life building and defending, and yet so much of it rang completely true. His life was in ruins, his Republic was in ruins, and yet this man seemed to be implying all this time that there was more to be done, and that he, Cicero, could do it. In spite of everything.

"Why me?"

"But who else, really? I once considered offering you a consulship. That I cannot do now, for obvious reasons. But I can offer you something else, perhaps something greater. I'm going to confess to you now, Cicero, here, between us, that at one time I was seriously considering the idea of becoming King of the Romans. As a king, I could designate an heir, and then it would be a very obvious and natural thing that upon my death, my heir would step into my place. And in most of the world, that would be, of course, my son, just as Alexander stepped into the shoes of his father when Philip was assassinated. But Alexander left no son able to succeed him, and his empire was carved up by his generals. Pardon the history lesson, you know all this, but bear with me."

Cicero nodded and gestured with his hand, as though to say, "Go on."

"All those generals, though, Seleucus and Antigonus and Ptolemy, after they had taken as much land as they could grab and hold, they just passed on their kingdoms to their sons, and so on for many generations. You know, I once had a kind of fascination with Alexander. I wanted to match him or outdo him as a general. Perhaps I've already done as much, militarily, I'm not the best judge of that, finally. But there's one thing that's become clear to me: Alexander lived a life of glory, but he died a failure, and that's precisely because he did nothing to ensure that the empire he created would last after his death. I mean to have an heir. We Romans, though, we've never liked this whole business of kings leaving their thrones to their sons, not since we expelled the Tarquins. Aristotle is quite right about this, whether we're talking about tyrants or kings: there just is no guarantee, no matter how smart and capable the ruler, that his son won't be an idiot, or a drunkard, or a maniac. So we vested the sovereign power in a pair of elected consuls, and let the paternal authority, so to speak, rest with the Senate. That worked well for hundreds of years, but as we've agreed, it's no longer working well."

Cicero said nothing, and his face showed no emotion; inside, however, he was in turmoil. What Caesar was saying, and where he was tending . . . It was like an abyss opening at his feet. The problem was, Cicero didn't really know which he wanted more: to run away, or to leap into that abyss.

"Plato," Caesar resumed, "imagined a perfect city, but he knew that even if someone were somehow to found such a city, the problem of succession would eventually bring it down. The ideal would be for intelligent and capable rulers to identify and train the most intelligent and capable among the young, and bring them up to be the next generation of rulers. But how to do that, in the real world? Now as for me, I have no son. I will never have one. Nor do I have a daughter, now, whose husband could take my place when I die."

Caesar paused, and looked straight at Cicero, who returned the look. Both men had lost adult daughters, and neither would ever really recover from it. There was no need to dwell on it now.

"I have found a suitable heir, however, and I mean to arrange things right, so that when I finally go where Brutus and the others wanted to send me, as Homer puts it, "before my time," then my heir can become the next Caesar. And no, to anticipate your question, I don't mean Lepidus, I don't mean Cleopatra's son, who for some reason known only to his mother bears my name, and by all means I don't mean Antony. I have plans for each of them, yes, but taking my place in the Republic is not part of those plans for any of them."

"Who is your heir, then?"

Caesar smiled. "Against my advice (but what does that matter?), my sister Julia married a man named Atius, and nothing good came of it except for a daughter, Atia, who grew up and married Gaius Octavius, an equestrian. They had a son, also Gaius Octavius, who is now 19 years old. When he was just a boy, his father died; Atia remarried, but her new husband wanted nothing to do with someone else's son, so Octavius went to live with my sister, his grandmother. Sorry for the tiresome family stuff, but I needed to explain how it happened that I got to know the young man, who is now 19, that I had some connection with him. Anyway, just before I was attacked last March, I drew up a will, in which I adopted young Octavius as my son, and named him as my heir. I mean to live a few more years, at least, and my hope is that, during this time, young Octavius will either prove to be worth the trouble I mean to invest in him, in which case he will replace me, or he will disappoint me, in which case I'll replace him. But after what almost happened, I'm not going to wait, after all, to adopt him posthumously, in my will. I've already set the process in motion. Within a few days, the city will learn that there is a young man with the resonant name, Gaius Julius Caesar Octavianius. Now I'm getting to the point, Cicero. I see you fidgeting, trying to be polite while I talk about family matters."

Cicero made a gesture that might have meant many things, but was probably intended to mean, "Please go on."

"I want to put young Octavius (Octavian, rather, to be correct, though it's not official quite yet) under your tutelage. If all goes well, I'd like to arrange for him to be consul for next year, and for the Senate to commission him to undertake a comprehensive program to restore the Republic. I think he should take two colleagues; these things always work best when there is a committee of three, don't you think? Say, Lepidus, a decent soldier who is loyal and industrious, but neither smart enough nor ambitious enough to be a danger to anyone. And you."

The look of shock on Cicero's face was, Caesar thought, priceless. He continued.

"We'll have the Senate make a resolution naming you, Octavian, and Lepidus (or whoever you prefer for a third), as 'triumvirs to restore the republic' or something of that nature. You would have a year, maybe more, to fix that crumbling bridge called "Republic," so that it will last at least a few hundred years more. And I have another task in mind for you that may please you even more. As you know, the last censors, the ones that were selected while I was in Gaul to make sure that everyone who would be likely to support my case in the Senate would be marked down as morally deficient and thus conveniently removed from the Senate— they left their office in such disgrace that the idea of selecting censors and having another *lustrum* just now . . . well . . .".

"It seems preposterous."

"Quite so. You may not be inclined to produce as many words as before, my old friend, but the ones you do produce are exactly right. The office is in disrepute, and just between us, I rather think one of the reasons for this attitude in the Senate is that no one really supposes that I would approve of having censors conduct a *lustrum*. But I've been thinking about this for some time now. Public works are neglected, the Senate has lost its bearings, no one knows who is who. These are problems I can't fix, even with the temporary powers the Senate has seen fit to give me, which, in any event, I mean to set aside at the earliest possible moment. Anyway, here's my idea: it's time to have a *lustrum,* and I think you would be perfect for it. In fact, I can't think of one other person in this city right now who could do this job. And it's a job that doesn't require any speeches, though it's all the more important for that. I don't need your eloquence right now, I need your intelligence and your wisdom. Or rather, the Republic does, as it's never needed it before. It's time to clean up the mess we've made, don't you think?"

Even if he had still been inclined to speak in torrents of well-chosen words, as before, Cicero would have been left speechless by the proposal Caesar had just made, at once awful and wonderful, terrifying and exciting. He opened his mouth, but closed it without making a sound.

When he saw that there would be no verbal answer, Caesar resumed. "I won't even ask you to say 'yes' or 'no' right now. This is an enormous burden that I'm asking you to assume, and you'd have every right to say that it's too much. Or, which may be even more likely, you may find the whole idea just too repugnant, not something you want your name to be associated with. But before you make up your mind, if you haven't already, I'd ask you to meet Octavian once or twice, size him up, see what you think of my choice. At the very least, if you think I've misjudged his capability, you can tell me, as a friend to a friend, that I should look for another heir. First that, then we can talk about the *lustrum.* But for now, just think about it, and please don't say no until you're sure."

Cicero's face, which had become more and more tense as Caesar talked, relaxed ever so slightly. He had been given a graceful exit. He nodded.

"One reason why I think you will hit it off, you and Octavian, is that he was raised, as you were, in a fine equestrian family, not in Rome, but in Velletri, a pretty little town that I think is not too much different from Arpinum."

Cicero grimaced. He was not really ashamed of where he came from, but over the last thirty years, no senator who mentioned Arpinum in his presence had meant anything good by it.

"I don't want to seem patronizing," Caesar said, faultlessly interpreting the wordless grimace, "but I really do think that people like you and Octavian, Italian but not Roman, noble but not patrician—you are the foundation upon which this city and its Empire rests. You've always talked about *tota Italia*, and though you may well not believe me, that slogan of yours has always appealed to me. Think about this, meet my nephew, and we can talk again later. All is up for discussion, unless you say no right now, in which case I promise never to mention it again, either to you or to anyone else. Agreed?"

There was really not much Cicero could do, at this point, but nod his assent.

Caesar

After Cicero took his leave (still saying little, but with ever so much more spring in his step), Caesar did not stay at the Regia, but rather called his bearers, the lictors, and the dozen extra armed guards who now escorted him any time he left his house, and made his way back to the Suburra.

Despite the late hour, the streets were far from empty. It was a very pleasant evening, as the sea breeze came in, cooling down the city after the warm September sun. But that was not the reason for the crowding. This was Caesar's own fault: one of his first administrative decisions when he returned from Spain, after Munda, and set out to put the city in order, was that there was to be no wheeled traffic within the city walls during the day. Before this decree, a half hour's journey through the city could take an afternoon, and when the center of the city was jammed with carts and animals, not even a cohort of legionaries could make a path through it. And all this was to say nothing of the appalling number of children who were trampled every day by mules and oxen. One could hardly claim to be a "man of the people" and allow this to continue.

Now, as his entourage made its way, slowly, along the streets, Caesar reflected somewhat ruefully on the consequences of his own decision: forbidden to clog the streets during the day, the carts all entered the city after sundown, and rumbled down the streets until nearly dawn, moving the food and other goods the city needed to survive. There was, in fact, no way of reducing vehicle traffic into this enormous city without causing major disruptions, mass hunger not excluded. Now, it was ever so much easier to move around in Rome during the day, and senators could no longer claim that they were late for a meeting because they had been unable to move through streets clogged with people, animals, and wagons. But Rome had become a place where the nights were noisier even than the day, and those who did not have very thick walls around their bedchambers slept fitfully, at best.

The irony of political power, Caesar thought, not for the first time, is that most of it, nearly all of it, is illusory. A city with a thousand thousands of inhabitants lives its own life, by its own rules. One might as well try to tell the tides when they can ebb and when they can flow, as try to tell so many individual human beings when they can go where. If an army of several legions is already a terrifying thing that only the best of generals can keep under some semblance of control, some of the time, then a city of this size is a monster above all others. Laughable, to imagine that you can actually govern it.

And if this is true of one city, what can be said of an Empire that stretches from one horizon to the other, from the cold, misty north to the deserts beyond Numidia? It would be interesting, to say the least, in a horrifying sort of way, to take a census of the whole Empire, to count all those people, using numbers that the mathematicians would probably have to invent. And for all of that, Caesar thought, I am responsible.

He glanced through the curtain on his litter. People were making way, the drivers pushing their carts and animals to one side so that the litter could pass. They knew, obviously, who was coming. Rich senators might well try to pass these streets at night, as Cicero had surely done not so long ago, but no one would make way for them. On the contrary, the drivers of mule carts took a perverse delight in slowing the progress of the rich and powerful, making them wait. But even the most prominent senator did not travel with lictors and an escort of tough-looking soldiers, so it required little deductive skill for almost everyone out on the street to conclude that the none other than Caesar himself was coming. And they would not block his way, partly, perhaps, because they feared his soldiers, but more so because he was their man, the one who had boxed the noses of all those arrogant senators they detested, and they genuinely wished him well. This was as least as much a part of his power as the swords of his legions. Sulla, after all, had had legions, but the people, the fathers and grandfathers of these people here on the street tonight, had hated Sulla, and that old bastard in turn never made any secret of his loathing for the people. The result had been, that Sulla's power had lasted for a year or so, after which the bitter old man had died a miserable death, and nothing he had done outlasted him even a decade—except the hatred.

Cicero feared the urban masses at least as much as Sulla hated them, but if he didn't learn to deal with his fear, all his brilliance would be for nothing. Cicero couldn't get past the yelling, the cursing, the dirty, worn clothing, the smell, the jagged-tooth smiles, and preferred to imagine a city of industrious provincial nobles like himself (or like Sallust, or Octavius, as little as those three men might think they have in common), decent, presentable, well-mannered in a way that real patricians seldom were.

As he listened to the shouting and jostling outside, intermixed with men calling to each other, "Look, it's Caesar!", he remembered how it was, thirty years ago, no, more than thirty, when he was still a very junior senator just beginning to make his mark. He could remember the day, in fact, when he was making his way through the streets to the Senate, and for the first time he had noticed passers-by stopping, pointing him out to others, watching him pass. It had been intoxicating, then. Now, it was something he often longed to escape.

He knew that, now, there were men, even a fairly large number of them, who seemed to have no better occupation than to lounge on the street near his house, watch for him, follow him, spread the word through the alleys: "Caesar is coming!" "Caesar is dining at Cicero's house!" "Caesar went to visit a wealthy widow and didn't leave till dawn!" He could do nothing, in fact, not even fart at a dinner party, that would not be talked about. There were times he thought that, if some god actually existed and offered him his heart's desire, he might well ask if he could just walk away from it all, maybe go and live quietly, anonymously, in the Ostia house, which was probably his favorite of all his many houses. There is a freedom in anonymity, and once you've lost it, you are as much a slave as any Thracian pulling an oar in the galleys.

What would it be like to be one of these men, out there? To be a driver of mules, to pass the streets unnoticed by anyone, to look at whatever or whoever interested him without anyone even caring that he was there, to stop in a tavern for a cup of sour wine, and then sit and drink it without any fuss; and if he happened to have a denarius or two, perhaps a whore, without any fuss about that, either.

But none of that was possible now, was it? Not much point even thinking about it. Strange to think, but even as I sit here, envying these men their anonymity, many of them are surely looking at this litter, knowing who is inside, and thinking how much they would like to be me.

It is probably as well there are no gods to grant wishes. I would probably enjoy my anonymity for a fortnight, and then I would be standing outside the Regia, wishing I were inside. In fact, the other night, when I slipped out of the house in disguise, through the servants' entrance, to see Cleopatra, I had a moment of anonymity, but I can't say I enjoyed it much. Well, yes, it was amusing to think, as I passed a party of drunken senators' sons on the street, what they would say if they knew who it was they just jostled. But if they'd discovered me, I'd have to make a joke of it, and go home, and try to think up another way to have that talk with Cleopatra.

And this brought his thoughts back to the future, to his plans, to the concrete problems at hand. He would always be a general first and last, even when it was not really an army he was leading into something that was not exactly a battle. His mind went over it all for the hundredth time at least: have I thought of everything? Am I ready for everything? Will everyone and everything I need be ready to hand when I need them? Have I considered all the possibilities, all the potential weaknesses, points of possible counterattack? And when (not "if") I am taken by surprise, will I be able to hit back hard and quick, and survive?

He had made by now all his preparations. All his resources were committed, the main players set in motion, each of them thinking they knew what was going on, and each being more or less mistaken about that. It was as it should be.

Without actually lying to anyone, he had let each of them follow their own line of thinking to a set of conclusions that would induce them to do what he needed them to do.

With Sallust, he had indeed been more honest than with the others. He'd told the man what he wanted from him, and in this case, what he said was exactly what he really wanted from him. The man could write, a magnificent, terse, dense, deliberately archaic Latin, as impressive in its own way as Cicero's magnificent, flowing prose, but without the torrent of words. Sallust probably didn't believe it, but it was true: Caesar had indeed read, with interest, all the letters Sallust had sent him, not because he wanted the advice (most of it was perfectly predictable and pretty useless), but because he saw here a thoughtfulness and a style that he could use. It was important to make sure that his story was told, and told well; otherwise, he would be like Sulla, a man whose work did not outlive him. In Gaul, and even during the Civil War, he had tried to tell his story himself, not without success; but even then, as the war went on, he had been forced to recruit Hirtius and others to do the writing for him. Sallust was ever so much better than Hirtius.

As for Cleopatra: it was hard to say whether she realized that Caesar neither wanted nor expected her to become Queen of the East, or for her son to rule anything more than Egypt (if that). Most of the men who had ever underestimated her intelligence or her ruthlessness were dead. Passion was a means to her ends, not an end in itself, which was the crucial thing all her previous enemies had failed to realize. Oh yes, she loved the luxury, and she loved power, and she loved the adulation only a Pharaoh can command, but she never lost sight of the fact that her position was precarious. If she had, it would have been her body the fisherman would have found in the Nile bulrushes, not her brother's.

She was a lioness in bed, aroused and arousing, but in all her erotic gymnastics there was calculation. It was all about power. That's what it means to be royal, that even your sexual organs are, so to speak, weapons in a war. And it was all done because all those other people out there, like these people here, on the streets of Rome, needed to eat, to make love, in numbers sufficient to keep the whole thing going. To what end? But Caesar immediately cut off that line of thinking, as he always did. Philosophy has it uses, but a sensible man knows when to stop.

So if indeed she'd seen through Caesar's manipulation, as he more than half supposed she had, Cleopatra would instantly realize that she must not give the slightest outward sign that she understood. She was a falcon, which he had just unhooded and released to chase a rabbit. She would fly straight and fast at the target, attack it, kill it, and pick it up in her talons. But she would not make this kill, as a soldier would, out of loyalty to him. She would kill because she wanted to do so, and she would bring the prey to Caesar—if, that is, it pleased her to do so. If it didn't, she would consume it herself.

Sex with her had been . . . exceptional, intriguing, a pleasure to remember, but largely because it was safely over. They had both used all their formidable erotic skills to please the other, but both had carefully held back from the surrender of self that Eros demands. He knew it, and he supposed that she knew it, too, but the whole point of the game between the two of them was never to mention it. After he had cut himself loose from her, to fight a quick war in Asia and then return to Rome, she had toyed with the role of Medea, but finally played the role of Ariadne, abandoned by Theseus on Naxos, waiting to become the mistress of a god. He knew that it wasn't the man, Caesar, that she was in love with, but rather the power that flowed from him, the power with which she could surround herself, so as never to be afraid again. And that was perfect, exactly what he needed from her at this moment. Now she would use those formidable skills, the bedchamber acrobatics, on another target, a target that would not even try to hold anything back.

The conversation with Cicero, then, had gone remarkably well. The man was no fool, nor a coward, nor a weakling, though there were certainly some who thought Cicero was all of those things. He would resist, for a while, the idea of cooperating in the establishment of a new order in Rome, but in the end he was smart enough to realize that the thing had to be done, and brave enough to take on the task. And his will and his mind were both strong enough to finish the task, once he had taken it on. The chance to create a philosopher-king (because that is what Octavian was going to be, though neither term would ever be used of him in public) would be impossible for Cicero to resist too long or too hard.

Cicero almost certainly realized, if he was in a position to think about it (perhaps he was, perhaps not), that he had been saved from the lynch mob that had made such short work of Brutus, Cassius, and the others, not by fate, or chance, or the kindness of the immortal gods, but by careful provisions, made in advance. The deaths of the five defendants had been a most regrettable necessity, to which Caesar had reluctantly given his consent. But he wanted Cicero alive. Well, things happen, it could have been much worse. A way had been found to make the best of the contingency, so all was well.

Which brought to mind the only other player of importance left to account for: Antony.

There had been no conversation with him, and would be none, at least nothing very serious, no more than the usual bantering that Antony preferred to any sort of real conversation. It was enough to set the falcon on the rabbit, and let the rabbit do what it could. Its chances of survival were not good. In a very public way, Caesar would announce that he himself would not go to fight the Parthians and recover the standards lost by Crassus, but would send his most able field commander, Antony, to perform that vital service.

Caesar knew, of course, that Antony had not meant for him to survive the Ides of March. It had been a serious error, underestimating Antony' capacity for duplicity, and like every one of the relative handful of such errors Caesar had made in his career, this one had nearly cost him his life.

In fact, if Antony had been just a little smarter, if he had done what Caesar would have done in his place (that is, had a contingency plan ready in case Brutus or one of the others had lost his nerve at the lost moment), then today, Caesar would be dead, Antony would have taken his place in command of the legions, and Rome would be his. All he would have needed to do, fairly quickly, would be to arrange for poor Octavian to have an unfortunate accident, not a hard thing to do when there is disorder in the city and gangs are afoot. But Antony hadn't made the right moves.

The plan itself was not that bad, though it was childishly easy to figure out, after the fact. Antony would use his foreknowledge of the conspiracy to make just the right use of Trebonius's clumsy attempt to delay his intervention; he would allow just enough time to be sure that Caesar was dead before springing his trap on the conspirators, probably killing all of them on the spot, before proclaiming to the city that Caesar was dead, but that he, Antony, had dealt justice to the murderers. The army already loved him, the city would learn to love him, and he could do as he pleased, no longer Caesar's adjutant, but king-in-all-but-name. Perhaps in name as well: Antony wasn't a subtle man, and he wouldn't realize that such a move would sooner or later bring another Brutus upon him.

It would not end well.

So Antony would be launched at the Parthians, thinking that he's the falcon, when in fact he's the rabbit. The problem was easily stated, but not so easily solved: Antony was too dangerous to be left alive, but Caesar himself could not be seen to have taken any part in eliminating him. So he would have to do this distasteful but absolutely necessary task by proxy. There will be so many logistical problems in getting troops and supplies to him for the Parthian expedition, problems that Antony doesn't handle well, since you can't solve them by cursing and swinging a sword. In the meantime, Cleopatra would have him by the balls, figuratively if not literally, and the combination of wine and sex would reduce him to mud. Either he will finally march against the Parthians, ill-equipped, underprepared, and end up as badly as Crassus did, or he will just dawdle and not march, until the Senate and the people, together, demand that something be done.

By then, one way or the other, there will be time for Caesar to what he does best: to arrive when he is least expected, hid hard and fast, and win the war before the enemy is completely aware that it's started. But his authority at home, combined with the complementary skills of old Cicero and young Octavian, will also have given the Republic a new foundation. So the die will be cast again, with this difference, that live or die, Caesar can't lose. Neither can Rome.

And let Alexander turn over in his grave.

Calpurnia

Caesar entered his wife's bedroom quietly, late at night, through the "private" door, through which neither of them had passed for several months now. Calpurnia, who had just begun to doze off, was momentarily startled by his sudden appearance next to her bed. Surely, he didn't want . . .

"I'm so sorry to disturb you," he said, "but I have a matter of some importance to discuss with you, and I really can't wait for a better time to talk."

"I've been your wife long enough now," she replied smoothly, covering her alarm with an effort, "to know that you will do whatever you choose to do at the moment that best suits you. I'm neither surprised nor annoyed that you've appeared so mysteriously beside my bed, and to tell the truth I'm really very pleased to see you here. It's the little things like this which tell me that life in this house is finally returning to normal. You've been neglecting your wife." She shook a finger at him in mocking reprimand.

"It's still too early for that, Calpurnia, though I do hope it won't be too much longer. I feel like an old man sometimes, and I don't like it much."

Calpurnia laughed. "I can wait a little longer, husband. But only a little."

Caesar smiled—and then, without ceasing to smile at her benignly, he changed the subject.

"Calpurnia, you did your very best, that day, to keep me at home. If you had succeeded, things might have gone very differently. Don't ever think for a moment that I don't know that. I should've listened to you."

For several heartbeats, time stood still. It seemed to Calpurnia that the moment had finally come, the moment she had been dreading, and still her first thought was to find some way to defer it. Caesar, like Caesar, showed no signs of impatience, but of course he wanted some kind of response. He smiled, he waited.

Calpurnia drew a deep breath and plunged into the abyss.

"If you had listened to me much earlier, Caesar, long before the Ides of March, none of this would have happened."

"What do you mean?"

"I mean the many times I tried to warn you not to trust those slimy bastards, that they didn't deserve the confidence you put in them, and especially Brutus. You think of yourself as a great judge of a man's character, and most of the time, you're right. But you've always been better at dealing with an enemy who announces himself as your enemy. You read Pompey perfectly, but he was too stupid, forgive me for saying so, to even try to deceive you about his intentions. You could read that fool Cato like a book, too, but again, that man hated you, for whatever reason, from the day he laid eyes on you, and he never let up, even for a moment. You beat them both, you beat that Gallic chieftain Vircing—whatever, I can't wrap my mouth around Gallic names—because you knew that beating you in battle was his only possible path to glory, and you used it against him. I read your commentaries, you know. But Brutus, Cassius, and even Albinus—you never seemed to notice how their eyes were always saying something very different from the words coming out of their mouths. Always."

"That's the woman's gift, isn't it? To know what's in the other person's heart, even when their faces and their words are telling a different story. Of course, if that intuition were so infallible as you women seem to think, how would expert seducers like me ever succeed?"

This sudden display of vulgarity was vintage Caesar, trying to put her off guard. Calpurnia refused to let herself rise to that bait.

"You succeed, you sons of bitches, because we choose to let you think we've been fooled. Men are so often surprised when they wake up the next morning and see who's lying next to them. Women never are."

Caesar laughed, and this time his amusement seemed genuine. "I take your point."

"That's as may be, my dear husband, but I don't think you've taken my point at all. You see . . .".

She drew in a deep breath and continued.

"You see, I knew exactly what was going to happen at Pompey's Theater that day. But it wasn't 'intuition.' Antony had told me everything, the day before."

The smile disappeared from Caesar's face. There was a flicker of something that might have been anger. "You knew? Then why didn't say so?"

"Because," she replied, "I also knew that you knew as much as I did about the Ides of March, and so if I confronted you with this truth, this reality that in fact we both understood, you would have been in an impossible predicament. You could either have dismissed my fears, knowing them to be entirely justified, or you could have said that you knew perfectly well about the danger you were facing, and you were going to go there anyway. So I gave in. There was no chance I could convince you to stay home, and anything else I could have said to make you stay would've made it so very difficult for us to stay married."

"Knowing that I was walking into mortal danger, you just gave it up?"

"It was the hardest thing I've ever done, not to throw myself on the ground screaming. Not that it would've done any good."

"But you realize that the main reason I decided to go was precisely that you had tried so hard to convince me not to go. Or . . ." But he didn't finish the sentence. His voice trailed off as he thought very hard for a moment. Then something appeared on his face that Calpurnia had only seen two or three times, and had hoped never to see again: a rage so intense that it was taking every bit of strength Caesar could muster not to attack her. With a supreme effort to keep his voice under control, he said, "Or is it that you knew all along that if you tried to keep me at home, I would be all the more likely to go? Is that what you wanted: for me to die? Had life as Caesar's wife become so unbearable?"

And in a moment, the rage vanished, and gave way to something very like collapse. For Calpurnia it was hard to say which was worse: the fire of rage that had just died in his eyes, or the absence of any light at all in his eyes now, as he seemed to age 10 years in the blink of an eye,

"No, Caesar, no! I will tell you the whole story, and then I will tell you what was in my heart, and why I did what I did."

Which is what she proceeded to do. She told him how Antony had come to see her, and how he meant to deal with the problem, so as to catch the would-be assassins with daggers in hand. She told him how she had initially agreed to go along with the plan, but changed her mind that fateful morning, because Antony himself, she had realized after a sleepless night of worrying, was no more trustworthy than the assassins. She could see how it could work to Antony's advantage to first allow the assassins to kill their victim, so that he could then destroy them, and claim the mantle as Caesar's avenger—and, of course, successor. So she had decided to trip Antony up by delaying his plans for another day, by which time, she hoped, she would have worked out a different solution.

As she spoke, yet another unfamiliar emotion gradually appeared on his face: amazement.

"You played me, Calpurnia, exactly as I would have played myself, if I had been in your place. Better, in fact. I had no idea, none whatsoever, and here's Calpurnia, out-Caesaring Caesar."

She shook her head. "I can only think of one outcome worse for me than what actually happened, and that is an outcome that was only prevented by Scaeva's bravery and skill. I still don't know why that man did what he did in Pompey's Theater, or what he has been doing for us ever since. Anyway, all I wanted to achieve was for you to realize, finally, that Brutus was not the son you've always wanted and never had. But I never would have let you be hurt so badly just to teach you that lesson. Never. I'm not sure I can ever forgive myself for what happened."

Some time passed before Caesar replied. He spoke, finally, without looking directly at her.

"I knew, yes, that Brutus and his associates would try to kill me, if not on the Ides of March, then at some other time soon, before I could leave for Parthia. But I was so sure I could play him, and in fact, I did play him. I called him "son," and at the moment when I repeated that word, he hesitated just long enough that Antony's men were able to stop him from killing me. But I waited too long to throw the dice, to use Brutus's filial piety against him. I had it all worked out in my mind very differently, and in my scenario, I would walk away without a scratch, once I had shamed Brutus into submission. It was stupid arrogance on my part to think that once these men got their blood up, I could snatch yet another victory from the jaws of defeat."

He turned to look at Calpurnia.

"I've put you through something you should never have had to endure, and all because I came to believe so strongly in this myth of Caesar that I've worked so hard and so long to create. I'm the one who should be sorry."

It was the first time Calpurnia had ever heard anything coming from the mouth of her husband that sounded at all like a real apology. Her heart seemed to quiver. It was a fine moment. It was utterly astounding, and it changed everything—or nearly everything.

"No doubt you're wondering," he said suddenly, after a pregnant silence, "why, if I knew Brutus was guilty, I put on that whole show at his trial, as though I wanted to save him from execution for treason."

"Let me guess," she answered. "It was you, not Antony, who ordered that all the defendants, including Brutus, be lynched after the verdict. You put on the "show," as you call it, so that you could first strip him of his honor as the assassin of a tyrant."

Caesar laughed, yet again, with real amusement. "You couldn't be more right. I simply didn't want him to die with the feeling that he was a martyr to the cause of liberty. I wanted him to be exposed as a man who, at the crucial moment, didn't have the belly to finish what he'd started."

"So I have to ask," said Calpurnia, "though I've never believed the gossip: are you, or could you have been, his father?"

"Of course not. Don't be ridiculous, I was 15 when he was born. I suppose that physically, yes, I could have gotten a woman pregnant at age 15, but really . . . Still, there was a time when I did love his mother, and a time when I wished I could have been his father, when I thought I was a better father to him than the son of a bitch who actually fathered him. You were right, though. I was blind about him, and it nearly cost me my life."

"Look at the two of us," said Calpurnia, after an interval of silence, as they both gathered their thoughts. "We are such players, we both spend all our time and energy not letting others know what we really think, and all the while we're looking into their souls to see what's really there. Mostly, to be honest, so that we can use them to win the game we're trying so hard to win. I suppose we deserve each other."

"But yes," he answered. "Look at us now. Look at how we've just finished revealing to each other the deepest secrets of our souls. And it feels . . . I can't even find the words. Liberating? I promise you, Calpurnia, that I will never again keep anything from you, no matter what is at stake. What could we not do, the two of us, if we were to start playing this game together, as one? The whole world couldn't stand against the two of us."

"I couldn't even begin to answer that, Caesar. But I promise you this much right now, that I am through trying to play you. What you are saying makes my heart beat faster than it has at any time since you looked at me the very first time, over dinner, and made me feel like a woman worthy of Caesar's full attention."

"So let me start this new life of ours," Caesar answered, taking her by the hand, "by telling you what I think I should do. I've just finished doing what I do best: I've identified three important people I consider essential to my future plans, and convinced each of them to play their part in my plans, without actually revealing those plans to any of them. I'm satisfied with the result, at least so far.

"The attempt to kill me, followed by my struggle to return to life, taught me some hard lessons I probably wouldn't have learned any other way. I'm not a walking myth, after all, but a man with some remarkable talents, and some equally remarkable faults. I can't remake the world. I'm not saying that I regret knocking down the whole rotten structure that Sulla left behind: far from it. But as soon as I knocked it down, I reached the limit of my possibilities. I've been flopping around like a fish on a hook ever since I came back from Spain, desperate to keep on winning despite the obvious fact that the game I'd been playing was now over. It's time for someone to take over, someone who knows more about building and less about knocking down."

"Who would that be?" asked Calpurnia.

"I'm not quite sure yet," Caesar responded, "but there isn't anyone that I see as ready to take over this enormous task tomorrow. My last challenge, I think, is to find the right person, train him to the task at hand, and help him get a good start. If I can't do that, everything I've accomplished so far will be worse than worthless.

"And now, just now, I've realized that the person who can help me the most in all this is right here in front of me. I need you, Calpurnia. I need your insight into people, I need you to shed light on the places that are dark to me, and the darkest of those places, as it turns out, are inside my own soul. And now, I need to find the strength inside myself to simply ask for your help, instead of ordering you to do it, or manipulating you—which is what I've always done, all my life, isn't it? Manipulating people into playing the game by my rules. So here is Caesar, asking his wife for her help. What do you say?"

Calpurnia laid her hand on his. "You could have had it without asking, but I love you all the more for asking. Now lie down here beside me, and let's start tomorrow."

www.ingramcontent.com/pod-product-compliance
Lightning Source LLC
Chambersburg PA
CBHW051136030726
47504CB00004B/896